GATES OF EDEN
A STORY OF RESISTANCE, REBELLION, AND LOVE

Charles Degelman

New York
Harvard Square Editions
www.HarvardSquareEditions.org
2012

Published in the United States by
Harvard Square Editions (HSE), Ltd.

ISBN: 978-0-9833216-3-7

Harvard Square Editions:
www.HarvardSquareEditions.org

Printed in the United States of America

Gates of Eden reflects a collective consciousness worth celebrating. To that end . . .

To Ronnie Davis for teaching me that art can change the world. For all the folkies, peaceniks, politicos, SDSers, Mime Troupers, communards, feministas, truckers, and free-city Diggers in Boston, Philly, San Francisco, Ward, Colorado, and Petrolia who demanded the impossible. For Betsy, Joss, and Jake who lived that life. To Charlotte Sheedy for urging me to begin and to Elisabeth Dyssegaard and Sharon Dilworth for their expertise. To John Rechy and friends for teaching me how to write different and to David Lowry and Paul Wales for their adamant support. To the Harvard Fiction writers for their smart words and to the readers in my Los Angeles family, especially Diane, Lorraine and Eric.

Above all, I embrace my partner, Susan Rubin, whose brilliant, loving, and hilarious spirit illuminates my path every day.

"Be realistic. Demand the impossible!"

— Ernesto "Che" Guevara

PROLOGUE
1970

GREENWICH VILLAGE

The explosion raised the townhouse roof off its top-story plate. It blew out every rippled, nineteenth-century windowpane from cellar to atrium. A wall collapsed. Broken glass cascaded from windows across the street. With a shriek of pulled carpenter's pegs and splintered wood, beams that had supported the structure for more than a century followed the bricks into the basement.

Two smaller blasts blew the rubble upward. Flames darted from a fractured gas main igniting shredded drapery and the splintered ends of plaster lath. Water hissed from ruptured plumbing.

A young woman stumbled through billows of brick dust, water spray and smoke. Naked and barefoot, dripping with bath water, she crouched like an animal, picking her way along a ragged ledge, all that remained of the living-room floor. Close-cropped hair caked with plaster dust, face and torso bleeding from a filigree of tiny cuts, she emerged onto the sidewalk.

A sturdy matron with iron-gray hair threw a plaid blanket around the young woman's shoulders, guided her through the rubble that littered the sidewalk and ushered her up the granite stairway of an adjacent brownstone.

Once inside the foyer of the elegant old house, the matron grasped the young woman by the shoulders and led her to a chair. "Are you all right?" she asked the stunned creature before her.

Trembling, her feet bleeding, the young woman covered her eyes and sat.

The neighbor hurried to the kitchen, returning with a tumbler full of water. "Drink this," she said.

The young woman took the tumbler in both hands and drank like a child.

The gray-haired woman put her arms around the young woman. "And no. I won't call the police."

THE
INHERITED WORLD
1945 – 1963

PITTSBURGH

Aperoxide blonde in a silk blouse and rayon slacks tiptoed into the studio and pushed the door closed with a pedicured toe. She carried coffee in two stained mugs. Aaron Friedman, Pittsburgh's paramount wartime disk jockey, took a deep breath and filled the room with a baritone boom.

"Gooood morning Pittsburgh! Breaking news here. Front page headline on the *New York Times*! Yes, folks, the *New York Times*! Says 'Japs Surrender!' Wake up, America, crack a great big smile, and say 'hello' to peacetime!"

Aaron dropped back into his chair. The blonde pushed a pile of records aside with her heart-shaped behind and handed him a cup of coffee. He opened a drawer and pulled out a bottle of Scotch. He poured a shot into each of the coffee mugs and kissed the blonde on her perfectly painted lips. "Here's a new one from Charlie Barnet," he crooned into the microphone. "Get you to the coffee pot on time."

The blonde swigged the coffee and whiskey and unbuttoned her blouse. She popped the buttons of his shirt. Aaron unzipped his trousers. "Be back with more

3

news," he told his listeners. " . . . in four minutes and fifty-three seconds flat." The blonde reached behind her back and unclasped an apricot brassiere. The colors of blouse, bra, and her creamy pink skin reminded Aaron of a bowl of fruit. "Breakfast time!" he shouted and dropped the arm of the studio phonograph onto the rapidly spinning seventy-eight. Charlie Barnet's brass and reed ensemble swelled over the monitors.

Head buzzing with whiskey, caffeine, and fatigue, Aaron trudged up the front steps of his home. Aaron liked his assistant. Hell, he liked all these wartime babies, so young, so pretty, so grown up. They carried a fatalism, a live-for-the-moment recklessness that flew in the face of the grim times. She liked to fuck anywhere, his girl Friday — the chair, the desk, the floor, even the turntable console. He devoured her, she consumed him. Why look a gift horse in the mouth when you can kiss it? She sure as hell didn't taste like the soft-nuzzled old nags that had pulled his old man's rag wagon.

He opened the front door. *What the hell*, he thought. *Things are gonna change now.*

Inside, Aaron's wife Nina, an auburn-haired beauty with long limbs and thin European features sat on the edge of a chair at the far end of the hall. She cradled her pregnant belly under a nightgown, breasts swollen, nipples huge.

"War's over, Honey," he said.

"Oh," she said. "When?"

"Last night. Yesterday. I dunno. Today is tomorrow over there." He walked down the hall, arms extended, and embraced her. "War's over," he repeated into her hair. The floorboards creaked under his weight.

Nina gripped her husband's hand. "It's coming," she said.

"What? Now? Oh my God!" " He pulled away. He stank of whiskey and perfume and lord knows what else. He needed a bath. "Now? Right now?"

"Yes," she said, sitting back down. "Right now."

He ran into the kitchen and splashed water on his hands, neck, face, anywhere his assistant's scent might lurk. He dashed back into the hallway, knelt at her side, put his lips to the tight flesh of her belly, struggling to ground himself in his own life.

"We better get going," she said.

He leapt up the stairs two at a time, grabbed Nina's suitcase off the bed and stopped. Sunlight trumpeted through gauzy curtains that covered a dormer window. The light streaked across the white bedspread and bounced off a wedding photograph hanging on the wall above the bureau. Aaron's parents, a rag picker and his wife, stood side-by-side in stark, formal simplicity, ringing down a half-century from the tarnished pewter frame.

I am a father now. The shock of recognition moved his lips. There will be a future for this kid, a peacetime future, filled with money and opportunity and a new technology. Radio, radiation and radar will merge into a phantasmagoric electronic orgy. I will raise a child while I unleash my ambitions and ride this new, photon-driven roller coaster — television! Coming soon to a world near you! Broadcasting with pictures! Nothing — no war, no poverty, no authority — can stop that phenomenon from becoming a reality, and nobody can stop me from boarding that train.

Aaron let the moment in. With the sun shining on a Wednesday morning, his child was about to be born, one day after the most horrible war the world had ever known had come to an end.

"Aaron!" Nina's cry collapsed into a moan. "Hurry!"

5

Beyond the distant booming of the stamp mills and the distressed cry from his wife, the peace seemed palpable, discernible, like a suddenly noticed silence.

MASTERS OF WAR
JULY, 1949

WASHINGTON, D.C. — "We're going to look pretty stupid if we don't answer this Oriental fella." President Harry S. Truman waved a sheaf of telegrams at a silver-haired patrician. He moved across the Oval Office to a massive antique globe suspended in a mahogany cradle. He leaned over the western shore of the Pacific. "Just exactly where is this Indochina place?"

George C. Marshall knew where Indochina was. He had been Roosevelt's ambassador to China, then the Armed Forces Chief of Staff. Now he was working on a plan to buy out the communists in Europe with a massive infusion of tax dollars.

Marshall was not the President's man. In fact, he considered Truman to be a rube. Roosevelt had brought Marshall to Washington as part of the New Deal's best and brightest. But FDR was dead now, and Marshall had to deal with Truman — a haberdasher from Missouri — as his boss.

"Can you imagine that?" Truman peered at a spot on the globe. "This fella Minh..."

"Ho." Marshall corrected the President. "Ho Chi Minh."

"Minh, Ho..." Truman spun the globe. "The man stole our Declaration of Independence. Almost word for word. Let 'em declare their own independence, dammit."

Marshall clasped his hands behind his back and stared out the window. The drapes in the Oval Office smelled dusty. "We've got to keep the French focused on their own territory, Mr. President," he said. The French obsession with Indochina threatened Marshall's post-war design for Europe. "We have the Soviets to contend with."

Truman ignored him. "We have the Communists marching across China. They're grabbing everything and everybody in their path. We have Ho Chi Minh shouting democracy in Hanoi and..." He poked at Marshall with a stubby finger. "Now we have the French crying in their *vin rosé*." Truman pronounced rosé as "rosie."

Marshall cringed at the slaughtered French. "Believe me, Mr. President. We do not want to get involved in a land war in Asia."

"Land war? Who's talking about a land war? Indochina? A crappy little country south of somebody else's border." Truman spun the globe eastward toward Europe. "We need to commit to the French, George. They want their damned colony back? We gotta help 'em. I don't want to be known as a shrinking violet on this matter."

"Roosevelt never committed to the French," Marshall replied.

7

"The hell he didn't. What was D-Day all about?"

"But not in Indochina," Marshall retorted. "Not even to fight the Japanese."

Truman leaned against his desk, rubbing his jaw. "What about that emperor... Bao Dai? He's the doggone king of Indochina. You can't tell me he's a Communist. Get the French to put him in the saddle down there in Saigon. Then we throw money at him. Keep the nationals happy, give the French their damned rubber plantations back." He spun the globe. "Maybe that way, this Ho Minh fella will stay in his own backyard."

Marshall eyed the dapper little hick. Backing Bao Dai, Indochina's playboy emperor, was a damned clever idea. Despite his mulish Missouri demeanor, President Harry S. Truman was no fool.

MANHATTAN

Eight years later, former disk jockey Aaron Friedman stood resplendent in a new suit and convinced a table full of burgeoning television executives that an atom bomb test in the Nevada desert would make an exciting backdrop for TV talk-show pioneer Dave Garroway and the "Today" show.

Garroway was an affable, long-faced man with horn-rimmed glasses and a crew cut. On camera, he appeared bemused by the world that paraded outside the ground-floor studio at Rockefeller Center. Spectators waved through the windows. Others stared into the glass-walled studio, held in awe by the cameras, the crew, the real-life Garroway persona and the magnetism of the new medium.

A chimpanzee named J. Fred Muggs appeared daily with Dave. His free-floating antics gave every man and woman in mid-50s America a glimpse of primitive and enviable freedom.

Several days before the bomb would be detonated, the network had shipped the entire "Today" show — including J. Fred Muggs and his trainer — from its Manhattan studios to Las Vegas, a rapidly growing gambling Mecca in the Nevada desert.

Before he left Manhattan, Garroway teased his audience. "Out there, we — and all of you viewers, too — are going to take a peek at an atomic explosion. Va-va-voom!" He wiggled his eyebrows behind his glasses. "From a long, long way off, mind you."

Mr. Weaver, the big boss of NBC, put Aaron Friedman in charge of production for the atomic broadcast. Aaron left days ahead of time for Las Vegas to make sure everything went smoothly with the "remote", as he called it. On location, Garroway sent an assistant to a war surplus store to purchase a gas mask and a tin helmet for J. Fred to wear on D-Day. Everybody at the studio had gotten a laugh out of that.

On the morning of the bomb test, Aaron's nine-year-old son, David, sat cross-legged on the living room floor high above Riverside Drive, wrapped in his bathrobe with the bucking broncos on it. The television, tuned to Garroway's "Today" show, sat between two windows that overlooked the Hudson River. David searched the screen for his father. Aaron Friedman was nowhere to be seen.

Television cameras scanned a tower jutting out of the Nevada desert where the bomb sat. They called the place ground zero. *Ground zero.* David had looked up the term in a new dictionary at school. The dictionary called it a point on the earth's surface where a nuclear bomb is exploded. It was still dark, way out there in the desert. Floodlights illuminated the sagebrush behind the bomb tower.

Other cameras panned over soldiers lined up in the desert. The soldiers had orders to watch the blast from close up. Zero hour approached. *Ground zero, zero hour. They sure use a lot of zeros when they talk about atom bombs,* David thought. The soldiers grinned, waved at the cameras and pulled on dark glasses. *They look like bugs.* They filed into the trenches.

"The military experts tell us we won't be able to broadcast the actual detonation," Dave Garroway said. "The intensity of the light would burn out the cameras. Besides, it's a matter of national security. You never know." He wiggled his eyebrows up and down. "The Russians might be watching."

David laughed at Dave Garroway but he felt scared. He knew about the Russians, too. He knew they weren't really the Russians. They were called the Soviet Union. His dad had snarled about the Russians and explained how drunk Russian Cossacks had raced through his grandparents' village back when it was called Russia. Despite his probing questions, David's dad wouldn't say what the Cossacks had done, so David went back to calling them the Soviets, like the television guys did.

He knew the Soviets had a bomb, too. The President had said the only way the Soviets could make a bomb was to steal the big American secret. So the Soviets must have spies. To steal the bomb secret. He knew a little about the spy stuff. During the trial of a mother and father named the Rosenbergs, David's dad had come home from the newsroom full of news about what the Rosenbergs knew and didn't know about the atom bomb and what they had given to the Russians. Or not. His father was full of questions about what had happened and what had not happened. And what the news broadcasters could and couldn't say.

The Rosenbergs were in jail. The judge accused them of giving stolen bomb secrets to Soviet spies. *Why all the talk about stealing*, David thought. *Couldn't the Soviets make a bomb of their own?* But the Rosenbergs had been found guilty. David's parents said there was talk about executing them.

David couldn't tell what Garroway thought about the Rosenbergs but David knew what he thought. He had read a book about the atom bomb the night before. He lay awake imagining the explosion. The book said that in a tiny part of a second, split-open atoms could make a fireball one million degrees hot. But what would stop the atoms from splitting? They had dropped a bomb like Harry on Japan a few days before he was born. They called that bomb Little Boy. It burned up a whole city. He knew that Harry was even bigger than Little Boy.

Now David stood in his pajamas and waited in the living room to watch the bomb burn up his father, Dave Garroway, J. Fred Muggs, the desert, the mountains, New York City, the Rosenbergs, and finally the whole world. It could happen right now, in one tiny second, because nobody, not even the grownups, knew for sure when the atoms would stop splitting.

On the screen, Dave Garroway said, "okay, one minute," then "okay, thirty seconds." J. Fred Muggs tore the gas mask off his face and hurled it on the floor.

"Keep moving, Sweetie" David's mother called from the bedroom. "You'll be late. And don't forget. It's Cub Scout day. Your uniform is clean and folded on the dryer."

Behind Dave Garroway's head, a low flash outlined the hills.

Chicago

Louis Guillory sat at his mother's kitchen table and stared out the window. Sounds of morning traffic murmured through the glass. The red and white linoleum squares on the kitchen floor were swabbed spotless, and a bowl of apples, oranges, and bananas topped the kitchen table.

"I got to go, Ma."

A parakeet squawked.

"Have to go," his mother corrected.

"Got to, have to . . . All Chicago's gonna be there."

"All of Chicago is not going to be there," she snapped. "And you, young man, will be among the missing."

Sophie Guillory was a beautifully composed woman with high, Caribbean cheekbones and a reddish tint to her complexion. Oiled ringlets of short hair framed the regal dome of her forehead, the arch of her eyebrows, and the stunning symmetry of her nose, eyes and lips. "Why do you need to sit witness over a dead child?"

"Because I knew him."

"Not hardly."

"He was a boy like me."

"He wasn't like you!" Sophie brought her palm down on the table. "Nothing like you!"

"He went to my school. You taught him, Mama."

Sophie refused to share the cross weave of her feelings about Emmett Till, not with her son, not thirty minutes before she had to stand up in her first-period classroom and try to teach forty Negro children out of the hell they had been born into.

The long worm of an elevated train crept along the rooftops of a distant block.

"I feel bad for the boy," she said. "I feel worse for his mother."

"I want to see him," Louis repeated. "Before they bury him."

Sophie knew Emmett Till's mother. Mamie Bradley's husband had died when Emmett had been little more than an infant. A decade later, curious about his family, Emmett had pleaded with his mother to let him visit their relatives. Mamie Bradley bowed to her son's curiosity and sent him to stay with his uncle in Money, Mississippi. She salved her anxiety with justification. "He should know his family," she explained to herself and her friends.

On a hot Mississippi afternoon, Emmett had taken a picture out of his wallet — a school photo of a towheaded Arkie girl from the South Side — and bragged that she was his sweetheart. The boast drew a challenge from his country cousins. "I bet you don't dare go sweet-talk the white woman in that store over there."

"Watch me." Emmett sauntered into a grocery store at the center of Money, Mississippi, bought a soda and said "'Bye, 'bye, Baby," to the white woman behind the counter. The story traveled like mercury through the isolated Jim Crow community.

Emmett Till was shipped back to Chicago in a pine box, his waterlogged carcass battered beyond recognition. His mother inspected Emmett's body inch-by-inch to find marks that would identify him.

"You know," Sophie warned Louis, "it isn't going to be pretty."

"I've seen dead people before." He wanted to see. How could a living, joking human being, an older boy that he had admired, be transformed into a broken, empty thing?

Like Emmett, Louis had done things on a dare. He had jumped into the Chicago Ship Canal on the first hot day in May. He had thrown a snowball at the cranky old pastor from the First Ebenezer Baptist Church. He had walked beside the tracks of the Rock Island line, so close that he had been blinded by the wind and dust thrown up by a fast-moving train. But he had never been kidnapped or chained and beaten, never had an eye gouged or skull crushed. He had never been shot in the face or thrown into an algae-filled backwater creek to rot.

"I can learn something, Mama." He put his dishes in the sink.

Sophie felt a familiar sadness settle into her neck and shoulders. Louis lived in the shelter of the South Side ghetto. He basked in the love of his mother. He engendered the respect of his teachers. He had friends and he was smart. His school was populated entirely by Negro students. He had never suffered direct hatred or violence stimulated by the color of his skin. She had worked hard to keep Louis from the ugliness of the world. "I don't want you to go, Louis."

"Ma!"

"You'll see such sights soon enough."

"But Ma! I can . . ."

"No!" She rose from the table. "I don't want to talk any further about this. I've got to get to school, and so do you," she said, picking up her briefcase. "And before you leave . . . Do something for that bird."

BRONCO, TEXAS

Twelve hundred and seventy-two miles to the southwest of Chicago, young Roger Wolfe watched the nuclear blast that Aaron Friedman had televised. But by the time Roger turned on the television, the news station had footage of the actual explosion. To Roger, the blast looked like a fiery cobra, arching up out of the desert, twisting, writhing in pain, looking for somebody to bite. *Bite with fire,* he thought. *The hottest fire in the world.* For Roger, it felt as if the fire had burnt his brain and he would never forget it, no matter how hard he tried.

That night, Roger's mom Dottie asked husband Bob not to douse the charcoal with too much starter. "It makes the damn burgers smell like gasoline," she complained. He poured the whole can of fluid over the grill and struck a match. Flames leapt into the darkening Friday-night sky.

"You asshole!"

Dottie's voice brought Roger to his bedroom window. Silhouetted against the skyrocketing flames, Bob took a defiant swig off the long neck of a Lone Star beer.

Dottie grabbed the garden hose and drowned the meat, the grill, the family dog, and Bob.

Bob threw down his beer, yanked the hose out of Dottie's hand, and turned it on her.

"Son of a bitch!" She ran into the house, sliding the patio door closed with a whoosh. The water from the hose made a rattling sound on the glass.

Roger had been painting a plastic model, a B-29 bomber, like the planes his mom helped build, back in California, back before he was born. He wondered if his B-29 model could carry an atom bomb in its belly like his mom had carried him. He imagined himself falling and hitting the ground where he turned into a cobra on fire, twisting and snarling flames.

Roger liked to look at the pictures of his mom in California. She seemed so happy, standing there by the ocean or leaning against a convertible. He wondered why she would leave all that and move to Bronco, Texas. It didn't make sense.

His father was laughing. "Bitch," he shouted through the door. "Stupid bitch."

The bathroom door slammed, locked, water poured into the tub.

Roger painted bomber parts while his father stabbed and flipped pieces of meat over the smoky flames. Fat flared in the growing dusk.

Dottie emerged, wrapped in a bathrobe with a towel on her head. Roger thought she looked pretty. Dottie and Bob sat on the sofa behind the coffee table talking in low voices. She lit a cigarette, the smoke drifting up into the lampshade held up by the half-naked Chinese lady on the end table. His dad had brought the matched pair — a yellow lady and a red lady — back from the war.

Roger retreated to his room with the chuck wagons and rodeo riders on the wallpaper. *Maybe they'll make up if I leave them alone,* he thought.

Bob Wolfe and Dottie Beemis had grown up fast while the world was at war. Bob had been stationed on a succession of shattered atolls as the Allies took the Pacific from the Japanese. He was responsible for keeping open the lines of communication between the base, the meteorologists, the trackers, and the B-29s — sleek, silver killing machines that droned north by northwest from the Marianas to Japan, pounding the Rising Sun into the sunset in abstract, bloody ceremonies conducted from 30,000 feet. Wreaking such carnage from the icy heavens demanded courage, pathos, patience, cooperation, even humor — all the best qualities of adulthood.

Dottie missed the camaraderie of the women she had worked with during the war. She missed the daily challenge to prove they could do the job as well or better than the men, crawling through the fuselage, stringing Byzantine mazes of wiring, oxygen and hydraulic lines.

Bob and Dottie had met at the Formosa Lounge in Hollywood. Beneath the autographed photos of movie stars, they drank stingers and talked about the planes. That was common ground enough. They went to her place that first night and fucked each other raw. They married two weeks later. It was the thing to do — to live for the moment.

After the war, Bob used his signal corps experience to work into an entry-level job with the OSS, the U.S. Intelligence service. He became an agent, parlaying his limited communications skills into undercover applications, striving to make himself useful. He would go anywhere on assignment — the jungles of Cambodia, the frozen misery of the Aleutians, the deserts of North Africa. He held on. The OSS, burgeoning into the CIA as the Cold War began to intensify was taking on practically anyone with four limbs, five senses, and war zone experience.

Roger entered first grade and Dottie rejoined the work force, but it didn't feel the same. The men had come home and were given their old jobs. Dottie's new assignments were silly, meaningless, "like stuffing jelly into donuts," she said.

The first ninety days of connubial bliss passed unnoticed into the subsequent two years of making do, complicated by Bob's frequent absences. Their fights grew progressively violent, suppressed only by her resolve to protect her son from the ugliness that flared between her and Bob.

Now, struggling to make up one more time, Bob pleaded with Dottie to accompany him to their favorite watering hole, the Old Oaken Bucket. "We can make up over steaks and a couple of drinks," he said.

Ever hopeful, she dressed, boiled a saucepan full of hot dogs, toasted a few buns, and set the table with mustard, ketchup, and sweet pickle relish. She felt bad about leaving Roger alone after she and Bob had been hollering at each other, so she put a plate of cookies on the Formica kitchen counter for extra love and kissed him goodbye.

After they left, Roger stuffed the green beans down the garbage disposal and ate the hot dogs in silence.

Greenwich Village

"Don't you ever stop, Dad?" Fifteen-year-old Madeline Singer stood in the doorway of the den, looking down at her father. He looked tired, hunched over his massive desk, poring through legal documents.

She hugged him from behind.

Paul Singer was a self-confessed workaholic, convinced that his daughter needed more attention than he had time to give, more affection than he dared show. She had turned into a lovely young woman, a teenager poised on the brink of maturity. His attraction for her frightened him. He often feared for her, darkening at the possibility that she might be treated the way he had treated so many like her. His good looks and aggressive practice — he was determined to save the world through his legal work — had netted admiration from a host of women.

Now only his wife Eugenia remained of the bevy of beauties that must have adorned his past. To Madeline and her father, Eugenia Singer stood alone, self-sufficient, smart and sardonic, preoccupied with her work. She, too, had found solace in the arms of others and — in her own interest — ardently refrained from disparaging her husband. From Eugenia's point of view, Madeline was Paul's little girl and she liked it that way.

Madeline noticed that her father occasionally spent Saturday or Sunday mornings with their neighbor Katherine, a bosomy woman Paul had known forever. The pairing seemed unlikely but Madeline never probed. She was fond enough of her dad to overlook his dalliances and worldly enough to countenance any scenario that might have unfolded between them.

"Another big day in court, huh Dad?

"Always is, I guess." He gave his daughter what he hoped was a fatherly pat. "I'm a bloody bore, ain't I?"

She squeezed him, smelling his hair oil, the remaining hint of the morning's Old Spice, the tobacco. "Hardly, Daddy. *Au contraire*, you're the most intriguing man I know."

"Stop it, Honey. You don't know all that many men." He glanced up, faking a frown. "Do you?"

She plunked down in the rich leather of the French club chair. He was handsome, his face lined with experience, his hair still thick. She loved to listen to her father talk about his work. He was always careful to explain the courtroom dramas so she could understand them. "Do I know many men? Ha ha. Boys is more like it, and certainly none like you. But back to more important things . . . the law! You know you're gonna win this one, too, even if you don't stay up all night."

"Hope so. Damned good cause," he growled. "Partners are getting testy about my *pro bono* stuff."

"Why?" She knew about her father's partners. Late middle-aged men with expensive suits who drank too much and had begun to look at her different whenever she dropped by the office. "Don't tell me." She shifted in the leather comfort of the chair. "They think you should drop the charity work."

He laughed. "You got it, Honey. As if this work was a threat to the firm's coffers. *Pro bono* is as old as the law itself."

"Uh, Dad?"

"Hmmm?" he asked, his voice already vague with preoccupation, his head turned back to his papers.

"Sunday I have to go uptown to the library . . ."

"The what?" He scribbled a quick note in the margin of a brief.

"The library. The big one."

"Hmmm." He watched her feet swinging, noting that Madeline was learning new ways to get what she wanted.

He hoped she would find a profession that would allow for her independence, the way her mother had, work that gave her parity with the men she would have to compete with. Or serve. He smiled, face glowing with the warm light cast by a green glass desk lamp. "Research?"

"For history class. Gotta read up on Cuba." He would like that. He was big on Fidel Castro and the revolution and all that stuff.

He stared at her briefly. Well, not at her, Madeline noticed, but around her, like the guys at school who didn't want to get caught peeking.

"Okay," he said. "But here . . ." He dug in his pocket and pulled out a twenty. "Research expenses."

"Thanks, Dad." She kissed him on the cheek and withdrew. Her mother would be away all weekend, leaving time for her dad to visit Katherine if he wanted and leaving Madeline with one less gauntlet for her to run before she was free to launch her Washington Square project.

MASTERS OF WAR
JANUARY, 1961

WASHINGTON, D.C — President Dwight D. Eisenhower liked to work alone in the Lincoln bedroom. Still in pajamas and a robe, he sipped coffee and hunched over a yellow pad, contemplating a last-minute revision to his farewell speech.

The President had polished the speech over a fortnight, but in the darkness of his last night in office, he realized he had made a critical omission. With the great house beginning to stir, Ike put blue ink to yellow paper.

*Until the latest of our world con-
flicts, the United States had no armaments
industry. American makers of plowshares
could, when called upon to do so, make
swords as well.*

He could hear Mamie moving about the
upstairs parlor. He knew that she would
be distressed. The transfer of power to
a young Catholic politician who traveled
in a sophisticated crowd would put her
in an uncomfortable spotlight. He also
knew that she had already taken her first
drink. He returned to his work.

*But now we have been compelled to
create a permanent armaments industry of
vast proportions.*

When it came to affairs of the heart,
Ike had found it was often better to look
away. He had always reserved his power
for ordering men into battle or rendering
final decisions that would affect millions. Mamie would do what she would do
and he would let her. He owed her that.
He turned his attention back to the page.
He did not want to monger fear.

*This conjunction of an immense mili-
tary establishment and a large arms industry is new to the American experience,*
he wrote. *The potential for the disas-
trous rise of misplaced power exists and
will persist.*

Beyond the closed doors of the Lincoln bedroom, a bottle shattered on the
parquet floor. Mamie exhaled a quiet, resigned "Oh, dear." Ike rose from the desk

21

and opened the doors. His wife wobbled
into the room.

Washington, D.C.

Sheltered by the egg-and-coffee smell of the Howard
University student union, Louis Guillory huddled over
an open copy of the *Washington Post*. On the front page,
a Greyhound bus sat abandoned on a highway shoulder,
tires flattened, flames bursting from broken windows. A
black man in a bloodstained white shirt, arms and hands
limp with shock, watched the bus burn from the grass
verge.

"Why didn't they fight back?" Louis' roommate, Sonny,
took a slug from his soda.

"They're not supposed to," Louis said, his eyes locked
on the image.

"Yeah? So what are they supposed to do?"

"Turn the other cheek,"

"And get their butts kicked," Sonny added. *"Shee-it.*
Since when does freedom mean you let some cracker kick
the shit out of you?" He bit into an apple. "Them people
are fools," he scoffed. "Alabama. Shit. That place never
gonna change. You thank your lucky stars you're sittin' up
here in D.C., gettin' a store-bought education." He pointed
the white apple core at Louis' chest. "A college education.
Put on a suit and show whitey that you can do anything he
can. That's how to fight for equality, Brother."

"They're putting their lives on the line. For all of
us." Louis pushed his plate away. "I can't sit here and do
nothing."

"You can't sit where and do nothing?" Diane Thomas frowned into the phone. "Howard University!" Half amused, half curious, she remained on the line. "Don't you have finals to finish?"

"Never mind that," Louis shouted into the phone. "After I saw those photos. That burnt out bus, those two men beaten . . . "

"There's been photos?"

"In the *Post* — that's the big paper up here in Washington."

"I'm familiar with *The Washington Post*. I'm in Nashville, not Lagos." Diane was standing in the Nashville headquarters of CORE, the Congress of Racial Equality, where she played an irreplaceable role in the coordination of the Freedom Rides, the organization's attempts to bring civil-rights violations of the interstate transportation laws to the courtroom.

"A picture of a Greyhound bus. Right on the front page. The bus is on fire, windows broken, smoke everywhere."

"Thank goodness, they are paying attention."

"After that, I couldn't study anymore."

"Meaning?"

"Meaning, I want to join the Freedom Riders."

"I'm sorry, Mr . . ."

"Guillory."

"Guillory. We're only taking people who've been trained."

"Trained?! Trained for what?"

"Nonviolence."

"What's there to learn?"

"If you don't know, you shouldn't come, young man."

"I'll drop my studies, anything."

"I admire your enthusiasm," Diane said. "But as you can see from the photo, the Freedom Rides are dangerous, bloody and possibly lethal expeditions. Now they know we're coming." She avoided mentioning the prospect that they could be killed. "Do we know how you will respond? No. Do *you* know how you will respond?"

"I can take care of myself."

"I'm sure you can. But we don't know you. You could come work with us this summer."

"I need to do this now."

"Your personal needs aren't of paramount importance, Mr. Guillory. I'm sorry." She hung up knowing she would like to know more about the soul that lay beneath that brash, indignant voice.

Three days and six hundred miles later, Louis stood in the aisle of a Greyhound bus bound for Birmingham and stared down at a diminutive but angry Diane Thomas.

"I told you not to come," she said.

He was surprised at her youth. Over the phone he had imagined a mature, churchy lady. Instead, a petite young woman in a white blouse and a straight skirt confronted him from her seat at the back of the bus. "I wasn't playing God over the phone. CORE has a policy. I tried my best to describe why you might be a liability." She stared out the window as the landscape began to move behind them.

"I had to join you," he mumbled. "I had to."

"All right," she sighed. "You're here." She contemplated her nails for a moment. Her power carried a softness with it, as if there were great reserves of strength that required no validation. She snapped her head up, her eyes boring into his. "Better be a credit to your stubbornness."

"Better be a credit to my people," he said quietly.

"You probably will be." She smiled. "Despite yourself."

The road unwound through the Appalachians, a ribbon of black twisting through a channel of green. In the distance, smoke rose from the blast furnaces of Birmingham and dissolved into the overcast sky. Troopers stood in the road, patrol cars barricading the highway beyond them.

Louis stood up to see better.

Diane pulled him back down. "Just sit tight."

The driver pulled the Greyhound over and opened the door. Two Alabama state troopers clumped on board. In unison, their eyes landed on two young Freedom Riders, one black, one white, sitting together in the front row. One trooper placed a gloved hand on each young man's collar and yanked both men out of their seats.

"You are under arrest for violating the transportation laws of the state of Alabama," the second trooper drawled. The first trooper hurtled the two Freedom Riders down the bus steps into a knot of cops.

Louis' mouth went chemical with adrenaline.

Diane stood and called out. "We have the right to equal protection afforded us by . . . "

"Shut up and sit down."

Men in plain clothes tramped onto the bus behind the troopers. The air grew hot, impossible to breathe. The cops stood in the aisle, blocking the light from the windshield.

"They knew we were coming," Diane whispered.

The plainclothesmen taped newsprint over the bus windows. The interior, already jammed with cops and riders, shrunk under the gloom cast by the print-covered windows. The troopers moved down the aisle like the Gestapo on a German train, checking tickets with their flashlights. Anyone who had a ticket from Nashville to New Orleans was deemed a Freedom Rider. Each was ordered to the back of the bus. Everyone else was labeled free of malicious intent. Wordlessly, full of relief, the uninvolved rose and squeezed through the phalanx of gloves, boots, and pistols holstered on Sam Browne belts.

"This is how they got the first bunch," Diane whispered to Louis. "Stay right by my side and do exactly as I tell you."

With a whine of gears, the Greyhound pulled away from the roadblock. The troopers moved back up the aisle while the bus rolled on. A labyrinth of starts, stops and right-angle turns kept the passengers off-balance. The newspaper-covered windows made the movement disorienting. The darkness was claustrophobic. In a small, clear voice, Diane began to sing.

We shall not, we shall not be moved.

MANHATTAN

Every Sunday afternoon, a group of folk musicians gathered by the fountain in Washington Square Park to play old Appalachian ballads and Texas country blues, Mississippi rags and Arkansas hollers. The impromptu band filled the air with finger- and flat-picked guitar, clawhammered banjo arpeggios and a nearly in-tune fiddle. A chubby mandolin plucker and a stringy-haired guy with a washtub bass bracketed the musical spectrum from high to low.

Sunday afternoon in Washington Square Park was not just for folkies. Coteries of cold-eyed teenagers from the Bronx watched the action with sarcasm. Boys from NYU cruised Capri-clad Italian girls from the neighborhood, old Polish women sunned themselves, their stockings rolled below the knee. Around the back of the fountain, young men in jeans and t-shirts leaned into each other with undisguised infatuation, kissing, caressing, fingering each other's crucifixes.

David Friedman, now fifteen, loved the lyrics of the songs the folk musicians played. He had never gone out on strike or laid down a deputy with a log chain. Nor had he ever murdered a pretty little girl on the banks of the Ohio River or toiled in the dark dungeons of a coalmine. But the tunes and their lyrics transported him out of the claustrophobic, steam-heated, career-obsessed, martini-driven, private-school shelter his parents had created on the tenth floor of a spacious Riverside Drive apartment. The songs carried him to another America, where he caught a glimpse of a more authentic world.

The players spiraled in a slow-moving galaxy before the fountain. Where they stood depended on their abilities. A nod from the core group and you took a step toward the center of the spiral. Players who didn't know the chord changes, played too loud, or couldn't keep up were banished with the turn of a shoulder. A devout audience gathered at the fringes, listening.

All summer, David lugged his guitar downtown, blue work shirt rolled up to his biceps, baggy dungarees and work boots signaling his intent to be mistaken for a ramblin' man just got into town. He never took the guitar out of its case but watched the players every Sunday. They inspired him to learn the chord changes, the finger-picking patterns and the lyrics to dozens of tunes — in his bedroom. Now, he was determined to play with the Washington Square folkies.

The musicians were picking their way through "Freight Train". David knew the tune. Hands shaking, he pulled his guitar out of the cardboard case and joined the circle. He worked inward verse by verse until he was surrounded by the wash of other instruments. The banjo player nodded encouragement until the band finished with a ragged flourish.

The crowd of onlookers applauded. The musicians scratched, stretched and shifted as if no one was there. The banjo player noodled the melody of the next tune while a gallon bottle of wine floated from mouth to mouth.

A young woman carried on the applause longer than the others. She sat cross-legged on the foot-worn cobbles, a dungareed hip wedged against the curve of the washtub. She wore a men's blue work shirt, and a small, spiral-bound notebook poked out of her left breast pocket. She wore scuffed-up saddle shoes without laces, and a yellow pencil nested in an unruly sphere of curly black hair that cascaded around her baby-smooth features. An olive-skinned shoulder disappeared under her shirt. She was more than pretty. She was beautiful in a grown-up, scary, exotic kind-of-a way.

I bet she gets around, David thought.

"Hey!" She looked up at him with dark brown eyes. "You're pretty good."

The banjo player started a new tune. A guitarist in a cape stepped into the circle. David recognized him as a regular at the Café Figaro and the Village Gate. He gave way, standing opposite so that he could watch the older musician's fingers. The banjo player turned his back and closed David out of the circle. That was it. He had been axed.

"Don't let those guys get you down." The girl pulled the notebook out of her shirt pocket. He felt warm-headed and flushed from the wine.

"What's your name?"

"Uh, David." He extended his hand.

Her pencil remained poised. "I mean your whole name, dummy."

"David Friedman. F-R-I-E . . . "

"I know how to spell it." She scribbled, not looking up.

"Why're you writing my name down?"

"Maybe you'll get famous. Besides, I'm writing a story about Washington Square Park."

"You mean, like a novel?"

"No. It's a story. For the school paper."

"Hey," David said. "That's pretty cool."

She looked up at him with a bemused smile.

"So, uh." David felt uncomfortable with the silence. Maybe he was acting like a jerk. "What's your name?"

"Madeline."

"Wow," David said. "That's French, isn't it?"

"*Oui*." She fluttered her eyelashes in *faux* flirtation. "*Très sophistiqué, n'est-ce pas?* My parents named me after this French girl in a kid's book, but I think it's sexy, don't you?"

"Sure." He blushed again, a fool with his guitar hanging out. He retreated to the park bench where he had left his guitar case.

"So how long have you been playing?" she asked, moving with him.

"I started last winter."

"You're kidding me!"

"But mostly I been playing alone. You know, with books and records. This was the first time I . . . "

"The first time? You really are good." She drifted lazily beside him. "Keep an eye out for them, though."

"Who?"

"Hank, Gino, all those guys. They're put-down artists. And they don't like guys who're better than them."

"I'm not better than they are."

"Maybe not now. But you will be."

"Better'n them? Naaah." He pulled his guitar case out from under the green-painted slats.

"I been watchin' that for ya, sonny." An old man sat on the bench, scratching his whiskers with a toothpick. "Should be worth somethin', shouldn't it?"

David dug out a quarter and gave it to the bum.

"Pretty gal you got there."

"I'm not his 'gal.'"

"Well, gawddam, sonny." The bum cackled through his gums. "You got yourself a tiger by the tail, doncha now." He pocketed the quarter and disappeared.

"You gonna be at the Wha? tomorrow night?" she asked.

"The what?"

"Mondays is jam night at the Café Wha?. You know, Macdougal Street."

"I know where it is," he said.

"Then come on down. You should play."

"Play? Jeez. I dunno. I got a lot of homew . . . "

"I'm gonna be there." She rocked back and forth in her sneakers, hands in the back pockets of her jeans. "I got homework, too, ya know."

"Uh, maybe." He edged away, caught between the orb of her attention and his need to report home.

She stood in the middle of the path, smiling. "That was a nice thing you did back there, giving that bum a handout."

"Poor people got to live, too," he said.

"I know that," She replied. "What do you think? I was born stupid?" She punched his bicep and strolled back to the knot of musicians.

MIDDLETON, MASSACHUSETTS

Connie Moore could not read the names of the actors through the blur of her tears. The tranquil blues of the Mediterranean Sea washed across the screen. She hooked her bra, pulled down her sweater, cranked open the window of Eddie Carpenter's '50 Chevy and lifted the speaker off the glass. She slipped out of the car, inhaled the cool air and stretched. The words of the finale blared through dozens of tinny speakers.

They had been watching "Exodus," the Technicolor epic of Jewish relocation, Palestinian loss, British cruelty, all thrashing around a tragic Shakespearean romance. Eddie had groped, Connie had nuzzled, her attention caught by the riveting world that unfolded on the screen.

The night air cooled her tears. Eddie sprawled in the passenger seat, crumbs of popcorn littering his chest. She looked down at his profile, the strong lines of his forehead and jaw, handsome and goofy with his crew cut and popcorn mess. His T-shirt gleamed in the dark, a white, phosphorescent triangle glowing from the top of his V-neck sweater.

The film had left her with an ache that had become as familiar as the dark pines that surrounded the drive-in. She longed to be gone, not from sweet Eddie, but from the sheltered confines of her existence. At sixteen, she had already concocted a future that dazzled with hope. She was good at languages, with straight "A's" in Latin and French. She would train as an interpreter for the United Nations — after four years of college, of course. She would travel to Paris and Luxembourg and Istanbul, where she would translate important conversations that would help feed the starving children of Asia and Africa. President John F. Kennedy had said it was time for that.

She would live in elegant old hotels, wear short hair under a beret and slacks under a trench coat. She would translate for diplomats and write descriptions of her work for magazines like *Redbook* and *Seventeen* and maybe even *The New Yorker*.

"Let's go down to Dominic's and get a meatball sandwich." Eddie pushed the starter pedal. "I'm wicked hungry."

She pictured the gang crowded into the leatherette booths at Domenic's. She heard the jukebox blaring, the smiling, made-up faces watching hers, knowing they'd been at the drive-in, pawing at each other but not — of course — going 'all the way'. Good girls knew what other good girls did and didn't do. There were no secrets at Middleton High.

"Let's not," she said, climbing into the passenger seat. "Let's drive. Find someplace where we can just sit."

"Okay. Sure." He was hungry, but he was getting used to the impetuous desires of the good-looking girl who sat beside him. With her clean, sandy hair and tiny features, she smelled of soap, even after all that groping. "Anything you say, Queenie."

They drove down Nashoba Road, the elms and maples arching over them. A birch tree flared yellow in their headlights, standing out against the still-green oaks and maples. "That was such a sad story," she said. "All those people struggling to reach their homeland."

"Guess that goes to show ya. There's no place like home." He switched on the radio.

Connie felt safe with Eddie Carpenter. He was easy to play with, not like the other boys, always so full of defenses and postures. Still, she was surprised by her affection for him. He wasn't passionate about the same things. He didn't want to live in Paris and he wasn't concerned about the plight of African children. She had learned not to expect that from her friends at Middleton High. What mattered was that he had an honesty about him. He was different.

Connie's father was an electronics engineer who drove off every morning to work in a pristine laboratory hidden in the trees of a genteel Boston suburb. She lived in a two-story colonial structure that had stood witness to the Revolutionary War. She was an only child, the sole reflection of her parents. She was college material. That was certain.

Eddie's life was up for grabs. His father was a locksmith, a sad, quiet French Canadian who owned a shop in Somerville. Eddie lived with seven brothers and sisters in a one-story house covered with fake tarpaper bricks. His father had tacked on extra rooms as each new child was born. Eddie and his siblings scrapped with each other like puppies while his father moved from room to tiny room like a zombie, rising from the easy chair, peering into the refrigerator, standing over the toilet, then floating back to the chair, recycling an endless stream of coffee, beer, and vanilla cream soda, which he called "tonic".

Eddie's mother worked nights for New England Bell as a telephone operator. During the day, she sat at the kitchen table, taut and irritable with fatigue, smoking Marlboros and drinking endless cups of instant coffee while she ordered her daughters through a litany of chores. The kitchen always stunk of home permanents, cigarette smoke and tomato sauce.

When Connie visited Eddie at home, he seemed loud and physical, his language peppered with evocations of Jesus, Joseph and Mary. At school, he was quiet, almost bashful, screening his thoughts and feelings behind a little grin. In the cruelty of high school culture, he stood alone, smiling easily, running with the pack during good times and cutting himself off from the cliques. He had a sense of fairness that hung on him with a gentle stability that no bully could disturb.

"Look," she said, turning in her seat. A full moon traveled over the passing treetops, grazing the forested hump of Mount Massasoit. "Let's find a place where we can walk in the moonlight. Before it disappears."

She wanted to hold onto the feelings of the film. Those refugees jammed in the tramp steamer, escaping their pasts, fleeing over the sun-seared Mediterranean to Israel. The arid landscape excited her as well, moved her to wonder if she didn't have ancestors who once roamed the desert. The heat of the dunes, the clamor of the market place, the suspense of Exodus' shipboard intrigue pulled at her like a magnet. To Connie, the world had grown sad and glorious and exciting all at the same time.

"Isn't it neat, thinking about graduating and going someplace else?" she said. "I can't wait."

"What's wrong with Middleton?" he asked.

The road climbed up the side of Nashoba Notch. An apple orchard perched on the steep hillside, soaking up the moonlight. A stone wall, covered with moss and blackberry vines, tumbled along the pasture beside them. She rolled down the window and sniffed the air. The fragrance of moist earth and a remembrance of warmth hung in her nostrils.

"Nothing's wrong with it," she said. "But I feel like it's now or never, Eddie. For life, I mean. Going places. Meeting people. Doing some good in the world. Like those people did."

"Jeez, you're quite the philosopher today," he said.

"The birches look like ghosts."

"Oh, so now you're the poet, too." He giggled. "Your feet show it. They're Longfellows."

She mussed his hair.

"Hey!" He rolled the Chevy to a stop by the stone wall. "Hands off the merchandise."

While Eddie brushed his crew cut, Connie leaned on the door and stared out the open window. The hillside was bathed in moonlight, every detail outlined in the clear spring air. A herd of Holsteins grazed on the far side of the orchard. A malingering crow called to its partner. A dog yipped from a barnyard beyond the ridge.

With the broad images of the movie still running through her mind, she felt pulled by a million thoughts and yearnings. It was time! The last year of school, the cloistering comfort of her parents' home, the monotonous beauty of the little town she had known since childhood, the swirl of the world situation, all fought with the images of the Mediterranean and the desert, the handsome young President, the megaton bombs, the Peace Corps, the first man in space, fallout shelters, the Bay of Pigs, the Berlin Wall and now, the brave Freedom Riders. Everything scared and excited her, made her want to hide or fly forward, sleep forever or live life, get things done, before it was too late, before it was all over.

"You know what?" She stepped out of the car. "We have to think about these things."

He stayed put in the driver's seat. "What things?"

"We've got the biggest bombs the world has ever seen. So do the Russians. The President wants us to build fallout shelters! The next minute, he wants us to help people in Africa!" She stared at the moon, her voice distant with meditation. "I mean, what are we supposed to do?"

He stretched, took a swig out of his pint of Southern Comfort. On the way to the drive-in, he had stopped at Ducharme's package store. The guy there would sell a kid a pint, or a case of Black Label, if nobody else was around. Eddie got out of the car and leaned against the Chevy's fender. The engine ticked as it cooled in the quiet night. "I bet you're going to fix all that," he said. "Workin' at the United Nations."

"Well, I want to," she said. "But I get the feeling we're running out of time. Bomb shelters." She looked out over the orchard. This might be the end. What if nuclear disaster or some other dark catastrophe lay ahead of them, cruelly heedless of their dreams or personal destinies? What if they denied themselves that one thing, that mystery, so mysterious, so beautiful, so exciting?" She turned to him. "Eddie."

"Yeah?"

"Will you go all the way with me?"

"Huh?"

"With the world the way it is now, we could miss out on something if we don't hurry," she said.

"All the way?" He shifted uncomfortably. "But, uh, we never . . . "

"That's what I mean," she insisted. "All of these terrible things are happening. What if we don't experience life to the fullest?"

"Wow. But I . . . "

"What," she said, scared by his hesitation. "Don't you want to?"

"Well, sure I do," he said. "It's just that I . . . " He studied the cows, took another hit from his pint and looked at her with the eyes of a twelve-year-old. "I kinda gave up on bringin' a rubber."

"That's okay," she said, jamming her hands in her jeans pockets. "I have one."

"You do?"

"Just in case."

"Jeez." He looked down at the figure standing before him, shoulders squared in her sweater, arms stiff.

"I'm not a professional virgin or anything," she said. "I'm almost seventeen, you know. Besides," she said, "I knew we'd do it some time."

After all she had heard about doing it, this was the first time she had actually contemplated going through with it. It was scary, but she could not fight off her own sense of urgency. Besides, the air was cold and it would be warm in the Chevy. He looked scared and incredulous but he was already walking around to the driver's seat.

"Wait a minute," she said. "We should get into the back. You know, for more room."

"O-okay." He giggled as he climbed into the back seat. "Doubt if anybody's gonna be out hayin' tonight."

Trembling, she let the darkness surround her. She handed Eddie the tinfoil packet and opened her heart to the swelling chords of the Exodus theme song. Her sweetheart came to her smelling of Brylcreem, Southern Comfort and hot-buttered popcorn.

MASTERS OF WAR
SEPTEMBER, 1961

SAIGON — The Majestic Hotel overlooked the Saigon River from a broad river-front boulevard called Tong Duc Thang. An elaborate gingerbread castle that still paraded the worn mantle of its former colonial elegance, the Majestic was grand and stubbornly French, making a lucrative name for itself as a romantic hangout for journalists, contractors and statesmen.

An American journalist and a U.S. Army Signal Corps officer sat on the hotel terrace overlooking the boulevard, its morning traffic and the Saigon River beyond. They were sipping coffee and talking about a woman, an expensive Vietnamese hooker whom the journalist referred to as "Pandora", a woman who, according to legend, was capable of translating her contempt for white-skinned males into stunning, sadomasochistic rituals that generated a guilt-ridden, slavish ecstasy among her clients, her rituals for revenge.

"Thing about Pandora," the journalist concluded, "she always winds up on top."

Before Pandora entered the conversation, the two Americans had been talking politics. Although many would argue that sexual commerce was as political as the reportage in *The New York Times* or *Stars and Stripes,* they had been discussing larger affairs. The journalist had not been pandering for the fun of it. He was seeking information.

"What does Kennedy think?" the reporter asked.

The press officer leaned back to let a thin, white-jacketed man clear the breakfast dishes. "I don't think Kennedy knows where Vietnam is. Or cares."

"Oh, he cares." the journalist said. "Kennedy may like Negroes and small children back home but when he smells a commie overseas, he gets downright bumptious."

"Suit yourself." The press officer had eaten breakfast on the journalist's tab. He wanted Pandora's number, but he hadn't put out much information. "Looks to me like the same-old, same-old. They send a shitload of obsolete equipment over, call it aid, the local generals get a few new advisors..."

"Come on," the journalist said. "Kennedy's up to something."

A flock of young girls in graceful ao dais cycled down the boulevard below the terrace rail, catching the press officer's eye.

The journalist pressed his point. "Think Bay of Pigs, pal. Think Khrushchev, roughing him up over the Berlin Wall. Now a bunch of Buddhists are burning themselves in the streets and Vietminh guerrillas are everywhere. The Vietminh are Communists, buddy."

"I don't think Kennedy's gonna touch it."

"Camaaahn!" The journalist pulled a small, spiral notepad out of his bush jacket. "Kennedy likes to show the world he's tough on Commies."

"Eisenhower warned him about this place," the press officer replied. "De Gaulle warned him personally. Called the place *un puits sans fond.*"

"A what?"

"A bottomless pit, pal." The press officer finished his coffee. "A bottomless pit."

A chill drifted off the Saigon River, drawing tendrils of vapor across the water. A monstrous gray hulk appeared out of the mist, rounding one of the great, graceful oxbow bends that loop the ancient waterway through Saigon. Looming over the shipping-channel buoys, the hulk materialized into an aircraft carrier, a fleet of helicopters lashed to its deck. High above the misty flight deck, a glint of sunlight gleamed off the glass in the carrier's bridge.

"Well I'll be goddamned!" said the journalist, dropping the notepad and rising. "Getta loada that!"

The press officer squinted at the craft looming over the mist in the river. "I don't see anything," he said.

The journalist looked long and hard at the press officer. "Right," he said, and tucked his notepad away.

"So," the press officer said, rising from the table. "You gonna give me that number?"

"What number?"

The press officer grinned. "For your friend, Pandora."

The journalist sighed, pulled the notepad back out of his jacket pocket. "You owe me." He scribbled a number in his notepad and tore out the page. "On two counts," he said.

MIDDLETON, MASSACHUSETTS

Connie and Eddie sat leg by thigh, holding hands on the crest of a granite wave that hung suspended over the steep, forested hillsides of the Nashoba Valley. Ages before, flinty New England farmers had torn the stones from the soil and built walls around the edges of their fields. Now oaks and ash and beech and pines had grown over the fields and the piled stones. In the distance, an army of bulldozers cut a dirt swath across the wooded valley floor to build a new highway.

Sunlight pierced the trees overhead, dappling the couple in autumn light.

"The army?" Connie asked. "You're going to join the army?"

"The Marines."

"Oh, Eddie." She hung her head to hide her tears.

"For cryin' out loud, I gotta do somethin'!"

"Don't shout. I'm right here, you know."

"They'll teach me a trade. Somethin' I can use to make a livin'. I hafta do that, you know? Make a livin'? I can't go to work for my old man. I don't want be a fuckin' locksmith." He spun a splinter of granite off the promontory into the treetops below. "You got a better idea?"

"I had a better idea. Back last fall when you could have applied to college like everybody else."

"Yeah. Fitchburg State Teachers College. Big fucking deal."

"You didn't try."

"So I messed up." He tossed another flake into space. Sometimes Connie seemed too thick to be smart. Couldn't she see? The kids who got into college, the good colleges, came from different kinds of families, with big homes and helpful parents who told them how great they were doing every time they blew their noses. The fathers all drove into Boston to work. They didn't drink beer on weeknights and work for the town. They didn't call their kids "Hey, asshole." People traveled on different roads and — once school was over — they wouldn't come together again, not here, not in college, not on the job, not anywhere. Couldn't she see that?

She put her arms around him. He seemed young, younger than her and thin, not the strong boy she loved to watch play basketball, not the boy who had found her body, kissed her breasts, lain between her thighs. They were entering another world. "You could apply again," she said. "Keep your job down at the greenhouse and hey! It's almost fall. Send away for the applications. I'll help you."

"Yeah, sure you will, from all the way down there, wherever the fuck it is, the campus cutie with all the Ivy League guys. You'll have plenty of time for me."

"Okay, I make you mad." She pushed him away. "You're making me mad too. I thought you were a fighter." She had an impulse to push harder, to shove him over the edge, to put him out of his misery, feeling sorry for himself. Joining the army. What a dumb, small-town thing to do. "I guess you have to make your own decisions." She sat back on the granite.

"You sure did," he said. "Now I got to make mine."

"I'm sorry you didn't grow up the way I did. I can't help that."

"Aw, come on, Honey." He sat down beside her.

She put her arms around him. "But I hope, Eddie Carpenter, I hope with all my heart, with all these bombs and everybody hating the Communists and all that, I hope you don't have to go off and kill somebody just so you can learn a trade."

The pine needles smelled hot and pitchy and the earth-movers snorted as they cut into the ancient New England hills.

"Maybe I could get a job drivin' one of those Caterpillars," he said. "That'd be pretty cool."

Connie dropped her head to her forearms.

MANHATTAN

All fall David and Madeline had rendezvoused at a low-lit, brick-bound, Hell's Kitchen hideaway, doing each other's homework, exploring each other's bodies, running away from home. The apartment belonged to her big sister, who loaned it to the two teenagers on workdays. "Just make sure the sheets are still clean before you leave, Midget," she had told Madeline.

They made love here for the first time — the first time for both of them, immersing themselves in the heat and humidity of a New York summer afternoon. They sat on her sister's bed.

He turned to sneak a peek at her. She seemed lost in thought.

"So . . . Here we are," he said.

Madeline turned abruptly, took his face in her hands and pressed her mouth to his. With her came the fresh scent of soap, lavender, and a hint of sweet breath. "You smell so. . ."

"So . . . What?" she asked, unnerved by her own temerity.

"I dunno." He grinned. "Lemme check again. To make sure." He turned until they were knee to knee.

She giggled and pulled them back on the bed.

"Wait," he whispered, "I want to watch you undress."

"But you've seen me before."

"I want to see all of you."

"Okay." She grinned hard, hoping he didn't see her fear. " But you go first."

"Okay," he said. "Shirts."

"Nope." She pushed him back and stood up. "Shoes." Leaning on his shoulder, she unlaced her sandals. "Come on."

He rose, grinning, kicked off his shoes, stripped off his T-shirt. He tugged at his belt, buckle clanking, and kicked out of his jeans. "There," he grinned, standing at attention in his boxer shorts. "Way ahead of the game."

Button by button, she opened her blouse and shook the gauzy madras off her shoulders.

Barely breathing, he stepped forward, traced the line of her neck and shoulders.

43

"Please." She pushed him away. "I want to show you." She arched her back and reached behind. With a twist, she opened her bra and shrugged it into her fingertips.

He dropped his eyes.

She unzipped her skirt, letting it fall, stepped out of her panties and stood before him, hands to her sides.

His mouth opened, a tiny 'o'.

"Stop it, silly," she said, sunning herself in his gaze.

He sat down and he pulled them back onto the bed. They kissed, fingers and palms caressing each others' curves and flanks, exploring their differences.

"No fairsies." Madeline snapped the elastic of his boxer shorts. "Get rid of these."

He rolled to the edge of the bed, kicked them off and — grinning — turned back to her.

She cradled the back of his head and thrust her lips against his, opening his mouth. He thrust back, their tongues dancing together, billing. She felt him harden against her. He pressed at the raised curve of her hip and knee, his hand sliding down her thigh.

"Wait," David whispered. He leaned over the bedside and reached into his jeans pocket.

She fell back, eyes closed, not wanting to invade his privacy. She giggled at the absurdity. *Privacy!*

"What . . ." he asked, startled.

"Nothing." She stroked his thigh. "Just . . . Thank you."

He had practiced many times before, but this time — sliding the ring over his cock — it felt real. *Not like looking at a naked girl in a magazine,* he thought. *"Not lonesome.* He kneeled on the bed, up-angled now.

She relaxed, one knee bent, thigh opening, feeling his hands straddling her shoulders, placing her palms on his hips as he maneuvered between hers. She laughed.

He froze.

"Don't stop. It's okay," she said. "It's funny, too." She pulled him to her, embracing his hips with her knees. Trembling, he felt a wet warmth embrace him.

She inhaled sharply. "Oh!"

He stopped. "Are you okay?"

"Yeah," she whispered. "Keep going," willing her body to take over. She felt him push further than her fingers had ever been.

Awkward at first, their gawky thrusts began to quicken and take on grace. He fell out, poked her inner thigh, they giggled. She guided him back inside. The dance intensified, their breath growing ragged, summer sweat slicking their bodies until she lost herself in circles that radiated outward from a place inside her that had no center. She heard a moan, a pretty moan, distant at first, then closer until she recognized it as her own. As her undulations subsided, his tempo increased. She felt, then heard a growl as he thrust, felt her body moved by the strength of his hips, his belly, his legs, until . . . he stopped. Breathless, he pushed up with his arms until he arched like a bow, taut, poised, head thrown back.

In suspended silence, she stroked his wet hair, ran her hands down his back and pulled him deeper still until he collapsed onto her and they lay together, their pulses slowing.

They returned to consciousness locked around each other, drinking each other's eyes, lips, victorious faces. Sweat had turned her hair to ringlets and he kissed each curl on her forehead, blew them from her eyes. Their hands found each other again, seeking sweat and secrets. After a moment they stirred.

"I want to get on top," she said.

David toppled sideways, slipping out of her, laughing as she straddled his hips and pushed him back inside. "Now I can really see you!" He lay back, hardening again, adoring her beauty, watching her drift from serene repose to fierce focus as she began to gyrate. His hands roamed from hips to her glistening face to her breasts, she dancing above him until they once again found a shared tempo, moving through and around and over in a duet they had never known before.

Now, gray autumn light filtered through the bars and panes of a basement apartment. David lay on his back beside Madeline, hands behind his head, humming. He broke out into a low lyric.

Please see that my grave is kept clean.

"I think it's sad," Madeline traced David's bare shoulder with her fingertips.

"It's the blues, bayyybeeee," he said.

David and Madeline lay side-by-side under a quilt. David surveyed their surroundings. *Not bad*, he thought. His guitar leaned against a straight-backed chair. Behind it hung an unframed print of a Modigliani nude. He looked from the guitar to the Modigliani to the ivory-toned body stretched beside him. Madeline, Modigliani, me.

He moved lower, finding the soft curls between her thighs.

"Hey!" She raised her head on one elbow. Hair tumbled across her face. "You got another rubber?"

"No."

"Okay, then. Hands off, Romeo."

"I could wash the old one out."

"Oh, *yuk*, David." She rose to her feet, swept the sheet and blankets around herself, and disappeared into the bathroom. 'You're disgusting." She giggled. "Cute disgusting."

Outside, a cold rain began to fall through the gathering dusk.

Shivering, he scrambled into his corduroys and turtle-neck sweater. He lit a cigarette and called home. "Hiya, Ma. I'm downtown. Just got out of, uh, basketball practice. No. We had it late today. Look, I'm gonna stay down here, okay? Madeline is gonna come over to where I'm playin'. She's fin-ishin' her homework. Yeah, yeah, I know. I'm getting mine done right now."

Loving his lies, he watched Madeline emerge from the bathroom, her long hair pulled in a wave across one bare shoulder. Wearing the sheet and blanket like a robe, she padded smoothly across the room, her gait rolling into her hips, eyes on the floor, her mind a million miles away. He felt like a restless young gangster in a French movie. "Yeah, Ma, I promise. Before midnight." He hung up. It wasn't a movie; the apartment was real; Madeline was real; their lovemaking was real.

BRONCO, TEXAS

Harry Levin left his lecturer's post at Harvard to take a position in President John F. Kennedy's new international aid program, the Peace Corps. He had been excited by the Kennedy promise of justice and social change. Despite his skepticism, he believed that — with the Kennedy crowd — things could happen. When they offered him a job, there was no question: He would take a sabbatical and help launch the Peace Corps round the world.

The appointment was delayed, a bad joke, a third strike following a broken marriage and a death in the fam-ily. He took a job teaching history at Bronco High. He saw his sojourn in backwater West Texas as a sardonic respite from the pompous swirl of Ivy League academia and the pressures awaiting him in D.C. In a further capitulation to impulse, he rented an Airstream trailer parked in a grove of cottonwoods down by the river and settled into watery, contemplative seclusion.

As school opened at Bronco High, Harry Levin launched a project to inject inspiration into his listless Texas students. "What's going on out there?" he shouted at the somnambulant teenagers. "What are these new governments in Africa all about? Who's Patrice Lumumba? Why is Guatemala mad at America? What are these crazy guys with the beards doing in Cuba?" He rattled on like a brainy Gatling gun, never waiting for answers.

The kids at Bronco High closed ranks against the Northerner. Levin's urbane sense of humor confused them. His enthusiasm seemed alien and inappropriate. Teachers were supposed to be staid, boring. They gossiped about him in the halls. He was a communist, a weirdo. The guys thought he was a homo. The girls thought he was cute.

Who is this guy? Roger asked. *Where did he come from? What is he doing in Bronco?* He was different, this Harry Levin guy. He didn't dribble out the usual worn-out, cracker-barrel West Texas worldview, and he seemed to have a life somewhere else, a real life that he revealed in jokes, passing comments, and anecdotes that always seemed to hold a lesson.

Unlike his classmates, Roger wasn't convinced that there was nothing new under the Bronco sun. He didn't believe that life consisted of getting born, putting up with twelve grades of public school, getting drunk, landing a job, getting laid, hooking up the old ball and chain, having kids, paying the bills, growing old. As far as he could understand, this new teacher guy believed life was to be learned as well as lived, that there were worlds beyond the horizon that offered excitement, adventure and purpose. To Roger, Harry Levin opened a window onto a world that was different from Bronco, Texas.

Roger thought about his old man, who spoke of the faraway lands he visited, not with a sense of adventure or purpose, but with drunken contempt. He'd sit in "his" chair, a beer or a bourbon in his hand, commenting on how filthy and disgusting "those people" were — Africans, Indians in Guatemala and of course, the deadly depraved Commies anywhere — China, Russia, Cuba. When Roger questioned his old man about his travels, Bob Wolfe would wave his drink in the air, blink with annoyance and snarl, "Mind your own business."

Conversely, Roger's questions seemed to give Mr. Levin a big kick. He always took time to answer. There was something about him that made Roger feel at ease, like eating French fries. He enjoyed challenging the new teacher — not about history, Roger knew nothing of history — but about Levin's opinions on everything from Presidents to rock and roll.

One day, after class, Levin took him aside. "You know, Wolfe, if you quit being such a wise-ass, you might turn into a human being. Stranger things have happened."

Roger had matured into a handsome teenager. His brown eyes warmed the straight-nosed Nordic features he had inherited from his mother, Dottie. She had also given him the flare of red that burnished his blond hair. "What're ya pickin' on me for, Mr. Levin?"

"I'm not picking on you, kid," Levin answered, talking around a toothpick that lolled from one side of his jaw to the other. "I'm offering you a shovel, hoping you might dig yourself out of this shit heap."

"What shit heap?"

Levin laughed. "C'mon, Wolfe. Look around you. What shit heap you think I'm talkin' about?"

"What." Roger frowned. "You mean Bronco?"

"Bingo, Roger. Bronco."

"What's wrong with Bronco, Mr. Levin?"

"Oh, nothin'. If you're a go-nowhere dumbbell with a future full of oil rigs and cow shit. Nothing wrong with that, Wolfe. Problem is . . . " He grinned. "There's something wrong with you."

"Wrong?"

"You're different. You don't have the same crapped-out attitude everybody else's got around this dump." His features softened. "You don't even know it, do you?"

"Don't know what?" Roger asked.

"That you don't fit in." Levin pointed a pencil at Roger. "You don't belong here."

"Who says?" Other kids had parents, a family. His mother had been diagnosed with cancer and he had stopped calling his father 'Dad.' He was a good-looking kid, blond and blue-eyed, popular among his classmates, most of whom he had gone to school with since he was six, but he often felt alone in Bronco. This man was telling him there was a reason for his loneliness.

"Look, I don't have time to fuck around. Neither do you. I'm outta here, verrrry soon. So I'm taking a chance here. I'm telling you the truth."

"What truth?"

"That you have a brain. You have a spirit. And somewhere, hidden beneath that atrocious cowboy hat and those dirty fingernails, you got class. It's your senior year, Wolfe," he told the boy. "Go to college. Meet some people." He chewed on the toothpick. "Go down to Austin. To the University. I hear they let cowboys in for free."

MANHATTAN

Madeline and David were now practiced in this lovemaking thing. It was romantic as hell, the stuff of *La Nouvelle*

Vague, the French New Wave, resonating with the passions that raged between Jean-Paul Belmondo and Jean Seberg. For the young lovers, this was what you did before dressing and sauntering down McDougal Street to the coffee house where David was booked for another Monday night solo gig.

John Henry's was named after the steel drivin' hero who died with a hammer in his hand. John Henry had worked himself to death, sacrificing his life to beat the steam drill, a devilish machine that, ironically, spared human muscle from the pain and monotony of hard rock drilling while it impoverished thousands of laborers, black men slinging sixteen-pound sledges onto the shining eye of a steel drill, driving holes in rock for the Irish dynamiters to fill, to cut the tunnels and level the grades for the railroads that had stitched together the parts and pieces of America to make one great land that David had fallen in love with.

An English entrepreneur, with a taste for aged American whiskey and young American girls, owned John Henry's. He lurked behind the bar, keeping a desperate eye out for what he called *totties*. He knew nothing of the music, and depended on his publicist to book the folkies who drew his customers. The cash register was his talent gauge. You rang up strong, he asked you back. Of course, the Englishman kept his bets covered. There was never less than a half-dozen folk hopefuls on the bill. Tonight, David Friedman was one of them.

He climbed onstage, flushing beneath the warmth of the lights. Madeline curled in the corner, watching people and jotting down her notes — sketches, she called them. She waved when he sat down and looked out, blinking past the lights. The cuffs of her jeans jacket covered all but her fingertips. She wore a red bandana in her hair.

While David sang, a lanky figure in a leather jacket and jeans slouched into the club. He leaned a guitar case against his leg and glanced around the room. David finished his set. The leather-jacketed stranger climbed on stage and pulled out an old, scarred Martin guitar, hung a wire contraption around his neck and fished a harmonica out of his jacket pocket. He blew a discordant wail through the harmonica, pulling the audience to him. He jabbed at the chords of his song with a choppy guitar style, feinting at them like a fighter, ducking the downbeat, side-stepping the backbeats, dropping measures, stretching out phrases, with no rules to follow but his own.

"He's writing that stuff himself." David sang old tunes, faithfully reproduced. The stranger's tunes sounded like folk songs, but they painted a fragmented picture, mixing Woody Guthrie's hillbilly understatement with an edgy anger that belonged to no one but the man behind the harmonica.

"Hmmmm. You're right." Madeline opened her notebook.

> Songs like a crack in a mirror. On one
> side of crack, ye olde folk songs, on
> the other side, beatnik poems, then
> a Lenny Bruce wise guy, then back
> to folk songs. He's . . . different!
>
> He sings about real stuff, not just love.
> About politicians with God on their
> side, murdered Negroes, masters of
> war. The letch who owns this joint
> calls him Bobby Dylan, so that's his
> name — for real? Is he for real?

During his own set, David couldn't get the stranger's voice out of his head. He stayed away from Woody Guthrie tunes and sang a song about a dirty old town and an angry young man who sets out to destroy the world around him. The song seemed simple-minded in contrast to the complex ironies that Dylan had layered into his music.

When he finished, Madeline had disappeared. He stepped off the stage and floated to the empty table where his guitar case lay open across his chair. The cider sat cold on the table, a thin streak of whiskey curling across the surface. Onstage, a trio decked out in identical madras shirts launched into a bawdy English ballad. In contrast to the stranger's bleak discord, the barbershop harmonies sounded silly. But where was Mad? And the stranger with the new songs? Where was he?

He had never before taken the step through the velvet curtains that hung across John Henry's "artists only" door. It was a haven where the older performers lurked, smoking, drinking, fondling each other in corners. He pushed through the curtains. A narrow stairway descended into the gloom of the brick-walled basement. The curtains closed behind him, muffling the song of the singers.

He heard the thin, reedy voice of the harmonica genius, then Madeline's laugh. He shuffled down half a dozen steps and leaned under the low ceiling. The bare brick walls were covered with posters of past performances. A scarred coffee table covered with old editions of the *Village Voice* squatted in front of a collapsed couch with an Indian print bedspread thrown over it.

Dylan lounged on the couch, one spindly leg crossed over the other. His boots dangled at the ends of his thin shins. Madeline crouched at the other end, pen in hand, open notepad on her lap.

David caught them in mid-laugh. "Madeline?"

She looked up at him, still smiling.

"'Madeline?' That's French, isn't it?" The stranger's Midwestern accent, so broad on stage, had disappeared.

"That's what he said." She jerked her head toward David. "When he first heard my name."

"Great minds." Dylan grinned, swinging his boot easily over one leg, swinging, swinging.

Madeline turned to David. "He was telling me he writes those songs so fast, he can't remember 'em."

"Yeah?" David clumped down the stairs. "That must be a lotta tunes you got there."

Dylan took in David with slight bemusement, stood, the leather coat hanging off his thin frame. "I better get upstairs," he said, glancing at Madeline. "I got a few more tunes to forget."

"See ya." Madeline giggled.

The stranger brushed past David, his boots disappearing softly upstairs. The music blared loud, then fell off as the door closed behind him.

David's mouth felt dry. "You want to go out with that guy or something?"

"I was curious." She closed her notepad. "I wanted to see what he was like. Maybe write something for the school paper."

"So did you get an interview or is it gonna take a little more time?" He collapsed on the couch. He lit a cigarette and inhaled angrily, his feet splayed straight out in front of him.

"Hey. We were just talking."

"You came down here lookin' for him didn't ya?"

"Yeah. So?"

"So, what do ya think he thinks now?"

"I don't know what he thinks." Her eyes blazed. "And I don't care." She leaned back against the couch. "I wanted to talk to him. He's interesting. Big deal. You're not the only one gets to do things. I could write a story about him. I'm sitting here, watching you play your songs. You sound cool. Really cool, but you don't care. It's more important for you to get jealous over some guy. And for what?"

"You tell me."

"I'm not your damned wife ya know, just because we do it together."

"'Just because!' " His mouth fell open. "You call that 'just because'? That's our own special thing."

"You're all bent out of shape because you think he's better than you are."

"How do you know?" His voice tightened with anger.

"I just know. It's always got to be a contest with you guys. Jesus." She pulled a cigarette out of her purse and lit it angrily.

"Gimme another one."

"You haven't finished the first one yet." She threw the cigarettes and the lighter on the couch beside him. "And you know what?" She squinted against the tobacco smoke. "He probably thinks he's a big fucking deal because some chick asked him questions about his dumb music."

"It's not 'dumb music.'"

"Now you're defending him? This is what I should write about. Not about some stupid folksinger. I should write a big, fat book about jealousy."

BRONCO, TEXAS

Roger stood at a workbench, listening to KLIF radio while he rebuilt the fuel pump on the Sheriff's aging DeSoto. He had skipped school. On Thursdays they always served this cheesy slop at school called Welsh rabbit. Forget about it. Now it was almost one p.m. and he was hungry. A bulletin alert buzzer broke into the doo-wop. "Three shots reportedly were fired at President Kennedy's motorcade today near Dallas' downtown section. We're checking out the report. Stay tuned."

Roger kept working. *That could never happen*, he told himself. He sat down beneath a cottonwood and ate his sandwich, soaking up the pale November sun. He drank a Coke but he felt itchy, puzzled. Still, the doo-wop kept playing, so what the heck. *Oh well, the joke's on that news guy*, he thought, and went around back to piss.

He reassembled the fuel pump and was cleaning up when the radio alert buzzed in a second time. A somber voice came over the speakers. "Ladies and gentlemen, the President of the United States is dead. John F. Kennedy has died of the wounds he received in an assassination in Dallas less than an hour ago. We repeat, it has just been announced that . . ." A long pause. "President Kennedy is dead."

Roger's vision blurred. The air filled with a gray mist and he felt hot. His heart began to pound and adrenaline shot through his limbs. He stood at the bench, listening to the news bursts. Strangely, the music played on between bulletins. That pissed Roger off. His head was filling up with questions and he didn't want to be alone. Not now. He rubbed his hands clean with a rag and gasoline, jumped in his truck and roared down to the river, to Harry Levin's ramshackle Airstream trailer.

He parked on the patchy grass and knocked on Levin's screen door. "Mr. Levin?"

No answer, only the sound of the opening and closing of drawers. Roger opened the screen door and stuck his head in. "Mind if I come in?"

A cabinet door slammed.

Roger walked into the dim light of the cramped trailer. Harry Levin was standing over his bed, folding a shirt in a chaos of scattered clothing.

"What are you doing?" Roger asked.

"Gettin' outta here," Levin growled. "Suddenly, Texas feels like enemy territory."

"Why?"

Levin spun to faced Roger. "Why?! Because they shot the President in Texas. That's why." He tossed the shirt into an open suitcase at his feet. "Do you know what's happened, Wolfe?" Levin picked up another shirt and snapped it into a crude fold.

"Yeah, well sure. The President got killed."

"President John F. Kennedy was assassinated by alleged unknown assailants. Be specific, Wolfe. This is reality."

"But why are you leaving? What's gonna happen now?"

"Who the hell knows, for Chrissakes!" Levin softened. "This is one of those times when something happens that is big, complex, full of portent, that . . . "

"What does portent mean?"

"Look it up in the dictionary. Wolfe, you gotta understand." He put his hands on Roger's shoulders. "I don't have any answers. This has never happened before."

"But what should I do?"

Levin turned back to his shirts. "Take it all in, Roger. Keep asking questions. Listen to the news. Read the goddamned newspaper."

"Okay. But . . . "

Down the narrow corridor, the phone rang.

"I gotta take this, pal."

He started down the hallway toward the jangling bell, then turned. "Do what I told you to do. Go to college." The phone rang on. Harry Levin winked. "They let cowboys in for free."

In the glow of the kitchen light, Roger could see Levin stooped over the phone, talking low into the receiver.

MASTERS OF WAR
NOVEMBER, 1963

WASHINGTON, D.C. — *Gusano* is Spanish for worm. Cubans also use the word to describe people who oppose *la revolución.* For example, the CIA-backed exiles who invaded Cuba at the Bay of Pigs were *gusanos.*

On the day of the invasion, President John F. Kennedy had ordered the attack and then driven to Virginia to play golf with his little brother, Attorney General Robert Kennedy. Thousands of U.S.-armed and hastily-trained Cuban nationals hit the beach, landing in a motley flotilla of private boats.

Once the invasion began, Kennedy refused to offer further support. Unmarked B-25s filled with bombs and armed with machine guns were not allowed to take off from Florida. No artillery fire came from the sea to support the landing.

The Cuban army, a people's army, was ready, trained and prepared for just such an attempt. The invading *gusanos* were killed, captured, or driven into the sea. Contrary to the stubborn predictions of the President's advisors, no Cuban wished to welcome any *gusanos* to their island. They were outraged, and repelled the invaders with cold fury. The "liberation" of Cuba was an overnight disaster. Jack

Kennedy's refusal to support the invasion angered certain people.

The *gusanos* in Miami were angry because Kennedy stood by while their children died on the beaches.

The CIA was angry because the President had castrated their battle plans.

The Mafia was angry because they had thrown their support behind Kennedy at election time. In exchange, they had expected to recoup their Havana hotels, brothels, and casinos after the invasion. Now, there would be no invasion, no overthrow, and little Bobby Kennedy had begun hauling them into Congressional hearings. The Mafia expressed deep disappointment in the President — to their friends.

Fidel exchanged the 1,113 *gusano* soldiers they had captured for $53 million worth of penicillin and baby food. This was too much for Jack and Bobby. Cuba had grown problematic.

The White House contacted Jean Daniel, a French reporter in Washington who was scheduled to interview Fidel for *L'Express.* Daniel rushed to respond.

"I would like you to broach the subject of *rapprochement* with Mr. Castro," the President told Daniel. "Sound him out. Off the record. We'll talk further when I return from Dallas."

Jean Daniel flew to Havana and met with Fidel at his bungalow on Veradero beach. Fidel began the interview with a discussion of Cuban cigars and national health, meandered through his love of American jazz and baseball, and landed, almost coincidentally, on *rapprochement.* "Do you think," he asked Daniel, "that Jack Kennedy has come to a better understanding of Cuba's needs and desires... since the Bay of Pigs?" He raised his eyebrows quizzically.

In another room, the phone rang. An aide came to the door. "It's President Dorticós, Fidel," the aide said. *"Es urgente."*

Fidel excused himself, picked up the phone, turned his back on the reporter and listened. The silence raised the hair on Daniel's arms.

After a brief, quiet exchange, Fidel hung up. He drifted back to the table, eyes glazed. "Kennedy has been shot," he said. "In Dallas, Texas." He sat down. "This is bad news. This is very bad news."

They sat alone together for a moment. The sound of the surf washed the beach outside and a breeze flowed through the gauze curtains. Fidel turned to the reporter. "I'm sorry, but I'm sure you understand. This puts an end to your mission of peace."

COMPARED TO WHAT?
1964 – 1966

MANHATTAN

June greenery burst out across the city. After a year of sporadic, mid-term *rendezvous*, Madeline and David lounged once again in her sister's basement apartment. In the darkening room, David was convinced that Madeline's body glowed. She looked ethereal, distant. "Here. Try some of this." He extended his hand.

She pushed him away.

Confused, he sucked another hit off the tarred brown paper. A seed popped in the glowing tip. He held his breath, pushing the smoke into his lungs. The backs of his knees began to tingle. "Do your knees itch?"

She stared over at the boy on the sheets, lying flat and relaxed, a tomcat on a hot day. *What is he doing here?* she thought.

"Well, not your knees exactly. " He took another pull and held the smoke behind his constricted throat. "More like the back of your knees, like the little hollow in back." He cupped the fingers on his free hand and thrust them behind her naked leg. "Right there."

She jerked her leg beyond his reach.

He caressed her naked shoulder. "Are my hands cold?" He raised himself on an elbow. "They can't be," he giggled.

61

"It's summertime." He took another hit off the joint. "It's summertime, summertime, sum-, sum-, summertime."

"Oh, David. Shut up."

Uptown, beyond the span of the George Washington Bridge, a rolling wave of thunder tympanied across the river and into the Manhattan canyons. The window fan hummed unevenly, the moan rising and falling with the drafts of an approaching thunderstorm.

"I'm sorry," she said. "I just feel . . . "

"What?"

"Far away from you." She felt coerced by his tireless affection.

"You're just not used to having me around." He forced a laugh. "We got all summer. We'll come down here, go to the concerts in the park."

"I'm gonna be busy."

"Doing what?"

"Writing for the paper."

"In the summer?"

"Yeah, 'in the summer'. You think everything should grind to a halt, 'cause you come home from school?"

He whistled low. "Wow. Madeline's mad." He gauged her dark look. His grin faded. "Why didn't you say anything before?"

"Life isn't going to just start right back up again, you know." She rolled out of bed, grabbed her skirt and blouse off the threadbare chair and crossed the room. The bathroom door swooshed shut, swaying the fringe of the Spanish shawl that hung there.

Dismayed, he sat up, hugging his knees, perspiration turning cold. The marijuana high turned to spikes of tense hyperawareness. She was acting like a trapped animal. "Just 'cause we were apart?" he shouted through the door. "People stay in love if they want to."

"People meet other people, too."

"Oh, wow!" He rose. "So that's it! Another guy, huh? While I'm stuck on campus minding my own business." He lied. Over the year, he had crossed paths with scores of academic lovelies sporting mini-skirts, boots to the knees, bangs cut low, eyes made sultry with Cleopatra mascara. In the coffee houses they flocked around any performer with a guitar and a wistful demeanor. There had been dalliances, but he always felt horrible afterward and avoided his one-night lovers. Madeline reigned supreme in his heart. *Why doesn't she feel the same way?*

Through the months that separated them, David had become a talisman of her former innocence and adolescent neediness. He seemed to have grown younger, not older, childish in comparison with the men she had recently met, men with their own lives, their own apartments. She could learn from them. "I've been with other people, you know," she said. "Right here in this room."

"'Been with?' What's that supposed to mean?"

"You know."

"You did it?"

"Yeah."

"Right here?"

"Yes." She swept her panties from between the sheets and stepped quickly into them. "It doesn't matter anyway," she said.

"Doesn't matter?" He watched her comb her hair in the mirror, snapping at it angrily, pulling it down over her red- and black-striped jersey. Her body had disappeared beneath her clothes.

Outside the window, rain began splashing on the pavement.

He stepped into his pants and pulled the belt tight beneath his skinny ribcage. "You cheated on me."

"That's a funny word," she said. "'Cheated'. Like I peeked at your hand in a game of fish? Like I stole money

63

from the Monopoly bank? Life isn't a game, y'know. Besides, I know what college life is like. You telling me you didn't meet any girls at school?"

"No. I didn't. I'm your boyfriend."

"You would've if you could've." She lipsticked her mouth in the mirror. For a moment, she saw her mother in the reflection — the same rapid, seemingly careless strokes of color that always landed perfectly on the lips.

"Would've . . . could've," he mimicked, getting angry now. "You sound like a school kid."

"Oh, yeah?" She stepped into her low-heeled Capezios and turned to face him, thrusting a hip against the short suede skirt. Her black hair shone wild around her dark features, her eyes flashing in the Cleopatra makeup, the red-and-black stripes of her jersey following the curves of her breasts. "Do I look like a school kid to you?"

A smear of white light flashed through the blinds, followed quickly by the racket of thunder. The drumming of the rain increased as if a gigantic hand had turned up the volume. She felt regret close around her. *Too late now,* she thought.

David stared at her with the hollow eyes of one of those corny Keane paintings. The apartment was no longer their hideaway, not after Tony the photographer and Mark the journalism T.A. and that weird guy who afterwards told her all about his wife. *His wife!* "You know, it's easy, once you get a diaphragm. No one has to worry about getting knocked up, nobody has to use a rubber."

"Shut up, Mad!" he shouted, his voice husky. "Why are you saying all this shit?"

Because that's how I was taught, she shrieked to herself. "Because you don't own me. Fucking is just a thing anyway. It's like going to the movies. It doesn't make you married to somebody. You and your stupid jealousy. God!"

He stood silently, head cocked, watching her. No words came.

"Why are you looking at me like that?" she demanded.

David had lost his ability to speak. Lethargy fogged his brain and weighted his limbs.

"I'm getting out of here." She strode to the door, Capezio heels clicking on the parquet floor. "Let yourself out."

The door slammed shut.

Stoned and alone, David listened to her heels scuff up the slate steps to the sidewalk. The rain settled into a steady drizzle, cooling the air. He walked to the window and opened the shutters on the rain-lit black and blue of the New York night. He struggled to make the world small, picturing the rain falling all over Manhattan, falling on roofs littered with television antennas, old chairs, water tanks. Rain falling. On people running with groceries, holding up improvised newsprint umbrellas, huddling beneath café awnings and diving into taxicabs, splashing past windows of one-room apartments lending privacy to lovers.

"Fuck you, Madeline," he said aloud to the empty room. "Fuck you."

BRONCO, TEXAS

The cigarettes that Dottie Wolfe had smoked since her teens ganged up in her alveoli and poisoned her cells. With her husband out of town, she turned to Roger, as she had many times before.

He accepted his responsibilities with a fear-filled loyalty. Every day he would stop home after school to make sure she had eaten, taken her medications or kept her doctor's appointment. Then he would race off to pump gas at the local Texaco. Despite his intentions, Roger never did get around to applying to Austin. Besides, with Mr. Levin gone, his grades weren't worth squat and he'd had no one to advise him.

Dottie continued to waste away. As she did, she retreated from the world, leaving Roger helpless and guilt-ridden. Why was she leaving? What was he doing wrong?

When she was too weak to walk, the doctor ordered her into twenty-four-hour care. Two orderlies took her — still strong enough to curse and look good at the same time — from Roger's arms and ensconced her in the county hospital. She died on a Thursday afternoon while Roger was pumping gas beneath a bright, blue Texas sky.

He called his father in New Orleans. "Mom died."

"Shit."

"What?" Roger couldn't believe his father's response. "What did you say?"

"Nothing. It's just bad timing."

"Yeah, well . . ," Roger said, anger rising, "it was really bad timing for her, too."

"What's that supposed to mean?" His father's voice turned surly.

"Never mind." He sighed into the phone. "Can you come home?"

"It's gonna take some doin' . . . "

Bob Wolfe stood at the fringes of the small cemetery crowd, arms crossed over a skinny tie and white shirt, watching his son Roger and a sprinkling of Dottie's friends grieve over his dead wife's casket. Afterward, father and son drove to the gas station.

Roger pumped gas into his father's rental car while the old man sipped coffee. The old man was heading back to New Orleans that night. "Don't you miss her?" Roger asked.

His father glanced sideways at his son. He took another poke at his coffee. "Sure I do."

"Don't you miss me?"

"'Course I do, son." He put down the coffee on the workbench. "That's one helluva question for you to ask."

"But you can't stay."

"No."

"You got important work to do, right?"

"You better believe it, buddy." He gave Roger's shoulder a squeeze.

"I took good care of her, Dad. Best I could, anyways."

"You're a good man, Roger."

"I'm a man now? That's what it takes? My mother dyin'?"

"Hey, take it easy, son. We're all pretty broke up here."

"Bullshit. You don't say 'shit' and 'bad timing' when you hear your wife is dead. You say 'shit' when you run over a skunk and it stinks up your tires."

Bob Wolfe turned cold, his tone measured. "I said, take it easy."

"You barely make it to the fucking funeral and now . . . you're gone again? You call that 'broke up'?" Tears blurred his vision. He clenched his jaw. He wouldn't let his father see him cry. "You're not supposed to treat your wife — the people you love — like that."

"I have my reasons for comin' and goin'. You know that."

"Yeah?" Against his will, grief wrenched a sob out of his gut. "Like what?" He jammed the gas nozzle back in its cradle with a clash of metal. "Like what?" he repeated.

"National security is a big deal in this day and age, boy. You know that."

"They can't spare you for a minute?"

"I'm protectin' you . . . "

"From what?"

"I'm not at liberty to say."

Roger laughed a loud, harsh bark. "Mom didn't need any fuckin' national security. She needed a husband . . . somebody who cared about her." He retreated into the gloom of the garage, looking for a rag to wipe his hands. "Only, knowin' you," he emerged from the shadows, "she didn't need that either."

Bob Wolfe grabbed his son by the arm. "Look, you little bastard. The world is a dangerous place. While you're fiddle-fucking around here with your girlfriends."

Roger stepped to the bench, grabbed a grease rag. "I don't have a girlfriend."

"I'm the one keepin' all you people safe," Wolfe growled.

"Thanks a pantload, Dad. You're my hero." He tossed the rag on the bench and turned to face his father.

"Better believe it, boy. I know my enemies. Do you?" He pushed his son backward with hard, flat-handed shoves to the chest. "You don't have to like what I do. Shit, boy, you don't even know what I do. But goddammit . . . "

"Listen. Your fuckin' protection racket is up for grabs." He thought about Harry Levin and the hilarious position he took about America, past and present. "You think the enemy is out there." He leaned against the car and waved his arms at the horizon. He didn't want his father to see him shaking with rage. "You're wrong. The biggest enemy is right here. It's the U.S. fucking government, that's who the enemy is, you fool. The government and the corporations and the banks." He smiled broadly. "And that includes you and your cheesy, dumb-ass spy outfit . . . Dad!" He spat the 'Dad' out with such sardonic rage that his father yanked him to his sour-breathed face.

"You don't know shit about it, boy." His face grew livid.

Roger laughed in his face. "If I hear one more time about how, if I knew the things you knew, I'd feel the same way you do. Shit. Mom dies alone while you get paid to play hero." He pushed his old man away. "You make me puke."

Bob Wolfe's hands locked around Roger's throat, throwing the teenager off balance. They stumbled against the garage workbench, knocking a tray of socket wrenches into the grease pit behind them. Bob Wolfe found Roger's shin with the inside edge of his boot heel and drove straight down onto his son's foot. Roger screamed in pain and, locked together, father and son fell into the grease pit.

Roger scrambled to his feet, at the bottom of the grease pit, leg and ankle burning from his father's boot stroke. Bob Wolfe lay still. Oil and a thin trickle of blood blended into a viscous mess on the oil-soaked floor.

Outside the garage, the afternoon light angled from the west, lengthening the shadows of the cottonwoods, darkening the cluttered insides of the garage. Roger knelt over his father's form. Beneath the palm of his shaking hand, the older man's chest rose and fell. Pressure built behind Roger's eyes. He couldn't cry, not again, not over this, not now.

Hands shaking, he drove the rental car behind the garage, parked it, and threw the key into the alfalfa field beyond. He drove to the bungalow where he had lived his life, where his father had shared his table like an alien, where his mother had lain in bed reading magazines and dying.

He opened the door onto the barren living room, neglected during his mother's demise, the rug filthy, the drapes dingy, one of the naked oriental lady lamps broken. The Texas sunset bounced off five hundred miles of red New Mexico dirt and burst into the near-empty home, projecting a perfect square of rich orange light across the living room wall. A picture that had hung there for years, a harlequin-suited clown with a white face, now sat on the carpet, tilted against the wall like a drunk in an alley.

He put on a Sinatra record, one of his mom's favorites, and limped into the bathroom. He turned on the shower and shed his funeral clothes. The whole front of his shin had been scraped blood red. "Bastard," he spat out loud, hoping his hatred would defeat the fear. He could picture his father lying in the grease pit.

Please don't let him die, too.

Raw leg smarting, he soaped down before the water got hot. He had to leave — that night. He was going to begin his life like Harry Levin said he should. He'd get out of town, head for Austin and the college they had there. 'They let cowboys in for free,' that's what Mr. Levin said.

Roger Wolfe hit Austin about ten a.m. and found a boarding house near the campus. He wanted an anchor, a place to land in the midst of his road-weary confusion. The place was filled with white, pasty-looking guys who called themselves "grad students". The landlady called them "beatniks", but they paid by the semester and rarely "raised a fuss", she assured him. She looked the young, red-eyed refugee up and down but, allowing as how you mustn't judge a book by its cover, she took his thirty-five dollars for the week and let him drag his paltry belongings upstairs.

That night he lay in the dark and stared up at his thoughts. He couldn't convince himself that it had been a mistake, the fight with his old man. The anger, when it came, was unmistakable. He felt that he had struck, not out of his love for his mother or personal rage, but from a deeper hatred of his father's ugly heart, his foul temper, his creepy job — everything about him.

The next morning, Roger took to the streets in the Ford pickup. A hot afternoon sun dazzled the windshield. Seeking familiarity, he gravitated toward a dusty neighborhood with sun-baked, run-down bungalows, old vehicles propped up on cinderblocks and rag-tag sofas on the sidewalks. He drove out to Austin's auto row, looking for work, knowing that his wad of cash would melt away quickly.

He cruised the dreary boulevard bordered by a parade of brightly painted cinderblock boxes advertising $29 transmission rebuilds and nine-dollar tune-ups. It seemed as if every garage owner had just hired a cousin or a sister's boyfriend. The doubts closed in again. He might have killed his father. The thought was unbearable and David moved quickly past it, realizing that — even if his old man survived — he was alone, a penniless outlaw in a strange town. He needed money. He needed a job.

A waitress in a coffee shop called him "Honey" and told him to come back later when the boss showed up. She had a way with the boss, she assured him with a wink. He returned, the boss never showed, but the waitress took him home to a sad apartment. In a bed adorned with satin pillows, she took him in, bucked and gyrated until she reached a shrieking climax and then clung to him, smelling of rose petals, liquor and tobacco.

Claustrophobic and hung over, Roger fled into the gray dawn.

Two days later, after his dwindling assets had strengthened his resolve, he returned to the coffee shop, hopeful of the promised meeting with her boss. He sat expectantly at the counter, grinning tightly, wondering how he would work, day after day, with a woman who had been so . . . needy.

She refused to acknowledge him with anything more than a cool, gum-snapping. "What can I get for ya?"

"That job we were talkin' about. I . . . "

She laughed and slid a cup of coffee down the counter. "Come and gone, Hon. You was a little slow on the follow-up."

He wasn't sure what "the follow-up" meant, but when he rose to pay, she put her hand on his forearm and said, "It's on the house, Cutie."

Manhattan

"You want to go where?" Face slack with surprise, Aaron Friedman stood in the palatial Riverside Drive apartment and confronted his son.

"Philadelphia," David repeated.

Blinded by the glittering expanse of the Hudson, the television executive squinted at the boy.

"It's just for the summer," David continued. "To work with this new group."

"What group?"

"Students for a Democratic Society."

"Students for a Democratic what?"

"Just what it says."

"We already got a democratic society."

"Dad," David began. "There's another America out there. With poor people in it."

"Don't get smart with me," his father snapped. "I come from poor people. You come from poor people." Aaron turned his gaze toward the river. The sun had turned the Hudson bright blue. Below them, the leaves sparkled green in the treetops of Riverside Park. Hadn't he pulled them out of a nowhere disk jockey gig in Pittsburgh, leapt at the network ladder? Hadn't he paid for this, all of this — the tenth-floor apartment with a river view, the help, the

Eames furniture, the dinners out, the Broadway shows? Yes, he had, goddamn it, bought it with sweat, ingenuity, long hours and frazzled coffee'd-up nerves. Now his son was about to throw it away. "What about the job at the network?"

"I can't."

"You won't be working for me."

"It's not about you."

Aaron's face darkened. "You're going to take this job I got you. Maybe you'll learn something. And — at the risk of sounding cheap and trivial — You'll earn some god-damn money!"

Nina emerged from the bedroom. "What's the shouting about?"

Aaron ignored his wife. "We're making sacrifices to put you through college."

"Come on, Dad." David stared out the window. "You're making calls to your broker."

"David!"

"I'll ignore that." Aaron jerked a thumb at his son. "This guy wants to go to Philadelphia for the summer. To work for free!"

Nina arched an eyebrow. "Philadelphia?" She sat on the edge of one of the matching Eames chairs, legs crossed beneath her silk skirt, slim feet fitting perfectly into elegant heels.

"He's gonna go work for 'the other America', whatever that is."

"You make it sound like a company, Dad."

She turned away from her husband. "Tell us, David."

"It's about poor people. Bringin' 'em together." He thought she might listen. When the network needed his father in Las Vegas, Texas, California or the new Nigeria, David and his mother had become partners, even confidants. "Welfare mothers and miners' wives. Don't you remember? I told you about it."

"I was under the impression you were studying," Aaron said dryly. "Not doing charity work."

"It's not charity work!" he shouted, frustration rising. "Jesus! They're teaching us how to fight the fucking system."

"Keep your voice down, Aaron," Nina crooned. She wanted to hear her son. "And what will you be doing to, um . . . Fight the system?"

"We're opening a poverty office. They've already found a storefront in the right neighborhood."

"A storefront?" his father asked. "You'll be fighting poverty out of a storefront?" He turned to his wife in dismay. "We're going backwards here, Honey."

"Wait a minute, dear." Nina put a hand on her husband's chest. Every morning, after David and Aaron left and before Dorothea arrived to begin her daily routine, Nina sipped coffee and read substantial portions of *The New York Times*, sitting at the dining room table in her robe. Her son's zeal for things beyond sports and girls made her curious.

After David had described the March on Washington the summer before, Nina had felt great stirrings over what she described as 'the quiet dignity' of Dr. Martin Luther King. She was fond of Madeline, her son's girlfriend, not for her wifely potential but for her independence. She quietly envied the young girl and the fresh new world she seemed to be building around her. "So this is important to you?"

"It's important to all of us, Ma. If we don't fix this . . . "

"Fix it?" Aaron interrupted. "You don't 'fix' poverty. It's a fact of life. It's been around as long as there was grain to hoard, goats to herd and priests to hustle you. I know that. Your mother knows that. We been there, David! I've done storefronts. My whole childhood was about storefronts — dry goods shops, locksmiths, butcher shops, boot shops, yentas behind the counter, penny-pinchers in the back room. Fuck that! You don't need storefronts!" Aaron swirled the ice in his glass. "What're ya gonna sell in this damned storefront?" he said quietly. "An anti-poverty pill? Misery medicine? Anarchy? Revolution? Emma Goldman delivering more stirring speeches? Sacco and Vanzetti?"

"Their kids go to school hungry," David replied. "We eat steak and lobster and if I don't like it, the waiter takes the whole fucking plate back to the kitchen and throws it out!"

"Jesus, kid, you're all over the map here." Aaron raised his eyes to the ceiling. "What's poverty in Philly got to do with the price of lobster in Manhattan?"

"You talking to God again, Dad? He's not listening."

"Try to make sense, dear," Nina said.

David rose and pushed past his parents to the window. "Ma, me and Madeline broke up."

"Aw, Honey." She put her arms around his shoulders.

"Shit." Aaron said. "You gonna let a dose of puppy love stand between you and a job at the network?"

"Hmmm." Nina glanced at her husband over her son's shoulder. "Interesting priorities."

MIDDLETON, MASSACHUSETTS

Exhilarating! That's how Connie described her first year at college. The tweedy professors, the varnished lecture halls, the old stone buildings on campus made her feel grown up, out in the world. The library, filled with silence and the smell of Latakia wafting from undergrad meerschaums propelled her out of childhood toward her dreams. She would master the languages of the world, her work would ensure that people spoke to one another, they would reach out to join hands across the seas.

Many of her classmates, particularly the girls, already led grown-up lives in New York City or Boston or Washington, D.C. Many had come from far-off places like Paris or Tehran and spoke foreign languages like flowing water, full of laughter at word play and *double entendre*, things that Mrs. Gladstone, her high school French teacher had never been able to teach. She soaked up Russian and Spanish. She revised her thinking about the Middle Ages and reveled in the intellectual history of Eighteenth-Century France. In the clamped-down, no-think climate of Middleton High, she had felt alone, an "egghead". Here, people listened carefully to her deepest thoughts.

Before exams began, Connie's father had already arranged a summer job for her with a colleague. Her new employer was a long-range meteorologist who tracked weather patterns from what he called "dusty old records". The meteorologist, a handsome, gray-haired Yankee with thin lips, crooked teeth and a perennial chuckle, warned her that tabulating ninety years of weather reports would be "pretty darned tedious." Still, the job would take her to Boston every day on the train. She could eat lunch by the Charles River. There was a ten p.m. train back to Middleton, so, on special nights, she could stay for the free rehearsals at Symphony Hall or catch the first set of a folksinger at a Cambridge coffee house.

Restless after her first few days at home — the job hadn't begun yet — she had driven her mother's Pontiac station wagon down to the lake after dinner. She sat in the car, the windows open to the velvet night, listening to the radio.

She hadn't called Eddie Carpenter since she returned for the summer. In her own eyes, she seemed cold, uncaring. How could she be so cavalier as to arrive home without contacting him? He was — at very least — an old and dear friend. They would not have to resume their romantic ties. Back roads and back seat passion were behind her now, but she must not spurn him. She would ask about his plans, give him loving advice.

She drove around the lakeshore and parked beneath the thin birches that surrounded the Carpenter family's sad, sprawling home, hardly more than an attenuated shack. What if he was home alone? How would she face his anger? His advances? His old Chevy was absent. What if his sisters were there? Wouldn't they be angry at her, too?

I mustn't let fear rule me. She opened the car door, then stopped. *I need to be honest with myself.* She didn't want to inhale the stink of home permanents. She didn't want to make nice with sister Carol of the long legs, the short shorts and the haughty stare. *To be quite frank*, she told herself, *I probably don't even want to see Eddie all that much.*

Grateful for her own admission, she got back in the car and jounced back along the dirt road that ran around the lake. The relief was fleeting. How could she have turned her back so completely on him? And where was he now? With another girl?

Enough of this foolish seesawing, she told herself. She would see him. It was going to be a long summer and she'd better set things straight from the beginning. Resolved to do something about the situation, she drove to Farnsworth's, the ice cream parlor that served as a summertime hangout for the kids at Middleton High. Maybe Eddie would be there. If not, someone would certainly know where he was.

The heat and humidity of the summer day clung to the evening. Connie spotted Franny Ducharme jerking sodas behind the windows of the ice cream parlor. Connie hadn't been close to Franny in school, but she felt relieved at the sight of a familiar face. Franny hadn't gone away to college. She might know of Eddie's whereabouts. "Hi, Franny. How's it going?"

Franny shrugged. Behind the screen, her face glistened with sweat. "What'll ya have?" She wiped the vestiges of the last order onto her apron.

"How about the usual?"

"What's that?" Franny stared through the screen, her expression as flat as her accent.

"Franny, it's been the same for years."

Franny stared at her.

"Okay. Sorry. Silly of me. An orange freeze, please." She watched her former classmate dip into the tub with the heated spoon, bending over, her uniform skirt rising above the backs of her knees, her sneakers slimy with melted ice cream and dirt. She opened the screen and thrust the gooey drink at Connie. "Sixty-five cents," Franny said.

"Wow, hey . . . " Connie caught herself. Most of the kids who worked at Farnsworth's gave away free ice cream to their classmates.

"No more freebies. They caught a kid last week."

"Sorry." Connie reached into her blue jeans for a dollar bill, feeling panicky and alone. "When's your break?"

"'Bout five minutes."

"Will you come talk to me?" Connie asked. "I'll wait over by the car."

"Why not?" Franny slammed the screen closed, shutting out the flies. She shifted her gaze to the next customer.

Connie scuffed through the gravel parking lot, sucking on the cold orange sludge. She leaned against her mother's Pontiac and waited. That new group was singing "I want to hold your hand . . . " through the tinny speakers. Some people had it harder than others. It could make them bitter. She hoped Franny's life wasn't totally miserable.

"So," Franny said, "what's up?"

"Have you seen Eddie?"

"You gotta be kidding me."

"What do you mean?"

"Eddie joined the service."

Franny had knocked the wind out of her lungs.

"Didn't he tell you?"

Connie looked down at the gravel, her vision swimming.

"You and him. You never talked about this?"

"Of course we did." She looked away to hide her wet eyes. "I told him he shouldn't go. I told him he should go to college. I even said I'd help him apply."

Franny waved at a boy in a convertible, a stranger to Connie.

"I didn't think he'd actually *do it*!"

"Why not?" Franny's question felt like a jab. "You were gone."

"I didn't mean that much to him."

"Honey. He worshipped the ground you walked on!" Connie lit a Marlboro.

Beneath the stained apron and the orange and white uniform, Franny was soft and round, her breasts hiked high, her hips wide, calves smooth. Her eyebrows were plucked in a harlequin arch, her lipstick glossy. Connie could imagine Franny and Eddie together. "Why didn't he say anything to me?"

"He's a guy! What guy says anything?" Franny's eyes narrowed. "You shoulda known what to do. It's your duty."

"My what?"

"Your duty. To your guy."

Strange, Connie thought. She had never thought about having a duty to perform with Eddie other than to be a good person. She dropped it. She was tired of dealing with Franny's righteous working-class attitude. Connie didn't feel much like a privileged college brat. "But you do know how to reach him."

Franny threw away her cigarette and crushed it into the gravel with great concentration.

Connie glared at her former classmate. "But you do know how to reach him, right girl?"

Franny looked up.

"You and Eddie? You kinda . . . " She wrinkled her nose. "Keep in touch. Right?"

"Honey, my break's over." Franny smiled. "I gotta go." She turned and crunched away on the gravel. "Ask the Marines why doncha?"

Connie drove home in a trance. The familiar hills and curves of Middleton's back roads rolled beneath the Pontiac, the trees cloistering the pavement, greenery looming black over the windshield. The Marines? Why had he done it? She was responsible. *She* had reached down, crossed the boundary between college prep and the shop kids. She had dragged Eddie out of the layered safety of his small-town beginnings, mussed his hair and laughed at the simplicity of his worldview. She had seduced him with the urgency of her ideas. Her eyes blurred and she burst into tears, sobbing, wiping her eyes with the back of her hand. She rounded the curve near Kimball's dairy farm. Eddie used to step on the gas here, to bounce her around in the passenger seat. She heard his laughter.

A clash of metal exploded on her eardrums. A shattered windshield fractured her view. Stunned, she sat still, the Pontiac's engine raced, the car went nowhere and two crooked headlights glared crazily at her through the spider-webbed safety glass.

"Stupid bitch! Look what you done to my car!"

The grandfather clock ticked ponderously in the hallway. In the low-lit sonority of the ancient house, a lone cricket scraped a crazy solo from behind the bookcase. Connie's right arm ached, her head throbbed and the tears and blood had dried her face stiff as a mask. She sat on the flowered slip of the sofa, her feet flat on the floor, her pocketbook beside her as if she were waiting.

The brass spring of the clock wound up. Boom. Boom. Boom. Three a.m. The floorboards creaked in the hallway and the urgent murmurs of her parents' voices rose out of the fading dissonance of the clock's timeworn chime. She heard words like "charges" and "insurance rates" and "sobriety test".

She had ruined the family car. Well, one of them. There was no use telling her parents that she had been upset about Eddie. Not now. They might not even remember him. After his mother had determined that he was too "nice" a boy to take advantage of their daughter, and her father had approved of Eddie's polite interest in his encyclopedic knowledge, they paid only distracted homage to the comings and goings of a townie who wasn't even applying to college. They rested secure in their daughter's good judgment. She would outgrow him and she certainly wouldn't allow him to "go too far".

Her parents entered the room in a ceremonial silence. Her father carried a cup of coffee in his hand, the flowered pattern on the china clashing with the rough plaid of his Pendleton. Unshaven, Saturday growth darkened his face and he still had on his orange hunting hat. Despite the heat, he had come out to rescue her dressed like a woodsman, driving the pickup that he kept for what he called "chores around the property".

"How are you, dear?" She sat on the couch beside her daughter, her bathrobe drawn neatly around her thin frame. She did not touch Connie, not to calm or comfort her, not to stroke her cheek or straighten her hair. It was not her style.

Connie nodded, a lump in her throat. "I hurt."

"We need to take her to the hospital," her father said.

Her mother straightened up and turned away from her daughter. "At this hour?"

"I'm all right, Dad."

Her mother put a hand on her wrist. "Sweetie, we need to know."

"That's not important now, dear," he snapped. "She's been in an accident."

Connie's mother ignored him. "Chief Hannigan was concerned."

"Why? I'm okay."

"I know that, dear. He wanted to know if you were drinking with those boys," her mother said.

"Drinking?" Connie's features fell in pain and amazement. "They were coming from the other direction! How could I have been drinking with them?" She *was* hurting. "Why are you asking me this?"

Her father glared at his wife. "I'm sorry, Honey," he said. "We just need to know, that's all."

"You're worried about my reputation? What about my well-being?"

"This is foolishness, Sweetie. You're upset." Her mother sat back on the impeccable flowered fabric of the sofa. "We're all worried. Your father, the Pontiac, those boys . . . "

Connie didn't wait for any further explanations. She knew there would be none. "I used to think you were like other people's parents. That you loved me."

"Connie! That's a terrible thing to say!" Her mother rose from the sofa.

Her father stood silent over her, looking puzzled, hurt.

Connie began to cry. "It's only been a *year*," she cried. "A stupid, single year and I'm a stranger. Not just to the kids in this town, this stupid little town, but to you, too." She looked up. Her parents seemed to lean back, away from her, as if she were threatening them. "You don't even know what to say!" She covered her face, embarrassed to show emotion to these strangers. "We're alone," she wailed. "We are all so fucking alone."

Her mother willed herself to tears. Connie had seen her assemble this histrionic display dozens of times before. "You have no business talking that way here," she sobbed.

Connie's father took a position before the cold fireplace. "This is your home!"

"It's *your* home!" Connie cried out. "I don't belong here!"

Connie's father turned to her mother. "We've got to get her to a doctor, Honey."

"Don't talk about me like I'm not here."

"She's got to get a hold of herself," her mother said.

"She's had an accident!"

"I said . . . Don't talk to me like I'm . . . "

"In my car! And it's ruined! And how will I get around town? In that damned truck of yours? That'll be the a pretty picture!" Connie's mother disappeared into the kitchen and began rattling of dishes in the sink. The garbage disposal moaned.

Her father joined her on the sofa. "Sweetie, your mother's upset. You know how she can be." Her father seemed sad, helpless, hopeless. As always.

Connie pushed herself up from the perfect sofa. "Don't worry about it, Dad," she said. "I'm fine." Wanting to be rid of them, she patted his arm and climbed the treads of the stairway to the bathroom. Safely inside, she locked the door and washed the blood and tears off her face. She toweled off the cut, no longer hoping for, instead dreading the prospect of footsteps creaking up the ancient treads to intrude. She knew no one would come. She went into her room and opened her suitcase, as yet unpacked from college.

She took out a leaflet that had been folded into fours, then eights, then stuffed into the flap of a spiral bound notebook that had served as her journal, the record of her first year at school, her hopes, fears and aspirations.

EQUAL RIGHTS FOR ALL
Join
MISSISSIPPI FREEDOM SUMMER

AUSTIN, TEXAS

Roger picked up odd jobs, helping the landlady's sister move, hauling trash to the dump, fixing gates and porch roofs, anything to augment his dwindling savings and buy the cheap breakfasts, cheese sandwiches and truckers' chili that he survived on.

After he played out his daily job-hunt ritual, he usually retreated to the campus where he would sit on the yellow brick terraces that rose, step-by-step, to the tower marking the center of the University. He watched the summer school girls walk by in shorts and pedal pushers, their books and notepads cradled against pastel-colored sweaters.

"Hey, you okay?" An affable face floated above him, suspended between a greasy fatigue jacket and an explosion of black hair. A husky figure in black jeans and sneakers stood before him, a sheaf of mimeographed leaflets drooped over one arm.

"Hi. Yeah, I'm okay. Who're you?" Roger had no idea how long he had been sitting there.

"Name's Albert." He extended a chubby, paw-like hand. "Like Einstein. The genius."

"I'm Roger." Albert's palm felt warm, smooth, comforting.

"You don't look like most of the idiots around here," Albert continued. "You in a fraternity?"

"No, I . . . "

"Good. You into politics?"

"Politics? You mean like voting and LBJ and all that?"

Albert laughed. "No, not voting. Forget that. I mean like throwing yourself on the gears of the machine."

"What machine?" Roger laughed. "Sounds pretty fucked up."

"It's a figure of speech."

"Okay. So, like I say . . . What machine?"

"The University. The machine. That's what Mario Savio calls it."

"Who?"

"Mario Savio.

"Uh, cool." Roger had no idea what this guy was talking about.

"They shut down a whole university. Over there in Berkeley."

"Where?"

"Wow. You really are out of it," Albert said. "Berkeley, in California. Near San Francisco."

That sounded cool. Mr. Levin talked about San Francisco like it was heaven. Roger had seen pictures. It looked pretty nice, with the ocean all around it. So Berkeley had a college. "So this college . . . Who shut it down?"

"The students. And this guy Savio. A bunch of other kids, even some professors."

"Why'd they do that? Didn't they want to go to school?"

Albert sat down on the brick wall next to Roger. "That's a good sign."

"What is?"

"You ask questions."

"Yeah, well," Roger said. "You say weird shit."

"Nothing weird about what I say, Brother." Albert stared down at Roger for a moment. "Look . . . " He stared at his feet for a moment. "Why don't you come to this meeting?"

"What meeting?"

"Students for a Democratic Society."

Students. Albert didn't need to know that Roger wasn't one of them, and maybe he could meet some other kids. He fell back into his cowhand cool, the only defensive position he knew. "Sounds all right, I guess," he drawled.

Albert grabbed him by the sleeve. "Come on, cowpoke. Let's rustle us up some communists."

Crossing the campus with Albert, Roger realized he hadn't thought about his father — or mother — all day. For the first time. Maybe there'd be a buncha chicks at this democratic society thing. This college thing was looking pretty good and he sure was lonesome.

GREENHILL, MISSISSIPPI

"We might not have much." May June Thigpen stood at the front of the SNCC field office and addressed the circle of travel-weary volunteers. Suspended above them from water-stained tiles, two bare bulbs lit the room, casting shadows on the pine floor and wainscoted walls. "But," she continued, "whatever we got, you got it too. Everything from ham hocks to tired feet."

The arrivals laughed and settled into their chairs, relieved by the big woman's joviality.

86

May June was a field secretary for the Student Nonviolent Coordinating Committee, SNCC or "Snick" for short. A thin-legged, broad-shouldered woman with a sloping shelf for a breast, May June was born black and poor in Greenhill County. She had no land and no vote, but she made damned sure she had a voice. By the time she had borne her first three children, she had taught herself to read and write. With the arrival of the fifth, she had book-learned her way through the history of her country and the ways of its government. "Nothin' scarier to the white man than a colored lady with the facts," she explained.

"But seriously now," May June continued, "we are proud to welcome you to Greenhill, Mississippi, not simply as our guests, but as our brothers and sisters. We share a beautiful dream." She laughed. "You proved that by draggin' your tired behinds all the way down here in the Mississippi summer."

More laughter.

"So now, we're all going to work together to make that dream come true, right here, right now."

Louis Guillory stood at the side of the room and watched May June speak to the new arrivals. He had grown up since the Freedom Rider days. His round face had thinned, emphasizing high cheekbones, deep-set eyes and a strong jaw. Wearing a farmer's bib overalls and an immaculate white T-shirt, his forearms reflected the exertions of country living — chopping wood, hauling water — a Chicago boy, stumbling behind a mule and a plow while his rural neighbors doubled over with laughter. He was a city boy bone-deep, "didn't know a hoe handle from his own ax", but they gave him big points for trying.

The winter before, he had huddled at the core of a small group of scared and exhausted SNCC workers who had dared to invade Mississippi armed with boxes of voter-registration forms. They wanted to step up the campaign as the election approached. Their invasion did little to stem the ongoing resistance to integration. A Negro man had been hit by a train in the next county, the torn body thrown into a hole in the ground without a death certificate being issued. No one raised an eyebrow when the engineer reported that the body had not been moving before the train hit it. Two Northern Negroes — Army Reserve officers — had been ambushed on their way home from spring training at Fort Benning, Georgia. Shotguns, shattered windows, swerving autos, a crash. Death. Violence everywhere. Striking anyone, anytime.

The SNCC people reasoned that an influx of college kids from the North might help get the job done and capture the attention of the Northern media. Their presence might shine a light on a society that conspired to keep the Yankee outside and Jim Crow in his rightful place. They reached out to campuses across America, warning of the risks, developing training programs. For months ahead of time, campus volunteers flooded the SNCC office with phone calls and applications.

Those like Diane and Louis, who had survived the Freedom Rides or practiced nonviolence at segregated lunch counters, taught what they had learned to their inspired new troops — nonviolence in the morning, political strategy and the ways of Jim Crow in the afternoon.

Now, Louis surveyed May June's audience. A dozen in number, wilted but expectant, they sat in a circle of wooden folding chairs, fanning themselves with handkerchiefs and notebooks. Sweat soaked their rumpled shirts and dresses, mud clotted their shoes. It had been a long, hot journey from the training sessions on an Ohio campus to the dark green fields, red clay roads and sharecroppers' shanties of Haines County, Mississippi.

He knew how they felt. Negro, white. It made no difference. Arriving in the Deep South jolted everyone. He could picture them, lulled by the vibrations of the bus as it rolled through Kentucky and Tennessee, then east through northern Mississippi, growing aware of the poverty as they rolled south on Highway 61, the specter of Jim Crow growing with every rest stop.

"We got a lot of territory to cover," May June continued. "Tomorrow we're going to figure out who's goin' to be doin' what." She laughed. "My guess is that — when it gets down to it — everybody's gonna be doin' just about everything." She winked. "Just about all the time."

The group laughed. Several groaned aloud.

They already trusted her, Louis thought. *Good news.*

May June popped a caramel into her mouth. "Folks out here are gonna be scared, suspicious, you name it. They're not used to people tryin' to change the order of things and some of 'em . . . " She sucked on the candy. "Ain't gonna like it."

"Now I know some of you folks are teachers. Hope you don't think you gonna get a summer vacation like your kids. No, no. We're gonna need you to keep at it down here in Greenhill. When it comes to ignorance, we gonna stamp it out. When it comes to votin', no holds barred. We're gonna coax, wheedle and plead for folks to register and show them the power of the vote or my name ain't May June. And . . . " She stepped forward and pointed her index finger straight to the ceiling. "When it comes to God's plain truth, we're gonna teach that, too."

Louis' gaze rested on the upturned face of a volunteer who sat upright, ankles crossed primly beneath the rickety chair, gazing raptly at May June from beneath a mop of sandy blond hair cut in bangs. The rest was tied back in a chaos of straggled ends. Heat and humidity flushed a flat, freckled nose, round cheeks and those attentive brown eyes. A sleeveless blouse revealed smooth shoulders, and a nametag written in a graceful but childlike hand identified her as "Connie".

Outside, hard-shelled June bugs batted at the screen door beneath the porch light. A flatbed truck ground up the rutted road, headlights flashing through the field office windows. It rattled to a stop, doors slammed and two young men slipped inside the screen door. They spoke in hurried tones to a man in a denim jacket. He twisted a porcelain switch on the wall and the porch light went dark.

The volunteers turned.

"Louis . . ." the denim-jacketed man called out softly.

"Something went wrong." Elmo, a slight young man with the limbs of a bird and goggles for glasses sucked at his pencil. A mathematician from Cleveland, he sported a short-sleeved rayon shirt, a clip-on tie and an ink-streaked pocket protector filled with ballpoint pens.

"Shhh." Connie didn't like being scared by someone more frightened than she. The air seemed cooler now. She could hear crickets roaring in the fields. Despite the humidity, the night air smelt sweet, full of the odor of green grass and dirt, sudden rains and manure, just like home. *Nothing could go wrong here, could it?*

Connie Moore watched Louis pad to the rear to huddle with the men at the door. He was very handsome and he walked leopard-style on the balls of his feet. Like most of the SNCC veterans she had met at the training sessions, he seemed hardened, mature, powerful and gentle all at the same time. Connie hadn't met many men like that.

The messenger whispered into Louis' ear. Louis looked down at his shoes for a moment and gesticulated to May June, who stopped in mid-sentence. The room went silent as the big woman joined the group of men.

"You've had a long trip."

Louis called to the new arrivals from the back of the room. He managed an uneasy smile. "We can start fresh in the morning. So." He clapped his hands. "Let's get you settled."

The song of his voice raised the hair on Connie's arms. Goosebumps followed. She had to reach out. "I'm sorry to interrupt," she blurted. "But if something's gone wrong here . . . "

Louis glanced back at May June.

"Maybe," Connie continued, "if you told us what's happening. It might help us, you know, gain experience."

Louis leveled his gaze to the girl in the front row. Connie.

"We don't know enough yet . . . " Louis began.

Connie turned in her chair, facing the cluster of SNCC coordinators at the back of the room. "We're going to be working together all summer. It would be best if we knew what was going on."

"She's right." May June joined Louis. "You all got a right to know what's happening." She sat on the sofa and patted the seat next to her. "Come on, Mr. Guillory," she said. "Let the teachin' begin."

Louis stared at his hands for a moment, then looked up. "Three of our new people have gone missing."

Connie's heart leapt, began pounding. *So this is fear*, she thought. *Real fear.*

"Over in Philadelphia — that's just east of here. They trained ahead of you in Ohio and arrived just last week."

"What happened?"

"Day after they arrived, we all drove over to the Ebenezer Baptist Church," Louis said. "The church had volunteered to host a Freedom School for the summer. We had a good talk. That night, the church was burnt to the ground." He sighed and spread his hands, his dismay palpable. "We felt responsible. Yes, the Klan did the torching, but our appearance sparked the tinder. So, yesterday, three of our people returned to Philadelphia. We felt it was critical to be there for the Ebenezer folks."

Louis paused. He shouldn't have told them. In a vacuum of information, news like this would be terrifying, intimidating. The three missing ones were probably fine and this story would reduce itself to a cruel false alarm. On the other hand, this Connie girl was right. In this field office they worked by consensus. Everybody got the facts, everybody helped make decisions.

"After they left," he continued, "they were arrested for speeding, brought to the courthouse, arraigned, fined and released." He contemplated the floor. "That's the last we heard from them."

Moments earlier, Connie had been basking in the reverberations of Louis' mellow tones. Now he seemed confused, fearful.

"They're dead, aren't they?" Elmo peered up at Louis through the goggles of his glasses.

"I sincerely doubt that," May June snapped.

The upturned faces looked so tired, so white, so clearly in need of guidance. Louis felt a great weariness, a need to get the neophytes split up and tucked away in the sad homes of Greenhill, Mississippi. He smiled and place a hand on Omar's birdlike shoulder "When we know, brother, you'll know, too."

Later, an exhausted Connie bedded down in the back room of a pine-plank shanty with May June Thigpen's two teenaged daughters. The room was large enough for their two beds, a shared bureau and a mattress that they unrolled on the linoleum floor. Today was the summer solstice, the day on which the earth, wobbling on its axis, reached apogee with the sun. Ancient societies knew of such things, the Mayans, the Celts, the Egyptians. It had always been so and she knew of it because her father had told her about it, standing in the summer fields of fresh-mown New England hay, the fragrant grass drying, waiting to be baled and stored in the barns that dotted the hillsides of tranquil Middleton, Massachusetts.

Now she lay in a different landscape, listening to her newfound roommates' heavy breathing, her thoughts stretched toward the universe full of stars that glittered heedlessly over an unimaginable act that had made three young people like herself, with families and lives and names and faces, disappear into the summer night.

Bronco, Texas

An endless wire fence rose from the shoulders of the highway, flared into the twin halos of Roger's headlights and disappeared behind him. Mesmerized, he rolled over the nighttime desert, timing his journey so that he would arrive in Bronco after midnight.

Albert and the SDS meeting full of smart kids — and some cute chicks — had strengthened his resolve. It was so cool, this SDS thing. Everybody acting like they could actually change things, even stop the war. Why not? Jeez. They knew about history just like Mr. Levin did, and they made slick plans smart and fast, plans to stop the Machine, they called it, a real-world monster made of profit and industry and television lies, snorting napalm, snuffing justice . . .

And, hey! The most important thing — they talked about all this stuff like they were really going to do it! Damn! Now he knew what Harry Levin had talked about. He wanted to be a part of it. For that, he would have to get into college. He would need his school records.

Now he was on the way back to his hometown — and the crime scene he had fled — to get what he needed. As the highway grew familiar again, his skin prickled. He didn't like being here. You can't go home again. Mr. Levin said that once. Now Roger knew what he meant. Home was dead, like the countless snake skins he had come across, shed by their inhabitants as they grew and moved on. "Call me da Cobra!" he shouted over the roar of the V-8.

He drove past the Old Oaken Bucket, its parking lot empty. The Bucket had been his parents' favorite watering hole. The gas station and garage flashed past, where he'd worked so long, where he'd left his father lying bloodied in the grease pit. Now it was just another crap heap surrounded by junk cars in the middle of a nowhere.

On the outskirts of town he slowed and turned onto Edna Mae Street. The house, his former home, now painted a different color, looked small and sad. Could this pitiful pastel box have been home? Without slowing, he returned to the highway and headed for Bronco High.

When he reached the school, he shut off the ignition and glided behind the dark hulk of the Depression-era building. As the quiet settled around him, he yanked open the truck door, pulled a tire iron from behind the seat and walked quickly across the parking lot.

He had attended school in this dark, turreted building for twelve years. He knew every door, every window, every hiding place. He jammed the tire iron beneath the sill of a window that opened into a supply room. The latch popped like a gunshot. He froze. A car whooshed by. He heard laughter and a cowboy holler. Late-night drinkers, probably people he knew. Poor bastards. Entombed here in Bronco. He scrambled through the window, pulling it shut behind him.

Guided by the varnished banisters, he climbed the creaking stairway to the locker-lined corridors. Outside, a streetlamp backlit the opaque glass of the principal's office. He needed those grades. He couldn't ask a single person in this school, where he had been a fixture, year after year, Cub Scouts, safety patrol, baseball, track, keeping to himself. He couldn't remember learning anything here. Until Mr. Levin came along.

Roger smashed the office door glass with a tight, backhand blow of the tire iron. A shard flew across his knuckle, glistening in the cold, blue light. Sucking blood, he reached through, turned the knob and stepped into the office. The taste of blood, the ease of entry exhilarated him.

Pushing through the swinging door at the end of the counter, he made for the familiar files that held the school records. He'd been here before. Any student in trouble made his way through this door and into the principal's office. Now the office belonged to him. He listened. No sound. No autos.

With the tire iron, he tore at the top lip of the first file cabinet. The drawer front buckled but did not yield. Quickly, hands shaking, he worked around the drawer front, lifting, prying.

Pop! The latch gave way. File drawers rolled out, revealing class after class of Bronco High academic records. 1956, '57, '60. 1963. He pulled out a dog-eared Manila folder, his name written in a teacher's careful cursive hand. Wolfe, Roger B.

Tucking the folder under his arm, he shut each drawer, wiping the handles and fronts with a chalk-dusted cardigan he grabbed from a coat rack. Retreating through the swinging counter door, he stopped to survey the damage. "Da Cobra strikes again," he whispered melodramatically. No one would discover a thing until Monday morning. He'd be long gone by then.

Greenhill, Mississippi

Pairing a black man and a white woman for a field assignment was forbidden, but a sharecropper's wife had agreed to talk — only to a woman — about registering to vote. May June had her hands full. The assignment had fallen on Connie and Louis.

Driving in from the highway to the sharecropper's land, a fast-moving wall of thunderheads rolled over them. The deluge rutted the road so badly that it mired the station wagon up to its hubcaps.

"We've got to get out of sight," Louis insisted.

"That barn." She pointed to a tin-roofed hay barn at the end of the field. "Bet that's where this lady's husband keeps his mules."

"How you know that, college girl?"

"He's a farmer. He's gotta have mules. Besides, silly, there's the hay loft."

Abandoning the stranded wagon, they dashed across the field while the rain fell in gray spikes against the forest beyond, soaking them.

Inside, two stalls, planks worn smooth by generations of animals, took up most of the space. Spare harness and tack hung on pegs. They clambered up a crude wooden ladder to the hayloft. Connie stood barefoot in the straw, dripping wet, letting her eyes adjust to the dim light. Louis stood by the bright square of an open window, backlit by the silver clouds racing by outside. The smell of warm hay calmed her.

He peered out the hay bay. "The road's already turned to mud. Probably just as well." The hay smelled sweet, even to a Chicago boy. "Guess I can get used to this," he said.

"This'll blow over soon," She leaned against a stall and laughed. "Jimminy! Look at us!" Back on the road, one of her sneakers had disappeared as she leapt across the muddy clay toward the barn. Her drenched cotton dress clung to her skin.

An early twilight descended behind the storm. The steady dripping of runoff from the tin roof and the sweet molasses and mown-hay musk of the loft lulled them into a drowsy silence. It had been — like all the others — a hectic week full of early risings and late-night meetings, with plenty of crises in between.

She felt a wave of relaxation spread over her. The loft held the sun's earlier warmth and the scent of animals and dry-tossed hay. Her gaze swept over Louis' shoulders and flanks, outlined against the yellowing sky beyond the hayloft door. She inhaled sharply, exhaled, and began un-buttoning the front of her dress. After the first time, Eddie had always come to her, and she loved rising to his earnest approach. This was different — she wanted to be next to him, without encumbrance. A calm confidence rose from inside, urging her to peel the wet, clinging garment from her shoulders and let it slide down her hips. She stepped out of the circle of soaked fabric and draped the dress carefully over a beam. She shed her bra and stepped out of her panties.

Louis turned and watched as she stood beautiful before him.

She smiled, tingling with warmth. "Mmmm. Feels like I just climbed out of my skin."

This is madness, he thought, but did not speak. His voice would shatter a mystery he had not anticipated.

Unnerved by his hesitation, she threw her arms around his neck, pushed her mouth against his lips and — undaunted — pulled his body against hers.

His hands found the small of her back and he em-braced her.

"You're trembling," she whispered, turning her head sideways against his chest. "Are you cold?"

He refused to answer. He dared not hear his voice for fear it would shatter his desire or bring down retaliation from the enemies that surrounded them.

"Here," she said. "Let me help you out of these wet clothes." She unhooked his farmer's overalls and pushed the straps past his waist.

He stripped out of his T-shirt.

They embraced a second time, her open palms seeking the mass of his arms and back, his hands stretching down to form a "V" at the small of her dimpled back.

They knelt together, then dropped sideways into the hay where they lay locked, tongues exploring mouths. She pushed her palms under his overalls, pushing them down his legs until he kicked them free.

They folded into each other's limbs, the hay prickling their flesh. They twisted and plunged into each other, defying the danger that hovered over the barn, deflected only by its rusty tin roof. Afterward, they drowsed in the darkening loft until the sharecropper coaxed his big animals into their stalls below.

Austin, Texas

Roger slapped a worn manila folder on the admissions counter. "Here's my school records. I wanna enroll."

A thin lady with harlequin glasses and a face caked with powder and rouge glanced at the folder from behind a desk piled high with paperwork. "Good start, Sugar."

"They let cowboys in for free, right?"

"That's right, Honey." She resumed her work, head down. "If they're from Texas."

"Well I'm from Texas."

"That's good, dear."

"So let's get started," Roger replied, leaning on the counter. "What's next?"

Without looking up, the harlequin lady replied. "Okay. First, you'll need your completed Texas Common application, two admissions essays with your name and Social Security number on each page, an official transcript on your school letterhead and the signature of your high school principal."

She clacked on stiletto heels across the room to a stained coffee pot. "We'll need a signed statement from your school describing its ranking policy and a grade-distribution list." She poured half a bowl of sugar into a mug, added coffee and stirred. "You'll want your SAT's sent here directly. Them scores on your high school transcript will not satisfy this requirement."

She returned to the counter sipping the thick, black liquid. "Then there's your non-refundable five-dollar application fee, and Hon . . . " She glanced over her glasses at him. "The deadline for the fall semester was February first."

"You're supposed to let cowboys in for free."

"You still have to apply, Sweetheart." The harlequin woman dropped a stack of application forms on top of his wrinkled Bronco transcripts. "Even if you're Gene Autry."

He snatched the papers off the counter. "I'll be back."

"I know you will." She thrust a form at him. "Fill this out and we'll let you know when it's time to apply for the spring semester."

"Shoot, Ma'am, I don't hardly have an address."

"That's fine," she answered vacantly, already on to the next task. "Give us what you have and keep in touch."

Roger scribbled his name and the boarding house address down on the form and stomped out, heels clicking on the marble floor.

Outside, he blinked through the sunlight at the pamphlet. An application fee. And what's an SAT? Signatures from Bronco. This required a dad on one side, a mom on the other, a phone number, a principal's support. He had none of that.

Days later, a tired-looking detective in a rumpled blue suit appeared in the admissions office, looking for a Roger Wolfe. The harlequin lady shuffled through the "Ws" in the files. "No Roger here. I got me a Deborah Wolfe."

"Deborah Wolfe didn't burglarize her high school, did she?"

The harlequin studied her face in the mirror of a compact. "Not to my knowledge, Hon."

"Uh huh." Irritated that he had been assigned a burglary case from some crummy little West Texas town, he headed for the door and lunch.

She snapped her compact closed. "Wait a minute . . . There was a kid in here last week. Wanted to enroll."

The detective returned, pulling out a greasy little spiral-bound notepad. "He fill in an application?"

"Started one. Told him he'd have to wait for the spring semester to apply."

"You still got it?"

"Naw. I threw it away, Honey. I try to keep a tight ship here."

"What'd he look like?"

"Cute blond fella. Hold on here. I think he filled in a card. For the application notice."

Roger passed the landlady in the foyer. "There was a man come around here today, askin' for you," she said.

Roger's heart corkscrewed. His father was after him. "Was he small? Dark? Did he have a little moustache?"

"Oh, no, dear, he's a policeman." The landlady stood up from the oven. "I know him. Went to school with my son." She had set a pan of corn muffins on the sideboard and fixed him with a sad, steady stare. "Have you done something wrong, dear?"

Roger found Albert at the student union. "Listen, Einstein. I gotta get outta here."

Albert looked up from his cheeseburger. "Wha .. ?" He surveyed Roger's grimace. "Siddown." He shoved the plate of fries toward Roger. "Ever been to the Windy City?"

Roger grabbed a handful of fries. "Never really been anywhere. 'Cept for Bronco and here."

Albert shook his head. "Bummer, man. You gotta get out more often." He finished the cheeseburger. "Chicago. SDS. National headquarters is up there."

Roger brightened. Maybe he could leave but not lose a foothold in this exciting new world. "Yeah? What do I do? Just go there?"

Albert dropped a couple of bucks on the table. "Grab yourself a cheeseburger, bro. I'll set it up for ya."

MASTERS OF WAR
AUGUST, 1964

WASHINGTON, DC — "Atlantic City. She used to be a queen, John." President Lyndon B. Johnson sat in the White House, swirling ice in a glass of bourbon and watching the opening gambits of the Democratic National Convention. On television. From afar. A shrewd politician, he knew how to work a room and — more important— when not to. "Now she's a relic."

"Sir?" John Steinbeck, a thin, swarthy man with a worm of a moustache on his upper lip and bright, black eyes, sat on a silk brocade sofa opposite the President and the First Lady. Steinbeck had volunteered to write a biography for Johnson's use in the upcoming campaign.

The offer had moved the President deeply. He admired Steinbeck's populist writing and was flattered, particularly if the biography could be slapped together before the election. Johnson invited Steinbeck and his wife, Elaine, to join him and Ladybird Johnson in the White House on the eve of the Democratic National Convention.

The author and his wife had been rushed by limousine from their Sag Harbor home to a local airstrip where a nasty-looking military plane awaited them, twin props whirling.

Now, Steinbeck and Elaine sat watching the Convention with the President. Elaine, a tough, pretty Texan born into a wealthy oil family, was no debutante. She had just finished a long run as the first-ever woman stage manager of a Broadway musical. Fascinated, she drank a vodka gimlet and soaked up the experience of sitting across from the President of the United States. She felt comfortable here.

On television, coverage shifted to the boardwalk outside the convention hall, where hundreds of Negro and white demonstrators circled, carrying signs. "We shall not be moved", "Free Mississippi", and "We've waited too long". Lips moved in song.

"Those people are killin' me," the President said, pointing his bourbon at the screen. "Mississippi Freedom Democratic mule-ass party. Shit. That's Bobby Kennedy's doing."

"You're the people's favorite, Dear." The First Lady smiled nervously at their guests. She always grew wary when Lyndon grew too familiar too fast.

Speak truth to power, the writer told himself. "You're a leader, Mr. President..."

"Lyndon, John. The name's Lyndon."

Steinbeck took a sip of Scotch. "Lyndon. That's a grassroots effort. Sharecroppers. The salt of the earth. They need to be represented."

Steinberg's wife Elaine watched her husband with admiration. She kept her surprise at his candor to herself.

"Well hoorah," the President said quietly. "Fact is..." He leaned forward. "We choose these freedom people over the regular Mississippi delegation, the whole goddamn South will secede from the Union." The President shrugged. "We'll all be up shit's creek."

Steinbeck flushed, embarrassed. He couldn't believe the man's crude candor.

"It's like the story of two women," Johnson said. "If I leave the woman I love. Like I love that Civil Rights Bill. And if I get involved with that whore of a war over there..."

"Excuse me." The First Lady rose from the sofa and walked out of the room.

The President eyed his wife's departure. "I'm gonna lose everything. My voting rights act, my poverty program. And..." He belted away at the bourbon. "If I let the goddamned Communists take over South Vietnam I will be seen as a coward and Goldwater will jump in there like a pig in a wallow."

"You're taking this personally?" Elaine Steinbeck raised an eyebrow. "Isn't that a painful way to play politics?"

"Played it that way all my life." The President sighed, his bloodhound face sagging with sadness and fatigue. "Truth is, I ain't fit for political life."

Steinbeck made a mental note: when you speak truth to power — you get a confession.

ATLANTIC CITY

The August day broke cool and gray, a strange feeling for the Freedom Democratic Party delegates from Mississippi. Crowded onto a charter bus, carrying their own food and water — they did not want to risk rest-stop violence — they arrived at the cloudy beach town to be seated at the Democratic National Convention.

Connie Moore stood at the pay phones in the lobby of their rundown resort hotel, chatting up a local pastor who had volunteered sleeping space for Mississippi delegates. She watched as Louis crossed the lobby and embraced a small, well-put-together young Negro woman. They spoke while still holding on to each other. Brotherhood, sisterhood, Connie didn't like it. She didn't like herself for not liking it.

Diane Thomas had changed since she had stepped into the maelstrom of the Freedom Rides. She had moved steadily, without ambition, from coordinator to program manager in Tennessee. When SNCC needed competent, experienced people to staff a Washington office, she was invited to join the effort.

She stayed on, a formidable organizer. Now she had the ear of the Black Caucus, a contingent of Negro delegates and politicians who had leveraged their way into positions of power in the Democratic Party.

"I bring you lousy news," Diane said. Normally she would have enjoyed standing in Louis' company. Not today.

"What gives?" Louis asked.

"Word's out. LBJ's office just announced it. Any conflict between the Freedom party and the Mississippi delegation would be a disaster for party unity."

"We're ready to talk."

"They're not."

"What? Why not? By every law we qualify as delegates."

Diane closed her eyes and raised a hand. "The Black Caucus is meeting tonight."

"The Black Caucus. Great! We'll work up a strategy together. My mother's on the Caucus. She knows my work and she certainly knows the MFDP."

"Then she'll be a life saver. They're meeting to discuss how to lock you out."

"My mother won't allow that. She's a powerful voice in the Caucus."

Diane looked deeply into Louis' face. *Your mother? Do you really think your mother will back you and not the Caucus?* "You're meeting with her first I hope."

"Of course," Louis snapped.

Diane took his hand. "I'm sorry."

"And I know how she'll vote at the meeting tonight." Louis worked hard to hide his fear beneath an outburst. "Goddamn!" he hissed. "We should be scufflin' with Mississippi bigots, not the Black Caucus."

"Louis," Diane whispered. "You keep that under your hat."

Connie materialized at Louis' side. "Hi, folks. From over there, this conversation looks pretty serious." She smiled at Diane but turned to him. "What's happening?"

"Louis and I are old friends." Diane let go of Louis' hand. "I dropped by to say 'hello.'"

"And to bring us a little bad news," Connie added. "Right?"

Diane nodded and turned back to Louis. "Make sure you get somebody into that meeting, Mr. Guillory. A lot hangs in the balance." She squeezed his arm, smiled warmly at Connie and walked away.

Louis Guillory hadn't seen his mother in years. He knew that his impulsive choice to skip exams and join the Freedom Riders had disappointed her. His refusal to return to school had further distanced her. Still, he was hopeful.

Sophie Guillory's privileged position within the Illinois delegation could help them carry the torch. They had recently begun to write each other, but only after Louis had reached out to explain his work and the victories of the voter-registration drive. Now, Connie and Louis sat alone in a sticky restaurant booth, silent with apprehension.

Sophie Guillory arrived in a red suit and matching pillbox hat. She stood before them while she received a stiff embrace from her son. As they hugged, Sophie studied Connie. The girl was attractive, and her happiness at watching the mother-and-son reunion seemed authentic to Sophie. Clearly she was more than a pretty white girl, but . . . *What was her son doing? With this girl. With his life. With this dangerous project.* She quashed an impulse to probe and slid in beside them.

"Louis, my God, boy. Look at you. So grown up and so good looking!" She leaned in to Connie. "He's the spitting image of his father."

Before Connie could respond, Sophie raised her eyes to the chalkboard menu — breakfast, chili, fried fish, hamburgers, macaroni and cheese. "I'll just have coffee." He looked wonderful to her. Strong, clearly defined, no question where the world stopped and he began. Her boy. "You two order anything you want. It's on me. You must be operating on some horrendous shoestring budget." She looked out through the glass at the rumpled delegates lounging in the lobby. "Are these all your people?"

"They're your people, too, Mama."

"Sixty-eight of us came North." Connie volunteered.

"And we have supporters, outside."

"Oh, I know all about that. To get our credentials, we had to pass through your picket line."

"Not a picket line, Mother. A protest. A real, down-home, Mississippi-style, piss-and-vinegar protest."

"Why Louis," Sophie laughed lyrically. "You sound downright country." Sophie's melodious laughter struck Connie as being forced and condescending. "He's been there a long time," Connie explained, annoyed by his mother's distance.

"I'll say. A long damned time." Sophie caressed her son's cheek. "My God, boy, how I've missed you. Changed into a man behind my back."

Sophie turned on Connie, startled by the envy she felt for this pretty girl who chose to speak for her son. "And you, Connie." She resisted the impulse to raise an eyebrow. "How long have you been involved with, ah . . . Louis' cause?"

The implication was clear. "I don't think any of us consider voter registration in Mississippi to be . . . How did you put it? 'Louis' cause'?"

"I see," she said, reappraising the spunky girl. "I can tell you've learned a great deal."

"She has a lot to offer, Mama."

"I bet she does."

"I make my offerings to the movement, Mrs. Guillory." Connie folded her hands on the table as if to say 'enough'.

"She runs the Freedom School," Louis said, enunciating each syllable.

Sophie turned back to him. "How about you? You ever think of going back to school?"

"There'll be time for that," he said. "After the people of Mississippi have representation in Congress."

"Amen," Sophie said. "And am I to believe you were chosen to lead this righteous expedition?"

"We filed the papers we needed to claim our place as Mississippi delegates," Connie said. "We had so many obstacles to overcome."

Sophie sipped her coffee. "It's an amazing thing what you people have done."

"'You people'?" Louis pulled back.

Sophie laughed and turned to Connie. "There you are!" she said. "That's the boy I know! Looking for those cracks and crannies. A way to get . . ."

"Mrs. Guillory," Connie interrupted. "We need your help. We're struggling to be recognized here."

"Your presence has been noted."

"Noted. But not recognized," Connie continued.

"Your interests are well-represented. Why, look at me." She picked up her badge and ribbons from off her trim, well-accoutered bosom. "A Negro woman with a delegate's credentials. That can't be all bad, can it?"

"They're going to seat those crackers, Mama."

"You let the people with the savvy bring this off. We have a champion in our corner."

"Who, Mama? Who's our champion?"

"Mr. Lyndon Baines Johnson, the President of your U-nited States. One and the same." She moved again in her seat. "I know you've been busy, Louis, but surely you are aware that just last month, President Johnson signed a Congressional bill into a law that will turn your dreaded Jim Crow into a dinosaur."

"Goddam it, Ma. Stop playing the innocent. Johnson believes the Civil Rights Act could push him under a bus and you know it. Now he's gonna do whatever he has to — including throwing us under another bus — to keep Dixie in his pocket."

"You sound cynical, Son."

"I'm no cynic. I'm simply observing the cynical actions of a cynical, self-serving man and his cautious, cynical cronies. Don't visit his political fears on me. I'm not afraid for my career. I have no career."

"More's the pity."

Louis ignored her. "What I have is hope."

"Louis, you can have hope and you can have courage. But you've got to understand the other fella's point of view."

"What's that mean?"

"I'm talking strategy, here."

"We have strategy," Connie snapped.

"No. You have convictions. Hope and convictions are the beginning but you've got to get with the program."

"If you can't beat 'em, join 'em. That it, Mom?"

Sophie held her temper at bay. "No. I'm talking about knowing when to fight and where. And how."

"We don't have time for that," Connie added. "People are dying."

"We've always died, Connie." She turned to Louis. "Out of respect for our shared love, I can safely say that you folks will be invited onto the floor as honored guests."

"What . . . to watch?" Louis asked.

"Yes, to watch and be seen."

"Children need to be seen," Connie replied. "Seen and not heard, isn't that the saying? Well, Mrs. Guillory, we aren't children and we have a voice. A strong and righteous voice."

Sophie watched the resolve harden Connie's face and felt a shivering fear. She wanted her son back. "What do you expect me to do?"

"You can fight for us, Mother."

"Pay attention to the march of history, you two. It isn't going to happen, not this time around."

Connie crossed her arms. Louis looked away.

Sophie Guillory sat straight-backed and still. She had come all this way, a black woman delegate at the Democratic National Convention, where planks become platforms and platforms become speeches and speeches become legislation and then policy. She had known that he would be here, too, doubling the delight of her accomplishment. Yet here she sat, estranged and off-balance, feeling a million miles away from her own furious child and the young white woman who crouched across the table from her, eyes blazing.

MASTERS OF WAR
JANUARY, 1965

WASHINGTON, D.C. — "It's a mess, and it's going to get worse." President Lyndon Baines Johnson sat at a wooden table in the White House kitchen and listened to the Senator, Richard Russell from Geor-gia, a silver-haired wreck of a man, who faced him. Two others, Robert McNamara, a hawk-faced man in a double-breasted suit, and General William Westmoreland, braced by epaulets and campaign ribbons, flanked the sagging Senator. They sipped coffee while the President wolfed down forkfuls of ham and eggs.

"Here's what you do," the Senator said.

A steward glided toward the table with a silver coffee pot. The Senator looked up and smiled. The steward stopped, turned, and walked away. He'd been privy to these conversations before. Best not to listen too closely.

"Get rid of that cocky little fella you got playing top dog over there in Saigon." The Senator spoke beneath the kitchen clamor. "That Generalissimo Ky. And his Dragon Lady wife. They act like they're An-thony and Cleopatra running ancient Egypt.

Put a civilian in there. Somebody nobody likes. No commie. No. Somebody who's a nationalist and mad as hell. Let him demand that the U.S. get the hell out of Vietnam. Turn him into the devil and then... we get to fight the forces of evil. He hunched his shoulders and gave the President a tired smile. "Give us a heckuva good excuse, wouldn't it?"

"I'd love to do that, Dick," the President said. "But we've got to work with who we got, not with who we want."

"From where I sit," General Westmoreland said, "either we bring in our own troops to run this show right... "

"No more troops," the President said.

"Then we bomb North Vietnam." The general stared at the President with bright, bird-like eyes.

"We bomb civilians, I'm gonna look bad," the President said.

"We have those targets pretty well sighted in, Sir," McNamara said. "Factories, railroad yards, military installations. I can practically guarantee... "

"Come on, Mac," The President said. "This is wartime. You can't guarantee shit." He rose from the table. "Fellas," he said, "I'm standing here in a goddam paper canoe. I lean this way, I topple over. I lean that way, I topple over. If I stand still, I sink to the bottom of the damned river."

His underlings stared up at him like children at the dinner table who'd just been told they couldn't have dessert.

The President looked down at his aides and laughed. "Okay, fellas, you can have your goddamned war. But if we're going to turn up the juice on this puppy, we're going to need an excuse. We don't have one yet. And until we do, we're gonna stand here in the sun and wait for the trolley car to arrive."

GREENHILL, MISSISSIPPI

Rainwater dripped into a chipped enamel basin that stood in the center of the Greenhill field office floor, playing a duet with the clack of typewriter keys. Connie and Louis sat opposite each other pecking out reports beneath a bare bulb that hung over a card table. A hyperactive battery of kids scribbled at homework assignments for the Freedom School.

The telephone rang. Louis picked it up.

"Louis, is that you?" Louis and Diane Thomas had grown closer during the tragic farce that had unfolded in Atlantic City. As the Convention rolled forward, the "outlaw" Mississippi delegates had refused to sit as guests on the floor of the Convention, an invitation the entire contingent, from sharecroppers to lawyers, had deemed humiliating and fruitless. They would go home defeated but with their pride intact, their hands unsullied. They did not share power with the managers of racist America and they would not pretend they did. Johnson was nominated and had been elected. With or without the Civil Rights

Act, nothing changed in Mississippi. Through it all, Louis and Diane had kept in touch.

"Diane!" He was delighted to hear her voice floating across the scratchy connection.

Silence.

"What's wrong?" Louis asked. "Where are you?"

"I'm in Detroit."

"At school? That's great," he said, turning away from the room.

"Louis. Shut up," she whispered, voice trembling. "Just shut up and listen."

"What is it?"

"They shot Brother Malcolm. This afternoon. In New York."

"That's not possible."

"He's dead, Louis."

From across the room, Connie watched Louis hunch over the desk as if he had been punched in the gut. She got up from her post behind the typewriter. Something was wrong, but she didn't want to interrupt the conversation. The way he cradled the phone to his face seemed . . . intimate. She walked behind Louis and put her arms on his shoulders. She felt him jump beneath her touch.

"What happened?" God, she was sick of having to stand by like this, to plead for explanations.

Without turning, he waved her away. "Reverend King say anything about this?" he asked. "Where does he stand?"

"He sent condolences to Malcolm's family. This could be the beginning of a terrible time."

"We're in the midst of a terrible time."

It was Diane again, Connie realized. Diane, the fellow Freedom Rider, the down-to-earth organizer, sharing a private moment with Louis as she had in Atlantic City. Connie turned to the kids and tried to concentrate on helping them with their lessons. After a whispered goodbye, Louis quietly replaced the phone in its cradle and crossed to the open door. Beyond the corrugated tin of the porch, a winter rain fell into the light, silver spikes flaring before they dropped into the red clay. A dog barked.

Connie stepped out onto the porch and stood beside him, careful to keep her distance. "What happened?" she repeated.

"They killed Malcolm X."

"What?" Her petty jealousy felt wooden. "Who did it?"

He laughed. She looked naïve, stricken . . . pathetic. *Always seeking the truth,* he thought. *Never knowing it.* "Elijah's people," he snapped. "Killing one of their own. In the temple."

"But why?"

"Because he wouldn't toe the line for Elijah Mohammed, the Wise. The All-Powerful. The philanderer. The Prophet. The self-righteous snake." He slammed his hand against the porch corner post. The corrugated tin roof rattled under the blow, breaking the rhythmic patter of the raindrops.

"The police could have been involved." She felt wobbly, weak-kneed. "They want him dead, too."

"Why should they bother?" he shouted. "Sooner or later, we do it to each other. They know that."

The children fell silent in the yellow light of the room. They sat in a cluster, big-eyed, muted rag dolls, watching them. "This is just your anger talking," she said. "The Movement is larger than . . . "

"What do you know about it?

"What?" Her fear of the gulf between them turned to anger. "What did you say?"

He shook his head.

"You bastard! How dare you? I know plenty about it."

He stepped off the porch into the rain.

"You better take that back." Connie followed him into the downpour. The wet spikes flashed cool against her hot face.

"You look like a school girl," he said.

"Go to hell, Louis Guillory. I am not a fucking school-girl." She cradled her arms beneath her breasts and stood her ground. "I am a field coordinator for the Student Non-violent Coordinating Committee."

"Only because you want to," he snapped. Through the rain, they could hear singing from the Baptist church down the road.

"Don't you talk to me that way." Her voice shook.

He stared down at her. "This doesn't work."

"Louis." She stepped toward him, reached out to put her arms around him.

He pulled away and grabbed her by the wrists, holding her at arms' length. "I don't think you should be a part of this any more," he said, gentle now. "We're fighting amongst ourselves. Now we're gonna have to heal ourselves. You people have given enough."

She laughed, a sarcastic bark. "There it is," she shouted. "'You people'. Just like you said. Any time you hear 'you people' . . . " she mimicked him, poorly, "'you know you're talking to a bigot.'" Her face had turned cold in the un-stoppable rain.

"No blame," he said.

"'No blame'?" Connie spat. "You self-righteous sonofabitch."

"I don't think it works."

"What doesn't work?"

"You, me . . . The whole blackwhite thing."

Connie took a step backward to look him up and down, rain streaking her face. "I didn't come here because I'm white. I didn't come here to meet you. I came because I could see all of us — black and white— gasping for breath."

He climbed back onto the porch. "You came here because you were pissed off at your parents."

"Oh, shit. You . . . You. . ." Sobs rose to close her throat. "We were winning, you asshole," she choked out. "Not just you and me. Everybody. And you sully our work with a family squabble!" She ran at him, beating him on the chest, the arms, the head.

He pulled her back under the shelter. "You'll find other ways to fight," he said, holding her wrists.

"You're wrong." Although she was sobbing, Connie couldn't hold back the words. "If you think I'm standing in your way, I'll go. I'll get out, you son of a bitch." She stepped off the porch, back into the rain. "But when I'm gone, you'll never hear from me again. Not one word. Not for a month. Not for a year." She stared up at him. "And you, Louis Guillory . . . You'll live to regret it."

Louis stood beneath the shelter of the rain-rattled corrugated tin and watched her walk into the darkness.

MASTERS OF WAR
FEBRUARY, 1965

SAIGON — National Security Advisor Mc-George "Mac" Bundy was taking a tour of the war. He was billeted at a swanky bungalow in the Embassy compound, wakened gently in the morning with coffee and orange juice, fed like a pasha, and airlifted to garrisons so beefed-up that a cockroach couldn't have entered the perimeter without getting blown away.

Dressed in fatigues and wearing a flak vest, "Mac" overflew rich, green, rice paddies and tidy villages that embraced

the landscape in a centuries-old marriage of nature and agrarian ingenuity.
Through it all, he saw nothing, felt
nothing, and learned little.

On the last evening of his tour, Mac
Bundy returned to Saigon. He showered
and took dinner with a mixed entourage
of American and South Vietnamese officers, diplomats, and a serious Command-
ing General.

After dinner, Bundy was driven to GHQ.
Still vibrating with alcohol, coffee,
and tobacco, "Mac" joked with the staff
while he filed his final report. It would
be coded and sent by cable across the
Pacific, where it would greet President
Johnson at the beginning of his workday.

Bundy was smitten by the romance of
it all, as if he were a young reporter
in the field, temporarily relinquishing
control to the Fates of War. He sat in
his shirtsleeves and typed while the radio squawked, hissed, and popped in the
background.

The caffeine and alcohol wore off,
he grew drowsy, but "Mac" had important
findings to report and he stayed on task.

About two a.m. the radio lit up. Staff
members leapt out of their seats. A small
American airfield near Pleiku, a market
town in the Central Highlands, had fallen
under attack. Mac and the staff could
hear mortar and machine gun fire in the
hiss-pop, cut-in, cut-out of the radio.
Adrenaline rushed into Mac's system.

```
    Crouching at the typewriter as if he
were under fire, Mac pecked out a hasty
addendum to his report, addressed with
highest possible urgency to President
Johnson.
    Unprovoked communist attack at Pleiku.
Estimated eight American dead. Several
aircraft destroyed. Suggest your trolley
car has arrived.
```

GREENWICH VILLAGE

Madeline picked up a leaflet from a kid at a table in the NYU student union. She liked the simple, straightforward logic of the writing.

> *The war hurts the Vietnamese people.*
> *The war hurts the American people.*
> *SDS says U.S. get out of Vietnam.*

The leaflet made its point without exhortation, letting the connections speak for themselves. The new group had mushroomed on campus since their appearance last fall and seemed to be speaking to new hopes — that society could be changed — and new fears — that government was a whole lot bigger and badder than anything Bob Dylan or the Rolling Stones could fight with just a song. *Damn!*. She needed to do more than write about music. She brought the leaflet to the next editorial meeting at the *Washington Square Bulletin*.

"I want to cover this demo," she told the assembled editors. "This new group, SDS. They want the U.S. to pull out of Vietnam."

"Shit, man." The sports editor, a blond preppy with Ivy League pretensions, had leaned forward, elbows on knees. "Viet-what?"

"Anybody even fucking know where Vietnam is?" queried another.

"The U.S. military knows where it is," Madeline said. "They been sending gobs of red-blooded American boys over there."

"Come on, Madeline." Jason, a college junior who already affected the attire of a *Washington Post* columnist — bow tie, suspenders, button-down shirt — rolled his eyes. "Those Army guys. They're advisors. They don't fight."

"Hah hah. Right, sure."

"If you ever read the *Times*, you'd know. They ran a whole series on Indochina," Jason said. "We're helping them establish a democracy there. What's wrong with that?"

"So the *Times* is predicting the future now? What if it isn't so easy to establish a democracy? For somebody else's country?" She folded her arms. The others shifted uneasily. "Just because the *Times* said it doesn't mean that it's true."

Jason waved the pamphlet in the air. "So you want us to believe a crappy mimeo'd pamphlet." He sat back in his chair. "Who calls this thing a war anyway? Except fucking SDS?"

"Hey, Madeline," the blond sportswriter interrupted. "Why don't you stick to what you know?"

"What's that supposed to mean?"

"I mean like music and shit. Why don't you go interview the Lovin' Spoonful? They're cute."

"Cute." She knew the Lovin' Spoonful, gawky guys who lived in the East Village. "What's cute got to do with it?"

"Hey, Mad." The sports writer elbowed Jason. "I'm gonna cover the Yankees creaming the Sox at Fenway

Park. Wanna drive up to Beantown with me?" He winked. "Watch the game?"

She ignored him.

"It's just another demo," Jason whined. "Civil rights, ban the bomb, now a war that doesn't exist. People are getting sick of this shit."

"You sure about that?" she asked.

"Okay," the sports writer said. "She wants to make a mountain out of a molehill." He shrugged. "Let her."

Madeline tore the leaflet out of Jason's hand and turned on the sports writer. "Listen, you moron . . . "

"Hey, hey, hey," Jason admonished. "You don't have to get hostile."

"It's not your place to 'let' me do anything, Jockstrap. Not until you own the paper. You under the impression you own the *Washington Square Times*?"

The sports writer sneered. Jason put his head in his hands.

"I'm going to D.C." She stopped at the door. "And I'll come back with a story so fucking strong . . . " She laughed. "You won't dare publish it."

Washington, D.C. reminded Madeline of Paris. She wondered how heartily the French had protested their government's earlier war in Vietnam. *No one will come to this demo*, she feared. What do Americans know about a little Asian country full of rice paddies and water buffalo? Why would they care? *Damn! They better come.* She did not want her hunch disproved for the benefit of the boys' club at the NYU paper.

Last summer, Vietnam had already thrust its way into America's myopia when a Buddhist monk sat down on the street and set himself on fire. Madeline knew that monk must have believed very strongly in something if he was willing to die in such a painful way. Life was precious. He was a spiritual man. *How could he do that?*

The burning Buddhist yanked Vietnam into focus. Televisions flickered with images. Skinny Asian boys in oversized uniforms snapped to attention before big white men in gray suits who emerged from black Citroens and shook hands with short, yellow men in white suits.

Americans watched over TV dinners as American boys in olive drab clumped down the ramps of amphibious landing craft, soaking their combat boots in gentle, lapping waves. It didn't look like Normandy. It didn't look like Iwo Jima. It didn't look like a war. Soon after the monks had burned, Walter Cronkite began to report that new battles had blossomed in the far away country. He called the Viet Cong attackers 'insurgents', 'guerrillas' and 'rebels', implying that they were bandits with an illegitimate cause.

Madeline disagreed with Cronkite. The term 'guerrilla' suggested romance to her, a noble calling with noble principles attached. Hadn't 'insurgents', 'guerrillas' and 'rebels' overthrown tyrannies as far away as Bolivia and Iran, and as close to home as the farmers in the American Revolution who fired at the British Redcoats from behind stone walls? Robin Hood was an insurgent, wasn't he? And what about Fidel? What about the handsome young doctor they called Che? She recalled her father's admiration for Fidel and his band of guerrillas. They were rebels, too, like the Vietnamese. She hoped the demonstration would cast light on what the newspapers and television refused to cover. America was at war — undeclared war. She hoped the demonstration would rattle the gates of Eden, entryway to the complacent garden that Americans assumed belonged to them in perpetuity.

The Washington Monument cast a perfect shadow across the Mall. In front of the White House, a slow-moving line of demonstrators dressed like churchgoers crowded the sidewalks. There were Negroes there, too. A white guy with a crew cut and black glasses held a hand-lettered sign:

One Man, One Vote — Selma or Saigon

Another proclaimed:

FORGET DEMOCRACY.
Make The World Safe For Hypocrisy

Madeline wrote down the slogans she liked in her notebook. The procession grew, flowing around her like a slow river, gaining power as it moved downstream. The air was filled with hand clapping, snatches of song, laughter. A poorly played bugle blatted into the bright April air. They gathered around the base of the Monument.

A tall guy in a baggy corduroy sport jacket clambered onto the scaffolded stage. He approached the microphone tentatively, looked out at the crowd that had spread away down the mall and grinned. "Wow! You should see yourselves out there. You look fantastic! There are so many of you!"

The crowd hooted and whistled.

He quieted them with a grin and an extended hand. "But this gathering? This only signals the beginning." He shifted on the podium and looked up, serious, intense. "Vietnam is like a razor," he began. "It's cutting away any illusions about our government. They are fighting a war without declaring war, operating as if they own this country and they can use us the way they want. But they don't own it. We do. And they can't use us. Not if we don't let them."

As she watched the speaker, Madeline felt a presence pushing toward her through the crowd. She spun to identify it, surprised at her own alarm, but the sun's glare blinded her. The backlit form seemed headed straight for her. Why? She stepped back to let the specter pass but he stopped at her flank.

"Mad? Madeline Singer?" She spun to face the speaker. How did he know her name? Who would have spotted her in this crowd?

She felt a rush of adrenaline. David stood beside her, too close for comfort, squinting into the same morning sun, his hair long and tousled, a red armband hugging the sleeve of his sport jacket. She hadn't seen him since she walked out of her sister's Hell's Kitchen apartment into the June rain. Over a year before. Surprising herself, her heart leapt. Embarrassed by her response, she turned back to the speaker.

"That's Carl up there." David stuck with her.

"There's a lot of people here," she said. "How did you find me?"

"Heyyy. Glad to see you, too, Mad. And I didn't come looking for you."

"This is a pretty big crowd," she said, grabbing for words. "I didn't think it . . ."

"Yeah, huge. You know, back when we started planning this thing . . . "

"'We'? Are you in SDS?"

"I went to Philly, joined an SDS chapter some friends started."

"Oh. That sounds cool."

"Didn't feel so cool. After we'd broken up."

"Listen, I . . ."

"But hey." He swept an arm across the crowd. "I guess I have you to thank for all this."

Madeline caught the edge of sarcasm. Same old David. "I doubt that." A shot of remorse ran through her. She had been cruel to him on that rainy summer night. She recalled his stoned, stunned, childlike response. His incredulity. She hadn't wanted to hurt him, she'd wanted out. She returned her attention to the podium.

"The guys at the National Office said an anti-Vietnam march would never fly," David said. "Then Johnson kicks off Operation Rolling Thunder and ka-boom!"

"That's kind of cynical," she said.

"What?" He sounded genuinely surprised. And hurt.

"Sounds like you're making political hay out of a bunch people getting bombed."

"You think that's what we're doing here?"

"No. Of course not." She turned back to the speaker, hating her anger, her envy. While she was staking her claim with older guys and pushing her way into the school paper, he had been jumpstarting a political group, doing things. And here she was, alone, trying to prove a point to a bunch of campus newspaper bozos. "So. You been playing any music lately?"

"No."

"Why not?"

"I don't have time."

"Look at Bob Dylan. Or Pete Seeger. They're political organizers, too."

"Yeah. Okay. But I'm no Bob Dylan."

"Oh. Bitter are we?"

"First I'm cynical. Now I'm bitter. *Shee-it*. Nice ta see you, too." He backed away. "I don't have time to let you bring me down again."

On stage, the speaker had grown hoarse with excitement and urgency. "A movement that will reach out to everybody! In Vietnam. In Mississippi!"

Madeline turned back to David. He was gone. Longing descended over her. She missed them together, who they had been, how sweet it was. His strong connection to SDS — a group she already held in awe — galled her. She turned her focus back to the podium.

"All right people." David stood on the platform, waving handfuls of papers in the air. "SDS has gathered these petitions from campuses all across the country. Signatures!" He grabbed another handful. "Fifty thousand strong!"

The crowd roared. She watched, fighting the ache inside her. She reined in her emotions, turned to her work. *Write it like you see it.*

> *The crowd seems ready to act on the*
> *strength of the speakers' words. They*
> *have a mission — to stop the pollution of*
> *democracy by a government that's sending*
> *its young men off to kill and be killed.*

David and a squad of blue-jeaned SDS cadre held the box of petitions aloft. They moved down the Mall, leading the crowd toward the dome of the Capitol Building. As they approached the Capitol, rhythmic shouts of "one, two, three, four, we won't fight your dirty war" and "U.S. out of Southeast Asia" overwhelmed the singing.

David and the SDS guys were going to carry those petitions up to the front door of the Capitol Building themselves, and leave the crowd behind. *Yeah, here they are again,* she thought. *The guys. Only they weren't the only people who wanted this war stopped.*

"Let's all go!" she shouted.

Echoing her words, the crowd rolled forward, gaining momentum as they flowed between the chartered buses parked along the boulevard. "Tell 'em no! Let's all go!"

A double line of helmeted cops waited at the foot of the Capitol steps. Grasping their nightsticks in both gloved hands, they linked arms, legs spread, forming a chain of sticks and arms. The protestors took on the speed of a river suddenly forced into a narrow gorge.

Let's all go, go, go, go!
Tell 'em no, no, no, no!

The ragged chant caught on, the crowd moved forward. They would storm Congress!

"Stop!" David shouted into a bull horn. "Please stop! Please!" The SDSers formed a line, a fragile barrier between the charging demonstrators and the blue police line. "This is a nonviolent demonstration, people! Stick to the plan! Please!"

The feisty vanguard subsided, hissing and murmuring like a spent wave.

Madeline stopped with them, breathless, shaking. She had wanted to rush the cops, to throw herself up against the wall of blue, to kick and punch and bite. But was that the way? To fly at a bunch of cops? Her real fury focused at . . . what? David? At a bunch of men? She walked away from the front lines to watch.

The SDS squad regrouped around the abandoned petitions. Diminished by the granite expanse of the Capitol, they carried the box like a coffin up the Capitol steps. A frightened clerk stood at the top, dwarfed beneath the great rotunda. The petitions were delivered into his arms.

The April afternoon cooled, the sun set behind brick and granite buildings and the crowd dissolved. Lines of tired demonstrators drifted back to their buses. Madeline drifted with them, exhausted by the collective exultation of the march and confused by her own emotions. She had never felt so alone, so isolated and — at the same time — so enmeshed with other human beings.

The morning sun flowed white across Madeline's pillow. Yesterday's longing swept over her again. She was hungry for the camaraderie she had shared with thousands of other protestors. Regret flowed, for the trouble she had caused, for the shameful selfish feelings of envy and fury she had allowed to motivate her. At least she had understood herself well enough to retreat, not let her feelings drive her. The demonstration had been very effective at . . . She wasn't sure what, but something big had happened down there in Washington, D.C.

She put on water for coffee, threw on yesterday's jeans and sweatshirt and loped barefoot down five flights of stairs to the newsstand on the corner. "Hiya, Morty," she said to the overweight newsie who ran the stand.

"Hiya, Sweetheart," Morty wheezed. "Another hot one today. And it's only April."

"Yeah," she said absent-mindedly, as she scanned the front page of the *Times*.

Washington Rally Attracts Thousands

"Thousands!" She muttered. "There was like, a million people there!" She flipped the pages, reading snatches aloud. *"A handful of adults!'* There were about a thousand buses, and people came from everywhere. *'Students clogged the sidewalk.'"* She glared up at the wheezing newsie. "Shit, Morty, they're lying! We were everywhere! We marched to the Capitol Building with a huge pile of petitions. Don't they even say that?"

"You was there?" He looked skeptical.

She thrust her face into the paper. "'. . . *beards and blue jeans!*' Who cares what they wore!" She read on incredulous, while he huffed and puffed in the background like an old-time steam engine. What about the petition? What about Joan Baez and those songs about the war? What about the guy who spoke? They didn't even give his name. He was so cool. And David. With the thousands of petitions. "This isn't the way it was, Morty. This isn't the way at all!" She handed him a quarter.

"Keep it, Sweetie," he said.

She kissed his cheek and walked back to her apartment. *So this is what they do*, she thought. They don't actually lie. Except about the numbers. It's what they left out. What *does The New York Times* have to lose from a bunch of people saying a war shouldn't happen? *We must have made too much noise on the other side of power*, she thought. *Cool.*

The kettle whistled. Madeline brewed the coffee, sat down at the kitchen table and opened her notebook. Even if the *Times* was full of shit, the boys at the campus were such elitists, they'd be all over Madeline's coverage of the demo. If *The New York Times* covered a story, it must be news.

PHILADELPHIA

"Give the gas three pokes, then turn the key until it coughs. Stop immediately. Wait ten seconds. Turn the key again and . . . "

A knot of well wishers stood on the South Philly sidewalk as a young SDSer showed Connie Moore how to start the Dodge Dart. Sporting accordion fenders, scaling paint and engine gremlins, the powder-blue wreck would get Connie and David to Chicago cheaper than two tickets on the Greyhound. David had never learned how to drive. Connie — the country girl from Massachusetts — had learned how to drive in a cow pasture when she was eleven. She would get them there, engine gremlins, accordion fenders and all.

The crowd that stood around the old Dodge knew each other well. They had worked and lived together, survived on spaghetti and oatmeal for weeks on end, argued and strategized in a knot. Gradually, the Philly SDS project had established a beachhead in the mixed neighborhood, working with the local longshoremen and a cadre of welfare mothers to put pressure on the city to develop social-service outlets in the neighborhood.

Now, as presaged by the growing national involvement in Vietnam, the focus was shifting from neighborhood organizing to the war. David and Connie were traveling to Chicago to help out with the flood of chores generated by SDS' new anti-draft campaign. At the behest of their government, every male student on every campus across America had become part of a much larger demographic — cannon fodder.

"On the road! Yeah!" David slapped the roof of the Dodge as they sputtered east toward the Schuylkill River, the dirty blue car bouncing over the cobbled waterfront streets. "You ever read Kerouac? This is what he lived for. 'Course, he wasn't worried about the draft. Hey, you want to smoke some pot?"

"What?" Connie snapped.

"Pot," he replied. "You know, weed, gage, maryjane, reefer. A joint, a muggle, a doob, a . . . "

"I know what it is," she said, irritated. "I'm surprised you brought it along."

"Okay, okay. We don't have to smoke." He pulled a tinfoil packet out of his jeans pocket and shoved it under the front seat.

"We shouldn't be carrying it at all." The Philly SDS project had a strict rule — No one was to breach security with drugs. They were regularly hassled by city authorities — fire and building inspectors, health workers, a small-business rep who wanted to see their DBA papers, everybody looking for an excuse to render their upstairs apartment and storefront office illegal or unsafe. He must have stashed the pot somewhere in the office. *Dangerous*, she thought angrily. *Very dangerous*. Now he was putting them both in jeopardy on the road.

She found the rolling patchwork of browns and greens comforting. It reminded her of home and gradually, she began to relax about David and his marijuana. "So catch me up," she said. "In Mississippi, nobody talked much about Vietnam or the draft. The army was mostly a way for the kids down there to get out of hell."

"Whew. I bet." He paused for a moment, thinking of the courage this mild, pretty girl must have had, how much they all had, immersed in the steaming, fear-filled wilds of Jim Crow Mississippi. He felt like a spoiled college brat, with his university protests.

"Hello."

"Okay. So the anti-war thing. At first, nobody paid much attention," he began. "Then Johnson starts bombing Hanoi. A ton of people show up at this demo." Madeline flickered across his vision. He brushed her aside. "The one last fall? Even bigger. This crazy kid climbs onto the podium, borrows somebody's Zippo and lights his fucking draft card on fire. Another guy gets up, grabs the Zippo and blip! His draft card is gone, too. Before you know it, the whole crowd is torching cards."

"And did you burn yours?" Connie asked.

"I was the crazy kid who borrowed the guy's Zippo."

At the office, David had seemed flippant, irresponsible, even arrogant. Yet he worked in a leadership position at the Philly office and had taken this major step, burning his draft card.

"My own personal napalm bomb."

The highway narrowed to a two-lane corridor. Cars and trucks hurtled at them from the opposite direction.

"That's gonna be a big mistake," she said. "Drafting the middle class is different from sending poor Negro kids off to war."

"'Negro'?" David cuffed her lightly. " We're talkin' black people here. Black. 'Negro' done gone the same way as Step n' Fetchit. Obsolete." He turned to her. "That what they still call black people down in Mississippi?"

The sound of Louis' voice — enraged, desperate, unfairly accusing her of white naïveté — barked at her through David. She yanked the little car around a slow-moving truck, taking them into the opposite lane. Up ahead, a black Lincoln Continental rose out of a dip in the road.

David gripped the dashboard.

The Lincoln flashed its lights. They were only halfway past the slow-moving truck. The Lincoln dove for the shoulder, disappearing in a plume of dust. They inched past the truck and Connie yanked the wheel and cut back to the right before a second car blew past them in the opposite lane. The truck driver blared his horn.

David glanced in the rearview mirror. The Lincoln had squirreled back onto the road. "Something I said?"

"Yeah," Connie replied. "Something you said."

CHICAGO

"I got the assignment?"
    "Of course."

"Yippee!" Madeline Singer shouted into the phone and danced around the NYU newspaper office.

In Berkeley, the editor of *Ramparts* magazine held the receiver at arm's length. The young journalist's enthusiasm irritated him. "Why not? You can write." He stared out the window at the still-green East Bay hills. He hoped she could deliver. They needed young people who had their finger on the pulse of a movement that was unpredictable and growing fast. "I can't give you an advance."

The article she had pitched to *Ramparts* was about campus draft resistance, how it was growing and how SDS was handling it. Everything fit. She was handling a big-time story about something important. "That's okay. I'll be there. Right after exams."

"Exams?"

"Yeah." She lied into the phone, moving to cover the hole. She had told the *Ramparts* editor that she was five years older than she was. "I'm an adjunct professor at NYU." She bit her lip, waiting to be challenged. In the NYU news office, the student journalists moved about the room in a springtime torpor. *Please get me out of here*, she thought. *Please. Get me to Chicago.*

"Five thousand words. No . . . that's too much. Make it three thousand. Tops. Get it to me by the end of next week."

"Wow! Thanks!"

"Stop it, Singer. You're unnerving me. You sound like a kid."

"Thanks, Gene. Really."

"Fine, fine. Get out there before your radicals have all gone home to Mommy and Daddy."

"These kids won't quit," Madeline said. "Not until they get what they want."

"Yeah, okay. Whatever. Later on." The phone went dead.

She was on assignment. Ecstatic, she gazed at the other students, at the scraps on the newspaper layout table, the mess of paper on the floor, the baloney sandwich by her Remington. She loved it all — the writing, the office, even the jerk-off male staff.

Goin' to Chicago . . .

She skipped out of the NYU office singing one of David's blues tunes.

Sorry but I can't take youuuuu . . .

She was going to write for *Ramparts*, the hippest, weirdest left-wing magazine in America. She was going to write about what was really going on in this fucking country. The world was twisting off its hinges and Madeline was going to be a part of it.

The national office of Students for a Democratic Society huddled on the second floor of a crumbling red brick building east of Hyde Park. Weeds and broken glass stretched away from either side of the decrepit hulk, and the scabby buttresses of the Chicago El wrapped themselves around one corner of the building.

Madeline snapped a few shots of the forlorn headquarters with her Pentax and climbed the worn granite steps. The door was open. "Anybody home?" *Strange*, she thought. Most movement offices kept their doors locked, even barred, a cautionary measure generated by repeated break-ins, trashings and other, poorly disguised forms of harassment, usually by the FBI and the local cops.

She climbed the splintery stairs to the second floor. Inside the office, her eyes adjusted to a room full of battered desks, improvised tables, greasy typewriters and an ink-stained Gestetner mimeo machine. In the kitchen, paint and plaster hung in curls off the ceiling. Over the sink, the bearded visage of Che Guevara confessed:

> *At the risk of sounding ridiculous, let*
> *me say that the true revolutionary*
> *is guided by great feelings of love.*

Next to Che, the arrow of a hand-painted sign pointed down at the sink:

DRAIN BROKE
USE BATHROOM

She snapped a shot that included both images. Down the hall, a toilet flushed. A phone rang from the parlor office. She wove through the maze of tables and rickety chairs, looking for the source of the ringing.

A blond guy in blue jeans and a T-shirt emerged from the bathroom. He strode toward her, buttoning his fly. He was well-built, the muscles of his arms and chest squared-off, his waist devoid of the usual politico paunch.

She picked up the phone. "Hello?"

"Hey, how's it going?" The voice at the other end of the line sounded familiar. "I'm looking for Brooks. Brooks Robinson."

"I don't know if he's here. I . . . "

The blond guy grabbed the phone and pushed her away.

"Hey!" she shouted. "Keep your hands offa me!" He smelled of soap, hair oil and sweat.

"National office. Roger speakin." He inspected her with soft brown eyes. "Somebody'll be around when you get here. You know where you're headed? Yeah. South Lakeshore. You got it. Right. Right. Yes. Later on."

"Who was that?" she asked.

"None of your business." He slammed down the phone. "So . . . Who the hell are you?"

"Madeline Singer."

"What're you doing here, Madeline Singer?"

"I'm a journalist."

"Oh, great. Which side are you on?"

"Wow," Madeline said. "Who put a hair across your butt?"

"Just tell me what you're doing here. I've never seen you before and that ain't good."

"I'm writing a story. About SDS and the draft . . . "

"For who?"

"For whom."

"Fuck you. Who you with?"

"*Ramparts.*" She said. "I'm doing a story for them. And you just got it off to a terrible fucking start, you lunkhead."

"Aren't you the fair and impartial one. You gonna write a story about what's going on here or call me names?"

Look," she said. "I talked to Brooks Robinson on the phone. He said to come on ahead. So here I am." She giggled. "And I'm sorry I surprised you on the shitter."

"'I'm sorry I surprised you on the shitter!'" he mimicked, then relaxed and grinned. "Forget it. Everybody's a little uptight here. We been hassled by the cops, spied on by the Feds and . . . " He glared at her. "We been dragged through the mud by the media. Plenty of times."

"Yeah," Madeline said. "By the *Chicago Tribune.* The *Sun-Times*, the Bumfuck, Nebraska, *Tweedledum.* Straight newspapers. That's not me."

"How am I supposed to know that?"

"Come on, Man." She presented herself to him, knowing the stance did double duty as disarmament and flirtation. "Do I look like an established journalist to you?"

"No." He scrutinized her faded black jeans, scoop-neck cotton blouse and giant hoop earrings. A blue bandana failed to contain an explosion of curly black hair. "Know how I can tell?"

"No," she said, impatient. "How?"

"Your boots. Scuffed-up. You know, like shit-kickers."

"'Shit-kickers'?" She wrinkled her nose.

"Yeah. Shit-kickers. You know." He turned the drawl up a notch. "Like you been on a farm. Not the kind of outfit a snitch from the *Tribune* would be able to assemble."

"Okay, Sherlock. So I got the right kind of shit-kickers. When can I talk to Brooks Robinson?"

"That's up to him." He let his eyes roll freely down her body. "I got work to do. You'll have to wait on your own."

"That's cool," she said. "I'm already working."

"How?"

"You're a story all by yourself, Buster. What kinda story, I wouldn't want to say . . . not yet anyway." She pushed a pile of clothes and a dog-eared copy of *One Flew Over the Cuckoo's Nest* out of the way and sat down on the end of the saggy cot that ran beneath a bay window. "So where is everybody?"

"Up at the University."

An elevated train roared by the window outside, shaking the building.

Roger sat down at a table surrounded by a pile of mimeographed literature. He folded a mimeo and stuffed it in an envelope. He liked her looks, her belligerence. He even liked her big mouth. She was . . . different. Sophisticated. Smart. He liked her, but he wasn't going to show it.

"Why aren't you up there with the rest of them?" she asked.

"I'm not a student."

"If you're not a student . . . " she asked, "what are you doing at Students for a Democratic Society?"

"So this is a sniping expedition." He spun in his chair. "You don't want to find out what's happening. You want to find out what's wrong!"

"I'm trying to get some information."

"I'll tell you what's wrong here," he said. "The fucking war. That's what's wrong. Why don't you go write about that? What's the matter . . . don't got any connections to the Pentagon? No inside line to Bob McNamara?"

"No, I don't," she said. "I'm trying to cover the Left, not The Man. Besides, I don't see anything wrong here."

"I'm so relieved." He turned away. "I gotta get this literature out."

"Can I help?" Without waiting for an answer, she sat down at the table opposite him.

"Thought you'd never ask."

Outside, a slow-to-come rain first spattered, then steadily increased, sending the smell of summer-hot brick and pavement wafting up through the open windows of the flat.

ON THE ROAD

By the time they crossed out of Ohio, David and Connie were swapping life stories. His first encounter with Madeline in Washington Square Park, their Greenwich Village adventures. He described — with surprising sensitivity, Connie thought — their tender sexual discoveries.

"You know, first time stuff. When I first met Mad, I thought she'd probably had plenty of um . . . worldly experience."

"Bet she didn't, huh." She watched as David's face relaxed and went sweet with recollection.

"No. We were both — you know — excited, scared, curious as hell." He tapped Connie's knee with a rapid, syncopated boom-boom, boom-boom. It was okay with Connie. He was endearing.

"Then we sort of fell over together and she kissed me." He turned to her suddenly. "You know what I think the coolest thing was?"

"I can guess, Connie said.

"No, no. Not that," he replied. "It was how much we helped each other out. I mean, kind of bumping around down there, I thought I was gonna be done in thirty seconds . . . "

Connie laughed. "Doesn't sound like it went that way for you guys."

"We trusted each other so much by that time, it was just . . . Everything was okay." David grinned. "We just kept laughing and caressing each other's faces.

"You sound like you really loved each other."

"Yeah." He looked out the window. "We did."

He watched the monotonous farmland glide by. Talking about her made David realize how much he missed Madeline. Did she miss him too? She had broken up with him so suddenly, with such fierce resolve, but he had not fought back, had he? He hadn't run after her through the rainstorm, acted out his passion for her. If he only had the guts, the foresight to fight back on that June evening. He had felt like killing himself that night. She must have felt some regret, some pain. But she had seemed so confident. So powerful. A goddess. She was no goddess, just a girl. She must still love him, somewhere. But no. He was kidding himself. She had pushed him away again at the Washington demo.

"Yeah, I miss her." He laughed. "It's funny I'm telling you this, but. . ."

"You can say it. After all, it's just you, me, and this junky old car out here in the middle of nowhere."

"I used to think I would die for her. And . . ."

"Yeah?" Connie was painfully curious, hungry for comparison. To know that others had felt what she felt for Louis. "Please. Tell me."

"Just right now, I was thinking. I would still die for her. Wow." David ran a hand through his hair. "What a cornball idea. Scratch that."

"It's a beautiful idea. Don't be scared about it."

"I'm not scared," David snapped. "It was just a rush, that's all."

Connie drove on, the road passing beneath them with the ever-present rush of wind.

"Eddie and I . . . " Connie needed to banish the silence. "We had nothing in common. Not like you and . . . "

"Madeline."

"But he was honest. And sweet. And funny. He had a great sense of humor"

"'Had'?"

She caught her breath. "Oh, dear. No. He's not dead." She shivered.

"Sounds like you outgrew him."

"Maybe. He told me he was going to join the Marines. I was so disappointed, we didn't really say goodbye."

" 'Disappointed'? Shit, man, maybe you were pissed off. I would be."

"Okay," she laughed. "He pissed me off. Because it was a waste, what he was doing. And nobody was really thinking about any war."

"What about this other guy?" David asked. "The guy down in Mississippi. What happened to him?"

"Drop it," Connie snapped. "Or I take another suicide run around that semi up ahead."

CHICAGO

At the Chicago SDS office, Madeline looked up at a tall, stoop-shouldered man standing at the top of the stairs. "I bet you're that reporter from *Ramparts*," he boomed.

"I'm only freelancing for *Ramparts*," she replied. "I write for the *Washington Square Bulletin*."

"Sounds classy," Robinson commented.

"It's the NYU student paper."

"From a student newspaper to *Ramparts*. Impressive. But how do you know they'll publish your article?" Not waiting for an answer, he extended a hand to Madeline. "Brooks Robinson here. Pleased to make your acquaintance." Brooks rumbled into the main office, collapsed on a sofa and patted the cushion beside him.

"I have an assignment." *This guy is a piece of work*, she thought, and remained on her feet.

"An assignment. And a publishing guarantee?" He grinned up at her disarmingly.

"See," Roger said to her. "We got you both ways. I'm hassling you 'cause you write for The Man while Brooks here . . . He thinks you're small potatoes. You can't win for losin', girl."

Brooks threw a tight smile at Roger and dismissed him with a good-natured wave of the hand.

"Yeah, right." Roger rose and retreated down the hall.

Madeline felt bad for him. Before, he had seemed so together. Now, he was acting like a hostile kid sparring with a crabby dad. She liked him better the other way.

"Cowboys," Robinson jerked his head toward the empty doorjamb where Roger had stood.

"Excuse me?"

"This new contingent of activists. They have these bucking-bronco notions about how to run a political organization. No sense of history."

"You mean 'tradition'?" She wanted to trap him.

"No. Tradition suggests stasis. I mean history. History is full of change. The dynamic cause-and-effect connection between historical events. Constantly in flux. Making it all the more critical to know history as a living, breathing entity. My point being . . . These kids don't know it."

Brooks surprised Madeline. He projected a calm, good-natured authority. Kind. Fatherly. But tension snaked through the rambling apartment. Was Brooks holding things back here? Was Roger truly a new breed of SDSer, at odds with the leadership? Should she dig for dirt? Or was Roger right? *Screw it*, she thought. *It's all about the war. The rest is bullshit.*

A contingent of Chicago SDSers crowded into the kitchen. Over a raucous spaghetti fest fortified by a gallon of bad Zinfandel and loaves of day-old bread, she peppered the staff and students with questions. How did they balance the draft protest with their studies? Would they stay on after the semester ended? She scribbled nonstop, sucking up spaghetti and flicking tomato sauce on her yellow legal pad.

After dinner, they drifted into the clutter of the office, where, sitting on desktops, the cot and the suspicious-looking sofa, the SDSers conducted a sweaty, freewheeling discussion about tomorrow's strategies. To Madeline, it seemed as if everyone had a voice, not just Brooks. Even the women seemed confident about participating, and — in Madeline's estimation — they had the most cogent observations to make.

The U. of Chicago students headed toward the El for the ride back to the university. One by one, the handful of weary staffers toddled off to bed until only Roger, Madeline and Brooks Robinson remained. There was only one bedroom left and they still had two travelers to arrive.

"That's okay," she said. "I can crash on the couch or get a hotel room."

"Ridiculous," Brooks hissed. "You're not venturing out. Not in this neighborhood. Not at this hour."

"Ah," she said. "Am I to believe that mixing with the people is dangerous for a lady?"

He blushed. "No it's just that I . . . "

"Stop." She found his vulnerability believable but smelled a trace of carnal opportunism. "Nobody wants to dig any holes here . . . do they?"

Robinson cranked up a bad mix of feigned surprise and boyish hurt feelings. Her quick parries surprised him. He struggled to recover. "Besides," he said . . . "You do want to get a feel for the place, don't you?"

"Oh, I'm getting that all right," she said.

Roger watched Robinson losing the duel. Full of admiration for this knockout beautiful, sharp-sensed visitor, he fell back into cowboy cool.

"So. Let's get on with it. Shall we?" She pulled the pencil out of her hair. "How would you describe the possible effect of this protest? Do you think the Chancellor's office is going to stop collaborating with the Selective Service?"

"Of course not," Robinson snapped. "The ranking system is in place in every college in the land. We simply want to raise the issue before the public eye."

"What he means . . . " Roger drawled, "is that we wanna kick enough ass to make us feel better."

"About what? Madeline asked.

"That the University is pimping us out to the U.S. gummint murder-meat factory. They really are a buncha cocksuckers, ya know."

Madeline laughed. "May I quote you on that?"

"Aw shucks, Ma'am." Roger tipped an imaginary Stetson.

She gave Roger a friendly kick on the boot, and scribbled in her notebook. "You got a way with words, cowboy."

"Thank yuh, lady reporter."

"By the way," Madeline replied. "You got something against cocksuckers?"

"Okay." Brooks slapped his knees and rose. "This conversation has deteriorated beyond my ability to participate. I wish you all a goodnight." He vanished down the hallway. A door slammed.

"Whew." Madeline tossed her notebook aside. "I thought that'd never end." She leaned over and lightly brushed Roger's lips. His breath felt warm and sweet, like a young animal.

Roger's mouth opened in a surprised smile. Eyes wide open, he gazed up into the aura of her hair and watched as she settled on the edge of the chair. Without a cue, they inhaled each other.

She rose and pulled him up by the hands. "You taste good."

He led her down the hallway in an exaggerated tiptoe, finger to lips. He stopped and opened a door. She followed him through and they embraced in the darkness, pulling each other closer, seeking mouths, arms, torsos. They sunk to their knees and began tugging at each other's garments.

A knock rattled the front door downstairs.

Roger sighed and threw his shirt on. He opened the bedroom door.

"Hey, cowboy," Madeline whispered. "You never answered me.

Roger turned, eyes liquid in the semi-darkness. "Answered what?"

"What's wrong with cocksuckers, anyway?"

"Ah . . . Nothin'." He retreated, leaving her alone in the darkness. Her eyes adjusted and she could make out a white-sheeted mattress on the floor, a lamp with a ruptured shade hunkered down beside it. She sat down cross-legged and let the last few minutes ripple through her.

CHICAGO

Minutes earlier, Connie had inched the Dodge northward around the shore of Lake Michigan. Road weariness silenced them both. David was asleep. Navigating alone, she turned off Lakeshore Drive and splashed over the rain-wet streets. Four-story tenements frowned down. Eighty-Seventh Street, Seventy-Ninth Street.

David stirred.

Cracker South had no monopoly on racism, Connie thought. The SDS National Office would be housed in another run-down, low-rent needle in another ghetto haystack like Philadelphia, like Mississippi. They rattled over potholes and plunged into the shadow cast by the Chicago El. Trains thundered above them in both directions. They stopped at a corner, heads craning out the window, seeking street numbers.

A gaunt-featured, long-wristed black man flattened cardboard boxes in front of a corner grocery. "You people lookin' for the program, ain't you."

"Students for a Democratic Society?"

"That what they call it?" The gaunt man raised a long arm and pointed halfway down the block. On the second floor of a dark brick mass, a single light glowed behind a filthy window. "That's where the program's at."

"Thanks, Brother," David replied.

"Ain't got no brother, and if I did," he laughed, "I sincerely doubt you'd be him."

They cruised down the block. The gaunt man went back to slashing cardboard. Connie pulled up beneath the single light and shut off the engine.

Stiff with fatigue, they grabbed their gear, climbed the front stoop, and knocked.

Silence.

The padding of bare feet.

145

Now the door swung open, the stairwell light silhouetting a compact figure, faceless in the dark. "Hi. You must be the Philly people." A Texas twang rode the sleepy voice.

David nodded, balancing his guitar and a duffel on the stairs.

The silhouette stepped aside. Inside, Connie blinked. In the light of the single bulb, the silhouette materialized into a skinny SDSer in blue jeans and a cowboy shirt.

"Hi. People're already crashed," he said. "The last bedroom down the hall is empty. There's a mattress there." He glanced at Connie. "Or . . . if you're not together, one of you can crash on the couch."

"That's all right," she said. "We're together."

David swallowed his surprise.

"Cool." The silhouette ambled down the hall. "There's leftover spaghetti in the fridge. We'll talk in the morning. I know Brooks wants to fill you in before we go up to the campus. *Venceremos.*" He held up a casually clenched fist. "And welcome to Chicago." He disappeared.

Roger returned to Madeline. He found her sitting in the low light of his shabby room, its faults dulled by a bandana she had thrown over the lamp. He shut the door and stood against it, watching her.

"What?" she asked. His stillness made her uneasy. He seemed to glow with adoration, as if he were giving thanks for a heaven-descended blessing. An unfamiliar fascination for him transported her to another reality, a free zone, disconnected from her own compulsion to observe. He was handsome, physical, with his tight belly and golden arms and chest.

He knelt beside her and they resumed their slow, serene duet. The languid motions of their explorations rose, peaked, and stilled. She luxuriated beneath the tickle of his fingers tracing patterns on her body. She fell asleep, her back cuddled against him, hoping that this lovely boy would not convert their experience into religion. Instead — she smiled to herself — she hoped he might rouse her again not now, but later, after she had drifted into sleep.

Roger leaned on his elbow, watching Madeline's slim, tapered back rise and fall as her breath slowed. Outside, the slow rain turned the sounds of traffic into a gentle, hissing wash. *Fuck it*, he thought. *Whatever it was, this was a life worth living.*

David and Connie were too exhausted from the trip to be hungry. They tiptoed down the hallway and opened the last door. An overhead bulb cast jagged shadows along peeling wallpaper. Cardboard-filled window panes gaped like broken teeth. A mattress sat flat on the floor, covered with boxes of *New Left Notes*. Army blankets lay snarled at the foot of the mattress.

"I can see why this is the last room."

She threw her sleeping bag on the floor and nodded at the boxes on the bed. "Your turn. I drove." She grabbed a case out of her bag and padded out the door.

He stacked the literature boxes in the corner, brushed the detritus off the mattress and gingerly inspected the blankets for life forms. He shook one, spread it out on the mattress and tucked it in. Neatly. He puffed up the two greasy pillows and lay down.

Connie reappeared in the doorway, skin shining in the dim light. She clicked the door closed and turned around. Her bra and jeans were slung over one shoulder and a T-shirt half-covered a childlike pair of cotton panties. "Thanks for that," she said, nodding at the bed. She got down on her knees and spread out her sleeping bag. "And thanks for putting down the blanket," she said. "I'd hate to think where this mattress has been."

"Or what's been living in it."

"Gross." She sat down cross-legged on the blanket.

"I'm glad you're here," she said. "I would have died, sleeping here alone."

"Come on," he whispered. "You been to Mississippi. You probably slept in places a lot funkier than this."

She thought of her first night in Greenville, sleeping on a pallet in May June's daughter's bedroom. She remembered the dangerous, stolen nights in Louis' shanty, the narrow iron bed, newsprint for wallpaper. Such a great distance she had come. In such a short time. She stripped off her T-shirt and stretched out beside him.

David turned toward her, surprised at her abrupt move toward intimacy. In the car, they had been travelling companions, fellow travelers on the political road, nothing more, nothing less. Then, her sudden easy declaration. 'We're together.' *Where had that come from?* And immediately afterward. *Who cares?* He was too beguiled by the prospects to question the source. He never tired of being granted that first look at a woman's breasts. He moved to her and they lay in parallel, limbs gleaming, staring at the ceiling. It was too hot for a sleeping bag or blanket.

A melodious sigh floated through the wall from the bedroom next door.

Her palm massaged his belly, spiraling downward.

"Uh, Connie."

"Mmmmm?"

"I wasn't expecting to . . . "

She traced her hand along the top of his thigh. "It's been taken care of."

She has one of those diaphragm things, he thought. *I don't have to wear anything.* Wow. Stiffening, he let her hand roam. He felt strange, letting her take the lead, but he could feel a bee-like buzz flow between them like low-voltage electricity. She closed her fingers around his erection, eager to break the last bond that held her to Louis.

A second, lyrical moan crept through the wall from the next room.

Down the hall, Roger woke into the morning light and gazed at the beautiful stranger who sprawled beside him. He dared not disturb her lest she disappear. Instead, he slipped into his jeans, pulled on a clean T-shirt, gently closed the door behind him and softly padded down the hallway to the morning bustle of the kitchen.

The new arrivals, faces puffy with fatigue, slouched at the table. Brooks pontificated at them over a cup of coffee.

"Hi. I'm Roger."

They nodded. "Thanks for your help last night," Connie said.

Roger moved to the stove and lit the burner under the coffee pot, mind hovering over the exquisite being who lay asleep in his bed.

A chair clattered to the kitchen floor.

Roger turned to see the new guy, David, sprawled on his back, legs tangled in the chair, head jammed against the refrigerator. He followed David's open-mouthed stare.

Backlit by the hazy glare of the office, Madeline stood leggy in the kitchen doorway clad only in Roger's cowboy shirt.

"Mad?"

"David?"

"You two know each other?" Brooks ogled Madeline's legs.

David scrambled to his feet. "What are you doing here?"

"I could ask you the same thing."

Silence.

Brooks broke the bubble. "Madeline's doing a story on the draft thing for *Ramparts*."

"Wow. *Ramparts*," David said. "You're keeping pretty hip company."

"Hi." Connie extended a hand to Madeline. *What's going on here?* she thought.

Madeline felt herself flush. She hadn't expected to find David here, especially like this, splattered on the floor. "Hi," She took Connie's hand.

"David and I came out together from Philly. We . . . " Connie stopped herself. *I don't have to explain anything to this girl.*

"I heard you come in," Madeline glanced at David. "Just didn't know it was you guys. Not really my place to say 'welcome.'" She fixed David with a stare. "Seeing as I just got here myself."

David peeled himself off the floor. "Funny," he muttered. "You look pretty settled in."

Madeline flared. "Meaning?"

"Hey, folks," Roger set the chair straight. "We got to get to the campus." *I don't have to give a damn about this*, he thought. The girl in his shirt was obviously not his girl, so fuck her. No! That didn't work. Madeline was already everything to him, a future, a path, something he would refuse to let loose.

"I'll get ready." Madeline smiled at Connie. "Nice to meet you," she said, and disappeared down the hall.

"Who's she?" Connie asked.

David rubbed the back of his head. "That . . . is Madeline."

"Ah." Connie felt tired. Nothing seemed to fit. She turned to Roger. "Can we go soon?"

"Yes, Ma'am."

Gray sky blew in from Lake Michigan, cooling the city. Roger drove them the short distance to the campus. Madeline punctuated the silence with questions. Roger, his attention split between her still-magical presence, the traffic on the streets and the electricity crackling between his passengers, answered in clipped sentences.

Connie looked out the window at the South Side's crapped-out, half-abandoned buildings. She felt weird. Claustrophobic. Why had she come to Chicago? What had she done, pulling this David guy into her life? And now, a dead romance that he had shared with her on the road had sprung back to life. Right in her face. "One big ghetto," she muttered at the landscape. "Forget the University. This is where they're getting their soldiers."

On campus, a banner draped on a wrought-iron fence shouted . . .

Extra! Extra!
Vietnam War Executes
Great Society

Others thronged around the big building entrance, passing out leaflets. A pretty blonde girl in a business suit ignored them. A burly man in a janitor's uniform stopped to read his copy. A clerk tore his leaflet into stamp-sized pieces. "My kid brother's over there." He threw the shredded leaflet onto the plaza bricks. "He didn't get no deferment."

Rain began to fall in fat, sporadic drops. The drops turned into a shower. Borne aloft by students, the Extra! Extra! banner flowed into the administration building. Roger and Madeline followed the flow.

Connie stood outside and watched.

"Connie! Whassup?" David held the door, looking toward her, his face a question mark.

She stood in the rain at the center of the terrace and waved him inside.

The rain increased. More students joined the first wave of shrieking, laughing refugees, dashing past David. He crossed to her, grabbing her arm. "What're you doing? It's wet out here."

"No." She pulled her arm from his grip. "I can't stay."

"What?" He squinted through the pelting rain to her bedraggled features, hair streaming down her face, an extension of the water. "Why not?"

"I can't."

"Why?" He reached for her arm. "C'mon, Connie. This is crazy."

"Leave me alone!" She pulled out of his grasp. "I came here to resist the draft, not get caught up in a soap opera."

"What soap opera?"

She laughed. "Don't play dumb with me. It's insulting."

"What about last night? You and me, I mean."

"It was a mistake."

He laughed, uncomfortable now. "No, it wasn't. It was good. We . . . "

"Not for me, it wasn't. I was trying to do something I shouldn't have tried."

"What are you saying?"

"Never mind." Louis floated in front of David. *And Eddie,* she thought. *Wherever he is now. Never had a chance to avoid his fate.* She grabbed David's shoulders and twisted him to face the administration building. "Go." She shoved him. "Do the work."

Dazed with surprise, he stumbled away from her. Thunder struck the campus windows with percussive force. Sheets of rain, driven horizontal by squalls off Lake Michigan, obscured the terrace. When he turned, she had already disappeared.

MASTERS OF WAR
NOVEMBER, 1965

ARLINGTON, VA — On a gray autumn afternoon, an American, a Quaker named Nor-
man Morrison, crossed the Potomac from
Georgetown and made his way into a small
garden on the grounds of the Pentagon.
Above him loomed the mass of the war
building, its five-sided design a universal symbol of unbalanced power.

The man had no entourage of priests or
acolytes. No one knew of his whereabouts,
not his wife, his friends, or colleagues.
He had, however, written letters to the
editors of dozens of papers, had marched
in scores of anti-war demonstrations and
had kept silent watch during peace vigils
organized by the American Friends Service Committee.

That morning, he had read a news story
about the accidental bombing of a Saigon
church by American aircraft. "My God," a
priest who was wounded in the bombing had
exclaimed to reporters, "these were innocent people. They had hearts and souls.
They had lives."

Now, Morrison sat down in lotus position on the green grass, poured gasoline
over his head and shoulders, and set
himself afire.

"Come here, Sir. Right now!"

Secretary of Defense Robert McNamara,
unused to being given orders by an aide,
rose from his desk and crossed his big

office to a window. He pushed aside the
drapes and looked down onto the gray,
gray-green garden. Giving off an almost
comforting orange glow, someone, a monk,
a lunatic, some fanatic, was immersed in
flame.

"Jesus," the secretary uttered. "What
do you suppose makes a man do that?"

HAVERFORD, PENNSYLVANIA

"Want to go to Hanoi?"

David stood in the winter sunlight and pulled the
phone away from his ear. He had left Chicago months
earlier. The striking students had occupied the building
for three grubby days and nights. The administration refused to budge. Madeline filed her story and the tac squad
moved in. Hundreds had been arrested.

Now he was back at school, broke, disgusted with the
non-conclusion of their efforts and out of touch with Connie, his parents and the rest of the world. The offer seemed
bizarre, impossible. "Hanoi?" David asked. "How?"

"I just got back from Vienna. I attended a conference
on the new European socialism. I read my paper. You know
I have been refining my thoughts on draft resistance . . . "

"Hey, Brooks, you just asked me if I wanted to go to
Hanoi. We're at war with Hanoi. We're talking on a phone
that could be bugged. You wanna get to the point?"

"I was approached by a group of professors."

"Professors? What's that got to do with a city in Southeast Asia which shall go unnamed?"

154

"These professors were, in fact, Polish diplomats, looking for an opportunity to put us in touch with the leadership of the Democratic Republic of Vietnam."

"Why do they want to meet with us?"

"Because they think we're for real, that's why."

"SDS?"

"The whole Movement."

"Damn." David had never imagined that — beyond the boundaries of their own struggle — the Vietnamese might be aware of the American anti-war movement. It was eerie.

Brooks continued. "They're curious. More than curious. According to them, there hasn't been an American Left Wing of this strength since the Russian Revolution. They want to know how big we are, how well-organized we are . . . "

"Jesus." David's heart was pounding. Yes, they were talking treason, but they would be joining hands with the greatest revolutionary movement since America's radical journalist John Reed traveled to Moscow in 1917 and wrote *Ten Days that Shook the World.* "Jesus," he repeated.

"I doubt Jesus has much to do with it," Brooks said. "Now get off the phone."

"No shit, Shakespeare."

NORTH VIETNAM

Villages floated below them like islands in a sea of rice paddies. Each cluster appeared ancient, earthlike, a part of nature, thatched roofs sprouting like morels out of the green and brown terrain. In the distance, Hanoi hunkered in the mist, a low, gray-blue sprawl with a silver river snaking through it.

"I don't see any factories," Brooks Robinson said, peering out the window of the Aeroflot turboprop. "I thought we were bombing factories," Brooks continued. "Where are they?"

An airborne network had leapfrogged David and Brooks eastward from Paris to Prague. After Prague, the customs and security guards stopped stamping passports. Now they were on the lam. Americans visiting Moscow were frowned upon, Peking was off-limits and visitors to Vietnam could be tried for treason.

Although David and Brooks considered their mission to be highly charged, their escorts treated them with a courteous nonchalance. Few seemed inclined to discuss the plight of Vietnam. Every diplomatic enclave seemed to have its own agenda concerning what they called "the American War".

The Muscovites had been the most fearful. At the late night parties where vodka flowed loose but not tongues, David's probes about Soviet-Vietnamese alliances and strategies were met with shrugs and evasive toasts to peace and friendship. Vietnam had its own history of resistance to unravel, the Soviet apparatchiks explained. The subtext was clear — the Soviets had problems of their own. They weren't eager to clash with the United States over Vietnam.

"That's not the way we've been hearing it in the United States," Brooks replied.

His naïveté was met with roars of laughter. "Try reading *Pravda* instead of *The New York Times*," the Soviets suggested, and lifted their glasses once more.

Peking, like Moscow, had done little to nurture the pilgrimage to Hanoi. The Chinese liaison was curt and close-lipped. He expressed his concern in impeccable English — Brooks' and David's well-intentioned information-gathering foray might betray the Vietnamese revolution.

As with the Russians, the Chinese believed that Vietnam had to follow its own destiny. "The Vietnamese people will fight to the last man, woman and child to banish the Americans. The Vietnamese revolution will prevail in Vietnam," the Peking diplomats suggested. "They don't need our help." They escorted David and Brooks onto the next plane bound for Hanoi. *So much for the domino theory*, David thought.

The Hanoi air terminal was nothing more than a large shed. David and Brooks were met by a small, dapper man who smoked incessantly and addressed them in an English that reminded David of warm water. He introduced himself as Nguyen Xuan Duoc, the head of the Peace Committee that had contacted the Americans in Warsaw.

They were driven into town in an entourage that filled two old Citroens — low, black, European sedans with flaring fenders and long hoods, the kind that David had watched chasing Jean-Paul Belmondo in French gangster films.

Duoc sat in front and spoke over the seat to David and Brooks. "Vietnam has a long history of resistance. Before the French and the Americans," he bowed his head in a kind of ironic homage to his guests, "there were the Japanese. And the Chinese. And the Mongol hordes. The monument you saw on the airport roadway celebrates a hero who banished Genghis Khan from this soil."

"Outstanding!" Brooks exclaimed.

There were few automobiles. Most Vietnamese traveled by foot or on bicycles, with equal numbers of shrill motorcycles and two-wheeled carts filled with straw, pottery and baskets of fish or vegetable greens, drawn by patient water buffaloes. No one appeared tortured, harried, mad or driven to desperation by the threat of bombing.

"When do they bomb?" Brooks asked. "Surely not now." He laughed too loudly.

"It depends," Duoc replied. "By day, their bombing is more accurate. At night, they are hit less by anti-aircraft fire but they often miss their targets." He laughed. "Your pilots seem to prefer the night flights. More bombs drop on people's homes but fewer shells hit their aircraft. They live to fly again. Sensible."

"Outrageous!" Brooks exclaimed.

The highway ended abruptly in a tangle of narrow streets and shops with floor-to-ceiling openings that could be closed with shutters. The neighborhood seemed patched and poor.

"This is the old quarter of Hanoi."

"Gorgeous!" Brooks said.

"Most of the streets here are named after commodities," Duoc continued. "Hanoi began as a market place on the river."

"Amazing!" Brooks exclaimed. "For more than a century, the rivers were America's primary means of transportation. You see," he glowed with goodwill, "we have much in common."

Duoc continued, unperturbed by Brooks' enthusiasm. "Bean Street, Copper Street, Chicken Street. It has been this way for a thousand years, only now the river doesn't protect us. It has become a shining beacon for American bombers."

"Bastards!" Brooks proclaimed.

Duoc smiled and gazed through the windshield at the quiet, crowded streets. "We are almost at your hotel."

"Outstanding!" Brooks said. "I'm famished!"

They were billeted in an old French hotel that sat facing a silver-gray river. Its lichen-clad granite façade hovered above the street, glowing like an impressionist cityscape. Without the sandbags that protected the first-floor entrance, David might have been standing before a genteel but over-the-hill casino on the French Riviera. Duoc bade them goodbye and asked them to be ready at seven a.m. A Peace Committee member remained behind, "at your service", as Duoc explained.

Alone in his room, David took stock of his surroundings. In the street below, foot travelers and cyclists flowed past in serene silence, smooth-faced, seemingly fearless. The war lay further away here than it did in America, unreal beyond the delicate décor of his room and the traffic that flowed along the street below, unreal beyond the rice paddies and villages he had flown over. His war lay in America. Here in Hanoi, all was peaceful. Peaceful and real. He fell asleep, fully clothed, in the soft night.

Light green paddies stretched outward to the dark hills that rimmed the horizon. Low and rugged, the highlands never seemed to get nearer or farther away. The road ran straight along the top of a dike that separated rice paddies, the shallow water reflecting both the gray sky and the young, green shoots. The road left the straight lines of the dikes and snaked up well-worn switchbacks. Halfway up, they pulled off the road and parked in front of cliffs covered with vegetation. They climbed out of the Citroens.

"Our surprise," Duoc announced. Behind the vegetation, brick walls and doors sealed off cave entrances. The envoy pulled a chain. A distant bell rang. After a moment, a thick iron door swung open. Brooks had to double over to pass beneath the portal.

When their eyes adjusted, the entourage found themselves standing in the oily gloom of an underground machine shop, surrounded by a small group of young men and women who had shut down a battery of lathes and drill presses. Rifles hung from pegs in the wall.

"Amazing!" Brooks said.

David had never seen people like this. Young, they were really just kids, but they carried a polite authority behind their smooth, serious faces that seemed to outstrip any adulthood he had ever known. These kids had known war since they were born. *What did a lifetime of armed resistance bring to its children?*

Brooks extended a hand to a round youngster in an oily machinist's apron. He took Brooks' hand with a mock-puzzled expression that said, "I know what this hand-shaking business is, but it is weird." A few compatriots giggled. Others simply stared.

Undaunted, Brooks proceeded to shake hands all around. He turned to address Duoc. "English speakers, any?"

Duoc declined to answer. "I will translate," he insisted gently. "To avoid confusion."

"Most Americans think you folks are puppets of the Chinese," Brooks said. "Do the Chinese Communists influence you?"

One of the women smiled as Duoc translated. In a raspy, birdlike voice, she replied. "Vietnam liberation isn't about pulling strings on puppet people," Duoc translated. "We do what is needed because we know why it is needed. This knowledge doesn't come from a party cadre or the government or from China. It comes from us."

"Fantastic!" Brooks continued. "But let's suppose you needed help with things you cannot do for yourselves. Can you speak directly to your government?"

"Of course," another girl said. "When you speak to the Government, you must always speak directly. They are very busy people with great responsibilities. They cannot afford to spend time trying to understand what you want. You must be clear."

"It is painful to be a liberal, is it not?" Duoc spoke to Brooks. "First you must believe in your wonderful government. At the same time, you must defy it. Don't assume we live under the same painful contradictions. We have other problems." He translated his remarks for the young machinists. Many laughed. Others did not.

"What do they think?" one young man addressed Duoc. It was the first sign of anger David had seen. "That we live in slavery? That we are not free?"

In the distance, a string of crumpling thuds rose in a wave to a crescendo of muffled concussions, then tapered off. A second string followed.

"The B-52s," Duoc said.

The angry young man rose and put a large tin of water on a propane burner and spoke softly. Duoc translated. "Tell the liberal he will be safe here. We brew tea because we want to know . . . " he grinned. "Will we survive until after the water boils? Will we live to enjoy the tea after it steeps? This village is a lucky place . . . if you are primitive enough to be superstitious." He pointed at Brooks.

"And if we do not survive," said another, "the water will not boil and we will have no tea to enjoy." She smiled. "Others will take our places."

David, Brooks, Duoc and the machinists sat drinking tea into the early evening while the workers fired quiet questions at David and Brooks. Gradually, Brooks fell silent. He looked travel-weary and confused.

David realized he had grown to hate America. The folk romance of a nation of wheat fields, hogs and cornball farmer-philosophers, of factories and smoke, of steel rails slinging freight trains across the nation a mile a minute, of New Hampshire town meetings and Greenwich Village bohemians, of Wobblies from Boise and salmon fishermen from Seattle, all his admiration for Yankee honesty and courage had disappeared beneath an obscene cascade of 500-pound bombs and napalm canisters that fell near, then far, then nearer yet.

Another string of explosions thudded dully, nearer now, rattling the machinery. "Now we must go our posts," one of the young women said. They rose as one, took up their rifles. A young girl stopped and said to Duoc, "They think we are slaves and yet . . . . We like talking with the Americans."

"And no one is punishing us," added another. She looked up at the vibrating roof of the bunker. "Except the American planes." The young woman smiled. "You must be very brave Americans to come here." She nodded good-bye and left.

The young man in the machinist's apron showed them to the iron gate. He clenched his fist in a black power salute, then smiled. "Have them tell the American people we know this war is not their fault," he said to Duoc. "Tell them we know this is the work of their government and a leader who is afraid."

Outside, the visitors huddled beneath the ink-blue canopy of the sky. The gate swung closed.

"They seem very calm," Brooks said to Duoc.

"They seem calm because there is no other way to be," Duoc replied. He moved quickly to the cars explaining that — despite the falling bombs — it was urgent that they return to Hanoi before nightfall. "The danger will only increase with the growing darkness."

MADISON, WISCONSIN

After years of escalation, Americans were taking notice of the war in Vietnam. Mohammed Ali refused induction into the army. "No Vietcong ever called me nigger," he said. At the New York Stock Exchange, Abby Hoffman and a band of Yippies tossed handfuls of dollars from the balcony to the trading floor below. The brokers scrambled for the green like starving children. Young men in olive-drab fatigues marched with hundreds of thousands of Americans in Manhattan. They gathered around a sign that said:

Vietnam Veterans Against the War

An Englishman called *The New York Times* from a wretched village in Bolivia claiming he could identify a perforated corpse as Che Guevara. A poster of Che, handsome even in death, appeared on university campuses everywhere.

Amidst the tumult, Roger operated with a growing repertoire of revolutionary ideas and a heart full of grief. The revolution he understood — or thought he did. The loss of his mother mystified him. Madeline had returned to New York, to resume her life in a place that Roger could only imagine. He missed her terribly and worked incessantly, keeping his anger, grief and loss at bay. He began travelling from campus to campus, creating liaisons for the growing SDS network.

Now, he stood on the campus at Madison, Wisconsin, distributing a pamphlet announcing that the Dow Chemical Company would be recruiting graduating students next week. "On Wednesday," the pamphlet announced, "we're going to stop them."

At a strategy meeting, a scruffy, plaid-shirted lumberjack spoke to three hundred people crowded into the main lounge of the Student Union. "It's hip to be anti-war," he began. "We used to be the outcasts, the weirdos, the freaks. Now, not one professor in a hundred would support the war. Still . . . nothing changes! The killing machine keeps cranking, the Vietnamese keep getting fried, and American kids younger than you and me keep losing arms, legs, and their lives."

"Business as usual."

"Last year we appealed to reason. We wrote letters. We begged. Nothing changed!"

"Business as usual."

"This year we resist. Dow does napalm. Dow's got contracts to fill. Dow needs us. Too bad. We are not going to allow Dow to fill their contracts. Not on this campus. We are going to stop Dow from recruiting our students as drones for the napalm machine."

Stop Dow Now!

The strategy meeting emptied into the plaza and marched across campus to the Earth Sciences building where Dow was interviewing bright, young prospects from the Chemistry department. Once inside the Earth Sciences building, the students sat down in the corridors and began to sing. Heartened, the campus police chief met with the scruffy lumberjack. "We get Dow to leave and you leave too. Mission accomplished, right?"

"Wrong. This is our university. Dow leaves. We don't."

Madison's roly-poly campus police chief was taken by surprise. In past demonstrations — he could never remember what they were about — students had gone limp for arrest. They sang spirituals while they were being dragged to the paddy wagon. It had all gone so smoothly.

Not so, this time.

Now they clustered together, locking arms, angry, chanting obscenities, spoiling for a fight. No spirituals lent moral purpose. The roly-poly campus police chief called the Madison police, who sent their just-trained, eager-to-perform tactical squads to the campus.

The roly-poly chief and the lumberjack left the building to meet with the University Chancellor. A cheer went up from the crowd. The cheer broke into a chant:

Stop Dow Now!

"We'll see how this works." A frizzy-haired redhead grabbed Roger's sleeve. "I got my doubts. Our chancellor is a prick. He doesn't make deals." She leaned against him. "Mars bar?"

Roger looked down into bright green eyes that clashed with a pasty complexion and red hair. She had a funny, freckled quality that attracted him. "I never seen you before," she continued. "What are you . . . a freshman?" She eyed him with mock suspicion. "You don't look like a freshman to me."

"I'm from Chicago. SDS. The national office."

"Outside agitator, huh?" She giggled. "That's funny. I thought that was a big put-on by The Man. Outside agitator. And here I am, sittin' next to one. That's rich."

The lumberjack galumphed down the hall in his unlaced boots. "Chancellor Fuckhead stonewalled the negotiations."

"Told ya." The redhead put the rest of the chocolate away.

"A bunch of cops in riot gear are gonna bust through those doors in just a minute," the lumberjack shouted. "I don't want to scare you, but if you want to leave, now's the time." No one budged. "Okay. If you wear glasses, take 'em off. Be prepared to pull your coats over your heads for padding . . ."

"Great," she mumbled.

"Girls, pocket your jewelry, 'specially earrings and necklaces. You got any buttons pinned to your clothes, ditch 'em."

The redhead pulled hoops from her ears.

"Grab a buddy," the lumberjack guy went on. "Make sure it's someone you know. Look out for each other."

Roger tucked the redhead's arm under his bicep. Her breast felt friendly against his ribs. *Funny what we notice, even when the shit's gonna hit the fan,* he thought. "Okay. You're my buddy."

"Okay, Mr. Outside Agitator. I'll be your fucking buddy."

They looked at each other and grinned, eyes gleaming with fear and excitement, but not too blown out to ignore the crosshatch of innuendo.

At the end of the corridor, riot sticks shattered the floor-to-ceiling windows. Black-helmeted troops in blue nylon jumpsuits pushed into the building, scattering broken glass over the seated students. There was no verbal warning, no words spoken, no more waiting. Those who stood were beaten down immediately.

"Shit!" the redhead squeaked, and disappeared under Roger's jacket.

The cops gathered momentum, rolling down the hall like a bizarre machine, clubbing at arms, shoulders, legs, heads, anywhere they could land a blow. They tugged the harvested students, dazed and bloodied, down the corridor and out the door on a gauntleted conveyor belt.

The students fought back. Roger grappled with one of their attackers, grasping his assailant's arms, slowing the blow. He caught a glimpse of the cop's Midwestern features behind the face mask. He didn't look like a killer. He looked like an overworked plumber.

A club glanced off Roger's left temple. A leather-gloved claw yanked him into a maelstrom of fists and clubs. Helmeted, blue-clad robots pushed him along. Clubs darted out to stab. He rode the screams of students and the grunts of the body handlers, his hearing and vision fragmented, his body numbed.

Roger landed on his knees in the courtyard. The redhead lay next to him, eyes wild, her hair matted with blood. "That bastard grabbed my tit." She collapsed. Roger caught her, bloodying his hands.

Dark uniforms surrounded a cluster of crawling students, hustled them to their feet and rushed them into a tall, black paddy wagon. When it was full, the troopers slammed the door and turned to face the crowd.

Transformed by the violence they had witnessed, onlookers attacked the paddy wagon, beating on the sheet metal sides with their fists. A brick smashed the windshield. A skinny kid in a ski mask darted from tire to tire. An ice pick rose and fell. The machine, its human cargo locked inside, collapsed over flattened tires.

The cops closed ranks. A helmeted figure climbed behind the wheel. A bottle flew through the broken windshield, covering the driver's faceplate with soda. With a grinding of gears and a roar, the deflated paddy wagon lurched forward, then stalled as clouds of tire smoke rose from the truck's wheel rims, spinning uselessly against the deflated rubber.

The crowd surrounded cops, shouting, "Let them go! Let them go!"

Roger glanced around, wary of both sides. The cops were a known entity. They'd beat the shit out of anybody they could isolate. But . . . *if a provocateur or somebody on our side throws a Molotov cocktail now . . .* He could imagine the flames, the screams from inside, clobbered students trapped. *Is that what my old man's dumb spook friends would like to see me do?*

Cops huddled around the back doors of the immobilized paddy wagon. After a heated discussion, they yanked the doors open, releasing the students. The freed protestors disappeared into the cheering crowd.

Stop Dow Now!

The crowd attacked the empty van, Roger joining them. The redhead screamed like a banshee and rushed forward with the others, rocking the now-empty vehicle onto its side. Exploding teargas canisters rattled across the pavement. A coughing fit tore upward from the bottom of Roger's lungs. Blinded, choking, betrayed by his senses, claustrophobia set in. Millions of invisible glass shards ground into the membranes of his eyes, nose, and throat. The redhead, hair knotted and streaked with dried blood, pulled Roger into a stumbling retreat.

NORTH VIETNAM

On the way back to Hanoi, a distant string of thunder signaled another B-52 drop. The small convoy of Citroens turned back onto Highway One.

"Now we must hurry," Duoc explained. "We are traveling on the most heavily bombarded thoroughfare in all Vietnam. You see," he said, turning and smiling at David and Brooks, the professor. "Your nation and ours . . . by golly!" He slapped the seat for emphasis. "We really are at war!"

On the darkening road they picked up the reflection of bicycles. It was treacherous. No one showed lights. Even reflectors on the backs of bicycles had been removed. As they passed the silhouette of a pagoda they heard the crump-crump-whump of bombs resume in the distance.

Duoc spoke tersely to the driver. To the right, a chain of flashes illuminated the cloud cover, moving along the ragged horizon. There were no jet sounds, no guns. A second string roared over the near countryside like giant footsteps moving at inconceivable speed. The concussions beat against David's chest as the two autos raced down a road now devoid of traffic.

A loud crack shook the car from behind. The atmosphere retreated, returned in a shock wave that pounded the senses into paralysis. A giant, invisible hand tossed dirt and debris over the Citroën, blackening the world. Beyond the sudden darkness, a red-orange ball of flame uncoiled and lashed at the windshield.

The Citroën plunged nose-down into a crater that had opened beneath the ball of fire, throwing the Americans forward against the front seat. Other bombs impacted the road ahead in a string of ringing detonations. Dirt showered down like a ferocious hailstorm and the stink of cordite saturated the air.

Silence embraced by darkness followed the explosions. Another string of bombs walked down the highway ahead of them. Flame ate metal. It flared and hissed into life, an orange-black ball eating the exploded vacuum.

Brooks sat in the back seat screaming, both hands covering his eyes. David and Duoc pulled his hands away, expecting to find blood. Face intact, Brooks stared into space and bellowed. Duoc and the driver climbed out. David followed them. Without an audience, Brooks stopped screaming and collapsed numbly, hands on his lap, staring through the windshield, saying "oh, oh, oh."

The little Citroën lay unscathed but half-buried by the stinking earth that had fallen back into the crater. A group of barefoot citizens ran out of the darkness, pointing up the road ahead. In the distance, a siren wailed.

Duoc and the driver ran up the road. David pulled Brooks out of the car and hauled him up the side of the crater to the roadway. Brooks was silent. David left him shivering in the darkness and followed Duoc and the driver. In the beam of their flashlights, David saw the smoking carcass of a bus. A ragged body lay on the road, its head missing. A half dozen passengers sat upright in their seats, frozen in death, exposed by the torn sheet metal of the bus body. A leg smoked on the pavement like an overdone ham.

Bristling with rifles, the local militia pulled up in the back of a battered stake-bed truck. Despite the absence of uniforms, the villagers looked eerily like soldiers. David recognized one of the young factory workers among the militia. She carried a medical bag. While some unloaded equipment, the young man with the bowl-cut hair climbed aboard the ruptured bus, checking among the charred carcasses for signs of life.

Brooks Robinson staggered into the light, a shell-shocked Frankenstein. "Oh, oh, oh," he chanted. He knelt down and picked up the severed, smoking leg. "Oh, oh, oh."

Duoc spoke rapidly to the head of the medical truck. He pointed to Brooks. The man climbed down and gently tugged the carbonized limb from his grasp. Childish with shock, Brooks fussed and struggled feebly until he was shoved onto the tailgate of the medical wagon and made to strip off his shirt. The doctor quickly scanned the big man's eyes and stabbed him in the rump with a syringe.

Brooks sighed once and collapsed. The stink of scorched flesh settled on the scene. David and his immobilized partner were shepherded away before the first bodies were loaded into the truck. A screaming schoolgirl was gently laid on the temporary table that folded down from the side of the truck. One side of her face and arm resembled the skin of a marshmallow scorched over a campfire.

A second siren wailed in the distance, moaning for the dead. Duoc, the driver, David and the zombie-like Brooks trudged to a sentry outpost where Duoc showed his papers under the lantern. He was immediately ushered into an inner office. The sentries stared at David and Brooks as if they were from another planet. Their curiosity held no emotion.

MADISON, WISCONSIN

Roger and the redhead joined an odd assortment of riot refugees in an off-campus apartment. They took turns in the bathroom, washing away blood, putting cubes of ice on bruises, making hospital calls to locate friends. A strange, calm fatigue set in. Wine and beer materialized from paper bags, an aluminum vat dispatched spaghetti onto paper plates, and Jimi Hendrix roared out of the phonograph. People folded onto the rug, put their heads between their knees and swayed. As the night grew still, the refugees dissolved by ones and twos. By midnight, Roger and the redhead lay on the couch, the lone survivors, feet up on the coffee table.

The redhead rose and squatted before an orange crate full of records. Roger lazily eyed the spread of her hips, the sweetheart shape of her ass. After the images of fire and bloody faces and flailing batons, the sight of her body filled him with peace. She pulled out an album, rubbed the vinyl with her sleeve and dropped it onto the turntable. A reedy mixture of clarinet and a bamboo flute floated into the warmth of dusty drapes and stained carpet.

Roger pulled her back on the sofa. She fell on him and their mouths met. Tasting the salt of sweat and blood on each other's lips, they traced gingerly around bruised biceps and shins. They twisted out of their clothing, cringing at nose-piercing pockets of tear gas still caught in the crevices of their garments.

Naked, oblivious to the sleeping house, the redhead straddled him, his hands warm on her thighs as she moved, glowing in the light of the burnt-down candles, twisting, eyes closed, hands bracing herself on his aching ribcage, indecipherable expressions flickering across her face. Both starved for tenderness after the brutality of the day, they moved in and out of each other, beyond time and space, dancing away from the bloody, tear-stained world.

North Vietnam

David stood in the delicate elegance of his hotel room, dazed and still stinking of dirt, cordite, ammonium nitrate and burned flesh. A wicker basket filled with fresh fruit and a single peony in a slim-necked vase graced the coffee table in front of a richly upholstered rattan sofa.

Brooks had been ushered to his room by two Peace Committee members. Uninjured and alone, David dared not wash his hands. He feared they would break off. His vision pulsated with flashes and his ears strobed from the aftershock of the bombs, creating a whooshing oscillation in the murmuring ambience of the street below. His senses hungered for the crack, slap and roar, the flashing light, the tumult of stinking earth that had so recently testified to his survival. Without them, there was only silence, only blackness, only death. With them, he was alive.

He should write this all down in his journal. A wave of urgency swept over him. He must capture this now. While it was still fresh. He stood in the center of the room, hands shaking. With Brooks a walking mummy, he felt sure they would be sent home tomorrow, their visit cut short. David felt neither anger nor disappointment. All he could sense seemed weird and perfect. He became ravenous. He wanted to devour the world he saw around him. The notes would have to wait. He washed his face and hands in a basin — there was no running water — left his room and walked out through the quiet lobby into the street.

There were no soldiers or armed police at the hotel entrance. Only the sandbags stacked at every portal spoke to the existence of a war. In the street there was only the sound of feet and the tinkle of bicycle bells, the chatter of voices. There were few children. They had all been evacuated to the countryside.

Along the brick sidewalks, concrete rings had been set into the ground. Round concrete covers lay slightly askew over each chamber. Bomb shelters. He imagined climbing into one of these circular concrete wombs, big enough for a small adult and maybe a child, assuming a fetal position and closing the cover as thunderous concussions walked lightning-quick down the street vomiting fire and steel.

On a park bench, two teenagers held hands while the boy whispered into the girl's ear. She smiled a small, sad, smile. An old lady shook a fist at a bicyclist who careened around the corner. Random citizens stared at David, curious, while others passed by, unaware of the Caucasian who stumbled among them. At the end of the park, he turned back into the dusky streets of the blacked-out city. He paused at a cascade of broad colonial steps that led to a grand hotel on the corner of a tree-lined boulevard.

Music drifted from tall, shuttered windows, a plucked instrument and a flute fluttering around each other like butterflies. He entered.

Across the lobby, a lounge glowed from a darkened alcove. The walls were covered in dark red. The room seemed enclosed in a time capsule. It could easily have been filled with Frenchmen in white linen suits and Vietnamese bar girls in silk dresses. But the French colonials had been banished by the Vietnamese and the Americans had not set foot here for over a decade. A sprinkling of Vietnamese couples and several officers in white naval uniforms sat at tables or stood at the bar.

For David, every image still glowed with radiation from the bombs. Light flared off the liquor bottles behind the bar and reflections in the mirror sparkled like flying splinters. A young woman in a *bao dai* floated like a ghost among the tables, carrying a tray of drinks. She smiled. Her teeth shone like ivory.

Stiff with fatigue, David lowered himself into a banquette behind a black-lacquered table. His companion from the Peace Committee appeared in the door. When David spotted him, the escort waved and disappeared back into the lobby.

The waitress floated over, bent down and looked into his face, startled. "English?"

"American," he answered, blushing with embarrassment. "But you speak English?"

"No," she mouthed the word. In a fluid moment, she curved her lips around the 'o' until their eyes met. David's mouth parted gently. He recovered and pointed to the glasses in the other drinkers' hands.

She tipped her head and floated across to the bar, leaving him to be caressed by music that flowed from the shadows.

After the other customers had departed, the waitress returned. Driven by a desire to communicate beyond language, he gestured and scribbled drawings in the margins of a newspaper until she understood he had been bombed.

The waitress looked down at him with great sympathy. She placed her tray on the table and slid onto the banquette beside him and placed her fingers lightly on his arm. With signs, signals, and sounds, he learned that there was a bomb shelter in the basement of the hotel and that she was the commander of the hotel's anti-aircraft battery. At the sound of a siren, they would separate, she to the roof to command her guns, he to the bomb shelter in the basement.

With the bartender cleaning glasses in the background, the waitress hovered near him until the fragrance of her hair dislodged the stink of burnt flesh from his lungs.

The bartender looked up.

The waitress rose, turned to David, made a fierce gesture of firing a gun, grinned like a kid, and disappeared up a stairway at the back of the room. He rose to follow her, but his Peace Committee comrade had re-appeared. He smiled and gestured David out the door.

He walked back to his hotel, mind rushing to embrace the moment he had lost. All his desire to explore Hanoi had landed on the waitress. How had he reached out? Why did she approach him? The other women he had met thus far were adamantly formal, full of the nonsexuality of cadres, or hostile to his white skin and European features.

Surely, there were no bar girls in Hanoi. In Cuba, prostitution was on the verge of disappearing. Wouldn't it be so here? So . . . *was he special to her?* He suspected the violence of the bombing had turned him into a projection machine. Nevertheless, *life is dear . . . and short.* He would return the next night to the same bar, seek her out on the rooftop where she fought her battles against the searchlit sky. He reached the hotel, took his key from the stooped woman behind the desk, and climbed the stairs. Caught up in thought and emotion, he neglected to return the wave of his Peace Committee comrade.

Later, wakening alone in his room, he knew he wouldn't return the following night. He would return to the draft, the college, his parents, the rat's nest of his American life,

while she remained in ancient, brave Hanoi, serving cock-
tails, studying at the university, and firing anti-aircraft
shells at Americans in F-105s and B-52s.

PHILADELPHIA

Connie wobbled into the storefront office of the South
Philly SDS project. She had paid for the cab ride from
the Philadelphia airport with the last of the money her
parents had sent her — as she had requested — for "den-
tal work". The request was strained. She had not returned
home since she had left to train as a civil rights worker.
Had they known the money had gone for an abortion —
an illegal procedure resorted to only by whores and errant
teenagers — they could rest on their conviction that their
daughter had fallen from grace. Connie knew they would
have turned their back on her. She didn't think that would
be such a loss.

"Honey, you're back. Thank God." Carol, Connie's
friend at the Philly SDS office, stood behind the office
mimeograph machine. Mimeo blanks and torn leaflets lay
like wreckage on the floor. Carol stepped over the detritus and embraced Connie. Finally, she stepped back and
looked into Connie's eyes. "How'd it go?"

"It hurt." There had been no question about what she
had to do. It only seemed strange that she had traveled
hundreds of miles in secret to undergo a simple medical
procedure. She felt a deep, saddening loss, a terrible an-
guish generated by her body and her love of life, but felt
no shame about the abortion. No one told her that women
had the right to control their bodies and lives, but her time
in Mississippi taught her she had a right to stand outside
the law. She could not carry the baby to term and the gov-

ernment would not allow her to abort it. It had been a terrible decision, and she had been forced to make it alone and implement it in secrecy. Fuck the government.

"Was he a real doctor?"

"I never even saw him. Some woman — his assistant, I guess — drove me out to this creepy farmhouse. She chattered all the way, wouldn't answer questions, drove me all over the place first."

"Why?"

"To confuse my sense of direction, I suppose."

"Like you would want to find your way back to an abortion parlor?" Carol snorted. "That's nuts."

"If they get caught, they'll be put in jail," Connie said. "I understand the caution."

The numbness lingered. She felt hollow, carved out, scraped raw. Why had this happened? What had pushed her toward sleeping with a guy she hardly knew? She was hardly promiscuous. Loneliness? Fear? The need for revenge on Louis? He was a Negro — no, a black man — under stress. He couldn't be blamed. *I fucked a guy, he was a good lay, everybody tries their best the first time around.* Her diaphragm failed. *Get over it.* Despite her rhetoric, she shivered. "She gave me a gown, I undressed in a room that looked like the back room of a barber shop."

"Was it clean?"

"Yes. It was all very clean. But it was a house, not a doctor's office. Then she put me to sleep and when I woke up, she was sitting there, nose in a *Reader's Digest*. I didn't even know if it had happened. She nodded her head and smiled and said 'You did good.'"

Connie sat down on a folding chair in the mess of leaflets and put her head in her hands. "In Mississippi we have Jim Crow on the run. But because I'm a woman . . . because so many still believe I'm God's property."

177

"Let me make you a cup of tea or something," Carol said, flustered. She clanked a battered aluminum kettle under the faucet in the messy little downstairs kitchen. "The welfare meeting went well. People from the projects showed up. That Mrs. Wyczynski is a spark plug," she said brightly. "She dragged a couple of dozen people in here."

Women doing the work. Again. Connie sat in the familiar fluorescent glare of the little storefront and stared into the street. A group of black teenagers walked past, the boys shoving at each other's shoulders, the girls' hips in motion. She was back in the drab poverty-stricken neighborhood only thirty-six hours after she left it, but it seemed a lifetime. She felt stiff and gray, the color of wash water.

Carol brought in the tea and a can of condensed milk. "You sure you're all right?"

Connie nodded. "I stopped bleeding." She looked up at Carol. "But it's hard to fight the feeling that some part of me got torn out. It was a little life, you know."

"No it wasn't, Honey," Carol said. "Not yet it wasn't. It was just a little . . . " she shook her head and clasped her hands in anxiety. "It was just a little thing, that's all."

The two women sat in the bright light and watched the wind blow Dixie cups and candy wrappers across the sidewalk grates outside.

"Oh, I almost forgot." Carol crossed to the cluttered desk and returned with a travel-worn envelope, small, the address handwritten in ballpoint pen. It was covered in official-looking rubber-stamped smears. "This came in the mail Saturday," Carol said. "Do you know somebody in Vietnam?"

Connie knew the handwriting. She had read school papers written in that handwriting, palmed notes passed down the aisle in class. She opened the envelope to a folded piece of lined paper torn from a spiral binding.

Dear Connie,
Well I bet your not too surprised about
where this letter comes from. I came
home on leave and Franny Ducharme
told me you were asking after me. But
that was a long time ago and a lot has
happened. I don't know if this letter will
reach you, but your mother said it would.

Connie looked up at Carol. "So he came home. And went back."

Who did? Carol asked.

"My high school boyfriend." She smiled. "He didn't even try to get in touch." She recalled her conversation with Franny in the parking lot. Franny's anger, the accident, her parents' indifference.

"He doesn't really sound like he was right for you," Carol said. "I mean . . . " She stood behind Connie and embraced her. "Oh, dear. I'm sorry. What am I saying?"

"This Franny girl. We all went to high school together. I'm pretty sure they started seeing each other after I left. Me to college. Him to the Marines. God, what a world."

"But you loved him. Back then. Right?"

Connie nodded, eyes tearing up.

"That's all that counts . . . Isn't it?" Carol rocked her gently sideways, kissing Connie's hair.

Connie pulled away and continued reading.

Anyhow, I re-upped. So, here I am, in
Vietnam. Again. Cant really say anything
about what the war is like, besides nobody
knows where it is. You go everywhere
off the base by helicopter or truck, so
it's all the front lines. You carry your

m-16 everywhere even to the latrine,
so we must be in somebody's war.

It's green here. You'd like it, except for
the heat. It is real pretty and the people
are strange and sweet and are they poor.
Most of them just dirt farmers, more
busted out than anything you ever saw
back home. But in this beautiful way.

At first it felt real bad and I didn't know
how I was going to make it, not for a whole
year. Now today doesn't feel any worse
than yesterday. It's hard to put into words.

I don't know what's going to happen,
but you'd be proud of me even though
Im a fuckup. I'm a sergeant. That counts
for something. At least, over here.

You can write me here (if you want to
that is). I'd like to hear from you and
I'm not mad at you anymore. Honest.

Your old boyfriend and still friend (I hope),
Eddie Carpenter

Connie burst into tears and doubled over, the letter clasped between her thighs.

"Sweetie, what's wrong?"

"He wrote his whole name!" she sobbed. "Like he was somebody I wouldn't remember!"

Carol bent over Connie and stroked her arms.

180

"What's happening here?" she wailed. "Why doesn't anybody know me anymore? Why don't I know anybody? What's happening to us? All of us?"

VENCEREMOS
1967

"The eagle is looking the wrong way," David mumbled.

"What?" David's father, Aaron, lay on the sofa behind the Sunday *New York Times*.

"The eagle. On this draft notice. It's fucked."

"Draft notice?" Aaron lurched to his feet and yanked the document out of his son's hand. The Presidential seal lurked in the corner of a drab government memo. An American Eagle grasped a cluster of arrows in one claw and an olive branch in the other. "You are hereby ordered for induction into . . . " His voice dwindled. "But you're a student."

"That doesn't matter. Not anymore."

Nina Friedman smoothed her dress in the nervous manner that David remembered from childhood. "You have a student referral, don't you?"

"Deferment, Ma."

His parents were still drinking martinis and eating steak like it was 1958. Where he had just been, a stick of bombs had disintegrated a bus full of people, vaporized a rice paddy and blown his vehicle into oblivion. "I have a

2-S, a student deferment." It was impossible for David to hide his contempt. He didn't try.

"Of course." She waved her hands in dismay. "Whichever."

"Okay, deferred student," his father said, suspicious. "What are you now?"

"Your President has decided to fill his cannon fodder quota from the hallowed halls of academia." He snapped the notice out of his father's hands. "Why don't you guys know about this?"

"Because you never told us." She tidied up the magazines on the coffee table.

"It's been in the news. For months." He turned to his father. "Even your crappy network covered it."

"We didn't hear from you for the whole semester," Aaron snapped. "You don't return our phone calls. You're gone over the holidays. Where were you?"

"Working my tail off." David crumpled up the draft notice and lobbed it into the wastebasket by his mother's desk. *Swish.*

The maid clattered pans in the kitchen while she cooked a pot roast. Did she have a kid in Vietnam? She was black and poor. Sure upped the chances.

Since his return, David had struggled to reconcile what he had experienced in Hanoi with the blind bustle of Manhattan. His home did not have an anti-aircraft battery on its roof or a bomb shelter in its basement. There were no holes in the sidewalks of Amsterdam Avenue for women to drag their children into during an air raid. His parents' world sat solidly at the center of its own universe in a nation still unaware it was at war, while the lean, animated Vietnamese he had talked to, touched, fallen in love with, had disappeared.

Now, David questioned the cavalcade of peace marches that rose, took their moment in the public eye and faded.

Something had to be done to respond to what he had witnessed in Vietnam. Something more drastic. "The draft . . . " He laughed. "That's the least of my worries."

"What worries do you have?" Aaron demanded. "You're young, smart, good looking . . . " He stopped. "You didn't knock somebody up, did ya?"

"I just got back from Vietnam."

His father sat down on the couch as if he had been punched in the stomach.

"Oh my God." His mother put her hands to her mouth and dropped onto the sofa beside her husband. "In the army?"

"Of course not," his father snapped. "He went there on his own damned volition." He turned to David. "How the fuck did you manage to do that? You get a press pass or something?"

"Nope. It's easy. You book a flight to Paris to Prague to Moscow to Peking, turn right until you hit Hanoi. You'd be amazed . . . "

"Hanoi!" Nina inhaled sharply.

" . . . amazed at how brave these people are."

"Are you crazy?" Aaron's voice switched into the upper octaves. "That's treason."

"Why? We've never declared war." David laughed sharply.

"They'll arrest you." Aaron began pacing. "They'll throw you in the can. They'll fry you like the Rosenbergs." He paused. "Where'd you get the money?"

"This war — it's got to stop, Dad. And you're not going to stop it, are you?"

"You don't stop a war," his father shouted.

"We do."

"Bullshit. You're not stopping anything. You're parading around your halls of ivy like a bunch of brats. You think the people in the Pentagon give a rat's ass about you, little man?"

"You know, some peoples' parents actually support their kids' political convictions."

"That's not fair, David," his mother replied.

"What's wrong with you?" Aaron looked carefully at his son. He saw a strong, sinewy young man, strain tightening the flesh around his eyes, black hair falling in a straight line across his forehead. Hardly a chip off the old block. He didn't even joke about pussy or getting laid.

"I thought you wanted to be a folk singer," Aaron said. "That was ridiculous, but not criminal." All this illicit political activity seemed to have sprung out of the kid's forehead, he thought. Fully formed, as Red as his great-aunt Gert, the suffragist labor organizer. Out of control. "Hanoi! Jesus!" Still, David was his son. And it must have been one hell of an adventure. "We'll get somebody out of Rights and Permissions to help you out."

"I don't want some corporate flunky standing up for me in court."

"David."

"Flunky, schmunky. Least you could have done is let me know." Aaron laughed. "Shit. We would have sent a camera crew with you." Mighty Aaron lifted his habitual shield of sarcasm back into place. "What a scoop! *Scion of NBC Exec Turns Traitor in Hanoi.*"

David had been a fool to think he could recover at home. He sat down on the arm of the sofa and touched his mother's shoulder. "The war is getting serious now." He felt as if he were explaining sex to a pre-teen. "And it's not going all that well. We weren't supposed to be there long, remember? Just kill a few commies, inject the place with a shot of democracy, get an election over and get out."

His mother frowned. "You think we don't understand this?"

"They've already drafted as many ghetto kids as they can get their hands on. Ask your colored maid in there . . . "

"David!" Nina was appalled at his sarcasm.

"She'll tell ya." David nodded toward the kitchen, where a Sunbeam mixer whirred. "They pretty much went through all the black kids. Now they're rounding up the middle class. I'm afraid it isn't going so good for us over there, Ma."

"What makes you so sure?" David's father rose and walked to the window, his head and shoulders outlined by the gray winter light that bounced off the Hudson.

"Because I've been there," David said. "That's why."

Light spilled out onto the frozen slush from the storefront windows of the Philly SDS office. David stood inside and stared past a hand-painted sign that splashed across the glass.

JOIN
Jobs or Income NOW!

Inside, a black kid in a thin jacket spoke to a dozen South Philly residents. Women in long coats and an assortment of Sunday hats overflowed the metal folding chairs they sat in. Two older men wearing corduroy coats and black leatherette caps hugged themselves to keep warm. The neighborhood was beginning to take the SDS program seriously.

Connie spotted David outside the office window. Her heart convulsed. She found that confusing. *He looks good,* she thought. *Kind, open, handsome. But the father of a kid? Now? In this world?*

David slipped through the door. Heads turned. Smiling, he crossed the room, a familiar figure to many, conspicuous with his duffel bag and guitar. He leaned over Connie. "I need to talk," he whispered. "Can we go upstairs?"

"Now?" She glanced around the room. "We're in the middle of . . . "

"Please." The urgency in his eyes read real. "Before I get caught up in this." He nodded toward the room.

"Okay." She rose and walked around the back of the room and up the stairs. He followed, waving to several turned heads as he exited.

She led him to her room and stood by the door.

"So, hey, Connie. Hi." He looked around the small, bright bedroom, a bastion of order and comfort in the midst of the chaotic apartment. He wanted to touch her, but her body warned against it. "It's been a while."

"Not since you dragged me into a soap opera." She did not invite him to sit down.

"How'd you get back East?"

"Greyhound," Connie replied. "My parents wired the money. Before I knew it, I was back at work. I feel at home here."

"Look." She put a hand on his shoulder. "About Chicago? I'm sorry for the disappearing act."

"It's okay, Connie."

She shrugged, covering hurt. *One night in the sack with this guy* . . . She had torn the consequences of that night out of her body. *All this misery?*

David dropped his bag on the floor. "Look, I got a few things to figure out. I . . . " He turned to close the door.

"Don't do that!" she snapped.

"Dammit, Connie." His hand fell off the knob. "I got drafted!"

"Oh." She closed the door, sequestering them.

"Yeah. Quite the homecoming present." He stepped forward to hug her.

She backed away. "You've got some time, don't you? Before they call you up?"

"I can keep ahead of the draft. But I was going to tour the country, talk to people about my Vietnam trip. Now . . . "

Downstairs, the meeting was breaking up. Footsteps tramped up the stairs. Knuckles rapped softly on the door. "Hey, guys. It's Carol. Everything all right in here?"

"Yeah, we're okay," Connie called through the doorway. She turned back to David. "So. What's next?" She pulled a bathrobe off the hook on the back of the door.

"Thought I'd head out to the Coast. The Mobe is laying plans to shut down the Oakland draft center."

"The Mobe." She cinched the bathrobe around her. Tight.

"The Mobilization Committee to End the War in Vietnam. We formed it after those vets threw their medals over the White House gates."

"I remember that. Long name." Connie struggled to keep her armor up.

"Yeah. So we call it 'the Mobe'. He shrugged, weary. "Look, Connie, I gotta keep moving. The draft. The Vietnam thing. I got two strikes against me."

She opened the door. "Three strikes." She padded down the hallway toward the bathroom.

David followed. "What do you mean?"

"When I got back from Chicago, I was pregnant." She began washing her face.

"Who from?" he asked.

She turned around slowly, face wet. "You wanna think about that for a minute?"

"What. From that one night?"

"Well, you see . . . " She rubbed her face with a bath towel. "When a guy and a girl get naked and lie down together . . . "

"Stop. Why didn't you tell me?"

"I didn't want to drag you through it." She turned back to the sink.

"Are you still pregnant?"

"No, of course not." She squeezed paste onto a toothbrush.

"You got an abortion then?"

"Why are you being so thick about this?" Connie asked, mouth full of toothpaste.

"Did you go alone?"

"Yes."

"That's a drag."

"I figured it was going to be okay. I mean, why burden you with my little problem?"

"Doctor Sunshine, I hope." Everybody on the East Coast knew about the enigmatic doctor who, for a price, performed secret but safe abortions.

"I never saw him. They put me to sleep, he came in, did whatever he did and disappeared. I woke up and got driven back to the train station. It was weird."

"I should have been here." He tried to embrace her.

She pushed him away. "It's okay. I don't love you. You don't love me. We made a 'little mistake', as my mother would say."

"You should come with me. To California."

"Jesus, David." She shook her head in disbelief. "How do you get there from what I'm telling you?"

"I didn't. I don't. It's just . . . " He shrugged, dismayed.

"Why the hell should I do that? Drop everything? And head for the Coast? With you?" She walked back down the hallway to her room. "You know, I keep tossing around stuff."

"Stuff? Like?"

"Like, observations. We fuck each other. You go to Vietnam. I get an abortion." She leaned on his guitar case. "How does that work? You know what else I wonder?"

"Why don't you just tell me."

"Okay. I wonder why it is that guys always get to go first."

"Go where?"

"Everywhere. Even in the Movement. Where to go, what to do, when it's the right time to drop everything and head in the opposite direction. Jeez, most of you even think it's okay if you have an orgasm first. Why is that? Do you know more than I do?"

"No."

"But people respond to you. They nod their heads, say 'right on' or call you an asshole."

"More often than not."

"But they listen."

"And they don't listen to you?"

"No. They don't. They move on, like they're embarrassed about what I said. Then they refer back to what Matthew, Mark, Luke, John, what they all said before me. Like what I said never happened. Why is that?"

Silence.

She handed him his baggage and gently pushed him out the door. "You go to the Coast. You didn't do anything wrong." She kissed him. "I was the one who dragged you into bed."

"I didn't mind." He grinned. "You know that."

"I know." She closed her eyes, shook her head, and gently closed the door, leaving David in the shabby hallway listening to the thump of his own heart. He turned to go. Halfway down the stairs, he heard the door open.

"David."

He turned to look up.

Connie stood at the top of the stairs. "Give me a name. Not your real name. So I can reach you."

"Why would you do that?" he said.

"I don't know."

191

"Okay." He sighed. "Write to Django. With a DJ. I'll let you know where I am."

"I'll know where you are," she said.

At the bottom of the stairs, he looked up. "Connie . . . "

"Don't. Please." She blew him a kiss. "Goodbye, Django."

David turned and disappeared into the empty office below. She heard the door close and his footsteps recede into the dark Philly street.

MASTERS OF WAR
APRIL, 1967

AUSTIN, TEXAS — Grass at the LBJ Ranch grew so green as to be unreal. It rolled away like Astro Turf from both sides of a white oyster-shell path that connected a sprawling ranch house and a fairytale gazebo. A whitewashed livestock fence undulated over the terrain, gathering the ranch house, outbuildings and corrals into a tidy compound. The entire landscape looked as if it had been assembled by a model-railroad fanatic.

Two men in white shirtsleeves crunched over the oyster shells, sipping glasses filled with bourbon, ice, sugar and mint. Between them, a high-ranking Army officer slowed his military stride to keep pace with his civilian superiors. Beyond the trio, dark-suited figures stood in the shade of a horse barn and a cluster of Texas oaks. A brace of black Lincoln sedans pointed at the gate like shotguns.

"Thought you was going to get away from that Oriental heat, didn't ya, Bill?" President Johnson stood half a head taller than the others. He wore a pearl-gray, flat-brimmed lawman's Stetson.

"Glad for the peace and quiet, Mr. President." General William Westmoreland flashed a crooked smile at his Commander.

In the shade of the gazebo, the three men sunk into rattan chairs.

"The troops I'm requesting come from a pool of the best-equipped, best-trained, and best-motivated soldiers in history." The General sipped his coffee. "Don't try to convince them they don't want to go."

"That's good to hear, General." A pair of square-framed black glasses dominated Jack Valenti's features. "We don't want to be sending the Reserves over there."

"We call up the Reserves," Johnson interrupted, "you're gonna piss off a lot of Americans — families, small businessmen." Johnson laughed and dropped the Stetson on his knee. "I got enough enemies as it is, don't I, Jack?"

"Great men can't avoid it." Valenti smiled confidently to reinforce his image as an insider for the General, whom he mistrusted.

A jet contrail cut a frosty incision across the sky.

"How many more people are you asking for, General Westmoreland?" Valenti asked.

"I want to get us up to a little over 540,000."

"He didn't ask that," the President said. "He asked how many more?"

"One-hundred and forty thousand men, Sir."

"That's a twenty-five percent increase."

"Yes, Mr. Valenti, that's correct."

Johnson stared down at the floor between his knees and toyed with his Stetson, spinning it by the brim. "I can't get stuck in the mud over there, Bill. If I don't conduct myself different from the French, we're gonna see history repeat itself."

"I think we're a little differently placed than the French were," Westmoreland replied.

"What does that mean?" Valenti asked.

"We're building a Nation, not ruling the Vietnamese."

"And what does that mean?" Valenti repeated.

"These soldiers are trained to extend a helping hand, not just exert force."

"Kinda like the Boy Scouts." The President looked grimly at Valenti. "With guns."

"Exactly, Sir. We're doing this as rapidly as we can. We've certainly taken steps to restrain the use of weapons."

"I'm sorry this isn't better expressed by the American press," Johnson said.

"The newsmen over there are damned kids," Westmoreland snapped. "They're young, ambitious, and arrogant. You ask

me — most of them are just out there
looking for a Pulitzer."

"Look, General," Johnson said. "The
American people don't like war. But if
they gotta fight one, they damned sure
want to win it. I got an election comin'
up. We're already getting grief about
this college draft, Congress is crawling
with Republicans who don't like my poverty programs, and I don't want this mess
to go on forever. So, General, please
tell me... " Johnson rose. "What is the
current status of our effort in Vietnam?"

"We're winning."

Westmoreland rose. He stood half a
head shorter than Johnson, staring up at
the man. He blinked. "Well we're... " He
paused. "We've stopped losing, sir."

CHICAGO

"It started at a blind pig."

"A what?" Louis struggled to hear Diane Thomas'
voice through a hiss of static.

"A blind pig," she repeated. "A juke joint, Detroit-
style." Diane had left her civil rights work in Tennessee to
study political science at Detroit's Wayne State University.
"The cops answered a complaint. Nothing serious, people
throwing a party for two guys who just got back from
Vietnam."

Louis could imagine the forces at work — two black
soldiers home from the war, survivors, surrounded by
families and friends. "And in walks The Man," he said.

"They arrested everybody."

He had heard the story on a Chicago newscast. Just as the last "suspect" was hauled away from the blind pig, someone threw a beer bottle at a cop car. And so it began. Now he was hearing it first hand.

Newark had gone up in flames days earlier after a black cabdriver was arrested. The networks had broadcast film clips of burning buildings, dead and arrested Negroes and National Guardsmen firing at New Jersey rooftops. Now Detroit was exploding. He could hear sirens in the background. "Are you all right?"

"I'm okay."

"Tell me the truth." He knew her stoicism well.

"They're looting." She began to cry. "Silly me. I thought we had a chance to make a principled stand. I went downtown and the streets were full of women and kids with their arms full of clothes and toys and furniture. I lost it."

"Why?"

"They destroyed any chance of a dignified response. Detroit cops shoot at anything black."

His mother's apartment lay quiet in the dusk of a single floor lamp in the corner. Louis glanced down the hallway toward her bedroom. He had just checked her — she had already wandered into a fitful sleep. He could arrange for the neighbor to come in to feed her. "Give me an address."

"Why?"

"I'm coming. Maybe I can help."

"Don't. They have roadblocks everywhere."

"I'll find a way."

"It's too dangerous."

"All the more reason to come." A siren wailed outside his mother's window. When would Chicago go up?

"What about your mother?"

"I'll get somebody in. I have a neighbor . . . "

Sirens wavered in the distance. "We haven't spoken in a long time," she said. "I don't understand what would prompt you to come here. And besides." She paused. "What about Connie? Isn't that her name? The woman you were with in Mississippi? How will she feel about this?"

"We went our separate ways." He felt heavy with fatigue. "Right after Malcolm X died."

"I hope I didn't have anything to do with that."

"You didn't. It was Malcolm. And the people who assassinated him. Them and me. I assassinated Connie and me."

The Greyhound cut a straight line eastward across dark fields of corn, the passengers quiet in the tired night. Louis recalled his journeys south with the Freedom Riders in the same silver tube. Then it was a prison. Now the bus was taking him to war. A war in America.

Angry black and yellow smoke rose into the dawn sky. federal troops would be checking the bus stations for troublemakers. To avoid any possible confrontation, Louis descended at a roadstead stop outside the city. He would get a breakfast and ask for directions.

Louis stepped into the diner and a white man in a greasy cook's apron stepped through the swinging door with a sawed-off shotgun. He shoved a waitress down behind the counter and pointed the barrel at Louis.

"Outta here, Nigger." Several customers hit the floor. "Or I'll blow a hole in your belly big as a dinner plate."

Louis raised his hands and backed away from the smell of coffee and eggs, out of the restaurant and across the dusty parking lot, not daring to turn until he reached the highway. He was shaking. He began walking. Cars passed him by, people staring. Someone shouted at him.

He realized with a shock that he had arrived in a war zone and he was the enemy. If he survived the trek, he would go into battle on an empty stomach.

MASTERS OF WAR
AUGUST, 1967

WASHINGTON, D.C. — President Johnson peered over his glasses at a Presidential directive. "'... therefore do I, Franklin D. Roosevelt, command such insurgents to disperse and retire peacefully.'"

Johnson let the document slip onto the desk. "That's how the Big Man handled this mess back in '43." The AP and UPI ticker machines clacked in the background.

"I've got an open line here, Mr. President." The Attorney General held up the phone. "Snipers shooting at firefighters? Whoever heard of such a thing?"

Johnson grabbed the receiver. "What's the story, there, Governor?" Johnson roared. "We're about to put your people under U.S. Army command."

"We urge you to, Mr. President." The voice on the other end of the line quivered. "The State Guard just isn't handling this well. They're shooting at anything that moves."

"You sit tight there, Governor," Johnson boomed. "The cavalry's on the way."

It was ten p.m. Nighttime traffic flowed brightly outside the White House grounds. Johnson hung up the phone and sighed.

"In a matter of minutes, U.S. troops are gonna start shooting into a neighborhood full of women and children."

"No, Mr. President." A U.S. Army colonel had been summoned to the White House. "Our troops won't load their weapons until the order is given."

"So who takes the sniper fire?" Johnson crossed to the Teletype machines. "Unarmed Guardsmen or unarmed Federal troops?"

"Both about equally," said the officer.

Johnson turned back to his advisors. "I'm going to sign this order. Then I am going on television to speak to the American people. But I want you to consider this: there's folks out there gonna say that we can't kill enough people in Vietnam..."

President Johnson put pen to paper. Without looking up, he asked, "So now we're gonna go out and shoot civilians in Detroit?"

DETROIT

"Halt! State your business." A duo of young Guardsmen jammed M-1 rifles in Louis' face. He froze, transfixed by the blood gutters that ran the length of their bayonets. The air stunk of burnt tar, soaked cinders and fear.

"I'm here to visit a student."

"The campus is closed. Turn around and move on. Slow!"

"I'm alone," Louis smiled and shrugged. "I'm simply here to see . . . "

"Move it!" The Guardsman straight-armed his rifle into Louis' chest, sending him stumbling backwards. A squad of Guardsmen double-timed it toward them from a troop carrier. He backed away, turned and trotted toward a boulevard busy with traffic. A squad car full of helmeted policemen barreled down the street, lights flashing.

Louis faded into a liquor store and slunk to the payphone. He dialed the number he had jammed in his pocket. "I'm here, at Wayne State." He crouched over a payphone in the back. "I tried to get on campus but . . . "

"Oh, God. I told you not to . . . "

"I had to."

"You're as stubborn as ever."

"Just tell me how to find you."

"Stay off the main streets. They see a black man . . . "

"Already been through that. I've never seen so many guns."

"They're pointed at you. Move north and east. Stay on the west side of Woodward. The Army has control there and they haven't shot anybody yet."

"So who's killing people?"

"The cops and the National Guard."

"Great."

"All last night, the cops and the militia let people loot. They stood around like they were watching a football game. The fire department let the neighborhood burn, block by block."

"Any chance for retreat? Let some time pass?"

"Rednecks, young blacks with guns? This isn't church country, Louis. This is Detroit."

"We've got to start somewhere."

"There's a tenants' group. They're working up a strategy to keep people off the streets tonight."

"I'll be there. Woodward, right?"

"Woodward. Stay on the west side of the street. You come up the east side and you're dead."

He emerged from the liquor store and blinked in the sharp, smoke-filled light. Soldiers held every intersection and alley. Broken masonry and charred debris littered the sidewalks. Parking meters smashed, windows shattered. In front of a department store, nude, white-skinned manikins lay violated on the pavement, torsos severed at the waist, heads and shoulders, breasts, arms and wigs ground into the muddy, cindered filth. A cluster of Guardsmen stood in the demolished store entrance eating a watermelon they had gutted with a bayonet.

An armored personnel carrier rumbled past, soldiers crouched behind its bulwarks. Bristling with weapons, the bathtub-shaped vehicle chugged against the wrought-iron fence of a small, green park. The fence collapsed and the personnel carrier took up a position beneath an elm, its machine guns following anyone who dared venture into the intersection.

Across the boulevard, two jeeps covered the corner. Guardsmen crouched behind the vehicles or stood at corners of buildings, rifles jammed through cyclone fences at rooftops. Detroit lay under siege and the soldiers were as white as the stars on their jeeps.

The more destruction he saw, the more he understood the "why" of it. People were angry, disappointed, helpless. Their lives had been made a misery, their children had no education, they were locked out of the labor market and now their sons and brothers and boyfriends were coming home from Vietnam, dead, shot up or half-crazy.

He kept his cool. He had places to go, things to do, engagements to keep with civil society. White society. To pass for white. In a black skin. Ludicrous. *Fuck white so-*

ciety, fuck civil society, he thought. *Burn the motherfucker to the ground.*

Chicago

Roger leaned over the open hood of a bedraggled Dodge station wagon, checking the timing on the SDS office's only vehicle. He worked in a garage tucked behind the Hyde Park residence of a sympathetic University of Chicago professor.

Polka music drifted over the back fence and the smell of barbecue wafted through the open garage doors. He doubted he could depend on this wreck to get him from campus to campus even in Illinois. Forget about using it beyond the state line.

"Well, well, well. Whatta surprise. Together again. In one more garage." Roger's old man blocked the garage doorway.

Roger slung an oil rag at him and bolted.

"Heyyyyy, slow down, kiddo." His father grabbed Roger's shirt and yanked him back inside. He shoved his son down into a chair and stood over him, out of breath. "Can you give me a minute?" he wheezed. "Please."

"'Please'?" Roger glared up at him, sarcastic. "Where'd you learn that word?"

"Can't we be family for just a minute here? Jesus." The elder Wolfe sat down on a crate. "You'll be the death of me yet." He glared at the cornered boy.

Roger watched a shiny green-shelled wood beetle inch its way across the garage floor. "How did you find me?"

"I got a little help from my friends."

"Who?"

"Oh, this fella, that fella."

Roger hated the phony nonchalance his father used to describe his clandestine dealings. His old man had stalked him, using the power of the CIA or the FBI or both. Anger crowded his senses. "Mom — you remember her don'tcha? Dottie? — She used to tell me you were selling cars."

"She had to. For your own protection."

"Bullshit."

"Okay, you don't want to talk decent to your old man. Fine. Then shut up and listen." He leaned against a workbench that ran along the garage wall. "You're a fugitive," he said.

"Maybe," Roger replied, wary.

"'Course you are. You tried to kill me. And all this time, me wonderin' why . . . " He sighed and shook his head. "Why would my own kid want to kill me?"

"It was an accident."

"Tell that to the fuckin' judge." Bob Wolfe wheezed out a laugh. "You crossed state lines to avoid arrest, right?"

"If you say so, Dad. You're the expert."

"You tried to kill me in Texas," Bob Wolfe snapped. "And here we are in Chicago! Federal prosecutors get hold of this story, what you did, what you're doin' now, they'll make damned good and sure you end up in the pen. The Federal pen." Roger's old man coughed up a glob of phlegm and spat it on the floor. "We got a war to fight."

"Okay. We got a war to fight." Roger shifted uncomfortably in the chair. *So familiar and deadening and old,* he thought. "So why're you trying to be such a pal?"

"There's an enemy out there, Boy. And if it wasn't for us holding the line over there in those shitty little rice paddies, we'd all be kissing the ass of some Commissar."

A glistening, green wood beetle inched around the ball of phlegm and continued its odyssey.

Roger stood up. "You didn't follow me all the way to Chicago to give me a lecture about the world situation. Didja, Dad?"

"We're family, Son. We need each other. You got a little problem with the law. I got a little problem of my own."

"And you want me to help you?"

"We need information and I think you got it. So . . . " He winked. "Yes. You and me. We can work something out. Something good for you, good for me, good for the U-nited States of America. How would you like that? Hey, Son?"

"You don't wanna know. You gonna turn me in?"

"No." Bob Wolfe extended a booted foot and smashed the beetle into the concrete. "I got a couple friends I want you to talk to."

DETROIT

Louis and Diane held each other beneath the vaulted ceiling of a church vestry. "Sanctuary," she said, pulling back from their embrace. "Let's get to work." The church was working hard to keep people, especially the youngsters, off the streets — and rooftops. They pitched in.

By late afternoon, they were driving door-to-door with a neighborhood leader, escorting jittery kids to the church. By early evening nine more citizens had been killed, twenty-three hospitalized and 1200 arrested in sweeps as the U.S. Army began moving into the burnt-out areas.

Exhausted from the effort of herding angry youths away from the death zones, Louis and Diane sat low on the steps of a rickety wooden porch behind a crumbling, three-story brick tenement. They were trying to talk down two teen-aged boys who wanted to join the resistance. They didn't want any loot, they just wanted to shoot The Man. One boy, barely fifteen, pressed a shotgun stock against his hip and stood spread-legged on the porch, Panther style. Louis grasped the barrel of the gun. "You got a license to kill?"

"Yeah, Brother," the youth replied defiantly. "Now I do."

"We're tryin' to make this place a free zone," Diane said. "A place where you don't have to worry about your grandmother. Over there . . . " she gestured to the fires, only blocks away, " . . . is the war zone. You go out there with a gun, youngster, say your prayers."

"You may think you own this place," Louis continued. "But Mister Charlie doesn't think that way."

The young man laughed dismissively.

"And he'll kill you just to prove it," Diane added.

Across the alley, two old women sat on a back porch. Three black men, bloody, one of them missing a shoe, ran around the corner from the street-front sidewalk. Shotgun-toting officers pursued them. Three shots exploded simultaneously, ringing off the walls. Two of the blasts roared past Diane and Louis. The third, fired wide, hit both the old women, knocking them backward off the bungalow porch, rag dolls caught in a rattle of birdshot.

The boy threw the shotgun into the bushes and ran.

Louis hears Diane screaming at him, but she sounds very far away. Her screams fade into church music. A casket floats on a bed of white lilies. Water-swollen black hands folded across a small boy's lap, the torn body surrounded by frilly satin. A suit too large, collar and tie hang beneath a face, a smashed black pumpkin. Lips twisted into a line no muscles can shape. A man with a flower in his lapel closes the chapel door. Trapped with the boy, the summer heat closes around him.

Louis opened his eyes to the humid Detroit sky. Hot rage flushed his face. Blood pounded in his ears with the tempo of a palpitating heart, Louis snagged the shotgun and ducked inside the house. More police swarmed down the alley and into the bungalow yard. They took cover behind the fence and the carefully tended bushes, ignoring the moaning women.

Louis scrambled up the outdoor stairway. He reached the rooftop and burst through the door. Dragging the shotgun, he crawled to the parapet and looked down. Emmett Till, Mississippi, Malcolm X. His turn to get Mister Charlie.

Wham! A weight landed on his back, shoving his face into the graveled rooftop. He turned, struggling to free the shotgun.

"Stop!" A whispered voice, ragged and breathless. "Stop!"

"Let me go! I'm gonna kill the motherfuckers."

"Go ahead, big man." Diane, her face streaked with soot and tears, sat back against the brick parapet, sobbing on the tarred roof. "You come all the way from Chicago for this. So do it!" She screamed. "Crawl over to that wall and shoot. Set your sights on Mister Charlie down there. Get yourself a Pig, Brother. But do me a favor. Kill me first."

A helicopter roared over the rooftops behind Louis and Diane and hovered above and behind them.

"Drop the gun," a flat voice ordered through a megaphone.

Diane and Louis turned as one.

"Stand up slow." Again, that flat, dead vocal pitch. "Hands behind your head."

Louis and Diane stood up slowly, backs to the rooftop parapet.

"Now move towards . . . "

Shots rang out from the alleyway below.

Louis and Diane pitched forward violently, collapsing face down on the hot gravel roof, while blood red roses burst through his shirt, her blouse.

Cʜɪᴄᴀɢᴏ

Roger met his father's spook friends at the Honey Bee Café, a South Side restaurant that looked like a cross between a tearoom and a butcher shop. Gigantic waitresses served sausage, *piroshky*, corned beef, stuffed cabbage, three kinds of sauerkraut. The girth of the clientele matched that of the waitresses.

He arrived late. His father sat wedged between a pair of men who, despite the heat, remained armored in baggy black suits. "This is my kid," the elder Wolfe said. "He'll listen to anything you got to say."

The first man contemplated Roger with hard, bright eyes. He was swarthy, lean-featured, an olive complexion pockmarked by acne scars. "What makes you so sure this is the man we need?" He never took his eyes off Roger.

"You must be a spook," Roger said, throat dry. "You talk like somebody outta 'Dragnet.'"

His father glanced nervously at the spooks. "We made a deal, kid."

Roger laughed. His old man must have promised he could "deliver" his son to these guys. Roger felt trapped, helpless, stupid for going soft. He should have forgotten the whole, messy proposition. Too late.

The second man stood up, pasted a smile on his red-flushed face and extended a hand. A beer belly had popped open the bottom button of his shirtfront, exposing a hairy navel. "Name's Smitty."

Roger shook Smitty's hand, then rubbed the sweat on his jeans.

Smitty nodded toward his partner. "This here is Kronos."

The swarthy operative glared at his partner.

Roger watched the exchange, noting a rift between the two men. Apparently naming names was a breach of spook protocol. *So this Kronos guy is a by-the-book kinda guy,* Roger thought. *Good ta know.*

"Let's start with a coupla questions," Smitty said.

"I'll handle this." Kronos said, cutting his partner off.

Smitty sat down.

Kronos leaned forward, elbows on the table. "What do you do?"

"What do I do?" Roger looked at his father. "What kinda question is that?"

"He wants to know if you got a job," his father snapped.

Roger had never seen his father edgy. A tiny thrill of victory ran through him. He searched for a waitress. "Who do I have to fuck to get a cup a coffee around here?"

"Answer their question," his father whispered.

Roger stared at his father. The old man seemed diminished, jammed between the two big men. Why hadn't he seen this before? These men clearly considered Bob Wolfe a nobody. If he was a loser now, had he always been? What role did he really play in the world of spies and intrigue, the world he had bragged about so often when Roger had been a child? And why had his mother defended his father's integrity? The guy was a bastard, a liar, a cheater, and a killer. Still . . . Roger might be able to turn the whole mess to the Movement's advantage.

Roger Wolfe leaned forward and folded his hands on the table. "Okay, Fellas, what do you want to know?" he asked.

OAKLAND, CALIFORNIA

Jaw aching from a pulled wisdom tooth, David bused his way west, hallucinating on Darvon. Next to him, a busty grandma delivered rambling monologs on her son, her husband and the Almighty God, in that order. He was wanted on federal charges. He was crossing state lines. Was there a warrant out for his arrest? Would every cop in every coffee shop have his image memorized? Would his photo be plastered up on the post office bulletin board of the next town? His jaw ached, his head hurt. The Darvon hypnotized him and anaesthetized his anxiety. He popped another pill and slept his way toward California, nestled in the cocoon of the busty woman's baritone.

The Greyhound pulled into the Oakland terminal at four a.m. By sunrise, he joined a mass of demonstrators gathered opposite the windowless hulk of the Oakland Draft Induction Center, the processing building for new recruits. Here, teenaged draftees would be poked and prodded, sampled and questioned, rejected or stamped G.I. — Government Issue. Once processed, clutching their new identities, each G.I. filed back onto the buses and headed for Ford Ord, where they would be cranked through boot camp.

The Oakland Induction Center was the largest soldier factory west of New York's Whitehall facility. The Mobilization wanted to shut the motherfucker down. Apparently, the plan suited a large contingent of protestors. At seven a.m. they hovered, jostling and gabbing, waiting for the draftees to arrive.

The first bus pulled in and stopped with a hiss of airbrakes. Eyes averted, angry, close to tears, the cannon fodder descended from the buses, clenched their jaws and fists and strode up the factory ramp, deadpan with resolve.

David pushed against the cordon of cops along with thousands of others. "You don't have to go," the protestors shouted at the inductees. "You don't have to go." Other buses pulled up. The demonstrators sat, stood and sang while hundreds of young Americans strode, slunk or stumbled single-file up a ramp to the Center's entrance. Cattle up the chute. Beaver Cleaver's mom was nowhere in sight. There was no more milk in the refrigerator, no more pickup games in the alley for these guys. A lone goofball draftee grinned and flashed a peace sign.

The first day was a bust. Thousands hunkered down around the drab Induction Center and waited. The cops ordered them to disperse. They did not. The cops hauled their limp bodies from the entrances, dumped them into paddy wagons and drove them away. After they had cleaned house, the cops re-grouped around the perimeter of the induction center, barring any access. The assembly line kept cranking kids out of buses, into the *abattoir*, and out the other side.

On the second day the cops doubled in strength. Before dawn, they surrounded the Induction Center and dispersed bands of protestors down side streets or beat them against the Center's concrete walls. This first assault turned out to be the last victory for the cops.

By sunrise, the spirit winds had changed.

Thousands of newcomers doubled the rebels' numbers. They converged on the battle zone from every direction, chanting, stamping, howling, embracing the bloodied veterans. Longhaired Samaritans brought food, water, bandages, gas masks, painkillers, and marijuana. Reinforced by their newly arrived comrades, protestors who had gone limp the day before could now change tactics. The battle-weary veterans regrouped at every intersection, teaching on the run.

All day, the throngs kept coming, pushing their angry energy forward, broadening the battle lines and opening new fronts. Small efforts expanded into larger actions. Successful tactics spread by word of mouth. *Go where the cops can't — alleys, rooftops, trees. When you got the fuckers surrounded, harass them. Roll potted plants and benches into the streets. Push cars into intersections and puncture their tires.*

David led one of the reinforced skirmish groups south on Shattuck Avenue. As they raced down the middle of the broad thoroughfare, he spotted a platoon of armored and shotgunned sheriffs clustered in an alley, midway down the block. He turned, running backward, warning his comrades. "Pigs. To your right!" he shouted, still backpedaling. "They've got guns!" He waved his arms. "Spread out! Don't let them surround you! Scatter! Split! Now! We'll regroup at the next. . ."

A gauntleted hand grabbed him by the back of the neck and twisted him off balance. He fell. A boot pinned his forearm to the pavement. Half blinded by dust, he could make out the khaki-colored uniform of a Highway Patrol trooper.

The trooper yanked him to his feet. Stunned from the fall, David felt himself hauled backward toward the center of an intersection where the cops had corralled a tight knot of protestors. If they booked him . . .

A jolt from behind sent David and the trooper spinning. Another combatant had joined the tumult. In a tangle of limbs, dust and fragmented images, David broke loose and scrambled, stumbling over the twisted wreckage of a cyclone fence. He turned and watched his rescuer, a shirtless protestor in a red headband, grasp the trooper by the back of his gun belt and spin him in a tight circle, faster, faster until they resembled a bizarre law-and-disorderly dervish. When the protestor let go, the trooper sprawled into the entangling mesh of the cyclone fence.

The trooper scrambled to his feet, frightened, crouching low, gun drawn, while David and the shirtless protestor took off down the street. In an empty alley, David grabbed his rescuer. "Brother!" he whispered, hoarse and breathless.

"My Brother," the protestor rasped. "Kicked that fucker's ass."

"No! Better than that! David pulled the man to him. "You grabbed the enemy by the belt."

"Fuckin' A."

"Dig it. It's a VC trick. You get so close to the enemy, they can't fight back."

"Wow! Cool! I just did that!"

"On your own!" David shook they protestor. "The work of a warrior."

"All right!" the protestor shouted.

Together, David and the shirtless protestor stomped out a short freedom dance before they melted back into the mêlée.

The rout of the trooper marked the beginning of a rapid ride to victory for the protestors. The cops found themselves surrounded, confused, exhausted. They were supposed to outflank these little commie bastards. Instead, the little commie bastards were outflanking them. "I order you to disperse," bullhorns flared. "In the name of the people of California."

"We *are* the people of California," shouted the thousands. All day they ran the cops ragged. Threats and epithets ricocheted off buildings and rose with the pigeons and the tear gas into the blue Oakland sky. That night, they built bonfires in downtown intersections and danced under the moon while the Pigs disappeared into their precinct caves.

The next morning, the buses did not arrive at the Oakland Induction Center. That afternoon, the buses did not depart with their payload of fodder. The Mobilization Against the War in Vietnam had shut the motherfucker down.

MASTERS OF WAR
OCTOBER, 1967

WASHINGTON, D.C. — Over coffee, LBJ told FBI Director J. Edgar Hoover that General Westmoreland had asked for one hundred thousand more troops. Hoover bulged against the pinstriped constraints of his three-piece suit. "If you take a hundred thousand more Guardsmen out of this country, Mr. President," he said, "I cannot guarantee national security."

Johnson placed his head in his hands and tried to massage comfort into his face. "You telling me these protesters are getting to us?"

"The protestors, the rioters, the Communistic elements."

"Why aren't you doing something about it?"

"We're doing everything in our power..."

Head still down, Johnson waved the FBI into silence. Hoover blinked like a snake. He was not awed by Presidential power and he found the dismissal annoying.

"You're beginning to sound like Westmoreland," Johnson said. "I don't want any more Pollyannas in here."

"Do I strike you as a Pollyanna, Mr. President?"

Johnson lifted his face from his hands and stared straight into the unwavering eyes of the Director. "Westmoreland is going to raise hell. You're sure about this troop business."

"Without a doubt. We are fighting a war now. At home. A second front, if you will."

"Great." Johnson dropped his face back into his hands. "We got a war on the home front. Me and Hitler."

OAKLAND

Days after the Tet New Year's offensive began in South Vietnam — as if the two events were connected — the FBI and the Blue Meanies raided the Oakland Mobilization offices. At two in the morning. The Blue Meanies — Alameda County tactical squad goons — wore powder-blue coveralls that covered their badges and behaved more violently than their namesakes, the villains in the Beatles' "Yellow Submarine".

If he got busted, David would be arraigned on Federal charges, tried for treason and thrown into prison. The Mobe people knew that. As the Blue Meanies hit the front office, a brace of bearded, sweet-faced hippies hustled David — burning with fever and hacking from a bronchial cough — out the back door and into a pickup truck. The missing wisdom teeth, the sleepless nights, the tear gas and battle exhaustion had conspired to kick his ass.

By sunrise, the pickup — weighed down by a redwood structure that resembled a witch's hut — wound north-ward along the seaside grade of Highway One. Brown Sonoma County hills fell steeply away from the gray sky, stopped for a moment's respite at the highway grade, then plunged to the sea. Lying on a madras-covered foam pad, David drifted in and out of consciousness, hypnotized by the whine of the tires and the ribbon of highway unwind-ing behind the truck.

In his haze, David didn't care where he was headed. Nor would his escorts tell him — they were traveling north to Red Hawk, a commune snuggled in a valley on the Lost Coast, a near-inaccessible stretch of forested ridgelines and ravines in California's far-north Humboldt County.

They stopped frequently along the quiet road. Se-quoia, a red-bearded carpenter, disappeared into the woods at every stop, always returning with bounty —a rusted wrench, a hawk's wing, bunches of wild onions or watercress. While Sequoia combed the landscape, Ezekiel, bald and dusky with bad skin and soft brown eyes, would clamber into the back of the truck and take David's pulse at neck, wrist, belly and legs. As Zeke worked, David felt a strange glow of relaxation radiate from an imagined hole in the top of his head, flow through his lungs and stomach, and settle as an orange glow around his genitals. "So what are you? Some kinda medicine man?"

"Maybe. Maybe I'm a quack." He shrugged and grinned. "Who knows?"

At mid-day they turned off the highway, bounced down a rutted farm road and pulled into a stand of fir trees. The sudden silence filled with the squawk of blue jays and the rustle of wind in the pines. Sequoia and Eze-kiel disappeared. Just before David slept, he heard a cello playing in the distance.

"Shit!"

David awoke to a whispered curse. A body sprawled across his lap, a soft body smelling of patchouli and something vaguely tropical. A pair of fierce eyes glowered at him through a tousled mop of dirty blond hair. "Sorry about that." They were on the road again. The body crawled down the swaying mattress and loosened the rope ties holding the canvas flap at the back of the truck. The canvas dropped like an unfurled sail, plunging the interior of the homemade camper into a rosy, glowing twilight.

"I was freezing." Her face shone honey gold, sprinkled with a constellation of beauty marks. "My name's Jeanine." She rolled a cigarette from a pouch of Bugler tobacco. The Zouave on her Zig Zag rolling papers leered up at David. *Qualité Superior.* Jeanine lit the end of her hand-rolled cigarette.

"Is that a joint?"

"Tobacco."

"It looks like a joint."

"Appearances can deceive." She winked. She resembled a peasant in a Goya painting, fleshy, a scarf tied gypsy-fashion around her head.

In the closed world of the moving camper, gravity swayed from side to side like a hula dancer's hips. Glass chimes, brass Tibetan bells and a brace of chipped enamel saucepans leaned to the outside of each curve, tinkling gently.

"You've got a bone in your ear," he murmured.

"Foot bone from a red squirrel. Perfect l'il thing, isn't it?" She inhaled through her nose and passed the cigarette over.

Since arriving in Oakland, he had been sucked into the ritual of sharing. Everything — food and drink at the Mobe, a liberated car, every joint, even a can of root beer — passed among all present as freely as conversation. He inhaled and choked, the tobacco stinging his raw throat and lungs. "I forgot it wasn't pot," he squeezed out through his constricted throat.

Jeanine giggled. "Amateur."

They stopped for the night outside a solid little shanty with a corrugated tin roof. Salt-sprayed windows opened onto the sound of the surf below. The sun set beyond silver clouds. Jeanine started a fire in a round sheet-metal stove. The darkening room lay close about them, furnished with only a hand-made table and chairs. The fire painted the walls with animated shadows and colors, dancing over a guitar and a few driftwood sculptures. Ezekiel made soup from mustard greens, seaweed, and mussels that he and Sequoia had gathered at the shoreline. They passed around chunks of bread torn from a loaf shaped like a coffee can.

"Digger bread," Sequoia called it. "We bake it in coffee cans. The coffee cans were liberated. The bread's free. We give it away in the parks."

The fire crackled and pelicans flew north up the coastline in the sunset afterglow. Fortified with tea, soup and bread, the travelers sat quiet. David took a pull from a green glass gallon of Zinfandel. His head felt light and the gallon wine bottle reminded him of Madeline and Washington Square Park. *Two hundred Sundays ago.*

He glanced up at the guitar and rubbed his fingertips together. His guitarist's calluses had disappeared from lack of playing. *I won't be able to play for shit,* he told himself.

He waited for regret to settle in over the calm of the moment, but none came. Instead, a peace glowed from inside, eclipsing the war, the law and the future. He reached up, pulled down the guitar. A flat pick lay entwined in the strings at the top of the guitar neck. He began to play, a low-stringed blues in E. The rumble of the lower strings felt good against his groin.

"Hey man." Redwood turned around at the stove. "You make that fucked up old thing sound good!"

217

"'...fucked up old thing'!" David lifted the guitar and peered into the sound hole. "This is a Martin, man. They get better with age."

David resumed playing. He stopped, tuned, fell back into the ballsy shuffle on the low strings. He laughed. It felt good.

Jeanine grinned. "Hey, fucker. You can play!"

"Just like ridin' a bike." He played a second twelve-bar chorus, head bent over the mellow little Martin.

Jeanine rose and jingled outside. She returned from the truck with a dulcimer, an Appalachian zither with an hourglass body. She placed it on her lap and began to strum. David stopped, tuned the guitar closer to the dulcimer. The guitar was a remarkable find, an old Martin 00-18, small and scarred, its strings rusted by the salt sea air. His hands felt strong and the frets and strings lay sweet beneath his fingers.

In a fog of marijuana, wine and recovery, they played into the night while Zeke and Sequoia wailed incoherently and clapped rhythms that had nothing to do with the tunes he was playing. Jeanine knew no songs but strummed like a fierce puppy against anything David played. The music was horrendous, but who cared, in the strange, detached otherworld he had entered.

They played until Zeke and Sequoia grabbed their sleeping bags and drifted outside. The kerosene lamps cast a glow on Jeanine's face. She and David looked into each other's eyes, set their instruments aside. He leaned forward and their hands fell on each other's shoulders.

Jeanine pulled back. "You were half dead in the truck back there. You got some kind of disease or anything?"

"No, not really. It's just the flu."

"Oh." She pulled the hair away from her face. "I don't get the flu. Besides, sex can cure just about anything." She hoisted her skirts, straddled his thighs and leaned back, smiling down on him.

David got his first glimpse of the Red Hawk commune when Sequoia's truck slid around a tight switchback and began inching down a steep grade, gripping the hillside, a ravine yawning down and away from the roadside shoulder. At each turn, David caught a glimpse of the Lost Coast, a narrow band of black sand littered with a high-water tangle of bleached driftwood and surf-rounded rock. Beyond, the Pacific glittered in the afternoon sun. Below them, miniaturized by distance and altitude, a row of tin-roofed sheds and a sprawling clapboard house hunkered between a muddy road and a river gorge.

He had never seen land like this — rough, wild, young. Compared to New England's worn hills, Humboldt's coastal ridges had been tossed up by eons of tectonic collisions, boisterous, powerful, full of compressed energy. Ragged spikes of Douglas fir marched like soldiers along ridge tops and down the steep slopes.

"North Fork of the Salmon River." Jeanine pointed to a silver slash that glistened through the trees in the ravine.

"So I take it there are fish down there."

"Shit, Brother" said Sequoia. "We got salmon that'll jump right out of the creek and kiss your lips."

Sequoia's truck rolled to a stop in front of the clapboard building. Kids and adults crowded around the truck while Ezekiel and Sequoia pulled out sacks of coffee and sugar, potatoes and onions, socket wrenches, bolts of canvas, two cases of canning jars and a rifle. The kids got small toys, trucks, tops, dolls and a bag of licorice.

David was sure he had descended into a twilight zone. The women wore long skirts or farmers' bib overalls, the men draped in layers of shirts and overalls and ragged jeans. Most sported a hat, headband or untamed mop of thick hair. They all had a shaggy look, like beasts who had endured a Siberian winter.

Jeanine planted a carefree kiss on David's lips and punched his shoulder. "Later," she said and split with a guy she called her "old man", who looked to David like Popeye's Bluto had mated with a French Canadian *trappeur*, complete with plaid flannel shirt and fringed, high-topped mukluks.

"They live in a teepee up on the ridge." Zeke stood beside David as he watched Jeanine's lithe form scramble up the hillside with the *trappeur* galoot.

"Get used to it," Zeke continued. "You are hers like she is yours." He chortled. "In other words, not at all. Come on."

He dragged David into the ranch house and sat him down at a long, plank table. They fed him rice and boiled greens, roast potatoes and the leg of a small animal that tasted like chicken. They drank coffee from a blue-enameled pot and smoked a mixture of hash and tobacco from a long clay pipe. The bowl was fashioned into the finely etched head of a black man.

A puckish man in an embroidered skullcap sat down across from David. His skin appeared translucent and his eyes bored into the new arrival. With him was a dark-skinned woman with thick, black hair, cobalt-blue eyes and the delicate features of a cat.

"Who are you?" the man asked.

"What do you want to know? Name? Rank and serial number?"

"We don't need no stinkin' numbers here, Brother." The puckish man grinned.

"I been working with the Mobilization Against the War."

"The Mobe."

"Yeah." David was impressed. These hippie communards might be dropouts, but they knew about the Mobe. As the war redounds upon the home front, ain't no place to run, no place to hide. *Maybe the boundaries are beginning to blur*, he thought. "I had to get out of Dodge. Your friends here . . . "

"Zeke and Sequoia . . . "

"They pulled me out of the Oakland office one step ahead of the FBI."

"Why is the FBI interested in you?"

David shrugged. "Draft evasion, crossing state lines, inciting to riot. Oh and . . . " Would they understand? Still floating in the journey bubble that began in the redwood camper, he continued. "They want to bust me for giving aid and comfort to the enemy."

"What enemy do you have?" The cat woman looked skeptical.

"I took a trip to Vietnam."

"There's half a million Americans over there," said the cat woman. "What's so special about you?"

"Most Americans are trying to kill gooks." The elfin man spat the word, making a mockery of it. "I have a feeling our friend here took a different route."

"Yep." David grinned. "I didn't deploy at Da Nang. I traveled underground to Hanoi. Via the Soviet Union and China. I talked anti-war strategies with the North Vietnamese. They know what we are trying to do over here. And they love us for it. Oh. Yeah. And I fell in love."

The puckish man slapped his hand down on the table. "Now there's a reason for treason." He grinned and extended a hand. "Elf." They shook, thumb to thumb, palm to palm, knuckle to knuckle. "Pleased ta meetcha. This is your home, Brother. For as long as you need it. All you gotta do is act right, learn how to chop wood, and haul water." He winked. "Lots and lotsa water."

The cat woman rose from the table. She touched David on the shoulder. "C'mon. Let's get you settled." She guided David along a footpath until they came to a domelike structure. The Salmon River tumbled below in a noisy cacophony. "The guy who lives here. He went hunting yesterday."

"Yesterday? You mean like he stayed out all night?"

"You really are a city boy aren't you?"

"The only night I ever spent outdoors I half froze to death. Boy Scout camp."

She held aside a skin that covered the door. David ducked his head and stepped inside. Light angled down from a square hole in the ceiling. The interior smelled of pine pitch, wood smoke and incense. A sooty tin pail hung over the grate of a round, cast-iron woodstove. A glazed pottery plate and bowl lay freshly washed on a cloth spread flat on a low, Japanese-style table. A soapstone Buddha meditated on a cloth-covered pedestal. Cupped in the roar of the water behind them, the lodge possessed an eerie stillness. The hair stood up on David's arms.

"I would like to welcome you to Red Hawk." She pulled her sweater over her head and hung it neatly on a peg. "Hi, David. I'm Willy." Her skin was dark, almost middle-eastern and purple nipples spiked her breasts. "I learn you, you learn me. To survive up here, we all need to know each other very well." She lay down on a low, broad pedestal covered in multi-colored quilts and a glossy black-haired pelt. Head propped on one elbow, breasts yielding slightly to gravity, she rubbed the pelt with her hand and smiled at him. "Black bear."

"So this hunter . . . He won't be back?"

"I don't know. But it doesn't matter." She smiled. "This is his lodge. He built it, but he doesn't own it any more than he owns me. Free city, free country, we all live in harmony here."

David grinned and lay down beside her, nervous about the fast, intense familiarity but grateful for the comfort of her presence. He was awed by the easy aggression of Jeanine, and now this musky, shaggy-haired cat woman. Her breath smelled warm and sweet like molasses. The smooth pelt of the black bear caressed them as they intertwined.

The fluttering sound of a helicopter beat its way into David's dream. He awoke into a cold, pitch-black void. He had no idea where he was. Willy had disappeared. The fluttering grew louder, compressing the dark air. Framed by starlight, a winged apparition steadied itself on the wooden frame of the smoke hole, claws grasping, feathers at full extension, wings beating like the paddles of an infernal machine.

Terrified, he dove under the protection of quilts and the bear skin. *Where the fuck am I?* an inner voice screamed. The fright reoriented him. He was in a teepee on a mountain commune somewhere in California. Red Hawk they called it. Red Hawk commune, Humboldt County, far north of San Francisco. The fluttering stopped. He emerged slowly, peering up at the smoke hole. The apparition, in reality a large, stubby bird, blocked out the patch of sky. He could make out powerful talons dug into the wood.

"Whoo."

"What?"

"Whoo."

"Who what? What's the matter with me?" David said aloud. "I'm talking to a fucking animal here."

"Whoo." The bird stared at him with round, yellow-green eyes, blinked nonchalantly and swiveled its head.

223

The flap covering the lodge entrance swept aside and a tall, dark form filled the room. In one smooth movement, the form darted to the bed. A boot pressed against David's chest.

"Hey!" David squirmed, trying to get out from under the form, but he was pinned. "Get off me!"

The dark form held a long-barreled gun up and away from David. "Who the hell aah you?" The voice carried a strong New England accent.

"Me. David. I-I just got here. Willy brought me over. Said I could crash here."

The boot lifted off his chest.

"I came up from the city. With Sequoia and Ezekiel. And Jeanine."

The form stepped back and lit a kerosene lantern. In the dim light, David saw a long-limbed young man about his age with a pump shotgun, now cradled in the crook of his left elbow. A straight shock of hair fell across his eyes like a veil. He was dressed in a checked shirt, baggy fatigue pants and Vietnam-style jungle boots caked with clay.

"Why?"

"I had to. The Feds . . . "

"Never mind. I don't wanna know." He set the shotgun against the wall and extended a hand. "Eddie."

Soundlessly, the owl dropped in a quick, spread-winged arc and landed on the corner of the low table. "And this is Giap."

"Like the general?"

Eddie glanced at David with a quick, clear look. "What do you know about General Giap?"

"I know he's the commander of the North Vietnamese army," David said. "I know he was a history professor. I know he beat the French at Dien Bien Phu."

"Now he's beatin' the Americans." Eddie sat down cross-legged on the plank floor of the dome and ejected five shells out of the shotgun into his lap. The North Fork of the Salmon River roared through the cataracts below. "When he was planning Dien Bien Phu, General Giap set up his command post by a waterfall in the mountains. The roar of the water let him think. I think that's wicked fuckin' cool."

This man Eddie knew history. He admired a North Vietnamese general. Between his talk with the Elf and now, Eddie, David had found kindred spirits in a world he had never known existed. He extended his hand. "Pleased to meetcha. And thanks for letting me use your place."

"Not mine," Eddie said. "Everything at Red Hawk belongs to all of us."

CITY OF HOPE
1968

MASTERS OF WAR
JANUARY, 1968

SAIGON — The United States Embassy building rose above the tree-lined street, its architecture failing to conceal that the place was a fortress. Surrounded by thick, windowless walls, it squatted on its corner, an ugly incongruity in the midst of the neighborhood's Parisian roots. Stars and Stripes flew above its ramparts, flaunting the impregnable power of the American presence in Vietnam.

In hours, it would become one of thousands of targets scheduled for the opening day of Tet, the lunar New Year.

As dusk fell upon New Year's Eve, nineteen Vietcong commandos moved explosives, guns and ammunition in trucks full of vegetables into the city and stored the material in an auto repair shop owned by a Vietcong sympathizer named Satchmo.

The shop was three blocks from the American Embassy.

At three a.m., Satchmo's commandos pulled up to the Embassy in a dilapidated taxicab and a truck. Moving with speed and precision, they turned into an alley beside the building, jammed the vehicles against the Embassy wall, leapt from the far side doors and detonated the vehicle. Before the final shards of concrete had hit the ground, they leapt through the breach, shooting everything that moved.

Seconds later, American soldiers lay dead in the Embassy courtyard, the commissary was in flames, and the Ambassador had been whisked away in his pajamas amidst the turmoil of gunfire.

Simultaneous attacks blossomed throughout South Vietnam. The opening attacks crackled amidst cascades of Tet New Year holiday fireworks. City, countryside, and town turned equally deadly overnight as Viet Cong and NVA squads attacked simultaneously, each focused on a pre-arranged target.

The next morning, American television revealed all in living color: Dazed American soldiers and South Vietnamese police and military ran down corridors and into offices, shooting at ghosts in four directions. The last Viet Cong commando in the Embassy was shot as he penetrated the second floor offices.

All over South Vietnam, attacks flew like hawks at American and South Vietnamese soldiers alike, darting on the wings of mortar barrages and small arms fire. It was impossible for the embattled Americans and their South Vietnamese counterparts to distinguish an ambush from the detonations of a string of holiday fireworks. During Tet, everyone played with firecrackers. It was a centuries-old tradition.

Under cover of the New Year celebration, the Viet Cong took out guard posts on Highway One, attacked helicopter bases with mortars and RPGs, invaded police stations and assaulted the Presidential Palace. The surviving attackers disappeared with the dawn, melting back into village life or fleeing into the jungle, leaving any pursuers to run into the sights of rear-guard ambush squads.

In the morning, General Westmoreland appeared in painfully starched fatigues and announced that the Communists had "very deceitfully" manipulated a Tet holiday truce.

At home, Walter Cronkite, the most trusted man in America, said, "What the hell's going on? I thought we were winning this war!"

HUMBOLDT COUNTY

Red Hawk barely survived the winter. Twice, the communards had been cut off from town by freezing rain and mud, then snow. Supplies ran low. Every week, pairs of volunteers hiked out to the little store at Forks of Salmon to procure staples — rice, beans, coffee, candles, licorice for the kids, a precious fifth of whiskey.

Eddie became their savior. One night, after a grim tally of Red Hawk assets, he rose from the stained kitchen table and crossed the compound to his lodge. He reappeared carrying an M-16 and a canvas bag. No one had seen the rifle before. Two days later, he returned, the canvas bag stuffed with rabbits and quail packed in snow. The commune went wild. Puckered parsnips and potatoes and a handful of wrinkled carrots appeared from the root cellar. A vat of beans simmered over the fire.

Ezekiel led the collective in a mantra thanking each animal for its sacrifice. After the raucous meal, Eddie and David returned to the lodge.

"Y'know," David speculated, "those animals might prefer to be alive, rather than be chanted at."

"You think I shouldn't have shot them?" Eddie asked.

"If we all went back to the city, we wouldn't have to murder our lunch."

"Somebody else would be murdering it for us."

"We could be fighting in the streets."

"Fighting in the streets? That's rich." Eddie put more wood on the fire. "You ever been shot at? Ever hafta shoot anybody?"

"There's other ways of fighting, y'know."

"Whooo-eee!" Eddie slapped his knee in an exaggerated minstrel routine. "No offense, but you sound like my old girlfriend. Full of beautiful ideas that can never happen. Besides," Eddie continued, "you go back to the city, they'll bust your fugitive butt and throw it — and you — in Leavenworth." He embraced David. "You're a fuckin' traitor, Brother, and I love ya for it."

When Sequoia returned from the next supply run, he pulled a stack of mail from one of the grocery crates. He passed out letters and boxes to various communards and held up a small, single envelope. "Here's one. Almost didn't bring it back, but hell, the handwriting looked so damned sexy . . . " Sequoia sniffed the envelope, raised his eyebrows and peered at the address. "Says here it's for a DeeJango, um . . . "

"Django?" David straightened up. "Like D-J-A-N-G-O?"

"Yeah, that looks right."

"That's for me," David said. "Friend of mine. I gave this address."

Ezekiel frowned. "You're supposed to be underground."

"I only gave the P. O. box. Asked them to use that name."

"Django. He's that three-fingered guitarist, right?" Sequoia asked.

"Right," David replied. "The other two got burnt off in a fire." He took the letter, feeling a pang of regret about placing the commune at risk. He recognized the handwriting. It was from Connie, and the smell of the stationery left him feeling remote and thoughtful. He sat silently through the evening meal, made rowdy by the consumption of an industrial-sized bottle of cheap whiskey that Sequoia had packed back down from Forks of Salmon.

After dinner, he announced to the quieting crowd, "If you don't mind, I'd like to share this letter with you. It's from a friend back East."

> *Dear Django* (he read),
> *I hope this letter finds you in good*
> *health. I wanted to say I'm sorry I*
> *treated you so badly. I was still . . .*

231

He hesitated. *Should I read this*? Ah, what the hell, he was beginning to see certain advantages to the loose, no-secrets ethic that permeated commune life. You shared what you wanted, kept private what you wanted. Avoiding pain — bringing someone else down — seemed to be the only criterion for whether or not to divulge, confess or otherwise blow confidentiality.

> *I was still in pain about the*
> *abortion back then.*

No one stirred or commented. Many of them had experienced the same difficulty. Getting a bootleg abortion turned an already miserable experience into a nightmare — a risky, expensive nightmare. Connie was not alone. Nor was he.

> *Not that I think we should be back*
> *together. I don't. And that's not why*
> *I wrote. But so much is happening!!!*
> *They tell me you're out in the boonies,*
> *you may not know about it. So . . .*

He read more clearly now.

> *Bernardine Dohrn got elected President*
> *of SDS. Bernardine, not Bernie. Not a*
> *guy. Not a girl. A woman. She's smart*
> *and gorgeous. She looks hot but that's*
> *irrelevant. She is articulate and forceful,*
> *has been a lawyer for years already*
> *and cuts to the heart of any issue. A*
> *lot of the guys can't dig it, but she got*
> *there by consensus. People are smart*

enough to recognize a leader, even if
it's a 'she'. Oh yeah, she wins the hearts
and minds of a lot of guys, too.

The men grunted. The women laughed.

We're organizing another demo, this time
in Chicago, at the Democratic Convention.
We're going to force the delegates to add an
antiwar plank to the Democratic platform.
A lot of people plan to confront the
delegates, no matter what the cost. March
outside, try to meet with them, the way
we did with the Mississippi thing in '64.

Wish you were here, again, not for me,
but for the Movement. It needs you.
Sorry, but true. On both counts.
Venceremos,
Connie

"Connie?" Eddie picked the envelope off the table. He perused the letter carefully. "Hey. That's my girlfriend's handwriting!"

BOSTON

What began as a work partnership turned sexual after Madeline joined the staff of the *Back Bay Rat*. Sam Nicholson, the *Rat's* editor and publisher, was aristocratic and ambitious. Money had accumulated steadily in his family's coffers since Massachusetts was a colony. Despite Sam's entitlement, Madeline liked him. He espoused a soulful political stance, had cast off his family's patrician values, he commanded a thorough understanding of history and journalism, and he was a walking encyclopedia. Once again she had attached herself to a man, albeit attractive, from whom she could learn.

Madeline was a girl playing in a men's club. She adjusted her strategy. She would write a commentary and submit it to the *Village Voice* under a male pseudonym. If they published it, she would announce her real identity and her reasons for the gender shift. A double whammy. Smiling to herself she began to write.

> *For the first time in years, I'm feeling hopeful. Hope came conflicted with the news that the Viet Cong and the NVA had overrun South Vietnam during last month's Tet Offensive.*
>
> *Hope grew jubilant when Robert McNamara disappeared from the scene, ecstatic with the knowledge that we wouldn't have to watch the hubris radiate from his smug features any longer.*
>
> *Hope came with comic timing as, on April Fool's Eve, President Lyndon Baines Johnson hung his hang-dog face into the boob-tube and announced "Ah shall not seek, nor shall ah accept. . ." You know the rest. April fools!*
>
> *The streets exploded with grinning, war-weary Bostonians. You'd have thought the Red Sox had finally won the Series.*

So long, LBJ. Good riddance to bad
rubbish. In the words of our national
poet, Bobby Dylan, "How does it feel,"
(Lyndon), "to be on your own, (Lyndon),
no direction home, (Lyndon), like a
complete unknown, like a rolling stone?"

I know how it feels for me, Mr.
Johnson. I'm freakin' out for joy,
and that joy gives me hope.

Hours later, Martin Luther King bled to death on a motel balcony in Memphis. People walked the streets cautiously, waiting for violence to explode. One city after another ignited in flames. Boston was no exception. The Back Bay went crazy. The *Rat* staff hunkered down and barricaded the row house they had rented on Roxbury's Fort Avenue. Dirty yellow smoke, stinking of roofing tar and burnt electrical wiring, swirled around them while the wail of sirens floated on the distance outside.

The mayhem made Madeline restless.

"We should be out there," she said, peering through the window.

Sam picked up a two-by-four and dropped it into the straps that bracketed the plywood-reinforced door. They had installed plywood backing on all the first-floor windows and doors to hold back the Federal counterintelligence goon squads that roamed around the nation on the taxpayer's dime, trashing Movement offices and underground newspapers, injecting lies for the media to get high off of, smearing, framing, and beating white leftists and assassinating black activists. The FBI called this top secret operation "COINTELPRO". So did everyone else.

235

"I can't let you go out there." Sam looked to the staff for support.

"Today," said the verbose copy editor, "on this very special day, every white person in Boston, every white establishment — including the *Back Bay Rat* — will be tagged as ofay — the foe."

"You guys!" Madeline looked around the room. "It's happening right outside our door, for Chrissakes. You don't want to do anything about this?"

"We're not supposed to 'do anything'. We're supposed to cover it," Sam said.

"What?" She laughed. "From behind a barricaded door? Our little fort on Fort Avenue."

"Very prosaic, Madeline," Sam said. "So what would you do? Run up on the roof with a bunch of street urchins and pissed-off snipers? Or run down Columbus Avenue messing up the neighborhood? It's futile."

"It's not futile." She retreated to the stairway. "And there is no wasted motion. The whole world will be watching them. Those people. Not us. The ones in the street."

Sam didn't move. Neither did the others.

Madeline stood watching the impassive little knot of collective members, arms folded across chests, conflicted but silent. "Jesus," she said, and stomped out of the room.

Upstairs she sat down at the table facing the bay windows and watched the flashing lights of the cop cars scream up Columbus Avenue toward the rioters. Tears flowed, not from smoke or fear, but from rage. Infuriated by King's assassination, the broken promise of peace, dumbfounded by the passivity of her brothers and sisters downstairs, she tore the hopeful *Village Voice* article out of the typewriter and began again.

*The same body politic that leapt
with joy at the news of a ceasefire
and LBJ's resignation is crying over
the murder of another leader. A real
leader. An irreplaceable leader.*

*We have grown so used to violence
that we now react as if we were a
platoon on patrol. We flinch, shout
"incoming!" and hit the dirt.*

*But a revolutionary never dwells on
hopelessness. Peace- loving, nonviolent
Doctor King saw the war in Vietnam as "an
enemy of the poor" and vowed to attack
it. The Peacemaker had drawn his sword.*

*We should take his declaration as
our own call. It's time to go beyond
the system. It's time for fundamental
change, not reform. Call it Revolution
if you will, but in this journalist's
heartbroken yet enraged opinion, there
will be no peace in America until these
matters are resolved. I promise you.*

A patrol car cruised beneath the window, announcing in the flat tones of the Boston Irish that a curfew had been imposed. Those found on the street would be arrested.

Madeline's tears blurred the lights of Roxbury.

RED HAWK COMMUNE

David sat beneath bowers of marijuana, waiting for the acid to kick in. The hemp shoots had grown into sturdy clusters of five-fingered leaves, spiky digits reaching for the sky, cradled in the compost and goat shit that he and Eddie had hauled up from the creek bed in gunny sacks. Now he sat, stinking of goats and garbage, gazing at the beautiful leaves quivering yellow-green in the sunlight.

The acid, bought from wandering freaks in a school bus, wasn't taking effect. Blotter acid. It had probably dried out, gone stale. It didn't seem to be holding a dose. He was half relieved. He had taken acid once before. It had evoked a deep depression that had pinned him to a couch, immersed in a loneliness he had not known existed.

Eddie sat cross-legged on the slope above the marijuana. Giap perched in the fork of a stunted pine, preening his feathers and periodically glaring at his human cohabitants.

"That owl's got an attitude," David said.

"Who . . . Giap? Shit man, we're gonna get high and Giap's gonna protect us. For him, it's a bore. He lives in a constant psychedelic state."

"Ah, bullshit," David said.

Eddie grinned. "You wait. When you get cranked and look out your eyes, you're gonna see where Giap really lives."

They sat, silent, listening to the wind stirring the pines. Still unfazed, David contemplated his past, the stepping-stones that had gotten him to a mountainside in California, waiting for a dose of D-lysergic acid diethylamide to trigger his synapses.

When the drug first made its appearance, he had interpreted its potential to expand consciousness to be a method to improve people's learning abilities. The growing onslaught of phantasmagoric, acid-induced voyages soon overwhelmed any notion that the drug could be used to help you study better. How could he have known? He was only a freshman when Alpert and Leary were first experimenting with what they called consciousness expansion. Some expansion. And this acid wasn't happening, not to him, not yet.

"So you were bangin' my girlfriend."

"Huh?" Eddie's voice snapped David out of the jumble of his thoughts.

"You got her pregnant."

He felt bad for Eddie. He remembered how he suffered when Madeline told him she was sleeping with other guys. Jealousy. *How "free" was free love?* he thought. *Who did it liberate?* "It was just a thing."

"A 'thing', huh? How'd you two meet?"

"We drove to Chicago together."

Eddie closed his eyes and fell backward into a brown warmth of pine needles. The delicate, five-fingered leaves began to dance in rhythm, broadcasting an aura around each leaf in the guerrilla garden. "Weird. You fall into Red Hawk, we get tight, now I find out you knocked up my girlfriend."

"I thought you said she wasn't your girlfriend."

"Not any more."

"She had a lot to say about you." David pulled yellowed, five-fingered leaves off the nearest plant.

"She tell you how stubborn I am?"

"She told me when you joined the Marines, how sad she felt for you. How much it hurt her."

"That's bullshit. She didn't care."

The sky pulsed, a bright blue abyss above the pines. "That's what you think."

"That's what I thought then. Now . . . "

"Yeah?" He coaxed Eddie, feeling a great tenderness toward him and what he had been through.

"Now I believe you." Eddie stared up at the sky, arms spread-eagled in a fatigue-clad crucifixion.

"She tried to get you to go to college."

"College takes smarts. Oh yeah. And somebody to pay for it."

"She told me you thought you were stupid." He laughed. "You know goddam well you're not stupid, man."

"Oh, yeah?" Eddie said, nodding his head like a child. "I gotta be some kinda stupid. That's what lets you shoot a guy." He giggled like a child.

"Huh?" David had never heard Eddie talk about killing. "What do you mean?"

"Hey. You shoot somebody. You don't know him so you're stupid about him — or her. If you're lucky you don't have to see who it is." Eddie's face fell under the weight of a deep sadness. "Oh and then there's the part about what happens if you don't shoot him. Cause for shit sure, you don't do him, he's gonna do you, motherfucker." He giggled again, shrilly. "See what I mean? The whole fuckin' thing is stupid, man. Stupid is as stupid does. Stupid to enlist in the first fuckin' place. Stupid not to quit when you grok what's happenin'. Stupid not to frag every motherfucker ever ordered you to lock'n' load."

While he spoke, Eddie morphed into a giant baby sitting on the hillside — an old baby, a big, old killer baby, dirty, cagey, dying from the secrets he held. Eddie's voice sounded far away, as if he were calling from across the gorge on a still September day.

"That was stupid. And that was what Connie told me. And that was what pissed me off. Because I was stupid to do that."

David could feel himself going up into the sky. He talked out loud, wanting to ground himself. "She told me you were funny."

"Class clown. In the yearbook." He fell back into the pine needles. "Ha ha. I been some fuckin' clown, last coupla years."

Giap glared at the humans, measuring their progress with unblinking yellow eyes.

"No regrets, though," Eddie giggled. The giggle turned into a laugh, exploded into a roar of convulsive guffaws and decayed into a coughing fit that left him red-faced and exhausted. He fell back into the warm pine needles and moaned.

Plasma molecules swam across David's retinas, reflections cast on the sandy bottom of a shallow stream by water bugs that skate across the surface tension. Sunlight impaled his eyes and pulled him past claws of pine branches that loomed overhead, tossing him into blue sky, the indelible blue sky.

"Oh, fuck!!!" Eddie sat up quickly, eyes wide. "I think this shit just kicked in."

From across the universe, a pan clanks against a sink in the big house, its sonority flowing easy through the trees, its tones sluicing like blood-red wine into the glass vase blown from a glowing, molten blob at the end of a pipe in a Medieval village in France where a goat bell jingles in the glass-blower's garden and the wine. What wine? Drinking wine? Alcohol isn't high. Wine makes sleep not thinking sharp bright thinking . Why wine? Why France. Here is mountains and creeks and sounds of birds and marching soldiers in news clip napalm, flowers and trees.

What of trees?

What of birds, the sound of birds?

Why suffer the suffering of others? Why not buzz from rock to water to tree, sucking boundless energy from tree-tops and pinecones and rocks, a hummingbird sucking all things living and dead. Auras pulsate around each spider, stone, fingers, bootlace, gunny sack, each alive with infinite detail, look at a hand for a lifetime, go no further. The sky melts and flows candle wax down the shaft of perception. General Giap sits motionless over the two human beings trapped in helpless no-think. He blinks a welcome into his wilderness with a brusque impatience, standing guard at the gates of the garden on the ridge top.

Eddie and David sat up simultaneously and stared at Giap.

"Took you long enough to get here," he blinked.

A drumbeat broke into their journey, its tempo measuring time, which has no relevance out there. Tempo, time, pulling the two travelers back into the world. Still shimmering, they retreated to the lodge, stoked a fire of pitch-filled pine knots until the stove glowed roaring red, stripped and brushed their bodies with hemlock and spat water on the cook stove, raising the temperature in the lodge with clouds of steam. They sat side by side, drinking green tea, their naked bodies sweating out the acid toxins, immersed in the roar of the cascading rapids below, staring at the flames in the firebox.

"I gotta go back," Eddie said quietly.

"Back to Connie?"

"No, man," Eddie said. "To the world. The things Connie was talking about."

"What things?"

"In the letter. To you." Eddie grasped a hemlock frond, dipped it in cold creek water from the rapids below and splashed crystal drops onto the glowing seam between stove and stove pipe. The droplets danced before dissolving into steam. "I saw the whole thing."

"What?"

"The war." Eddie stared at the droplets dancing on the stove.

"You saw the war? While you were tripping?"

"Yeah."

"How did you stand it?" Hours and eternities earlier David had hallucinated light patterns that morphed into the orange and black blossoms exploding around him on Highway One south of Hanoi. A bad moment. "What did you see? The killing?"

"No, no," Eddie replied. "Not that war. The other war. The one here." Eddie stood naked, staring into the fire, glazed with sweat.

"What about it?" David looked at his hands as they softened in the wet heat.

"The Vietnamese, the NVA, they have this battle tactic," Eddie continued. "They get in so close you can't bring fire to bear on them. Mortars, artillery, air strike, napalm — without destroying your own people. 'Grab the enemy by the belt,' they say.

"Grab the enemy by the belt," David repeated. "Close in, where they can't swing at you."

"We got to do the same thing here," Eddie said. "Right here in the U.S. of A. It's time to grab the enemy by the belt."

Chicago

Connie Moore had come to protest the Democratic National Convention against her better judgment. She should have stayed in the overworked Philly office. But radicals had no faith in Eugene McCarthy, the 'peace candidate'. Silver-haired, humble-talking, affable Senator McCarthy had already sucked too many left-leaning idealists back toward the center. It was easier to go 'Clean for Gene' than it was to . . .

> *Dare to struggle!*
> *Dare to win!*
> *Dare to tear*
> *The roof off the motherfucker,*
> *Roof off the motherfucker,*
> *Roof off the motherfucker,*
> *Roof off the motherfucker!*

The SDS contingent knew that one more kid for McCarthy meant one less kid for the Mobilization. Connie's SDS brothers and sisters had insisted she go to Chicago, to assess how politically aware the Chicago demonstrators were and — if possible — to contact the McCarthy contingent. She didn't know a lot of people in the Mobe but she had the gift of persuasion.

As the sun climbed into the August sky, the rumors were not good. The crowds weren't showing. Onstage, the speakers seemed strained, anxious, like performers waiting for an audience to show. They spoke among themselves, only sporadically addressing the crowd through a bullhorn.

Beyond the park, clusters of uniformed men gathered. They wore the light blue summer uniforms and checkerbanded hats of the Chicago Police. The National Guard, helmets shining dully under streetlights, rifles with bayonets fixed and gas masks strapped to their legs, stood waiting at parade rest in the canyons behind the ornate façades of Chicago's lakefront buildings.

The Chicago cops had shot a young Sioux named Dean Johnson in the park that morning. Dean had threatened a cluster of cops with a knife. Or was it a gun? Or a fork?

They chased him into an alley where they had to shoot him — so the report read. Word of the shooting spread. The crowd's low-key response hardly seemed bizarre to Connie. Things didn't surprise people these days.

By noon, only a thousand demonstrators had gathered in Grant Park. A trio of bearded, bare-chested men stepped on stage. One of them embraced a small, pink piglet.

Connie watched them from the back of the crowd, arms folded. They seemed to be having a wonderful time. She wondered how they could be so full of hilarity, so full of themselves. It must be good to be with friends.

"Brothers and sisters!" A cheer went up from the scattered thousand. "Tomorrow, the delegates to the Un-Democratic Convention will be oinking and rooting and defecating in the hallowed halls of their fucking Convention Center."

A man with crinkly blond hair and ammunition bandoliers crossing his chest held a baby pig aloft. "We call him Pigasus!"

The pig grinned a pink, beatific pig smile.

The man hugged the pig.

The crowd roared. "Pigasus! Pigasus for President!"

Onstage, the bandolier man kissed Pigasus squarely on the snout. "We stand here, outside the headquarters of The Man and we will be heard. As the obscenity of this war drags on, The Man will eat our truth! Pigs of the world, heed Pigasus, our candidate for President. He has just begun to fight!" His crossed bandoliers held cigars, flowers and hot dogs in the cartridge loops.

Connie wasn't there to endorse a pig. She pushed forward toward the stage. "I want to speak," she told the bearded, blue-jeaned coordinator.

"Who're you?"

"My name is Connie Moore. I'm from the Philly SDS office."

The beard was clearly confused. "Cool, but you're not on the list and . . . ."

She grabbed the bullhorn and strode to the front of the stage. "Hey everybody!" Although she had no speech, no notes, nothing prepared, she felt calm. "Welcome to the Democratic National Convention! Our version of it, that is!"

Cheers.

A drunken boo.

"We may be on the outside, but before this week is over, we'll be the talk of this Convention, of the Nation, maybe even the world. I know. I was at the last Democratic Convention. I went there with the Mississippi Freedom Democratic Party."

People looked up, attentive.

"Those Mississippi farmers. They made people watch. They made people listen. And they didn't raise a hand in violence. Not once! Not ever! Now we have to do the same!"

"Naaah! Let's kick their ass!"

Connie ignored the heckler. "The eyes of the world will be watching what happens here in the next few days."

"Right fuckin' on, sister!"

Applause.

"We will make them listen. They will listen. And we will do it without violence."

"Tell that to the fuckin' Pigs!"

"Forget the Pigs!" she shouted. "We're here to talk to the delegates. To the 'Clean with Gene' folks, maybe even get 'em a little dirty. Most important, we're here to bring the war — the war in Vietnam and this war, the war at home — right onto the convention floor!"

The crowd broke into applause. "We Shall Overcome", started slow and low, swept through the park in a rising wave. Connie joined them. She hadn't expected such a reaction.

A garbled voice shouted into a bullhorn from outside the park. "This is an illegal assembly. You are hereby ordered to disperse!"

A scuffle broke out. Girls screamed, young men shouted in anger.

Disperse where? There was no place to go. Traffic rushed along the edge of the park forming a deadly, moving wall. The police charged. Tear gas bombs exploded with a dull thud. Choking gas came swirling, hitting Connie as if she were inhaling tiny slivers of broken glass. She tried to cover her face but the gas burnt into her skin like phosphorous.

She ran with the others, pushed along by the crowd, walking, half running, stopping to help those who fell. Others scooped up smoking tear gas canisters and lobbed them back at their attackers, a line of white-helmeted cops who waded into the crowd from the south end of the Park, gas masks making them look like insects.

She grabbed the hand of a panicky girl and pulled her along. Canisters exploded ahead of them now. There was no place to go but out into the traffic of Michigan Avenue. Cars squealed to a stop. Horns honked. She had seen no one she knew, not Louis, not David. Where was everybody? The people she ran with became her comrades, all of them dodging between the autos, choking on the gas, going nowhere, moving blindly across the broad boulevard and down the streets, away from the police and the tear gas and moving forward, moving toward . . . what?

In Boston, Madeline Singer had hustled a press pass from an infatuated reporter she knew at the *Boston Globe*, borrowed a friend's Volkswagen and driven straight through to Chicago. By the time she arrived, the cops had already cut off the lakefront, keeping the freaks cordoned off. She dumped the VW on a quiet street in Hyde Park and rode the elevated back to the Loop. A helicopter shot overhead, its rotors reverberating off the cliffs of the lakefront buildings. To the north, she could hear sirens.

A river of delegates with pot bellies and seersucker jackets flooded the hotels along Michigan Avenue and State Street. Cronies threw themselves into each other's arms, slapping backs behind roadblocks, at ease in their denial. Their cornball gaiety stunned Madeline. Grins appeared as grimaces. Did hysteria lie far beneath? Didn't they know there was a war going on? How can they be so blind? She wanted answers to her questions. Powered by her phony credentials, she left the conventioneers and crossed Michigan Avenue from one world to the next. Across from the bright, delegate-filled lobby of the Hilton, scruffy paralegals sat on the grass, taking affidavits from bloodied demonstrators about the police action the night before.

Madeline interviewed a diminutive protester who looked like she should be selling ice cream in Iowa for the summer. "We were crashing in the park. I was wasted, just from getting here and all." The protester looked up wide-eyed at Madeline. "They said it was okay."

"Who said what was okay?"

"The Pigs. Then the Mobe guys."

"The who?" Madeline knew what the term meant. She wanted to test this teenager.

"The Mobe. For Mobilization. The committee who put this . . . " The little girl threw a suspicious glance at Madeline. "You don't know what the Mobe is?"

"Yes." Madeline nodded. "I do. Just checking."

"Are you a snitch?" The little girl fingered Madeline's press pass. "The *Boston Globe*! That's a straight paper!"

"Look at the name. Do I look like somebody named Everett Sanford? My name is Madeline Singer and this story goes to the *Back Bay Rat*. These credentials help me get through police lines."

"Okay." Kids all over the country knew all the underground papers like the *Rat*. They were everywhere. "Cool. The Pigs let the Mobe guys keep the bullhorns, but they won't give them a permit."

"Who won't?"

The kid shrugged. "Maybe the Mayor. How would I know? You think I was at the meeting?" She laughed. "I'm a chick, man."

At Grant Park, David and Eddie lay on the grass with a thousand others, eyes closed, listening to Phil Ochs sing a song about a universal soldier. The well-known folk singer had often played in Washington Square Park alongside David. Now Ochs stood on the back of a flatbed truck and sang, his guitar ringing over the Park.

David felt no regret about their divergent paths. For him life was unfolding on its own terms and at breathtaking speed. They had left the wilds of Humboldt County just weeks earlier, entrusting the burgeoning weed crop to the Red Hawk communards. Now they lay between Lake Michigan and the canyons of Chicago, hooked up with the Mobe.

Despite his absence, David was still well known within the movement. His trip to Hanoi added weight to his past work. Here in Chicago, most of the Mobe leadership was still in jail after last night's bust. Movement lawyers were working overtime to spring them, but bail money was tight. Within an hour of their arrival at the Mobe's Grant Park encampment, he had been appointed to serve as messenger between the Vice President and the entire anti-war movement. His mission? To persuade Humphrey to endorse the Mobe's anti-war plank to the Democratic campaign platform. David had convinced the nervous Mobe underlings that Eddie's presence would lend authenticity to the meeting. They had no choice but to agree.

"Shit, man," Eddie had said. "A chat with the Vice President. Hadn't expected that."

"Neither will Humbert H. Humphrey." David grinned. "C'mon. Let's go grab the enemy by the belt."

David and Eddie crossed Michigan Avenue to the Conrad Hilton Hotel where Democratic Party Headquarters was ensconced on the sixteenth floor, high above the mêlée. A wind blew off the lake, tugging at hair and clothes.

"So I betcha Connie's here." Eddie scanned the crowds in front of the Hilton. "What do ya think?"

"She's here."

"Yeah? Well. Keep an eye out. I probably wouldn't even recognize her." He gave David a jab in the ribs. "You been a lot closer to her than I been lately. Right?"

"Right."

David hoped Eddie wouldn't turn the search for Connie into an obsession. He needed his help in this meeting. *Screw it*, he thought. He'd been through too much with Eddie at Red Hawk to have doubts about him now.

A white-shirted politico stood on the sidewalk in front of the Hilton.

David had been told the politico was a speechwriter from Humphrey's entourage. Yes, he was part of the establishment, but he understood the power of the Left. If there wasn't total chaos . . . if there wasn't a revolution, a Left-leaning leadership might move into positions of power in the years to come. Regardless of the outcome, the Mobe, SDS, the Congress of Racial Equality were not going to disappear. He had used the same argument to persuade his boss, the Vice President, to meet with the Mobilization people.

Humphrey had grunted his consent to a five-minute huddle just before he was due to make an appearance at the Convention's opening night inaugural.

"It's a go," the speechwriter told David. "Humphrey's cuttin' us five minutes." His attention fell on Eddie. "Who's this guy?"

"Eddie Carpenter."

"And?"

"He's a Vietnam vet."

"Actually, I speak English," Eddie interjected. "You can talk to me and I'll even fuckin' answer. Pretty cool, huh?"

"Okay," the speechwriter turned to Eddie. "What're you doin' here?"

"I think your candidate should hear about Vietnam from a fool's point of view."

"You think he needs a lecture?" The speechwriter checked Eddie out warily.

"I don't care what he needs, brother." Eddie draped an arm around the speechwriter's shoulder. "Don't have a cow. I said I was gonna deliver a fool's point of view, not make a fool of myself. Not even in front of your Vice President."

"My Vice President?"

"You heard me." Eddie nudged the politico forward.

"Hey! Roger! Roger Wolfe!" In Grant Park, Madeline stood on a faux-classic concrete balustrade and watched the blond cowboy weave through the crowd. Dressed in jeans and a denim jacket, a gritty red bandana tied around his blond hair, Roger looked like a Texas wrangler on acid. She remembered the sprawling Chicago SDS office, the languorous sex with the good-looking boy. She recalled what had attracted her to him. He was different from the cautious Boston and New York radicals she was used to. This guy wore his go-fuck-yourself politics on his sleeve. She liked his wildness. He promised a different road.

Roger stared up at the backlit figure on the concrete parapet above him. Press credentials and a Pentax hung around her neck. A stack of yellow pads jutted out of a tie-dyed canvas bag. Her sleeveless T-shirt revealed smooth, dark-skinned shoulders.

"You don't recognize me, do you?"

He squinted up at a goddess dressed in black, her Egyptian makeup framed by a corona of curly dark hair. The shock of recognition called up images from that night at the SDS office, the gray morning light, his empty, ugly room filled with her beauty, the languid feel of her limbs. "Wow! Madeline. I mean, 'Hi.'"

"I may not want to marry everybody I fuck, but I usually manage to remember them."

"I remember you." He laughed. "Took me months to get over you, actually."

"You're over me now?" She giggled. "Wow."

"Okay, I never got over you." Roger clambered onto the pedestal. "What's with the camera?" He tugged at her canvas bag. "And these credentials? Y'all covering us for *Life* and *Time*?"

"These are phony." She lifted the credentials. "I write for the *Back Bay Rat*. Heard of it?"

"Sure." He looked out over the crowd. "Saw your *Ramparts* thing. Looks like you hit the big time, missy."

"I hit the big time one time only. Big-time boys don't let small-time girls write big-time stories."

Roger's delight at seeing Madeline carried an edge. He hated the prospect of hustling her for facts. But he had to lay a pile of credible inside info on his father's stooge buddies before he could roll over on them. But picking

Madeline's brain? Or notebooks? *She was sooo sharp. How could he pull off such a trick with her?*

"At last," she said. "They're getting people here."

Down the length of green, the crowd had congealed into a growing mass of protestors that milled around the makeshift podium. Incense mingled with the smell of roasting meat. On the flatbed truck, Allen Ginsberg sat in lotus posture and chanted mantras over the reedy tones of a squeezebox harmonium.

Madeline spread herself out on the grass. "Tell me what you think is going to happen."

"I don't know." He leapt down to join her. "But I do know what should happen."

"Yeah?" She pulled a yellow pad out of the tie-dyed bag.

"We should go up against them."

"They're gonna kick our ass."

"Let the world see how they fuck us up. We take it, then let them shovel themselves outta their own bullshit."

"It's a good rap. For a provocateur." She threw him a sharp glance. "You a provocateur, Roger?"

His heart jumped. "No," he replied. "Watching the Pigs fuck us up will give everybody in television land a special view of America. Spelled with a 'K.'"

"Why not negotiate?"

"With who? Humbert H. Humphrey? The 'H' stands for hack. For halfway. For halfway honky hack. Shit." He pushed at her knee. "You know that."

She flipped a page on her yellow pad and kept writing.

He watched her scribble, wondering how much she had captured in those notes. If he could only get a hold of . . . "And speaking of hacks, how about 'Clean with Gene' the Peace Candidate. Haw! I didn't see no fuckin' Clean Gene McCarthy at no Pentagon demo."

"No, but that doesn't mean . . . "

"You think these kids out here . . . " Across the park, a flood of people streamed onto the grass with each turn of the traffic light. "You think they want to strike a deal with a copout like 'Clean Gene McCarthy'? Man! They see us with him, they're gonna think we're ratting them out. And we will be."

"Why?" She scribbled furiously without looking up.

"Because," he snapped. "McCarthy may wear flowers on his tie, but he's still a stooge. They elect him, you think we'll stop bombing Hanoi? *Shee-it.* He'll just wring his hands harder than the others. The fucking guy's sucking the fire out of a bunch of potential young radicals who still think electing stooges to the Presidency is the answer. Shit." He tore out a clump of grass and threw it at her. "Clean Gene don't have the answer."

"Who's got the answer?"

Roger eyed her with suspicion. "You're with me, aren't you."

"I'm interviewing you."

"Okay." He lowered his voice and leaned into her. "I got the answer."

"Okay," she replied, leaning toward his warm blond features. "What is it?"

He grinned. "Stop the fucking thing."

"What thing?"

"The whole fucking machine. Now. Right here. Shut it down. Do the Rosa Parks thing. Stop the buses, stop the work, close the gas stations, boycott the subways, turn off the television, quit writing letters to Congressmen, stand up and kick 'em in the moneybags."

"Damn, man." Madeline closed her notepad. "You sure know how to talk dirty."

Inside the Hilton, delegates guffawed, shook hands and rubbed bellies. Couriers darted through knots of conversing politicos. Elevators gaped and swallowed knots of conventioneers. Disheveled demonstrators cadged a snooze in the big leather club chairs and hunched over the counter in the lobby coffee shop.

Taking advantage of the chaos, David, Eddie and the scriptwriter slipped into a labyrinth of service corridors. Using a key he had hustled off a McCarthy aide, the speechwriter opened a door leading into an empty stairwell. They emerged sixteen stories high into a corridor full of men in gray suits, women in pink, and security goons in dark blue serge. The goons blocked their way. The speechwriter waved a packet of credentials. "We have an appointment."

"Who says?" A two-way radio spat from the fist of a second goon. "And how'd you get in here?"

"You've seen me here before," the speechwriter barked. "What's your name again?"

The goon turned his attention to Eddie and David. "Who are these individuals?"

"The Vice President is expecting us," David said.

"Who's 'us'?"

"The Mobilization."

"Who?" The goon looked down his nose.

"Hey, bro," Eddie said. "What unit were you with?"

The Secret Service guy deadpanned him.

"Hmmm," Eddie said. "Tough guy. You're not a Marine, that's for shit sure. Must have been 101st. You ever make any combat jumps, or did you go right into the *Polizei*?"

The goon puffed up, reinforcing Eddie's guess.

"It's okay." Eddie jabbed at the goon's arm. "I forgive you. For bein' an asshole and all."

The goon pinned him against the wall. "I don't give a shit what you forgive."

A set of cream-colored double doors flew open beyond the Secret Service duo. Humphrey emerged, flanked by two aides, a tuxedo jacket hooked over his shoulder.

"Mr. Vice President, sir," the speechwriter called past the goons. "I've got Friedman with me. From the Mobilization group, Sir. Remember?"

"Yes, yes, of course. Unfortunately, I'm late." Humphrey looked like a frog with his bulging, wide-set eyes.

A flash bulb popped.

"David Friedman, Sir." David thrust his hand at the Vice President.

"We wanna talk to you." Eddie pushed toward the Vice President. "About your anti-war plank."

The goons pounced, wrenching Eddie's arms behind his back.

"What's the matter with you people?" Humphrey glared at the goons. "That man's a veteran."

The goons froze.

"Let go of him," Humphrey barked.

Chagrined, the goons dropped Eddie's arms.

Humphrey scrutinized Eddie's shock of black hair, the greasy fatigue jacket, the scuffed GI-issue jungle boots. "We're going to take a minute here." Humphrey turned and strode back into the suite.

The goons closed the doors behind them.

Humphrey perched on the edge of a candy-striped ottoman. "So you, sir." He extended a hand to David. "You must be head of this Mobilization group, right?"

"Yessir," David said. "For the time being."

"For the time being?"

"The leader, along with several of his colleagues, they're all in jail right now."

"How the hell did they get there?"

"Chicago Police," the speechwriter interjected. "They made a sweep of the Park last night."

"What park?"

"Grant Park. Across the street."

Humphrey rose and walked to the windows. He looked down on the treetops. "Looks peaceful enough."

Was it possible that he didn't know? "We got roughed up pretty bad last night, Sir," David said.

"Ah, yes. I hear things got rowdy out there last night. We'll have to look into that." He looked meaningfully at the speechwriter. "This anti-war plank." He picked up a document and waved it at David. "You can back this up?"

"Yessir. If you adopt it." David spoke with a clarity and assurance that belied his dry mouth and shaking hands. "As you know, the whole nation is leaning away from the war these days, Sir. The casualties . . . "

"And you represent the whole nation?"

"I think you know how broad this shift in sentiment is, Sir. And I don't have to tell you what it signifies."

"Are you a black man, Friedlander?"

"Friedman, Sir," the speechwriter interjected.

Humphrey ignored him. "Can you deliver the poor people of Detroit and Newark? And how about all those regular, plain-vanilla folks in Sheboygan or Cincinnati. I believe you call them 'the straights'. Isn't that right?"

An aide chuckled.

Humphrey turned to Eddie. "How about you, son? Can you deliver your brothers-in-arms? Are they all against the war?"

"Pretty damned close."

The speechwriter groaned.

Humphrey chuckled. "I admire your candor."

"I got nothin' to lose, Sir."

"What are you trying to say, son?" Humphrey spoke gently, condescendingly, as if he were talking to a troubled teenager.

"You survive two tours of duty, Sir, it puts things in perspective."

"What kind of things?"

Eddie glanced at David.

David nodded at Eddie and grabbed his belt.

"When I joined the Marines," Eddie began, "I didn't have the damndest idea what I was getting into. And if I had . . . " He paused. "I never would have gone. First coupla weeks in-country opens your eyes. A lot of the guys put two and two together. Fast. Here, you see one side of the war, Sir, no offense. Over there, we see another. And it's ugly. Brutal, senseless, stupid and ugly. We're hated everywhere. Except in Patpong."

"Patpong?" Humphrey looked puzzled.

Neither Eddie nor David nor the speechwriter chose to elaborate on the fact that Bangkok served as a whorehouse for American servicemen and had grown enormously during the war, both economically and in the numbers of Thai farm girls — many of them still children — who had been forced into employment in the brothels and dance clubs of the Old District.

"All wars are ugly." Humphrey sighed, looking *faux* philosophical. "And stupid, I suppose."

"A lot of guys feel let down, lied to. And the truth is there to find. This is a bogus war and it's killing a lot of people and they don't like what they're being told to do. You're going to want those guys with you, not against you."

"You endorse the anti-war plank, Sir, these folks'll bust their hump for you," said the speechwriter. "You know that."

"Here's what I know, Gentlemen." Humphrey put down the proposal. "I know that people's positions on the war are fluid. I know that a long list of young men like you, son . . . " He nodded to Eddie. "Made the ultimate sacrifice over there."

"You mean getting blown away, Sir? Dusted?"

"Yes, I do." He stood up. "'Dusted. Blown away.' I thank you for your service. We take your sacrifice hard. No one wants to lose their kids."

"Neither do the Vietnamese." Eddie folded his arms.

Humphrey eyed the two young men for a moment, then took a breath. "You fellas are obviously passionate in your convictions. That will get you far." His eyes glistened with *faux*, sentimental sincerity. "But I have to answer to the whole nine yards. The American people may not have all seen combat. They might not grow their hair long or believe in free love, but most of them are not all that different from you fellas. Many — no, most — want to see an end to the war. What's not clear is how we're going to do that."

"Nossir," Eddie said. "It sure isn't."

That night, the Chicago cops announced that Grant Park would stay open. Roger and Madeline climbed a knoll where they could watch the crowd settling in, dotting the lawn with blankets, backpacks and sleeping bags. The smell of pot mixed with patchouli floated on the evening air. A green gallon jug made it up the hill. A joint the size of a cigar came with it. For a moment, everything was all right.

"So, miss reporter chick," Roger said. "How many people d'ya think are here?"

"Not enough. I know the Mobe guys are freaked. No turnout."

"I hear your boyfriend got to Humphrey."

"Ex-boyfriend." The wine and pot were slowing things down for her.

"What's his name?"

"David." She settled into Roger's shoulder. His arm was corded with lean muscle. "Mmm. Grapes and grass," she said.

"David what?"

"Huh?"

"What's your boyfriend's last name?"

She twisted to look at him. "What you want to know that for?"

"I like to know who I'm workin' with." And he would find out. He leaned forward to kiss her.

"I'm a reporter," she said, pushing him away. "You don't want me to reveal my sources, do ya?"

"He's a source?"

"Might be. Hey. You're not jealous are you?"

"Well . . . ," he said and kissed her fingers. "Maybe. Just a little."

"You too, huh? Guys."

"Okay, okay," Roger said and wound his fingers into hers. "I guess I'm just curious. He's a big shot in the Mobe, right?"

"If you know already, why are you asking me?"

He shrugged and put his arm around her. "I dunno."

They settled back against the parapet. Roger's flesh smelled warm and she felt a slow pull tighten from crotch to belly, a familiar warmth spreading from the groin. People would be humping all night in sleeping bags and quilts. Under cover of darkness, the anonymity of a crowd opened people's hearts souls, arms, mouths, legs. Madeline wasn't fond of fucking in Mother Nature. She liked big beds, clean sheets and soft down comforters. Still, this boy . . . "I have to pee."

"I'll alert the media."

"Wise guy." She unwound herself from his arms, kissed his forehead and uncoiled to her feet, slinging her bag over a shoulder.

"Hey, I'll watch your stuff for ya."

"No way, man."

Roger was more relieved than frustrated at her announcement. He didn't want to purloin her stuff — not even for the sake of his plan.

"Besides . . . " Madeline pulled a roll of toilet paper out of the voluminous bag. "I never go anywhere without this." She sauntered down the grassy hill, leaving him lounging on the grass.

When she returned, Roger was gone. She was surprised, more than a little hurt. They were having such a good time of it. He carried an amazing perspective, a point of view that needed to be covered. Besides, he was cute. He offered distraction and shelter against the storm. Where would he go now? And why? She stopped a frown before it tightened her brow. *Whatever. Do I need this guy?* she asked, and forced herself to relax.

The wine jugs circulated. A corn-fed Midwestern girl in an embroidered denim jacket passed Madeline an orange. She leaned back against the base of a statue at the top of the knoll and pulled a blanket around her shoulders. Idle, her thoughts turned back to Roger. She couldn't deny it. His disappearance hurt her. Pissed her off. And it made her uneasy, like somehow . . . she'd been had.

Eddie and David straddled two stools in a coffee shop around the corner from the Hilton. David sat with his back to the window and nursed a beer. "No way we got any antiwar plank across to Mr. Humphrey."

"No way you're gonna get dick across to Mr. Humphrey," Eddie said. He turned and looked around the coffee shop. "What a fuckin' bust. Shit. I hope Connie ain't here. This place is fucked up, man."

"Yeah," David said. "We gotta find her"

261

Eddie looked down at him. "What for?"

"C'mon, man. You want to see her."

"I dunno, man. I mean, between you and me . . . "

"She got us here, Eddie. Besides . . . " David stopped. "I want you to see."

"See what?"

"I don't mean shit to her," David said. "I was just somebody helped her to get over . . . "

"Over what? Not me. That's for damned sure. "

"Quit feeling sorry for yourself. She's bound to be around here somewhere."

Eddie sat silent for a moment. David felt the exhaustion begin to drain him. *Got to keep movin',* he thought.

Eddie lifted his head. Fast. He flicked his fingers at the window facing the street. "Incoming" he murmured coolly.

Whump! A dull thud compressed the plate glass window. Whump! Whump! Two more followed in rapid succession.

Outside, a wisp of tear gas swept past, thickening into a cloud. A figure rushed by, then two more. The jabbering coffee shop commotion turned the outside scenario into a silent movie. The gas thickened into a cloud, its windborne micro-shrapnel glistening beneath the streetlights. More demonstrators flashed across the view afforded by the plate glass window, looking back toward where they had come from, their shouts muffled through the glass.

"Let's get outta here. One of those gas grenades explodes in here? Gonna be a shitstorm." Eddie rose. "Look. We get separated? Don't go to the Park. We'll never hook up there. Come back here. Got it?"

"Got it." David dropped a buck on the table for the beers. Outside, the chemical sting hit their lungs. Both pulled out bandanas to cover their faces. Where were the freaks? Where were the cops? A violent blow struck David from behind, forcing him to the sidewalk, grinding his elbows into the concrete.

Eyes blinded by gas tears, he could hear running feet, tens, dozens, maybe hundreds. Grenade launchers sounded off in increasingly rapid succession, building to a crescendo like popping corn. He felt himself being pulled upright by the back of his collar as a wave of demonstrators swept past them.

"Up against the wall, Motherfucker!" The assailant slammed him against the empire marble of the hotel. Down the sidewalk he could see Eddie flailing beneath a herd of blue shirts and white helmets. David tried to face his attacker but the assailant kept him pinned against the wall. The marble felt cool against his cheek.

"Friedman!" He pushed David's face harder against the marble. "David Friedman!" He twisted David's arm behind his back.

"Yes!" David shouted. Anything to relieve the pressure on his shoulder, his face.

"You're under arrest."

Terror jolted him. Treason. Federal prison.

"You have the right to remain silent."

They had found him.

"You have the right to an attorney."

But how had they found him?

"If you cannot afford an attorney . . . "

How did this guy know his name?

"One will be provided to you . . . "

Had they followed him out of the meeting in the Hilton? Did Humphrey or his goons rat him out?

A platoon of gas-masked cops double-timed past David and his captor.

When he looked back, David saw Eddie, pinned to the sidewalk by one cop while another kneeled on his back and twisted his arms behind him. Beyond that, he caught a fleeting glimpse of a blurred figure talking to the police, a denim-clad hippie, his long blond hair bound by a gritty red bandana. He looked familiar.

David went blank.

Roger stood in the shadows of the precinct station and watched as scores of bloody, shackled protestors were thrown from paddy wagons and dragged into the holding tank. His mind flew, overloaded from watching the law-enforcement carnage. Had he gone too far? Yes, he had built his cover, but at what cost? There was no handbook for double snitches. Confused, exhausted, he sat in the shadows of the precinct station, keeping his head down, hoping not to be recognized and monitoring the arraignments.

Roger's heart pounded when they dragged David in, bruised and cuffed. Madeline was right. He was jealous. He respected David, was intimidated by his knowledge and dedication to the Movement, and the guy had been Madeline's main squeeze. Now the object of his envy was in handcuffs, helpless, headed for arraignment. It didn't make him gloat. He felt like crap.

Beyond that, Roger feared David would recognize him from the SDS office. *What have I done? What am I doing?* "Fuck!" he muttered aloud. He took a deep breath. *If I follow through on this, I'll be deep in the pockets of the FBI. Then I will attack,* he assured himself.

The other street fighter stumbled in dazed and beaten, flanked by two cops. He looked like a vet, clad in the usual greasy fatigue jacket, the scuffed black leather and green nylon boots. He was in jail, too, bloody and beaten, simply because he had been with David, because Roger had pointed them out. These dumb bastard stooges actually found these guys and busted them. Having to admit that the goons had succeeded was infuriating, unbearable. *Screw the plan.* He would have to find a way to spring David and his vet buddy. Roger strode into the makeshift FBI office.

Smitty, the red-faced operative, was sitting behind a temporary desk, feet up, scratching at a crossword puzzle.

Roger grabbed him by the arm, lifted him out of his chair and dragged him to the crowded holding tanks. He pointed at the two men hunkered down in the corner of a tank. "You gotta hustle those guys outta here," he whispered.

"I can't do that," Smitty said.

Roger grabbed his arm. "Just do it."

"That's not part of the routine, kid. Besides . . . " he wheezed. "Take it from me. Your old man don't mean shit to the Bureau."

Roger hardened. "Screw that. You're dealing with me. I gotta have those guys back out on the street."

"Whaaat?"

"You know the routine, Smitty. They lead me to the big shots."

Smitty contemplated Roger. He had to admit that this kid — filthy, long-haired Commie that he was — had a lot more moxie in him than his old man. Or Kronos. Yeah, Kronos. It was Kronos had sent him to cover this shit assignment. He hated this kind of crap, hanging around a urine-stinking precinct station, always a stranger. But these kids — the way they acted. They weren't scared, not even in the can. Even the girls — these so-called "hippie chicks" — had a lot more balls than most of the jerks at the Bureau.

Roger's voice brought him back to the precinct. "You want to nail the biggest birds you can. I can assure you, these two ain't it."

"Lettin' people go ain't part of the plan."

"Okay, Dumbbell." Roger turned to walk away, then spun and faced the startled operative. "You want to take the rap?"

"Whaddya mean, 'take the rap?' "

"When I explain to Kronos that Smitty the fuckup refused to . . . You know."

"Bullshit."

"Yeah, man. 'Bullshit.' Think about it." He pushed close enough to smell the Four Roses on Smitty's breath. "Fuckin' Smitboy. He was the one who ree-fused to bait the traps. Uh huh."

Roger watched Smitty's eyes narrow with suspicion. "Think about it, man. I'm the only one of us can spot what's happening out there. Kronos knows that. You know that. You better fuckin' cop to it . . ."

"Huh?"

Roger sighed and rolled his eyes in feigned exasperation. "I mean, you-should-ad-mit-that-you-know-what-I'm-talk-ing-a-bout. Get with the fuckin' program, fat boy." Roger fanned his face. "Jesus, dumbbell. You smell like shit." He raised his voice. "What's that you been drinking? Four Roses?"

Smitty looked around, nervous. "Shut up, Wolfe," he whispered.

"Then kick out the jams, Inspector Smitty." Roger leaned into the corner, arms folded.

"Wha . . .?"

"Just spring those guys, *compadre*. You'll be thanking me later."

Smitty squinted at Roger, then at his hands, then at the shadowy ceiling of the precinct. "Fuckin' precinct ain't gonna like this."

"Fuckin' precinct won't know, Smitboy." He nodded at the desk sergeant, inundated with cuffed youngsters.

"Look at that guy," Roger said. "He's so blown out, he'd book his own daughter without lookin' up."

"Like I said." Grunting with effort, Smitty rose and pulled his trousers up under his belly. He glared at Roger. "Sit down and shut up." He waddled off toward the holding tank. "And quit callin' me Smitboy."

The cell door rolled open with a metallic grind. David pulled his head up off his knees. A bailiff in a bulging uniform filled the opening. "Let's go," he chirped in a light tenor voice. "You got a friend waitin' for ya."

Bleary-eyed, confused, David followed the bailiff's chunky butt down the corridor. Dawn light filtered through the grates and grime on the high-set station windows. He expected to find a Federal marshal waiting for him. Instead, a goatee'd Mobe lawyer stood at the clerk's desk signing release forms.

"They releasing me?" David whispered.

"Yep." The lawyer handed the papers across. "Bailiff walks over, asks if I had some guy named Friedman on my list. When I said 'yeah', he disappeared. A minute later, you showed up."

"Whew," David said. "Maybe there is a God."

"Naaaah," the lawyer whispered. "You got lucky. They busted so many people, I think they overloaded their system. They aren't checking the Federal sheets."

"Listen, I got a friend back there in the tank."

"Never mind." He pushed David to the front desk and slapped down the release papers. "Get your stuff and wait outside. Before they get to your rap sheet."

"But Eddie. We gotta . . . "

"Go!"

"Okay," David said. "But I'm headed back to that coffee shop."

"Why?"

267

"We made a deal."

"Who?"

"Eddie and me."

"Fuck!" the lawyer whispered, exasperated. "What deal?"

"If we get separated, we meet back where we got busted. So I'm gonna sit my ass down at that counter until he shows up." The wheezy desk sergeant dumped David's wallet, watch and a dribble of cash out of a worn-out manila envelope. David scooped his belongings into his pocket and walked into the sunlight.

David and the goatee'd lawyer took the El downtown. At the diner, they slouched onto counter stools. You think your guy's gonna show up?" the lawyer asked. "In this mess?"

"What can I say," David said. "I take the guy serious."

In front of them, a big blonde with a stained apron splashed coffee into a couple of mugs.

The lawyer lifted his cup. 'Hope springs eternal."

David reached for the mug. He ached all over.

"And speaking of hope . . ." The lawyer took a slug of coffee. "Humphrey went back on us."

David froze, mug at his lips. "He did?" A rainbow swirl of grease floated on the black fluid. "How do you know?"

"I talked to one of his aides," the lawyer said. "He said the Southern Dems were all over Humphrey last night . . . "

"And?"

"And by the dawn's early light, our man Humphrey was putting the finishing touches on a plan to sabotage 'Clean with Gene' McCarthy. Hubert the Hawk, tough in Vietnam, the man to beat Nixon."

David scratched the stubble on his jaw. "Hubert fucking Humphrey. Knew it was too good to be true."

"Yeah," said the lawyer. "That's what Stalin told Hitler."

"Okay," David said. "That's it. Now we've got to get to the delegates. If the leadership won't move it, the people got to."

"Are you shitting me?" the lawyer said. "Have you seen your 'people'? They don't get to sit their fat asses in a convention hall because they represent the people, for Chrissakes."

"Then we're fucked."

"Naaah." A voice growled. "Now we get to grab those motherfuckers by the belt."

David spun around.

Eddie stood behind them, grinning, eye gone purple, sporting a busted lip and a big grin.

David stood and they embraced. The lawyer watched, open-mouthed.

"You okay?"

"Yeah." He sat down. "Fuckers kicked my butt, though."

"How'd you get out?"

"He's been drivin' me nuts." The lawyer jerked a thumb at David. "He said he wouldn't leave without you. But you weren't on the list and I . . . "

"They sprung me. Some stooge in a shiny suit comes to the drunk tank bars. He points at me and . . . BLAM! They pull me out. I'm thinkin' I'm a goner. They're also makin' me look fuckin' wicked. Like I'm a snitch."

The waitress swiped at the counter beneath their elbows. "You people gonna be around here long?"

"No, not long," the goatee'd lawyer said.

"Good," she said, and slapped down the check. "You all smell real bad."

Roger arrived back in Grant Park just as a shirtless boy shinnied up the flagpole, a cloth in his back pocket. The antiwar plank had been voted down in the Convention Hall and people were angry beyond despair. Embracing the top of the pole, skinny legs wrapped around the staff, the shirtless boy slashed at the flag halyard with a switchblade. The Stars and Stripes fluttered to the ground.

The police charged. They pulled the kid off the pole, beat him senseless and retreated helter-skelter, without orders or organization, an armed mob.

Roger knelt beside the shirtless boy. A medic arrived. He pressed a towel against the head wound that was turning the boy's hair thick with blood. Roger yanked a blood-stained T-shirt, from the boy's jeans pocket. Jamming it into the back of his belt, he shinnied to the top of the flagpole and tied the bloody shirt to the halyard. He dropped to the ground as the police moved in again.

"Roger!" Madeline shouted, her voice husky with stress.

They embraced, oblivious, crazy with the moment. For both, every detail of their faces, his crooked teeth, the grit on her face, stood out in high detail.

"Why did you do that?" she asked. Roger's earlier disappearance seemed irrelevant.

"To get even." He had gone beyond caring. He never wanted anything to do with the cops again. He never wanted anything to do with his father. Not unless he could kill them all.

The police line hit the knot of protestors gathered around the fallen boy. Several cops in the vanguard made for Roger and with him — Madeline. They ran, hand-in-hand, a sweaty Adam and Eve fleeing, blighted and tagged, through the gates of Eden and into the streets of Armageddon.

In the Convention Center, a haggard senior Senator fought his way to a podium and tore the microphone from the moderator. "Do you know what the Chicago police are doing to our children out there?" he shouted.

From the front row of the delegate seating, Mayor Richard Daly called the Senator a Jew bastard and shouted up at him to "shut the fuck up." Daley's voice was not recorded, but news cameras from ABC, NBC and CBS transmitted the words around the world to those who could read the Mayor's lips.

Undaunted by the Mayor, the Senator finished his announcement. "They're beating our kids to a bloody pulp."

Squads of National Guardsmen clustered at intersections and blocked bridges over the Chicago River. They crouched behind jeeps with wicked-looking barbed wire plows fixed to their front bumpers. Helmeted, flak-vested gunners stood behind .30-caliber machine guns mounted in the back of every jeep, shaky hands pointing the barrels down the broad avenue toward the enemy — unarmed peers, brothers and sisters who massed beyond the tear gas haze. The soldiers began to roll toward the demonstrators.

"Get to the Jackson Street bridge! It's still open!" David and Eddie bolted up Michigan Avenue with hundreds of demonstrators, looking to break free of the cordons by crossing the river. Legions of police and Guardsmen rushed to fill the gap. Hollering war whoops, the street fighters vaulted over the balustrades onto the bridge. They pounded across the undefended span and streamed onto the open streets beyond.

Cheers and slogans erupted as they outflanked the Guardsmen. The breached bridge would allow them to make an end run around the blockades, to rush through the streets to the Chicago Amphitheater where they would mob the front entrances of the Convention Center. They ran crouching low, aware that — at any moment — they could be raked with machine-gun fire. One trigger-happy Guardsman and Americans would be killing Americans on the streets of Chicago. Why not? They had already done so in Watts and Newark, Detroit and St. Louis. Of course, on those battlegrounds all the casualties were black.

"Look!" Halfway across the bridge, Eddie stopped and pointed back toward Michigan Avenue.

David turned. Others crowded to the bridge railing.

Moving slowly up the gas-hazed corridor of Michigan Avenue, a procession of marchers led team after team of great, glistening mules, harnessed for the plow. The procession clopped past the knots of street fighters and police cordons, past the National Guard jeeps, the machine guns, now aimed skyward, their gunners standing loose-limbed and hypnotized.

Marching to a cadence laid down by drums muted with black cloth, the mule train moved slow and unhurried, carrying the Poor People's Campaign banner that Martin Luther King had raised just months earlier, before his death.

Connie Moore watched the mule train progress, slow and silent, indifferent to its surroundings. She shouldered through the crowd, trying to keep abreast of the somber parade as it rolled up Michigan Avenue. She was looking for Louis. Jostled at every turn, she scanned the procession. *He's got to be here*, she thought, somewhere in this group of black men and mules. She knew him too well — he would, by now, be back in his hometown, working on just such a campaign. Her certainty filled her with desperation. She ached to see him again. She would have to find him.

David and Eddie regrouped at the vanguard of the massed students. Many wore helmets and carried makeshift shields. The group surged toward the outflanked cluster of cops massed behind the barbed-wire jeeps. Turning, the cops began firing tear gas into the crowd and cops on horseback rushed against them in the opposite direction of the mule train. An animal reared, tangling its partner in their harnesses.

In the midst of the chaos of tear gas, sticks, and horses, Eddie caught a glimpse of Connie, walking dreamlike through the violence. He grabbed David. "There she is!"

David turned, only to be jolted from behind by the surging demonstrators. He fell forward, scrambled to his feet, trying to catch a glimpse of Connie.

Shoved by the crowds, Eddie held her in sight long enough to see her standing unprotected in the mayhem. "What the fuck is she doing?" He went down, chopped on the shoulder by a club-wielding horse trooper. When he scrambled to his feet, Connie was gone and David was dragging him forward with the crowd.

They ducked into a doorway, Eddie still peering over the mess, looking for her. "She looked spaced out, Man. I gotta get to her." David grabbed him, jammed him into the doorway corner. "She'll be all right," David said. "She's bound to head back to the Park when this dies down."

"Lemme go. They'll kill her out there."

David hung on to his buddy. "You try to get back there now you're gonna . . . "

From horseback, a cop fired a tear gas grenade directly into the doorway. Stunned by the explosion, Eddie fell to his knees, picked up the grenade and threw it back into the chaos of horses and cops. "Hate to do that to an animal." Both men collapsed in paroxysms of coughing and spewed saliva.

High in the Hilton Hotel, Senator Eugene McCarthy's staff converted his campaign headquarters into a make-shift first-aid station. Horrified young 'Clean with Gene' volunteers, faith in the democratic process shattered, tore Hilton sheets into strips, pilfered bales of towels and set to cleaning and bandaging scores of beaten protestors.

The Chicago Police assaulted the Hilton, kicking down doors to McCarthy headquarters. They ransacked rooms and suites, arrested bloody, bandaged street fighters, and beat up McCarthy's innocent staff.

The Guardsmen, badly outflanked by the demonstrators and too cumbersome to maneuver in the city streets, regrouped in underground garages peripheral to the war zone. Young Guardsmen, embittered by the role they had been forced to play, hunkered down on garage floors where they sat exhausted or snarling their discontent.

"Fuck!" a young Guardsman blurted out. "I can't believe we did that."

We didn't do shit. They ran circles around us."

"We had orders. What're you gonna do?"

"Shit. I'd do the same thing them other kids was doin'." The first Guardsman ground a cigarette butt into the concrete. "For the same damned reason."

"Yeah? You'd go over to the other side? And get shot for mutiny?"

"Don't sound too bad to me," another Guardsman growled.

"Took balls what they did."

"Bullshit. Fuckin' cowards ran quicker 'n my dog."

"You're full of shit, peckerwood. Up against guns and bayonets?"

"You'd be an idiot not to. Admit it. They stood up to The Man."

"Yeah. They stood up to The Man all right," the first Guardsman snarled. "And The Man was us." He hunkered down, face in hands, his heaving shoulders the only sign of the grief and humiliation he felt.

When word reached the City Council that the Chicago Police had trashed the Hilton, the Council members called an emergency meeting and forced Mayor Daley to acknowledge that cracking kids' skulls might give the city a bad name. Red-faced with fury, an irate Mayor called off the police, who melted away to huddle in their precinct stations. Within the hour, the violence stopped.

Chicago lay prostrate, desolate, a naked city-state exposed to the morning light. Curtains of tear gas hung in the air. Battle-smashed police barricades, an overturned military jeep, spent tear gas canisters, a split helmet, a single shoe littered the streets. The battle had been fought, won, and lost, all at once. The anti-war plank had been voted down by the delegates on the floor. McCarthy retreated unnoticed. The Party had spoken. Hubert H. Humphrey, the Great Compromiser, would run for the office of President of the United States.

The delegates melted away in twos and threes, the National Guard companies withdrew. The media, with no more information to gather, coiled up their cables and drove off. The Hilton Hotel, now a breached fortress, shouted outrage from its upper-story windows. Festoons of red-lettered bed linen hung from the ransacked McCarthy headquarters.

Shame on Chicago

The Whole World is Watching

Mayor Daley + National Guard = Fascism

Worn out, bloody and exultant demonstrators had retaken the parks. Morning sun fell on the massed rebels. The gathering resembled a refugee camp in a ravaged Third World nation. Summer humidity shrouded the demonstrators in mist, blessing them with silence. The exhausted protestors sprawled against trees and walls, slept on the grass or clustered in small groups, talking fervently. No one could possibly have gauged the extent of their victories . . . or defeats.

Connie made her way back to Grant Park and collapsed on the grass. A girl with a swollen cheek unzipped her sleeping bag so that she and Connie could doze side by side in the warmth of the rising sun. She awoke to find a tall figure standing over her. Her eyes, bleary with tear gas, struggled to focus on the gaunt figure. His wrists dangled from a fatigue jacket, a mop of black hair and aquiline features metamorphosed into a familiar face and body.

The figure knelt. "I knew I'd find you here somewheres." He stroked her hair. "Jeez, Connie. I saw you back in the crowd last night. You looked like a fuckin' stoner. Are you okay?"

Connie sat up, frightening the girl next to her. She should have known. Why hadn't she recognized him?

"It's okay," the figure said to the swollen-faced girl. "We're old friends. Wicked old."

"'Wicked'?" the girl asked.

Connie squinted through her half-sleep. Behind the bruises, the bloody scalp, the sweat and the acrid odor of tear gas, even without the Old Spice and the hot-buttered popcorn, she could smell Eddie. Her Eddie. Her same wicked sweet Eddie. With a whimper of recognition, she opened her arms and embraced him.

"Ouch," he said.

"Um . . . I'm gonna go get something to eat, the swollen-faced girl. "I'll see you guys later."

"No!" Connie said. "Your sleeping bag."

The girl looked at Connie, then at Eddie. "Please." She gathered her belongings and melted into the crowd.

Following the swollen-faced girl's departure, Connie imagined she saw David threading through the sleeping bags. *Are they all here?* She thought. She buried her head in Eddie's shoulder and brought his tired body down to hers, grateful for the shelter. Comfort turned drowsiness to sleep. Nothing else mattered.

Madeline and Roger sat back-to-back on the hill beneath the bronze general and his magnificent steed. Dazed and sleepless, they followed the motions of the camp below, stubbornly holding onto their layered roles as observers, street fighters, compatriots and — for Roger — as a snitch trying to forget his recent deeds.

"Fuck this," said Madeline. Her camera had been destroyed, crushed under a trooper's boot. All her ambitions, her desire to tell the truth with the pen as a sword, dissolved in rage at the stupidity and brutality of the police, the failure of the Left to mount a real opposition, the blood, the fury, the wasted motion. "No more protests," she snarled. "No more fucking protests."

Connie and Eddie awoke to find themselves intertwined, their bodies thrusting against each other. Still glowing from the sleepy lovemaking they had awakened into, they lay side by side and began to catch up.

"So you know a friend of mine." His bruises had turned dark purple.

"Who?"

"I met him in California. After I come back. He seemed to know you pretty well."

277

"Quit teasing," she said. "Don't you want to go to the aid station?"

He ignored her. "I'll give you a clue. We're all here today. You, me, him . . . "

"Cut it out." She struggled to remain playful. *Could Eddie have met Louis?* Although he was clearly hurting from the beating he had taken, his voice was full of adolescent innuendo. She had no energy left to spar with him.

"When I met our boy," he continued, "he was a mess. Burnt out, on the lam from the Feds, totally fucked up and paranoid. A Good Samaritan shipped him out of Oakland to Humboldt."

"David." The figure walking through the sleeping bags. "So he is here."

"Yup. We came together. He's my buddy now."

"Did he get my letter?"

"That's how we got here. And . . . " he crossed his arms behind his head and stared at the sky. "That's how I made the connection."

"What connection?"

"That his Connie . . . "

"I'm not 'his Connie." She sat up. "I'm not your goddamned Connie, either, Eddie Carpenter."

"Okay, okay," he acquiesced. "But face it. We all had each other in common."

"How did you know that?"

"Your handwriting. In that letter." He shifted his position, grimacing. "Imagine my surprise."

"Enough." She pulled the sleeping bag around her. "You're sitting here, half beaten to a pulp and you pick at this sex thing?"

"Jeez." He looked hurt and confused. "Forget the pulp."

"It was a coincidence, Eddie. Shit. We're both acting like jealous teenagers."

"I'm no teenager. Neither are you."

"Come on," she said. "You're forgiven. I'm forgiven. Let's go get something to eat." She rose and, together, they made their way toward a Red Cross tent.

From her hilltop, Madeline spotted Connie with some guy in a fatigue jacket. He looked beaten up pretty bad but what the hell, so did everybody. "Connie!" she called out, grateful to find a familiar face in the throng, curious to hear their story.

Connie wasn't happy to see Madeline. She had revisited the past plenty in the last forty-eight hours with memories of Louis and now Eddie. David might be following Mad around. She stopped herself. *Forget about the who-fucked-whom soap opera,* she told herself. *A battle of historic proportions had spread itself across the streets of Chicago while the whole world watched. What had Madeline and this guy Roger been through? David was here. What had happened to him? What would happen next? What did they see for the future?*

They hiked up the knoll where Roger and Madeline perched at the foot of the bronze general and his horse. The four converged into a tight circle.

The regroup reminded Eddie of the times after messy firefights — checking out his own limbs, scrambling to account for his troops. Were they dead, alive, maimed? Was that a gutted V.C. shrieking in the crapped-out jungle? Or one of his buddies? And why did it make a difference, V.C. or American? He shook it off. "Anybody seen David?" he asked.

Roger remained silent. Any careless comment might reveal his collaborations with the enemy. *Shit,* he told himself, *it was probably easier to tell the truth than to keep track of all your damned lies.* He clenched his jaw and resolved to hold out. He would transform his duplicity into a single-edged sword set to slash back at The Man, the Machine, the fucking System. "Wherever he is, by now, he's gonna be hungry," Roger offered.

David stood outside the Red Cross kitchen tent, scanning the Park. He knew the movement of people in crisis. Everybody had to eat and drink. Here, at the source, he would find Eddie, possibly Connie. Maybe even Madeline. His eye picked up a knot of demonstrators, tiny dots on the faraway knoll where the bronze general pranced on his bronze steed. The knot moved downhill toward the tent with uncharacteristic purpose. There was something familiar about them.

The group converged slowly, messily, fatigue setting the tempo. Despite their long, intertwined experience they had never before assembled in one place at one time. But when Madeline spotted David, she raced ahead and embraced him, making him drop his mug full of hot liquid.

"Hey! Ow!" he shouted, happily, stroking Mad's familiar hair. He turned to embrace Eddie, while Roger and a reluctant Connie looked on.

"Hello, David," Connie said and reached out to stroke his arm awkwardly.

Madeline introduced Roger to David. Despite the fact that Roger's eyes never left the ground, David sensed something familiar about the guy but couldn't place it.

"Come on, Eddie said. "Let's eat. Maybe we can find a place to talk, catch up. The quintet queued up at the soup kitchen and gratefully accepted the watery scrambled eggs, soft white bread, coagulated cereal and thick, black, vat-brewed tea.

The entourage moved to the side, avoiding the stumble-hungry crowd, and hunkered down to talk about what they had seen, what might happen next.

"Time to tear the roof off the motherfucker." Roger was anxious declare which side he was on.

"Tear the roof off?" Connie asked. "You and whose army? I haven't seen the people of Chicago exactly lining up to follow our example these last few days."

"No more protests," Madeline said. "We gotta move on. No more dancing in the streets and getting beaten for it. We need to act. We have power, too.

"No you don't, Madeline," Connie chided, sharp with exhaustion. "You're alone."

"Alone?" Madeline asked quietly. "Shit, woman, we're everywhere."

"Who's 'everywhere'? I'm not ready to play power games with the U.S. Government." Connie swept her arm over the desolate landscape. "Look what it did."

"Think about what we can do," Madeline replied. "I saw this. You saw it, too. We push them, they push us. Now it's our turn to push back. On our terms, not theirs."

"With what? We're all dead here. You don't have any guns and you don't have any mass support," Connie snapped. "You don't even have much New Left support. Not with SDS, not with the Mobe. Not with anybody."

"You've got to join us," Roger said. "We can't do it alone."

"Shit," Connie said. "You don't even have unity amongst yourselves"

Roger's eyes narrowed. "Join us or fuck you."

Eddie leaned into the circle. "You don't want to go down this road, guys." He focused on Roger. "You're Custerizing this whole mess."

"Custerizing?" Madeline looked at him skeptically.

281

"Yeah, like the great blond Indian fighter," Eddie continued. "You're going to urge people into situations where they got no power, no control, no options. Bad strategy, all for the hell of it. A New Left battle of the Little Big Horn."

David picked up an expended tear gas canister and hefted it in his hand. "We've tried everything. Wrote to Congress. Voted for Kennedy. Marched the leather off our shoes. Meditated. Sang folk songs about dead workers. Practiced nonviolence and got our heads caved in. Practiced violence and got our heads caved in. Organized the neighborhoods. Didn't work. Did it?"

"So you're gonna take up arms?" Eddie asked. "Shit, man. You call that revolution? Kids with guns. Stupidest thing I ever heard of."

Connie grabbed David's hand. "You guys are on a death trip," she said. "Where will your army come from? Most people can't make the connection between their tax dollars, a string of B-52s destroying a village, and profits. Why the hell should they fight to the death?"

"You guys didn't think we'd get it right the first time around?" Eddie laughed and shook his head. "Did ya? Give it up for a hot minute. Take a break. Think about it."

"Come on, Eddie," David continued. "Who knows how this horror show's gonna mutate in the years to come? How long it will go on?" He leaned forward. "How long?"

"I dunno," Eddie spat, exasperated. "And neither do you."

"We got no choice," David said. "We're going to have to take the whole thing apart now or it's going to keep breeding." He sighed and tossed the tear gas canister away. "We been standing outside the Gates of Eden too long."

Tears swelled in Madeline's eyes. She embraced David, the familiarity of his hair, his skin, his limbs filling her with love. He leaned his head against hers and they fell silent.

"When all recourse to the courts has failed, it is time for revolution," Roger said.

"Lenin said something like that," Connie laughed. "You think you're Lenin, Roger?"

"You know what Lenin said in the next breath?" an outside voice asked quietly.

The group looked up at a small, stocky man with gray at his temples and streaking his goatee. His hands jammed into the pockets of a field jacket and a tight pot belly pushed at the buttons of a plaid shirt. "Lenin said 'One must learn to fight.'" He looked around the circle. "Anybody here ready for that? Or do you already know how to fight?" He laughed.

Roger stood up. "Mr. Levin?"

The newcomer frowned at Roger. "How the ... "

"Mr. Harry Levin?"

"Yeah ... " The gray-haired man now stood warily, rocking back and forth on the balls of his feet. "How do you know ...?"

"It's Roger, Mr. Levin. You remember. Bronco High?" He grinned. "They let cowboys in for free?"

Levin squinted at Roger, then ran a dirty hand through his disheveled hair. He looked like he'd seen a little action the last few days. "Well, I'll be damned."

"Wow, Sir, what're you doin' here?"

"I have a right to be anywhere I goddamned well want to, Roger." He grinned. "You know that."

Roger turned to his brothers and sisters. "Mr. Levin here. He was my high school history teacher. He ... "

"Yeah," Levin sighed wearily, laughed and put his hand on Roger's shoulder. "Exhibit A. From cowboy to revolutionary in ... " He turned to Roger. "How long has it been, Wolfe?"

"I dunno. Few years, I guess."

Levin laughed. "Aged in the barrel. Be careful, sinners, ere ye reap what ye shall sow. So . . . "

David guffawed.

Levin grimaced. "What the hell got you into this mess, Roger?"

"He did," Madeline said. "He got himself into it. With some influence from the right people." She smiled up at the handsome, smallish man. "Like cool teachers."

Levin took a step backwards shaking his head. "Teacher no more. Government hack now." He turned up his collar with a phony dramatic gesture. "Shouldn't be here, but hey! I was in the neighborhood."

Laughter.

"He was always like that," Roger said, relaxing in his mentor's presence.

"Still am, Rodge. Different time, different place. Same guy."

"He'd crack the whole class up," Roger explained.

"First," Levin retorted. "I'd have to *wake* the whole class up. So . . . " Levin continued, "you folks contemplating something a little more serious than marching and chanting? After this victory? Uh, debacle? Uh, media pageant? Whatever?" He kicked his feet in the dirt. "Couldn't help but overhear you ah . . . debating. I'm with the vet here." He nodded at Eddie. "Don't you think you should wait a while, see how things shake down? You prepared to go further?"

Silence.

"Yeah? Okay, then. In what direction? What's the plan. What'll the consequences be?"

"See," Roger said, excited. "That's what he used to do. Ask all these goddamned questions!"

"So, mister history teacher Levin," David said. "Are you prepared to fight?"

"Not until I know I can win," Levin said.

284

"We can win," Madeline said.

"You prepared for what 'win' means?" Levin said in a fatherly tone. "It means fight. And it leads to massacre. One armed protest on the lovely green Capitol Mall and you get machine-gunned by the U.S. Army. Not pretty. Makes this mess we been through a walk in the park." He looked around. "Get it? Not funny. Thousands dead in an hour. Where would you be? What would you be? Revolutionaries? No. Survivors? Maybe. Survivors rounded up slowly, steadily, thrown into ah . . . let's call them detention camps. For your own protection. 'Okay,' you say. 'Of course, dummy . . . direct confrontation is stupid. Right,' you say. 'We know what's next. Fidel, the mountains. Paris, Regis Debray talking shit about how the Vietnamese are teaching us. The guerrilla way is the cool way.' Right? So . . . " he grinned again. "A protracted guerrilla war. You got the political machine in place for that, boys and girls? Fighters have to understand what they're dying for. Every minute. Every move reasoned out. Taught. Workable. Convincing. Considerate of the people. Right? Can you swim, as do the Viet Cong, like revolutionary fish in the sea of the people? It works for the V.C. Would it work here for you? Here? In America?"

The weary knot of street fighters sat silent, looking up at the little man.

"So what side are you on, Mr. Levin?" Roger asked.

"I am on the side of study. Of application of the scientific method. It's the same with history. And yes, despite my degenerate appearance . . . " He winked at Roger. "I am a student of history."

"We all are," David retorted.

"Well then," Levin continued. "You already know that Ho Chi Minh began his resistance movement in Paris. Twenty years before he went underground. Is Chicago your Paris? Surely you don't think this skirmish is your

Dien Bien Phu!" He laughed, forcing his audience to laugh with him. "I don't know shit about what happened or what should happen next," he said. "And I sure as fuck don't know what to do about it. " He shrugged. "How would I? How would anybody know? Wouldn't make any hasty decisions, that's all."

Madeline shivered. There was something so familiar about this man, his position. But his history-bound view of the world. It made for poor strategy. No, it made for no strategy at all. She was going to war. *What finality, what absolute inevitability, what lunacy.* Loony or not, it was the only way.

"I know how to fight," Eddie said. He turned to David. "Take it from me, brother. We aren't ready to grab the enemy by the belt."

"That's not what you said a month ago," David said, smoldering.

"Takes more than a month to build an army," Eddie said.

"Listen to him," Levin said.

"All the more reason to get started," Roger said.

"Shit." Eddie shook his head.

Connie leaned against Eddie, near tears as she found herself — after so many years, after so much had gone down and come around — in harmony with her high school sweetheart, her sad, simple, beautiful young Eddie, now turned so hard, so fiery, so savvy and calm and so . . . so damned . . . wise! "Count me out," she said.

"Think about it, you all," Harry Levin said. "Roger." He extended his hand. "Good to see you again. Glad to see you have come all this way." He grinned a crooked grin. "I hope you find yourself a way to go further." He walked into the morning sun, never looking back.

PRAIRIE FIRE
1969 – 1970

CHICAGO

Connie had never visited Sophie Guillory while she and Louis were together. Still, the apartment felt familiar. A bright-colored cloth and a bowl of fruit adorned the kitchen table. The windows sparkled, keeping guard over the same red-brick, tarred-roof landscape that Louis must have known from childhood.

Sophie remembered Connie well from their meeting in Atlantic City. This young woman was hard to forget, after their collision over the Mississippi Democratic Freedom Party. Stricken with Lou Gehrig's disease, she could no longer speak. She had been forced to resign from her teaching job, the engine of her existence. Her symptoms had not subsided, but her powerful grace extinguished any hint of self-pity toward visitors. Instead, she projected a wry humor that was often wasted on her solitude. Now she sat across from her son's lover, a legal pad at her elbow, pen in hand, waiting for the question.

"I can't find Louis anywhere, Mizz Guillory. It's very disturbing. Do you have any idea where he is?

Alive inside a mind where synapses no longer transmitted thought to the spoken word, Sophie wrote in a clear, steady hand. *Louis was murdered by the police.*

Connie felt the muscles of her face fall, her mouth open soft, the pain building, like a child about to break into a wail of sorrow. She put her hands to her face and moaned.

He was shot down in Detroit last summer, during the violence. Sophie Guillory stabbed a period into the yellow pad with her pen.

Silent, Connie rose, came around the table and stood behind Sophie. Heart throbbing, eyesight misted, she embraced Sophie. The older woman put down the pad and placed a hand on Connie's forearm. The gesture flooded Connie with tenderness and allowed her to feel her softness pressing against the lean planes of Louis' body. Hiding her tears, she kissed Sophie on the hair.

ON THE ROAD

Out on the prairie campuses, Roger found kids who — in less than a year — had grown as militant as he. They didn't want theories. They wanted to bring the motherfucker down. They had suffered the war since they were children. Many had lost friends, classmates, big brothers, their communities forced to accommodate the haunted souls of those who returned, dead or alive. Many shared Roger's hardscrabble background and wanted to get things done. Now.

He missed Madeline. Yes, there were other people who believed that it was time for revolution. Yes, there were co-eds like the redhead, taken by his looks, fervor and charisma. Ensconced on their dreary Great Plains campuses, they reminded him of Bronco and his unhappy past.

Madeline held the key to a different and exciting world, a world he wanted to learn about. He had spent the first seventeen years of his life in Bronco, Texas. She had grown up in Manhattan. When she retreated to Boston after the Convention, Roger was left with nothing but the fear of loss. He called her frequently from the road.

"I'm going up to Woodstock," Madeline announced as Roger fed dimes into a prairie roadside payphone. "To cover the concert. I don't hope for much, but it'll get me away from Sam."

"Sam?"

"Yeah. Sam. The editor of the *Rat*."

"Uh, huh." He sensed a wariness in her voice as if she feared she had told him too much. A truck whined past on the highway outside the phone booth.

"Come on, Roger." Her voice sounded tired. "You want that driving you?"

"No. I don't." But it did. Jealousy had driven his choice to put David on the wanted list in Chicago. He regretted the impulse. *Jealousy has no place in the Revolution*, he thought. They should be sharing intimacy as they would share bread and roses, guns and ammunition.

The personal is the political. Women had started using the phrase in meetings, in battles with their boyfriends, dealing with the struggles to keep movement offices and collectives functional. The Revolution starts in our hearts. Che had said it. "At the risk of sounding ridiculous, the true revolutionary is guided by great feelings of love." From Che, from the women in the movement, it made startling sense to Roger. Yeah, they all pulled together for the Revolution, but what a brother or sister did with his or her life was his or her business. The fear of loss persisted.

Ridiculous, his head told him. The heat behind his eyes told him it wasn't. Goddamn! If only she knew. If only she would acknowledge what they shared, what they did for each other, what they meant to each other, how close they had become.

"You still there?" Madeline asked.

Madeline. *Is she pissed of at me? Tired of me?* Another truck rocked the booth. He grimaced, cursed the endless prairie and the big sky that separated him from her.

"Yeah. I'm here."

"I'm gonna let you go now, Roger. I have a deadline. But be safe out there. Okay?"

"Right on." *Act casual, Rodge.* "Talk soon?"

"You bet." Click. He pushed the doors open onto Big Country quiet. *Ridiculous.* He'd have to think his way out of the blues. *I'll clean up this mess,* he vowed. *I'll turn all these fucking* feelings *into action.* He'd come this far in his infiltration. He would thrust deeper now, engage the enemy and deliver the blow.

As he moved from campus to campus, many of the Midwest SDS chapters vibrated with a clandestine revolutionary plan. They would use the broad power of SDS and the Mobilization to overthrow the U.S. Government. They would liberate free zones through force of arms. In the free zones, they would create new communities that showed the people how life could be lived if you fought your way out of the belly of the capitalist beast.

Roger returned to SDS headquarters in Chicago full of the new radicals' rhetoric. "Come on, guys," he exhorted the staff. "I been all over the Midwest since the Chicago mess." He rose off the couch and began pacing. "These kids? They want to tear down the motherfucker. And they come up with heavy-duty, practical, kick-ass tactics."

"So do provocateurs," said another long-time SDS staffer. "They come up with kick-ass tactics, too."

"I'm not sure 'tear down the motherfucker' is the best way to describe how we want to proceed," Brooks Robinson pronounced. "It feels too hasty, too impatient, uninformed by past experience." Brooks bellowed. "Do any of these kids read history?"

"Take a look at the Panthers stuff," Roger continued. "Take a look at *Prairie Fire.* They're forging coalitions with other oppressed peoples. And they're succeeding. I'm telling you . . . Weatherman is here to stay."

"This is crazy," Brooks replied.

"Hey, Brooks," Roger interrupted. "No offense, but we gotta move on. Chicago taught us that."

Robinson exhaled and stared at the ceiling. "Suit yourself, Roger. But before you take command of your Revolution, you better check the office. You have a letter."

"What?" Roger stopped pacing. "When did that arrive?"

"Didn't you tell me once that your old man . . . "

Roger snatched the mail out of the pigeonhole and retreated to his room. If Brooks and the others found out he was talking with the FBI, they might as well have carved "snitch" on his forehead. He opened the letter, the address scrawled in his father's awkward handwriting. Postmarked Pittsburgh, Pennsylvania, it began, "Dear Son,"

> *I know things are not so good between*
> *us. But I am still your father and you*
> *owe me respect. This time, the situation*
> *will be better. Here's where I am. You can*
> *get a bus due West from Philadelphia to*
> *Pittsburgh. It's not to far. See? I'm not*
> *even following you. From your father*
> *who still loves his son, after all of the*
> *bad times we have been through.*

Roger reread the letter. His brothers and sisters in the Movement hadn't uncovered his snitch persona, he was golden with the Feds, and he had bested and humiliated his old man. So far so good. The only person who knew anything about Roger's turnaround was Smitty. Could fat, unhappy Smitty keep a secret from his boss? *Sure,* Roger thought. *If he didn't want to get his ass kicked for conspiracy.* Cloaked in the power of possibility, Roger felt the excitement build. Who knew what might come of insider contact with these FBI stooges?

MIDDLETON, MASSACHUSETTS

Connie couldn't believe the luck. Her parents had left for an off-season European holiday, leaving her alone in the old house on Foster Street. She had little money left after her Chicago foray, but her parents had left the car keys and a charge card at the grocery.

She missed them in her grief, but she could never have told her parents that she had fallen in love with a black man. That they had been lovers, had risked death for their love. How could she have repressed the pain she felt when he turned against her after Malcolm X? Did she want to watch them react to the news that he had died violently in the arms of another woman on the rooftop of a Detroit tenement? How could she explain it to herself?

She kissed her parents goodbye at Logan Airport. Her dad slipped an envelope full of twenties into her hand. "Have a good time, Honey," he whispered. "See if you can get a little rest. You have some thinking to do."

Now, she cruised through the sad streets of Ayer, Massachusetts, a crumbling New England burg that served

Fort Devens, training ground for Vietnam's artillery divisions. She was looking for the Stinking Rose.

The Stinking Rose was housed in a rented storefront on a side street that climbed the hill behind the Greyhound bus station. The place took its name from the Italian word for garlic and kept its doors open to any G.I. who wandered in off the streets.

The makeshift café sported an aluminum urn of institutional coffee and a back-room kitchen that churned out vats of spaghetti served with tomato sauce and garlic, carbonized whole-grain muffins and obscure vegetable soups, one flavor indistinguishable from the next.

Bulletin boards with announcements peppered the brightly painted walls. The Stinking Rose was a link in a chain of similar havens where G.I.s could hang out, eat, talk, read anything *from Mad Magazine* to political pamphlets and weekly underground papers like the *Back Bay Rat*. The plan was to encourage lonely G.I.s to relax first and ask questions second.

Connie enjoyed the low-key temperament of the Stinking Rose. No movement heavies frequented Ayer, Massachusetts, and the military authorities were dismissive of its presence. Occasionally a drunk "doggie" harassed them from the door but most often the G.I.s came curious and alone, not willing to risk derision from their fellow warriors.

No one who worked at the Stinking Rose ever considered these scared, lonely draftees to be "baby killers". That epithet they saved for Richard Nixon, the Secretary of Defense, Congress, and the Generals.

"Hiya." A G.I. crossed the portal and flashed the peace sign.

Connie invited him to sit down. "You want a cup of coffee?"

"Aw, shucks," he drawled. "Got any beer?"

293

"Nossir." She laughed. "I wish we did, but we can't."

"Okay," he replied. "Guess that's why you call it a coffee house." He watched her hungrily as she walked away. "Right?"

"Right on," Connie laughed. "Coffee house." She handed him a mug. "Coffee." She sat down again. "What's your name?"

"Haskell," he drawled in a slow Appalachian. "I got a sister who's a hippie."

"Does that mean she's against the war?"

"I dunno."

"So what makes her a hippie?"

"She's into free love, that kinda thing."

"What's free love?"

"When everybody gets to uh . . . I don't know, really."

"Okay." She knew better than to push past the boy's inhibitions. It would only put him on the defensive. "So your sister, does she worry about you?"

"Yeah." He licked his lips nervously.

"When does your unit get shipped out?"

"Can't say."

"You'll be all right," she said. "They train you pretty well, don't they?" She felt great tenderness for these kids. How could they — or she — possibly imagine what lay ahead of them?

"Say," the G.I. said. "If you ain't gonna preach against the war and all, why'd you folks take the trouble to set up this store? I mean, we're gonna be deployed, no way out. Ain't we a lost cause already?"

"You don't have to go," said a voice behind her.

Connie frowned. They didn't like to jump on a newcomer like that. Take time, build a little trust, have him talk with the regular G.I.s who frequented the place.

"Does he, Connie?" Eddie stood over her, draped in the same service jacket and scuffed leather and nylon jungle boots that he had been wearing in Chicago.

"Oh." Connie felt a rush, reminiscent not of Chicago, but of high school. She pushed at the stubborn nostalgia. She was working with a scared young soldier. Eddie had no place here. But of course he did. She felt embarrassed, confused, then angry at his reappearance and her long-abandoned heartthrob emotions. "Hi." She turned to the young G.I. "Now this soldier . . ." She pulled at Eddie's sleeve. She couldn't help it. He felt simple, reminiscent, longed for. "He wanted to go." He looked craggy, handsome in the gathering dusk. "Didn't you, Sergeant."

"Yeah," Eddie said. "Before I knew any better."

They embraced. She placed her head on his chest. He folded his arms around her.

"Home to see the family?" she murmured.

The young G.I. looked back and forth between the pretty woman and the tall, haggard vet. "You two know each other?"

"We went to school near here." She couldn't take her eyes off Eddie. She stopped fighting her feelings. "A long time ago."

The young draftee stared. His face and features went soft.

"Hey, Sarge? You think if I went AWOL I could find a girl like . . ." He stopped. "Oh, jeez," he said, his face flushing red, "I'm sorry, Miss. I don't mean to . . . "

"You don't have to be sorry." She put a hand on his arm. "Just do me this one favor."

"Sure, Miss," the young draftee said.

"Promise me you'll keep your eyes open, take care of yourself, and keep a journal. So when you come home safe and sound you can tell your friends what you learned about the war."

"Keep your head down," Eddie said. "Take care of your buddies. And try not to kill anybody."

"Okay, Sarge." The young soldier turned to Connie. "I'll do that," he said. "I'll do it for you." He grinned and looked at both of them. "For you two, the both a ya's."

PITTSBURGH

Roger found his way to the address his father had given him. The FBI field office skulked above a row of stores in a dreary industrial outskirt. Steel mills boomed in the distance. He climbed the stairs and rapped on the frosted glass. The door opened and Roger's father stood before him, hand extended. A crooked smile slashed his face.

"Hiya, Dad!" A flash of pity surged through Roger. "How they hangin'?" He patted his father's back.

Bob Wolfe played into the greeting. He needed to appear in control. "Hello, Son," he said in his best baritone.

"Heya, fellas." Roger extended a hand to each operative, first Kronos, then Smitty, throwing down the Movement handshake, fingers up, grabbing each unsuspecting agent by the thumb then twisting back to a traditional palm-to-palm handshake and back again to clasp the fingers. "Power to the people, right, guys?"

Smitty fumbled the handshake. Kronos simply batted Roger's hand away.

"Hey, Sir," Roger said. "You got to get that move down, make it second nature. Gotta know how the enemy throws down, dontcha now?"

Kronos sat back in his chair spinning a ring of keys around index finger. "We don't work the field."

"The hell we don't." Smitty winked at Roger. "You sent me to Chi-town to work with this smartass, didn't ya, Boss?"

Roger looked carefully at Smitty. The red-faced cop had sprung David. Probably Eddie, too. *Which side was he on?* Roger took a deep breath and surveyed his surroundings. Two gray desks and a brace of file cabinets were all it took to fill the shabby little office. He devoured the critical features — the locked-down files, the stacks of memos, the books swollen with mug shots and wanted posters, the entrances and exits, the windows.

"So . . ." Bob Wolfe clapped a hand on his son's shoulder. "They tell me my kid was a pretty big hit in Chicago." He grinned and pulled Roger to him. "Tagged a lot of perps."

Roger cringed. "What's a 'perp'?"

"A perpetrator," his father snarled.

"According to my report, you did," Smitty said. He pulled a cruller out of a pink box.

"You use my name?" Roger asked. "In the report?"

"Of course not." Kronos smiled. "You're an asset."

"An asset." Roger pondered the impersonality of the term.

"Even Smitty says so. You guys did the right thing, springing those two guppies."

"'Guppies?'" Roger asked.

"Bait," Roger's father chimed in. "To catch the bigger fish."

"We need people like you," Kronos continued. "In fact, we've got another assignment for you."

"That's why I wrote you, Son."

"Yeah, well, you almost blew my cover."

Old man Wolfe shifted uneasily in his chair.

Smitty snagged another cruller from the box.

"We call it Project Omega." Kronos opened a filing cabinet and pulled out a file, shielding it from Roger.

Smitty dunked the cruller in his coffee. "We at the Bureau believe you people are into black magic." Smitty took a sip. "Are you?" Cruller crumbs stuck to his cheek.

"Black magic?" Roger stepped to the window. He noticed a fire escape dropping out of sight into the alley.

"It's bullshit, right?" Smitty pushed the rest of the cruller into his coffee. "Even if the damned memo came down from . . . "

"Never mind that." Kronos shot Smitty a withering look. "It's all from credible sources."

Smitty shook his head and rose. "Be right back. Coffee just kicked in."

"Keep me posted on that," Kronos said.

After Smitty puffed out of the room, the swarthy operative turned back to Roger. "So. Black magic."

"Okay," Roger shrugged, rolling with the stupidity.

"Like, when you people planned to float the Pentagon." Kronos continued. "Levitation, I believe you called it." He smiled condescendingly. "You didn't really think you were going to raise the building off the ground, did you?"

"Aw, hell, no, Sir," Roger replied. How could he explain the gleeful Yuppie campaign? Gather enough freaks around the Pentagon to float the building off its foundations? They'd never understand. They'd never read an R. Crumb comic. They'd never tried to unravel the lyrics to a Dylan tune, never fucked to Otis Redding singing "Try a Little Tenderness", or fell out on a ratty carpet to dig the Mothers of Invention singing "Who Are the Brain Police?" How could they understand why half a million freaks converged on Washington to levitate the Pentagon, not as a reality but as a unifying strategy that swarmed around the five-sided temple of war like a single organism? How could they know?

"We also know you people believe in pagan symbols." Kronos pointed to a crudely drawn peace sign at the bottom of the memo. "That's Greek, right? A Greek magic sign."

"No Sir. Actually it isn't." Roger shrugged humbly. "It's a peace sign."

Down the hall, a toilet flushed.

"Not according to this report here." Kronos read aloud. "'The peace sign is an ancient and powerful symbol of the Antichrist.'"

"Uh, well, not really, Sir."

Kronos wrote a note on a pad. "According to this memo, newspapers call it part of a 'mystical renaissance.'"

Smitty wheezed back into the office, one shirttail flapping.

"I see." Roger had to stifle a laugh. The memos were pathetic. These jokers didn't have a clue. But he wanted those papers. He wanted them bad. He nodded solemnly at Kronos. "Go on."

"This mystical tendency gives us an opportunity."

"Sounds interesting, Sir." Roger leaned forward. He wanted to puke, but that would destroy the plan. "What opportunity?"

"We create paranoia amongst your ranks," Kronos said. "Our artists have sketched out mystical symbols you can use." He read from the file. "Drawings of a mythical Siberian beetle bearing captions such as 'the Siberian beetle is black', or 'the Siberian beetle can talk'. These would be sent to New Left leaders to confuse them, breed paranoia and conflict within the ranks."

"Ah . . . Right on!" Roger struggled to suppress a smirk. "Makes sense."

Kronos fixed Smitty with a 'told-you-so' stare.

"So," Roger said. "This Project Omega. What do you need from me?"

"We need a list," Smitty said.

"A list of leaders who would make suitable targets for breeding paranoia," Kronos said.

"Let me give it some thought," Roger risked a second glance at the file cabinets. "I should be able to help you out." He could probably bolt cut the locks. He needed a moment to himself. "Okay if I use the restroom?"

"Down the hall," Smitty replied.

"Can't miss it," Kronos snarled. "Especially since Smitty here just took a dump."

"Jesus H. Christ." Smitty sat down and folded his arms.

Roger wondered how these two avoided killing each other, jammed into a tight field office in a filthy city that stank of sulfur. The hallway opened onto wooden back stairs that zigzagged down the outside brick wall to a parking lot below. Okay. Entrance to the building.

In the bathroom he stood pissing, mind whirling. He could break into the building easy enough, but they kept everything in those files . . . His eye caught a glint of brass beneath the toilet. There, sprawled in a little cluster on the dirty tile floor was a tight ring of keys, identical to the ones Kronos had used.

"*I love you, Smitty,*" Roger thought. *Either he's doing me another big fucking favor. Or he's an incredible fuckup. Or . . . He's setting me up.* Roger didn't want to lay odds on any possibility. He scooped up the keys and flushed the toilet. If he could get in and out before the key loss was discovered, he would have access to a huge stash of classified information. Heart pounding, he returned to the office.

"I'll get you the names and addresses ASAP," he said.

Kronos looked up at him. "When?"

"Tomorrow." Roger grasped the keys. He would have to break in to the office tonight. He looked over at the fat, red-faced operative. Did he catch a hint of conspiratorial smugness? An ally, a slob, or a spider laying a trap?

Kronos gave him a thumbs up.

Roger turned to his father. "Thanks, Dad." He embraced the elder Wolfe a second time. "No hard feelings, right?"

"No hard feelings."

Roger nodded to the operatives and slid out the door, heart pounding. The building reminded him of his old high school in Bronco — thin doors, ancient locks, windows waiting to be jimmied, file cabinets full of documents. He fingered the ring of keys in his pocket. The stooges would get no leadership list, his old man would be crucified, but he knew what he would do with the files in that shabby little office, once the lights went out.

BOSTON

"I can't do anything with this." Sam Nicholson thrust Madeline's Woodstock article at her. "The people you trash in here? They bought a full-page ad in the *Rat*. You think they'll do that again?"

"Wow." She batted the manuscript away from her face. "Listen to you!"

"No, Madeline. Listen to you!" He read aloud:

> *Nature can be elegant. Nature can be*
> *messy. Woodstock was messy. Why?*
> *Because it was promoted by guys who*
> *wear their hair long, smoke dope and*
> *are in it for the money. At Woodstock,*
> *the peace train rolled for profit.*

"You know these guys paid your way up there?"

"They bought an ad to push their sleazy event. Big deal. What am I supposed to do? Suck dick or write what I see?"

Sam continued reading:

301

If swimming naked in a muddy
cattle pond or fucking everybody
in sight spells freedom, then we
were all free at Woodstock.

"Look," Sam said, "we're trying to make this paper cover its own nut for a change." He felt on edge. He adored Madeline but felt vulnerable. She knew how to fight in a way that his Yankee upbringing had never trained him for. Shouting was not allowed around the Nicholson home. Madeline raised her voice whenever she felt provoked and could argue circles around him on any subject. "You want us to keep running girlie ads?"

"Yeah." Madeline leaned forward. "I'd stick with the girlies. They don't tell us what to write." She felt betrayed, unclean. This guy, her lover, was bullshitting her. Sam was smart, funny, principled. She loved his body, the cut of his shoulders, chest and thighs, his earnest but awkward attempts at intimacy — a romantic trapped in the body of a White Anglo-Saxon Protestant. Lothario, no. Endearing, yes, but he had the stubborn instincts of a bow-tied Yankee patrician. "Aren't you embarrassed?"

"Embarrassed?" Sam reddened. He always flushed when angered. "About what? Trying to keep this paper solvent?"

Now those patrician instincts, generations deep, were pushing him back into the system. Couldn't somebody get it right? She knew *she* couldn't, but she desperately wanted somebody to show the way. She grabbed the copy pages and picked out one sheet. "Let's get to the point, Sam."

For those who think that Revolution
means peace and love and rock and roll
and living in mud and bum tripping
on bad acid and getting the clap . . .

"You think that's the whole story?" Sam shouted. "Hell, never mind the ads, these guys could sue you for slander."

She continued reading, more insistent now.

> *The sad part is, they'll have to settle for*
> *that hippie rip-off in upstate New York as*
> *the only evidence that they were part of a*
> *revolution. And that, brothers and sisters*
> *— given the critical nature of our struggle*
> *— is the real tragedy of Woodstock.*

"There." She threw the single last sheet at him. "Just print that paragraph and I'll get off your case."

"No," Sam said. "Absolutely not. Unacceptable. You can't fight a revolution if you don't have a press. And this press won't exist in another month if we keep going the way we are."

"Shit, man, we don't need the FBI to raid the *Rat.* You've already raided it." She could feel the anger rising in her. "They won't have to tell you what to do. You already know."

She picked up a large manila envelope from her desk. It carried no return address, but was postmarked Philadelphia. She pulled out an official-looking paper with an FBI seal at the top. Scrawled across the bottom in thick pencil:

> *Mad — There's more where this came from.*
> *- the boy from Chicago*

She stuffed the FBI memo back in the envelope. "To hell with Woodstock," she said. "This is a real story."

"Lemme see."

"Nope. I'm taking this to the Free Speech News. They don't have to answer to a bunch of hippie entrepreneurs."

"Fuck you."

"No, man," she sighed. "Fuck you."

After Sam left the office, Madeline re-opened the envelope and read.

```
United States Government
Federal Bureau Of Investigation
COINTELPRO
Memo: Project Omega
Objective — Disruption of the New Left

    Recent issues of the underground press
have been squabbling over a split that
has developed within the Free Speech News
(FSNS). One faction remains in New York.
The other has relocated to Apple Valley,
near Amherst, Massachusetts, a univer-
sity hotbed of radicalism.
    Take advantage of this split. Intro-
duce Project Omega (Egyptian Beetle) to
further disrupt the underground press
and attack the New Left.
```

She reread the note that had been scrawled in thick pencil across the bottom of the memo: *More where this came from.*

The next morning Madeline stuffed clothes and journals in a duffel bag, left a note for Sam and took off for the Free Speech News commune. The COINTELPRO plot, ridiculous though it was, targeted the FS News Service, and they needed to know about this malevolent stupidity. A brown Egyptian beetle. Mystic symbolism. *Please.*

MIDDLETON, MASSACHUSETTS

In the quiet emptiness of her parents' home, Connie and Eddie ate scrambled eggs and banana pancakes, drank beer, and smoked a bowl of his gray-green Humboldt pot.

"Did you get shot at?" she asked him.

Eddie connected with the level gaze of her deep brown eyes. "Yes." He looked away. "These pancakes remind me of 'way back when your parents were gone like this." He smiled, his lined face going soft. "Remember?"

"Of course I do, Eddie."

"Remember that day we sat up on Summit Rock and you chewed me out for going into the service?"

"Yes. Of course I do."

"I thought we'd never see each other again."

"So did I. But these days, life seems to bring people together in the most mysterious ways."

"Ain't no mystery. You know. . ."

Eddie and Connie had reunited on common ground — the war at home, like the war in Vietnam, tore people apart . . . and brought them together. Both understood the forces. Call it chance, call it coincidence, call it weird, they understood. They cleared the table without a word, stacked the dishes in the sink, and climbed the stairs, she leading the way.

At the top she turned and looked down at him on the step below. He grinned up at her and she found herself overwhelmed with a tenderness that was too real, too present to be nostalgic. *After running from Louis for so long, here I am, turning the tables. How different this feels. How perfectly strange.*

She had slept with David in a vain attempt to rid herself of Louis. Now she was sleeping with Eddie, but it felt new. She could embrace both. Her grief over Louis, her care for Eddie had fused and turned into gentle desire. She led Eddie down the hallway to her bedroom, pulled him inside and closed the door.

Inside, she stood against the door, holding the knob in both hands behind her back while he wandered around the room, revisiting the old posters, the pictures, the books on her shelves. "Wow," he said. "It's pretty much the way it used to be."

"My parents. They like to pretend I'm still here."

"My baby sister Theresa moved into my room about three days after I left."

She watched him move from photo to photo, reconstructing the past, his familiar form draped in ragged military leftovers.

"Did you have to kill anyone?" Shocked at the sound of the words, she did not retract them. She had wanted to know since she saw him in Chicago, not knowing what difference it would make. Now, alone with him in her bedroom, it seemed to matter, not because she was afraid for herself but because she was afraid for him, for the damage war might have — must have — done.

"Yes."

"What did it feel like?" She regretted asking the question. Too late. "I'm sorry." She traced the back of her fingers down his cheek. "You don't have to answer."

"It's okay. Usually I lie. But with you . . . " He sat down on the edge of the bed. "I wanna." He looked up at her. "One of the things you do when they put you in command of a platoon." His shoulders hunched. "It's your job to . . ."

She crossed the room and stood before him. Her fingertips dropped to his neck.

"I dunno. It gets all mixed up. What happened when. Other times it's clear. Different things happened different times." He opened his hands, splayed his palms, and raised his eyes. "I'll tell you a story."

She leaned down, put a hand on his arm. "You don't have to."

"I lost a buddy this one time. We got ambushed and he took an RPG round right through the chest. One of those Soviet jobs. Eighty-five millimeter. Blew him apart."

She straightened up. "Eddie, I . . ."

"No," he said quietly. "Let me tell you. It'll help you understand." He leaned forward, elbows on thighs. "Anyhow. When the shitstorm was over, I found him. He was off the trail in a little clearing, lying on his back. What was left of his back. His legs were still where they were supposed to be but his arms . . . They were kinda lying around, smoking, his hands curled up. Like a baby's.

"He was far away. On the other side of the clearing. So I crossed over and. . ." He laughed a little laugh. "I picked up the pieces and . . . I tried to put him back together." He made a gathering motion with his hands. "I figured if I could rebuild him he'd be okay. I don't know how long I tried. My lieutenant found me kneeling there, trying to fit the parts together — he was a pretty good guy for a lieutenant and all. He got a couple other guys. They took me away and this lieutenant . . . He shoved the parts in a body bag. It seemed to make sense at the time. Try to make something whole again. You know the feeling."

"No, I don't."

"It's like — over there? You're always trying to make sense out of things you can't make sense of."

"Now that I can relate to!" She peeled the coat off his back.

He helped her, shrugging out of the olive drab of the fatigue jacket. He reached up and began unbuttoning her blouse. He traced his fingers over her bare shoulders. "Now you . . . " He laughed gently. "You are whole."

Undressing each other, they slipped onto the big bed, side by side. He lay naked, revealing a red, ragged trail that ran along his shoulder and down his right arm.

"So. You were shot." She leaned over, kissed the still-angry line, traced the tight planes of hip and thigh with her fingertips. She reached down and stroked him gently at first, then harder as he sighed and arched up toward her. She straddled him as he stiffened, and took him into her easily, massaging his shoulders, chest and belly as she moved over him, hoping — not to reclaim their past, but — to heal something in him, some wrong, some wound that he hadn't been able to describe and that she could not confirm was even there. And to heal something in her.

APPLE VALLEY, MASSACHUSETTS

Madeline took a bus through the August humidity to Amherst and called the number she had for the Free Speech News collective. Knowing her work from *Ramparts* and the *Back Bay Rat*, the collective sent a bushy young journalist to pick her up at the Amherst Greyhound station. After her short answers calmed his questioning, he settled down and drove her to the rundown dairy farm that served as the collective's headquarters. Under the light of a full moon, a clapboard farmhouse spread its broad porches over an untended lawn at the center of the farm's lush fields and rolling woodlands.

She delivered Roger's Project Omega memo at the editorial meeting the day after she arrived. It caused quite a stir. "This is too stupid to be real," the bushy young journalist suggested. "This has to come from those fuckheads at the New York collective."

Paranoid, she thought. Little wonder. The Free Speech News had become one of the major mouthpieces of the New Left. This underground press network was making trouble for the power structure. *When you push,* Madeline knew, *the Machine pushes back.* The system's responses flared up everywhere. Underground papers across the country were raided and trashed. Under these circumstances, it was healthy to be paranoid.

Sam and Madeline's fight had come about as the result of the second, more effective tactic than raids and decimated mimeo machines — co-option. Under pressure from their cronies in Congress, tobacco companies and music execs were beginning to withdraw their ads from the papers. The papers, their circulation overextended, had become dependent on the tobacco and rock n' roll ads. When they lost the revenue, they failed to keep ahead of their bills. The alternative papers had allowed themselves to be sucker-punched by the great urge of capital to expand.

Provocateurs also did their damage. The combined tension and pressure had caused splits in the burnt-out staff members of more than one paper. Where had all the anger gone? Inward. It became easier to battle with the guy sitting next to you than with the great enemy beyond. So, too, with Madeline's new haven, the Free Speech News.

Under the charismatic but hard-to-follow leadership of Marshall Bromley, the new collective had broken off from the more doctrinaire New York collective. They had stolen the presses and fled to the farmhouse near Amherst after months of acrimonious battle. For the Movement, paranoia had at once become a necessity and an enemy within.

"This stuff is not from the New York collective," Madeline insisted. "I can vouch for the source." Doubt shadowed her guarantee. *Could Roger be trusted?*

Bromley rubbed his tired eyes. "If the FBI really came up with this shit . . ."

Madeline finished Bromley's sentence. "They don't have a fucking clue."

Many were suspicious of the messenger. How had Madeline gotten this information? Was she sent there to plant this memo, real or fake? Still, Marshall Bromley invited her to stay on.

Madeline kept largely to herself, toiling nonstop in the newsroom, editing the daily dispatches that Free Speech News sent to underground papers across the nation. She had no desire to take part in the nightly experimentation that manifested itself in intense, fast-growing liaisons. Private property was antithetical to the Revolution. Everything was to be shared. The collective members overcompensated for their largely middle-class upbringing by swapping partners in the same way they passed bread and wine around the big kitchen table.

Overall, Madeline believed in collectivity. But she didn't want a dose of the clap or to get knocked up. She wanted rest from what seemed to have been an endless cavalcade of boyfriends that stretched back to David, respite from the legacy left by her philandering parents. *Dad's probably still screwing Katherine, for God's sake!*

Besides, the communards all seemed so serious and humorless about their experimentation and — regardless of their intent — she could still see the power flowing from male to female. In every pair-swap or threesome that morphed out of the collective will, there always seemed to be at least one reluctant hostage who went along without conviction for the often-painful ride. The only saving grace, it seemed to Madeline, was that the unhappiness was never gender-specific.

Madeline heard the bark of the Volkswagen long before it bounced up the twin-rutted road that led to the farmhouse. Although the VW was not part of the arsenal of wrecks that usually graced the commune's front lawn, its authenticity was indisputable. The exterior was pocked with dents, the paint worn to anemic splotches. Salt from winter roads had terminally scarred each mismatched fender and door. The windshield was cracked and the muffler had rusted out.

The Volkswagen passed the funk test, but its arrival made Madeline uneasy. She was alone. Most of the Free Speech communards had gone down the road to help a local farmer bale and stack a field of alfalfa before the usual afternoon thunderheads dropped cloudbursts on the precious fodder.

The VW chugged to a stop. Through the glare on the cracked windshield, a familiar looking profile hunched over the steering wheel.

Who was this guy, what was he doing here and what did he want? Still, he looked vaguely familiar. She stepped to the front of the broad porch, shielding her eyes, trying to identify the enigmatic form behind the windshield. Finally it stirred and, grunting, pulled itself up and half-way out the driver's side window. He waved sheepishly at her. "Door's jammed." He kicked free and landed on the ground, blue-jean cuffs half stuffed into the tops of a worn pair of cowboy boots.

"Roger!" Madeline walked down to the car, unsure of what to expect. What was he doing? How did he know she was here?

Roger leaned back against the VW and held her. For a long time.

Wary of his presence, she also felt the attraction. She found herself softening. "So . . . " She pushed her head back but still held him, belly-to-belly. "How are you going to complicate my life this time?"

"I got stuff," he said.

"What kinda stuff?" She backed away from the car and let him pass.

Immediately, he sat down on the front stoop, establishing a beachhead. "I need a place to hide the papers." He lit a cigarette.

"Papers?"

"Government papers. FBI memos. Like the one I sent you."

Adrenaline rushed through her system. Yes, she had understood the power of the memo he had first sent. And she had used his offering as leverage to storm out of the *Back Bay Rat* and Sam's life. Still . . . *He can't have brought them here.* There was bound to be a snitch at the farm, someone who was reporting to the rival New York faction. She grabbed his shirt. "You didn't bring that crap here, did you?"

"It's not crap." Grinning and squinting past his cigarette smoke, he lifted the VW's trunk. "And yeah, I did bring it here."

Inside, two boxes full of documents and file folders hunkered behind the spare tire. Every document carried the FBI imprimatur. "It's been a freaked-out ride. I have to stash this stuff somewhere. And quick."

She tried to control her panic. The Free Press people would be returning from their haying expedition. What if the Feds showed up? "Is anybody following you? Did you pass anybody coming up here?"

"Of course not."

"And you drove up here in that hippie wreck? You probably got stopped by every state trooper from here to eternity!"

"You don't want these documents? I brought them for you."

"You coulda brought the Feds for me, too. And for the whole commune."

"Hey, Miss Righteous, I could have taken these papers to the New York faction."

"Why didn't you?"

"Because you're with these guys, not with them. I trust you. These folks are gonna wanna look at this shit. These boxes . . . " He patted the covers. "Full of strategy papers and reports. Skinny on the Mobe, the Panthers, all of us."

"Who's 'us,' Roger?"

"Huh? Whaddya mean?"

"Right now, motherfucker, you're acting more like a 'them' than an 'us,' " she said.

"Just help me hide the fuckin' papers, Madeline. I'll explain later."

"No!" She grabbed his arms and shook him. "Explain now, before Marshall and the rest get back and start asking questions that I can't answer."

"Okay, okay." He yanked away from her. "I paid a visit to my old man."

"That's your explanation?"

"You can figure it out, can't ya?"

She raised her hand. "Don't play games with me, Buster."

He looked so forlorn, so miserable, so uncharacteristically scared. She wanted to sit down beside him, but refrained. Heads had to rule here, not sympathy, certainly not simple attraction. "Maybe you better start from the beginning."

"My old man's in trouble. He figured if he could rope me into bein' a snitch, he'd get in good with his spook buddies. He had it over me because I beat the crap out of him back home. He pressed charges. I been on the lam ever since."

"Yeah? You and a lot of other people. So?"

"So my old man called me. Told me he needed me. At first I said 'forget it', then I thought . . . Hey, this might give me a window into the Feds. So I said 'okay.'"

"Like you're spying on the spies?"

"They brought me to this FBI office."

"Where?"

"Hey, Madeline. This is not a fuckin' interview for your fuckin' newspaper."

"Okay. Talk."

"The office was in Pittsburgh. What a hole."

"I know, I know. Whatcha got?"

"They showed me this." He showed her a copy of the COINTELPRO write-up about the Egyptian beetles. "This crap."

"Yeah. The stuff you sent me. I read it. It's ridiculous. That's the work of the much-feared, all-powerful FBI?"

"Yep. So I went along with it. And hit pay dirt. I'm sitting there listening to these guys talk at me and I'm looking at file after file of these papers. Too good to pass up. So I took the assignment."

"You're here to spy on the Free Speech News?"

"Yeah. And to introduce crap like that beetle memo. Only now, all they know is their documents got stolen. Probably by me. Shit." He ran his hands through his hair. "Who knows what they know? And what they don't?"

"Dammit, Roger, you're twisting this around." She shook her head in disbelief. "You took an assignment to sabotage us, then you . . . now you . . . what? Have a bunch of FBI files?"

He grinned that sly soft grin. "Just a select few. Heh."

She softened. This lunatic had smuggled a box of documents over state lines, documents that could get him imprisoned for treason. He couldn't be a snitch . . . Could he? "Now you're turning them over to the Free Speech

News?" She smiled and pushed at his chest. "Why are you telling me this?"

"Because I'm going to get my old man, that's why."

"That's not a reason. Every guy on this commune hates his old man."

"Yeah, but every guy on this commune ain't got an old man who works for the FBI. I broke into the office."

"Jesus, Roger."

"I found a set of keys."

"Where?"

"Behind a toilet."

She put her hands to her head and screamed in frustration. "Stop it! Stop it! You're lying, I know it!"

"Am not! I went through hell to get this shit." He broke, put his arms around her.

"Shit, Madeline. I love you. I . . . "

She couldn't push him away. She rested her cheek against his chest. "Don't you understand, Roger? You set these people up. You set me up."

"Madeline. Work with me. Please. I got a dead car. I got no money. And now I'm on the lam from the Feds. Times two. Big time."

"Like David," she said.

Roger held her tight. "I love you."

She could feel his strong body against her and nuzzled him. "Boy." She pounded his chest, her hand pausing, open palmed with each small blow. "I sure know how to pick 'em."

"So how about it? Madeline?"

She pushed away and stood, hands on hips, staring into the dirt. Finally she raised her head. "Okay. But we gotta talk to Marshall and the whole collective."

"No! Not yet."

Madeline folded her arms across her chest and scrutinized him. Hard. All she could see was the scared, cute boy who had the honesty to say he loved her. And she knew. She knew she had feelings for him, too. Dangerous feelings for a dangerous boy. *Clear*, she told herself. *Keep clear*. "Why *not* tell them now?"

"They don't know me. How do they know I'm telling the truth?"

"How do *I* know you're telling the truth? You've been acting squirrelly since the Chicago battles." She put her face in her hands and leaned against the VW. "I sleep with you one night and . . ." She didn't want this. She wanted Greenwich Village. She wanted her Dad. She wanted her fifth grade teacher, not these paranoid, driven revolutionary crazies. Yet she, too, was one of them.

She raised her head, surprised to find tears blurring the hay fields. "First you tell me you're supposed to be spying on this commune. Then you tell me you stole these documents for the Movement. Which is it? Is that what you did last summer in Chicago? Is that why you were acting so weird?"

"Sort of. That was the first time I was supposedly on the take."

"Did you rat anybody out?"

"Maybe."

"'Maybe.'" She shook her head, shocked and disappointed at the same time. "And now you want me to believe you're not a snitch?"

"Dammit, I told you! My old man had it over me. He could have busted me. 'Way back before the convention. I listened to him and his pathetic buddies. I decided not to roll for them."

"Jeez, Roger." She felt dismayed. "You sound like a gangster." This Movement. It started with folk music and peace marches. Now it felt weird, complicated, dark. "You have to be clear, right now, Roger. Really, really clear."

"What is this? The Inquisition?"

"No! Just the opposite. The Man is the Inquisition. We are the field hands, the slaves, not the Inquisitors. Remember?"

He stood before her, a clown down to his last dime, one step ahead of the law, all or nothing, a desperado, carrying his own truth around his neck like a talisman. And enough information to blow a hole in COINTELPRO. She got into the VW. "Drive me around to the back of the barn. And you better not fuck with me, Roger Wolfe."

MIDDLETON, MASSACHUSETTS

Eddie responded to their lovemaking with the same amazement her advances had evoked in the back seat of his car, years before. Afterward, they lay collapsed and sweating in the quiet darkness of her flounced and flowered bedroom, catching their breath amidst the tumbled bedclothes while he pushed wet tendrils of hair away from her face and kissed the sweat from between her breasts. Gradually they both fell silent, lost in their own jumbled thoughts and feelings. He seemed happy to please her and she wondered how he had kept that precious part of himself intact. What had gone on in this man during his time away? Sex with him had not given her any answers.

Eddie broke the silence. "You know when I first met David, he was totally fucked up. Totally fucked up and paranoid. Some Good Samaritan shipped him out of Oakland to Humboldt."

"Humboldt?"

"Humboldt County, north of San Francisco. God's Country. I was trying to get the napalm out of my system. It was a natural fit. I was a mess from the war, he was a mess from the anti-war."

317

"We all are."

"I taught him to hunt. We needed the meat. He hated it. Hunting. In the spring, we planted a patch of wicked kick-ass dope, him and me. The city freak and the farm boy, scratching in the ground, hauling water up to a ridge top. It was wicked cool. He talked a lot about you. Of course, I didn't know he was talking about my girl Connie." He laughed, a sharp, sarcastic bark that sounded doglike.

"Enough." She untangled herself from his thighs, sat up, and swung her legs over the edge of the bed.

"Huh?" He leaned on his elbow, watching her back. "What did I do?"

"You . . . I . . . I just . . ." She felt hot tears of frustration swell her eyes. Her throat felt tight. She felt naked. She rose and put on her blouse. "Can you stay with your parents?"

"Jeez, Connie . . ."

"This is the second time you brought this up."

"What?"

"In Chicago you had to tell me . . . "

"Tell you what?"

"That you knew David and I had slept together." The words began to flow. "As if that was all we did. We're all part of the anti-war movement, right? I met this guy. You met him, too. It was a coincidence."

He sat up, pulled a package of Camels from his jacket pocket.

She pulled on her panties. She wanted to wash him out of her. "You're making it sound like I'm a slut."

"'A slut'? Where'd you get that?"

"I need to clean up." She left the room.

When she returned, she found Eddie sitting cross-legged on the bed, smoking a Camel. "Hey, Connie . . ." His Zippo lay gleaming on the sheets, its Marine Corps insignia worn smooth. "Are you sure you need to fight this battle anymore?"

"What?" She frowned. "Of course I do. Why do you even ask?"

"I was over there. We're losin' the fuckin' war. Everybody knows it. Let it go. The whole fucking mess is gonna collapse anyway. Look at what it's doin' to you guys, fighting a dinosaur that's already dead. Jeez. Look at your boyfriend David."

"Dammit," she shouted. "He's not my . . ."

He put three fingers on her lips.

There was that touch again — so gentle.

"And . . ." he added. "He isn't the only anti-fucking-war freak out there who's shell-shocked."

"Do you have to smoke?" She was irritated, not by the smoke, but by his large, sudden return to her life. *But his eyes,* she thought. *At least his eyes are still soft.*

"Come with me."

"Where?"

"Back to Humboldt County. All you can hear is the crows and the hawks and the wind in the pines. Out there . . . It gives me peace of mind."

"It gives you peace of mind, Eddie, not me." She took the cigarette out of his hand and leaned her forehead against his shoulder. "I need to stay here."

"The Red Hawk people, they're against the war too."

"Everybody's against the war," she replied. "They just aren't doing anything about it."

"They made a choice."

"To run away from the struggle."

"Not everybody's a warrior, Con." "They should be. We need them."

"What they're doing up there . . . that's political."

"By running to the wilderness? Living in the mud and raising rabbits?"

319

"They're saying they don't want any part of the machine."

"While the machine keeps right on grinding. Grinding at us . . . and them."

"You are so fuckin' stubborn." He snatched the cigarette back. "You could use a break."

"I don't need a break." She pulled on a pair of faded jeans. "We're different people now."

"Yeah? So?"

"You need peace. You deserve it. I need to stay here."

"You weren't talkin' that way in Chicago when those people wanted to tear the roof off the motherfucker . . ."

"Yeah," she said, angry now. "There are other ways to fight beside blowing up buildings."

"Those people are full of shit. That Roger guy? Bullshit. And David? I'm fuckin' surprised at him. Even Madeline. She seemed a lot hipper than that. Armed fucking revolution? In the middle of the United States?" Eddie pulled on his jeans. "Them and their slogans. 'Power grows out of the barrel of a gun.' Bullshit. Power grows out of who's got the most guns. And it ain't David and Roger and Madeline."

"That's their way. I don't agree with it, but they know we need to fight. And that fight isn't going to happen in Humboldt County."

"It's gotta happen everywhere. Every which way."

"Right on." Connie walked out, into the hallway. "You go your way. I'll go mine." Framed by the door she looked back at her childhood sweetheart. "That way . . . we'll each be doing our part."

Apple Valley, Massachusetts

In the barn, Madeline swam to the surface of a dream. She had discovered a body decomposing in a grove of bare-limbed birches and fallen yellow leaves. The skull grinned up at her and a gaping wound flowered from the desiccated skeleton's sternum. The poor soul had been shot in the back. Heart pounding, she sat up and stared into darkness. The animal smells of the barn cloyed her nostrils but located her.

Measured breath rose from a mop of blond hair, further confusing her. She had not slept with anyone since she had left Sam. The vestiges of a night's lovemaking seemed odd, even dismaying, as if she had awoken with a stranger whose name she couldn't remember. But no . . . this was Roger.

She lay naked beneath the puff of an old quilt, hands behind her head. She would have to force the issue with Roger. *If he's a snitch*, she thought, *he won't want to tell the News Service people about the box of documents or this dumb Egyptian beetle caper. If he means what he says — that he's there not to spy, but to turn over the box — then he would have to deliver the documents to the collective or pack them into the VW and split at dawn.* She could always explain his quick come-and-go as a reunion gone bad.

"Okay, Roger Wolfe, double snitch or sonofabitch." Madeline shook the sleeping fugitive awake.

He opened his eyes, disoriented.

"Show time," she said. "We're gonna take the papers to the house and explain the whole thing — the complete fucking nightmare — or you go. Now. Before the dawn's early light, brother."

He turned to her, sleepy, horny and happy to see her. He reached out.

He looked adorable, smiling, hair mussed, eyes closed, arms extended. The cutest little snitch-thief, spy, double spy, who the fuck knew? "This is serious," she said. "D-Day."

He leaned up on one elbow and gazed at her intently. "Okay," he said. He put a hand on her arm. "Stand by me?"

She put her hand on his warm wrist. "Depends."

They dressed and lugged the boxes of documents to the farmhouse. The collective's editorial crew was sitting at a kitchen table covered with copy and paste-ups and homemade bread and coffee. An odd group, all men, they sprouted a wide range of hairstyles — from anarchist shag to straight-guy — and an equally wide range of dress, from blue jeans and sports jackets to militant fatigues and mystic robes. Regardless of appearance, all were feeding facts to the underground newspaper network that stretched from Maine to California.

The newshounds clustered around the boxes, pulling out one document after another. Roger had chosen well from the rifled files. Each bore evidence of COINTEL-PRO's intent to infiltrate and destroy the New Left, the civil rights movement, the Black Panthers, and anybody else who got uppity. The only sounds were of quiet, concentrated amazement and the occasional low whistle as the papers were passed from one hand to the next.

"Careful with those docs," Bromley insisted. "It's all in chronological order." Marshal Bromley was a thoroughbred intellectual, *magna cum laude* from Yale, his clean, white, graceful hands a contradiction to the clownish Bohemian clothes, explosive mop of black hair and an outrageously droopy handlebar moustache. "Okay," he asked quietly. "Where'd you get these?"

"From the FBI," Roger said.

"How?"

"My old man."

"Great," Marshal said. "What the hell are you talking about?"

"He wanted me to snitch for the Feds."

"And?"

"And I had to. He had leverage."

"What leverage?"

"I threw him into a grease pit after my mother's funeral."

"Happy couple?"

Roger ignored the comment. "He pressed charges. There's a warrant out for me in Texas."

Bromley turned to Madeline. "Can you please interpret for this guy? I don't have the vaguest fucking idea what he's babbling about."

"His father is FBI. He needed a stooge. He knew Roger was working with SDS. He knew he could pin him with a felony. So he tracked him down and threatened to turn him in."

"Turn who in?"

"Roger."

"Jesus." Bromley shook his head in dismay.

"My old man was going to drop the dime on me if I didn't go to work for him and his FBI buddies," Roger added.

"But ol' Rodge here, he didn't do that. Did he?" She threw a look at Roger as if to say, *and if this is bullshit, you've fucked us both.* "Instead, he took advantage of the situation."

"And this," Roger swept his arm over the spread of documents, "is the result."

Bromley stared intently. "Where did you get this stuff?"

"Pittsburgh," Roger replied.

"They keep this kind of information in a fucking FBI office? In Pittsburgh?"

"They send these files around by the truckload. I wouldn't doubt you could find these papers in any field office," Roger snapped. "If you had the balls to look."

"Doesn't it seem possible that you . . . " Bromley turned to Roger. "You can see, can't you? That your sudden appearance here might make us nervous."

Roger shrugged. "Stealing those documents made me nervous, Bromley. You can see that, too . . . can't you?"

"We live in nervous times."

"Forget it, Marshall." Another news freak grabbed a sheaf of the documents. "Nobody could have forged this crap."

"I don't have any problem with the message," Bromley replied. "I have a problem with the messenger." He glanced at Madeline. "The messengers."

"You don't believe us?" Madeline asked.

"I don't trust him," Bromley replied. "And now I don't know what to make of you, either, Madeline. Matter of fact," he blinked, "I'm getting a funny vibe off the both of you."

"'A funny vibe'? " Madeline mimicked Bromley, angry now. "What the hell is a 'vibe'? How do you measure a 'vibe'? Column inches? The density of the aura the viber puts out? Or does the vibee get to determine when bullshit is real?"

Bromley put up a hand. "You're acting hostile."

"You're acting paranoid." Roger sifted through the documents. "These papers are hard-won. Weapons for the Movement. Ammunition. I took a lotta chances, copping this material."

"Hold it! Let's be scientific about this." The second newsfreak leaned into Roger. "You bring a box full of hot documents you 'pilfered' from the FBI, and you tell us this story about how you hate your father. How do we know you stole them? Maybe they gave them to you. Otherwise, how come they didn't come after you? And if they did . . . They'll come here."

"The FBI? They won't even discover this shit is missing for days. I used a key, not a pry bar. And dumped the keys back where I found 'em."

"Behind a toilet," Madeline added.

Bromley groaned and stuffed his knuckles into his eye sockets.

"Uh huh. Maybe. Maybe not," replied the newsfreak. "I may get stoned from time to time . . . "

Another editor laughed.

" . . . but I'm not stupid. Or naïve."

"I don't trust the source," said a third collective member.

"This whole fucking circus feels like trouble."

Madeline had made up her mind. These guys were fucking around. She no longer felt close to them. "What do we do with these papers, Marshall Bromley? C'mon . . . " She picked up a handful of the memos. "Shit or get off the pot."

Bromley took them from her and threw them at Roger. "We think you might be a fucking snitch, okay?" He turned to Madeline. "How's that for shitting?"

People in the kitchen froze.

"Fuck it." Roger pushed the box of FBI docs across the table. "Keep it."

"Why" asked the forthright journalist. "So you fuckers can call in our coordinates to the Feds? Stick us with a pile of top-secret FBI memos that are so hot they glow in the dark? Thanks a pantload."

"Getting busted with these . . . that's tantamount to treason," Bromley said.

"Drop the 'tantamount' part, Marshall," said the newsfreak. "They'll hang us from the roof beams."

"Fine," Roger said. "Do what you want with them. Burn them if you think they're too hot. It's your loss, not mine."

In silent support, Madeline laid the Egyptian beetle memo on top of the pile of FBI documents.

"There's one document I want to keep," Roger said. "Sort of as a commission." He reached across the table and lifted a booklet out of the cardboard file.

"What's that?" The scientific journalist eyed him suspiciously.

"A list of Federal offices and military research centers. We're going to need this," he said, tucking the booklet into his shirt. He stood up and stared down at the Free Speech journalists. "For our next action."

"Oh really," Bromley said, his tone lofty. "And what might your next action be?"

"Shit howdy, brother." Roger spread his broad, pearly smile across his handsome face and dropped into his old Texas drawl. "Whatever it's gonna be — sure as the sun don't shine outta my asshole — it's gonna be a whole helluva lot different from that which you're doin' right here, right now."

Austin, Texas

The National Convention of the Students for a Democratic Society was held in Middle America so everyone could make the scene. The college liberals, the ragtag revolutionaries, the bright-eyed sopho-mores converged in derelict VW vans, on dusty motorcycles, in trains, planes, buses, or riding their thumbs. One freak walked from Wyoming.

Most Middle Americans had known nothing about SDS until the long-haired youngsters took to the Chicago streets the summer before. The tear gas- and outrage-shattered fiasco that had climaxed with the embarrassing nomination of Humbert H. Humphrey. Now, Tricky Dick Nixon was in the White House, and the people who met in Austin had stopped writing their Congressman years ago.

National hounds clustered around front doors of the Gothic mausoleum that would house the Convention. After they reached critical mass, a striking young woman in black — surrounded by an entourage of SDS cadres — emerged through the lobby doors to address the press.

"No mainstream vultures will be allowed inside unless you register." Ensconced behind large sunglasses, looking like a left-wing Sophia Loren, the young woman spoke without waiting for the microphones.

"Don't worry about recording this. I'm addressing you, the news workers, not your clients, the advertisers, or your commodity, the readers and viewers. If you come inside, your names will be recorded in the books. Our books. We can, however, warn you that — as usual — Pig spies will weasel their way into this meeting."

"Can you give us your name?" asked a reporter.

"I'm a Sister." The young woman pressed on, not waiting for a response. "Once you register, your names will appear on our books, without distinction, without qualification, like every other SDS member, like the rest of the revolutionary freaks behind these doors. If your name appears in our books, you, too, will become a revolutionary freak. We are all the same in the eyes of the authorities."

The journalists shifted uncomfortably on the sidewalk.

"If you are not daunted by the thought of joining us as future comrades in the struggle, come inside. We only ask that you deviate from your normal practice and tell the truth about what you witness here."

After the reporters and camera crews had retreated from the scene, the delegates to the National Conference of the Students for a Democratic Society filtered into the drab, varnished meeting hall to begin hashing out what they were going to do with the fledgling movement they had built.

The constituency quickly polarized. Intellectuals in corduroy jackets clashed with prairie firebrands in leather jackets. Fueled by the urgency of war and the commitment of days, months, and years of struggle, inspired by the new manifesto, and sparked by the passions of the moment, friends shouted down friends and

```
finally, under the weight of days of con-
flict, the organization shattered.
```

POUGHKEEPSIE

In the aftermath of the Austin Convention, David made a pact with Roger and Madeline. Heartened by the desperation of their enemies, they would take the cue and push the resistance forward — by any means necessary. There would be little communication between cells. They shared the same resolve — forward movement from resistance to rebellion, to Revolution.

The trio split up. David headed to Philadelphia where he could work with the low-profile Philly SDS office. Madeline and Roger found a place to live outside New York, where — according to the list they took from the FBI files — most of their targets lay. When they found a suitable base of operations, they would contact David. The message would be waiting for him at his parents' Riverside Drive apartment. Regardless of his revolutionary fervor, David could not suppress the image of Madeline, standing barelegged in a kitchen doorway, draped in Roger's shirt. So long ago, and yet how fresh his emotions burnt.

Roger and Madeline drove the last gasp out of the VW, landing in a motel on the outskirts of Poughkeepsie. They scrapped the VW for cash at a junkyard, rented a shabby pink row house and bought an old Pontiac station wagon that reeked of leaking transmission fluid and suburbia.

They contacted the Philadelphia SDS office via a phone in the Poughkeepsie bus terminal.

"Hi," Madeline said. "Is David there?"

"David who?"

Madeline didn't know the voice. The person didn't recognize hers either. Good. "Just tell him to come home. Okay?"

"Sure," the voice replied. "I don't know if he'll . . . "

"That's okay," Madeline replied, in a hurry to get off the line. "He'll understand."

"Sure, but . . . "

Madeline hung up. They were ready to escalate. Full resistance.

"I don't like it," Roger said.

"Why?" Madeline asked. "He was the only one with us in Chicago."

"I have a funny feeling about him."

"Yeah," she said. "And the funny feeling is me."

"Goddammit," he shouted. "Stop making this so fucking personal. You think you're the center of the universe?"

"No, I don't." She sat at the kitchen table. "But you do." She pulled him into a seat opposite her. "Come on, Rodge." She leaned across the table and kissed him on the lips. "We made a deal. All three of us."

"Okay." *No more tricks. No more double-talk*, he vowed to himself. "A deal's a deal."

"Cool." She knew David's presence would be a steadying influence on him, and — in a place still visceral from childhood — she wanted her old friend and lover beside her. She grabbed two beers from the 'fridge and sat down across from Roger. "Here's to the morrow!" She took a swig.

The next morning, Madeline took the train south to Grand Central Station, where she sidled up to a polished, brassy wall of mailboxes. Her father had rented #1147 years ago as a catchall for anonymous communications, As a kid, he had brought her there, building the excitement, turning a petty intrigue into a big spy story. He would let her dial the combination and . . . presto! A secret missive!

The combination came to her easily now. She twirled the two dials, heard the familiar click. Her heart rose to her throat. At the shadowy end of the box lay a thick envelope. *What was it?* A seamy communiqué for a private investigator, a disreputable tipster, maybe even a lover's note. She pulled out the envelope. Scribbled on the outside in her father's spastic handwriting . . .

For Madeline

She opened the envelope, hands shaking. A folded paper read:

> *Hiya, Mads. Just in case you were in the*
> *neighborhood and remembered the fun we*
> *used to have at our secret message place.*
> *Hope this comes in handy. Love, Dad*

She unfolded the paper. A stack of one-hundred-dollar bills, ten of them, fanned into her hand. Teary-eyed, incredulous, she replaced the envelope with her note to David. His gift, such a clumsy, familiar gesture of love, filled her with longing. In junior high school, she often received a coded hint over dinner, an attempt to hold onto the old bond between them, a bond that had weakened as she became independent. "Got a train to catch?" he'd ask innocently across the table. Her mom never caught on. She would follow the lead, spin the dial and spin the dial. An envelope containing a twenty or more always waited at the other end of the rainbow.

Now she ached to visit home, but she knew that time spent with her parents would require explanations, particularly for her father. She would want to acknowledge his gift, declare her love for him. Most important, Mad-

331

eline had no words for what she was about to do. *It was madness,* she thought.

Nevertheless, she found herself migrating downtown until she crossed 14th Street, zigging and zagging south and east until she reached the Greenwich Village block where she was born. She stood alone on the sidewalk in the gray afternoon light, peering up at the drawn curtains of her father's study. The desk lamp glowed green through the drapes and she could imagine his comfortable presence in the cloistered office, his posture loose and relaxed from his Saturday squash game, poring over legal papers or digging into one of his beloved tomes on American history or constitutional law.

She retreated to a drug store on the corner of Sixth Avenue, closed herself into a phone booth, dropped a dime, hesitated, then made the call.

"Paul Singer here."

She smiled. Her father always answered the phone as if he were at the office and his secretary had just stepped out for lunch. "Hi, Daddy." Unlike many of her male comrades, she still loved her father. He had treated her with love, and she had never used him as a proxy for the outrages of the Machine. "How's it going?"

"Hiya, Sweetie! Shouldn't I be asking you that question?"

"I'm okay."

"Just okay?"

She sighed. This was going to be tough. Paul Singer knew his daughter. "I'm fine. Really. A little tired. We're so busy."

"Of course you are." He tried to sound relaxed, good-natured, but he was probing. "Busy doing what?"

She felt an urge to tell him but couldn't imagine an explanation that wouldn't come off sounding ludicrous. And alarming. 'We're planning to step up the Resistance,

Daddy. We've broken into cohort groups and we're making plans to resist the Government of the United States — by force of arms.' Uh huh. Dramatic, stupid, almost corny. She stopped. She had to have faith. They hadn't come this far to go out with a whimper of self-doubt. But you have gone beyond everything you know, believe in, were trained for . . . What happens next? When you have right on your side, she asked herself, who will teach you what is right? What is wrong?

She cradled the phone on her shoulder and rubbed her temples, trying to massage away the hollow, headachy feeling. *This is absurd. We're crazy.* They were crazy. And yet she and many of her brothers and sisters had arrived at the same place together. She was relieved that she hadn't dared go home. She would have lost her will power, would have been trapped by her father's Socratic interrogations, suspended in an obsolete womb. Who knows what she would have confessed?

"Are you there, Honey? Anyone with you?"

Startled, she returned to the conversation. "We're setting up a community center here . . . "

"Where's 'here'?"

"Upstate New York."

"Big place, upstate New York." He laughed. "Kinda backwater up there, ain't it? Especially for a sophisticated Manhattan girl like my daughter."

"You got that right." He was right. She wouldn't be caught dead in Poughkeepsie under normal circumstances. But these weren't normal circumstances. "The folks I'm working with are great."

"I bet they are."

She heard loneliness in his voice. Perhaps her isolation was coloring her emotions. "I miss you."

"I miss you too, Madeline." There was a pause. "Your mom just got appointed department chair," he replied. "Not too shabby, huh?"

She pursed her lips, felt sorry for him. Attentive to his wife, careful with his dalliances, wary of his daughter's emergence, never wanting to hear about whom she was with, as if she might blurt out some horrifying particulars of her sex life or recite a list of the drugs she was taking.

But she must remain wary, too. He was a lawyer and knew how to corner people. He had done it plenty when she was a teenager, a fatherly Socratic method that nailed her to the wall. She smiled. She ached to prolong the discussion, to savor the comforting drone of his voice.

"So when is my sweetheart going to take a break and come visit?"

"Soon. I have a lot of responsibility — to the group and all."

"That's my gal." He laughed. "Bringing economic justice and racial harmony to upstate New York. You writing? I don't suppose there's much raw material for a *Village Voice* article up there." His laughter sounded strained.

"Nope. Not much up here for *The Village Voice*."

"So back to my question. When are you coming home?"

"Aren't you and Mom going to Puerto Rico this spring?" she retorted, dodging the question.

"Your mother can't wait to get out of the slush and into the sun."

"Lemme guess," Madeline said. "You don't give a damn about Puerto Rico. You've got work to do."

"Got it in one."

"How long are you going for?"

"I dunno. Ten days or so."

The timing couldn't have been more perfect. She felt ashamed for being so calculating, but they could use the house as a base for their first action. By the time her parents left, they would be ready. She shook herself back to the present. The future was too frightening to contemplate. She longed to sit in the kitchen and talk, kidding around, just the two of them, while her mom worked late at the University.

"When are you leaving?"

"Your mother knows the dates."

"When you get back, I'll be there."

"Promise?"

"Promise."

"Great. Something to look forward to."

"After you return to gray, old Manhattan."

She fought the urge to drop the phone, walk down the block and up the long flight of granite steps, to push open the heavy, black-enameled front door, burst into his study and hug him. "I'm gonna let you go now, Dad. See you with a Caribbean tan, okay?"

"Okay, Sweetie." He sounded resigned. "Stay warm up there."

"Give my love to Mom. And tell her congratulations."

"As soon as she gets home." There was such longing in his voice. *Had he forsaken his trysts? What about Katherine, next door? No longer available?* "Goodbye, Madeline."

"`Bye, Dad." She hung up, brushed the tears out of her eyes with the sleeve of her jacket and returned to Grand Central Station. She took the 5:45 and cried all the way back to Poughkeepsie.

MANHATTAN

David climbed the granite steps and pried open the wrought-iron doors that guarded his parents' apartment

335

building. Gaining entry in the gusty November wind required all his strength. He wondered how he had managed to seek shelter as a child, when the blasts had blown like this off the Hudson. He had lived in the same grand, old building on Riverside Drive since before he could remember. Now the place no longer seemed like home. He was no longer the kid who had inhaled blues and folk tunes alone in his room and rendezvoused with Madeline in a roach-ridden, Hell's Kitchen apartment. He was no longer the boy who had written about Fidel and the Cuban Revolution for his senior paper, who had played folk music as a celebration of history, who had joined a fledgling organization called Students for a Democratic Society because, dammit, the world needed changing and they were going to change it. He still believed in all that, but now? He had become an outlaw.

He pulled the heavy doors together behind him, shutting out the cold blasts. In the warm silence, he removed his hat and gloves, watching the wind strip the last of the autumn leaves off the branches of the elms that bordered Riverside Park. *Hostile fucking environment.*

He turned away from the doors and froze. A new doorman perched behind the concierge's podium. David had timed his visit to avoid the doorman. Willy had always come on after four p.m. He nodded and headed for the elevator.

"Excuse me, Sir . . . "

David stopped. "I guess you're new here."

"Yessir. So you know the building?"

"I have friends here."

"Great, Sir. And their names?"

"Wow." The guy was screening him. This was his home but— as a fugitive — any challenge carried a charge. "This is new."

"Yes, Sir." Implacable, congenial, very professional.

"Well, then." Panic tugged at him. "Call the Friedmans' for me." He tried to sound imperious and hated it.

"And you are?"

"Just tell them that David is here," he snapped.

"Oh! Yes! Of course. You're the Friedman boy. Right here on the list. So sorry Sir. I didn't . . . "

"Please!" David's annoyance showed through the smile. "You don't have to call me 'Sir.'"

"No, of course not." He gripped David's hand firmly. "Guess you've been away to school, eh, young fella?"

"Right." He'd been marked. Upstairs, he'd have to get to the point — fast. "Gotta go." He pressed the call button for the elevator.

"Of course, Sir."

"Uh-uh." He held up his hand again. "No more 'sirs', remember?"

The doorman winked and shot him with a finger pistol. "Gotcha!"

The door closed David into the elevator.

'*Gotcha*,' he thought. *Great*. The windows rolled past on each floor, the old cage shaking its well-worn shimmy up the shaft. He had rehearsed no lines for the visit. He knew what the conclusion had to be.

Tenth floor. A pounding heart kicked at his sternum. He stepped out of the elevator. The little brass plaque with its black apartment number stared at him as it had forever. He pressed the button.

"David? Is that you?" His mother's voice lilted through the door.

"Yesss." He eyed the hallway nervously. He didn't want another encounter, particularly with a neighbor.

His mother opened the door. "The doorman called ahead. Don't you have your key?"

David laughed and hugged her. Somewhere between Haverford, Hanoi, the Oakland street fighting, Humboldt

County, Philly and Chicago, he had lost the key to Riverside Drive. He realized he hadn't seen her for a year. Sadness seeped into him and he hugged her convulsively.

She pushed him away and looked into his face. "Where have you been? Why haven't you called?"

"Haven't I?"

"Please, David."

"Sorry, Ma." He looked over his shoulder as the elevator knocked and rattled back down to the lobby. "I've been on the road a lot. I lost track of time."

"For heaven's sake, come in." She backed away from the door, and stood contemplating him for a moment. How strange it felt, to formally invite her own son into their home.

He stepped inside. His mother seemed so purposeful, her features focused. Had she aged? In a year? He wasn't used to looking for signs of wear on his mother's perennially beautiful features.

"Aaron! Look who's home!" she called out. Grasping his hand, she dragged him into the living room. The Sunday *Times* lay scattered over the sofa and coffee table. Bagels, lox and cream cheese dried in crumbly disarray on the dining room table.

His father emerged from the bedroom, blinking his way out of sleep. He looked stooped and tired. *Maybe it was the nap*, David speculated.

"Well, well, well," Aaron growled, pulling up his suspenders. "The prodigal son returns." He gripped his son in a bear hug.

David felt the old, overwhelming mass of his father's bulk, but there was a trembling, desperate feel to the embrace. He frowned. His father shaky, his mother grim, focused, unfamiliar in her clarity. Had he done this to them? Of course he had.

He sat down at the dining room table, choosing the chair with the most direct line to the door. He twitched, wanting to stay light on his feet. He remembered his second-grade teacher asking him in front of the class, 'Can't you ever sit still, David? Is someone chasing you?'

"Great to be home," he grinned.

"Are you hungry?" Nina asked. "How long can you stay?"

Aaron entered the room and, silent, crossed to the liquor cabinet. He filled a glass with ice and poured a Scotch. "You stink at communication, kid." He pointed the whiskey at his son. "You know that?"

"Aaron, he just got here."

"Do you have any idea? Any fucking idea what it's like? To jump every time the phone rings, hoping it's you? We're not a couple of teenagers in love here, fella. We're your parents."

"I'm sorry. Look, Ma, I'm really sorry. I . . . "

"How about a sandwich? Or some pot roast? Dorothea cooked pot roast for last night's dinner."

"Sure, Ma. A sandwich. That'll be fine." The visceral comfort of home battled with the guilt and adrenaline that shot through his system. He had no appetite, his stomach twisted in a knot, his heart tripping double time since he stepped out of the elevator. Home was probably the most risky place for him to be. He couldn't afford to linger, hated to delude them any longer. He'd better get down to it. Still, it was so comforting, the cluttered Sunday table, his mother rattling plates in the kitchen. "Look, Ma. Dad."

"I am looking," Aaron said. "I see my son. For the first time in maybe a year." He pulled on the Scotch and began pacing. "So how long has it been?" He was getting his voice back.

"Dad. Please! Let me talk here."

His mother set down the sandwich on the table with a glass of milk. A glass of milk! He hadn't drunk milk since he was in junior high school.

"Got a beer by any chance, Ma?"

"We're Jews, Buster," his father said, finding his sarcasm. "Jews don't drink beer. Germans drink beer. Jews drink vodka." He pulled at his Scotch and cackled. "Except for this Jew."

Nina sighed. "Of course we have a beer, Honey." She rose.

David put a hand on her wrist. "I can't stay long."

Nina sat back down. "Why not?"

"Because I . . . " He couldn't drop the bomb — not yet. "Um, did I get any mail recently? A letter?"

"I put all your mail in your room. On your dresser." His mother rose.

"That's okay, Ma." He leapt out of his seat. "I'll look through it in there."

His bedroom seemed frozen in time, as if he had left for the weekend — or had died. The bedspread lay stretched impeccably taut, the same pictures and political posters adorned the walls, his books and records sat dusted and unmoved on their shelves.

An envelope tilted between his alarm clock and the blue ceramic knock-off of an ancient Egyptian hippopotamus from the Metropolitan Museum of Art that Madeline had given to him. A long, long time ago. *Time isn't measured by the ticking of a clock,* he thought. *It's measured by the things you do.* He stuffed the envelope into his jacket pocket and left the room without looking back.

"Letter from a girlfriend?" Aaron winked as his son returned.

"Yeah," he grinned and pocketed the envelope. "You might say that." Watching his Dad try to relax, act congenial, made him want to hug him.

"Don't worry, kid," Aaron said. "It's that time for you. I don't suppose I had much to say to my parents by the time I was your age." He paused. "'Course they were both dead by then." He barked a laugh. "Tough job, pissing off the dead."

His father's sarcasm pushed him forward. "Look, folks," David began. "I'm kind of passing through, here."

Nina stared straight at him, her usual myopia absent. The "pleasant" mom, the "nice" hostess disappeared. "What's going on, David?"

"You mean they haven't called?"

"You're referring to the FBI." His mother leaned forward, elbows on the table. "That's why you're so damned edgy, isn't it?"

"They called here," Aaron added.

"What did they say?"

"They asked for you. They wouldn't say why."

"What did you tell them?"

"What did we tell them?" Aaron retorted. "We told them the truth. That we had no goddamn idea where the hell you were." He downed the rest of the Scotch.

"We tried to reach you." Nina placed the sandwich on the table. "It was futile. But you know that." She stared at him wide-eyed. "You might've checked in from time to time."

Finally. From behind his father's bombast came real feeling. From beneath his mother's saccharine façade came clarity and demand.

"Okay. Here's the deal." He spoke in clipped phrases, heart pounding. "The trip to Hanoi. My draft status. My work with the Mobe."

"The what?" His father grimaced.

"The Mobilization to End the War. Never mind that." He paused for breath. "I'm wanted. By the FBI. I'm a Federal fugitive."

341

Nina covered her face with her hands.

Aaron frowned. "That doesn't make any sense."

"'Doesn't make any sense'?" His father's confusion irritated him. "What does that mean?"

"Well, dammit? If you're such a goddamned criminal, why didn't they shake us down harder, try to find you?"

"Maybe they didn't want you to tip me off."

"You made damned good and sure we couldn't do that," Nina said. "Didn't you."

"Honey," Aaron said. "Wait a minute." He turned to his son. "So you've been on the run since you went to Vietnam?"

David walked to the window, looked out over the Hudson, shining silver-gray in the November light. "Yes."

"This is serious. Isn't it?" His father's voice had lost its edge. "Like I said. Treason."

"Yeah."

"You see?" His father pounded the table with his fist. "I knew it! I told you when you came back, the shit was going to hit the fucking fan on this. Goddammit!"

"Oh, shut up, Aaron."

David wanted to cry. To say he was sorry. To admit he was scared. But he couldn't. And they didn't ask him to. Aaron sat silent, lost in thought. There was no room for fear. This was wartime, and in wartime even the middle-class learns to triage its emotions.

"That's outrageous," Aaron muttered. "You go to a pissant little Oriental colony we've been bombing into oblivion? And you get busted for it? They don't have better things to do?" He poured another Scotch. "This country has gone to hell."

The room went quiet, the silence letting in the sound of traffic swishing below.

"You've got to turn yourself in," Nina said. "We'll get the best lawyers . . . "

"No! Please! Don't mess with this." David put both hands up. "Right now, they have no idea where to find me. This is the most dangerous place I've been in months, sitting right here in your living room."

His father sat down opposite him. "You're really committed to this thing, aren't you, kid?"

"Yeah. I am."

"In the last year, I gotta admit. I've let myself think you've been . . . right, dammit. That you've been right all the time. I see this horror, this stupidity rattle across the newsroom teletype every day."

"I know, Dad."

"Cronkite and those guys, they love to say we're tearing the shroud off this war. Bullshit. We just keep shoving the real news into a body bag."

"I know."

"The stories that get filed from over there. The real ones? They never get broadcast. Because of you, I began to understand. Not while you were arguing with me, not while you were trying to convince me, but afterwards, after you'd come and gone, when I saw the truth come in on the Teletype and the lies go out on the airwaves. Body counts." He snorted through his nose. "Shit. What a way to win a war. Count the dead people. And the whole time, I stand there like a dickless wonder, doing nothing. Totally helpless. As a matter of fact, I think we fanned the flames. Not just us. All the networks. All the papers. Everybody."

"I think you did, too."

"I'm sorry, kid." Aaron leaned over his son and embraced him. "I'm really, really sorry."

"Don't be." David patted his father's arm, confused by his father's unraveling. "You're just a cog in the wheel."

"'A cog in the . . .'" Aaron turned red. "Now wait a God damned minute. I . . . "

"So," Nina interrupted her husband's bluster. "What are you going to do?"

"I gotta go. Now."

"Where?" Nina asked.

"Underground."

"What the hell does that mean?" she asked coldly. "Underground what?"

"I've got to disappear."

"What? Why?" His father stood up. "Jesus, Son, you've got tremendous resources at your disposal. We can get you cleared of this crap. A cog in the wheel? I'll show you what a goddamned cog in the . . . "

"I don't want to get cleared. Getting cleared means another white, middle-class kid gets off the hook. Working class kids go AWOL. They don't get a break. The Panthers, they don't get a break."

"God, what have we come to here?" Nina looked at her hands, her wedding diamond, the anniversary sapphire.

"I have to go now," David continued. "I can't tell you where I'm going. I don't know where I'm going. But I promise you. I will contact you whenever I can."

"What should we tell people?"

"You still embarrassed about me?"

"God!" Nina reddened with hurt and anger. You really think I'm shallow, don't you? Jesus!"

"I'm sorry, Ma. I . . . "

"Just shut up and listen." She spoke quickly now. "We need a story, something credible. Something that will work for us. For the neighbors, for the FBI, for everybody. And we can't fabricate one. It needs to be authentic. So you better get to work, kiddo, and figure out a story people will believe. Otherwise, we are going to be an open window. A mark, a big, fat, finger pointing straight at you."

David dropped his head on his forearms and wept. When the spasms stopped, he raised his head. "Of course.

You're right. I'll work up a story you can use. But give me a little time."

"There is no time. That nosy new doorman spotted you." Nina sighed. "You'll need to come up with something fast."

"I will keep in touch. I promise."

"You'd better, Buster," Nina said.

"Shit, kid." His dad made a pathetic attempt to lighten up. "Anything will be better than the total and complete silence of the last year."

"Don't go." Nina softened, grabbed his arm. "Please."

"Honey, he's got to."

"I know." She said. "I know." She began to cry.

Hot tears flowing down his face, David rose. He hugged each of his parents and took a last, long look around the apartment, its bookshelves, the grand piano, the African prints and statuary, the afternoon light bouncing from the Hudson painting the walls orange. He opened the door and fled to the elevator.

David walked to Broadway and 101st and sat on a bench, soaking up the thin winter sunlight. He sat there until his hands stopped trembling and the hot, wet pressure left his eyes. The corner, the cabs rushing down the Great White Way, the bodega with its neon beer signs, the cut-rate luggage outlet, the Cuban Chinese restaurant, the aluminum-sided storefront where his mother had taken him every September to buy school shoes, it all looked different. From ratty blankets spread on the sidewalk, street vendors sold the same used books and records, hawking paperbacks from a world that was rapidly receding from his frame of reference. No one knew his name, no one knew his past. Had they known his future, they would have feared or hated him. He sat on the bench, legs casually crossed, a pariah in his own world.

He pulled the envelope from his jeans pocket. It was addressed in courier type, the characters punched hard through a faded ribbon onto the envelope face. He stripped it open.

> *Go where the sun shines through the*
> *big windows. Remember? There was*
> *always a treasure there for me.*
> *1147*
> *13-right*
> *19-left*
> *24-right*
> *Buy a Rand McNally pocket*
> *atlas — 1969 edition*
> *Kisses*

Chanting the box number and the combination into memory, he proceeded down Broadway to the 96th Street IRT entrance. How would it be, living, working, hiding underground with her? And Roger. He brushed his questions aside. More important things to consider. Before he descended the gritty IRT stairway, he stuffed the letter in his pocket, tore the envelope into bits and threw it into a trash basket.

At Times Square he took the Lexington Avenue shuttle across town. When he reached Grand Central Station, he tore up the letter and stuffed it into a second trashcan. Half of Manhattan separated what remained of the envelope, the address and its contents.

Punching his hands into his pea jacket, he ascended the great marble stairway toward the diffused light that shone down from the station's leaded-glass atrium. He found the corridor of brass-faced mailboxes and knelt at the top of the stairway, re-arranging the belongings in his student knapsack while he watched the commuters funnel past the mailboxes. After ten minutes of mundane trafficking, commuters coming and going, he slung his backpack on his shoulders and cruised past box 1147. Was it being watched, marked in some Federal agent's sights? He took a seat on a bench at the opposite end of the corridor and fidgeted.

"Waitin' for thomeone?" A bag lady with a harelip offered him a pretzel from a wrinkled cellophane bag.

"No."

"Go ahead." She thrust the bag at him, her knuckles filthy with grime. "You know you want one."

He reached into the bag.

"Nithe and thalty," she lisped.

He crunched the pretzel in his teeth. It was months, possibly years old, rock hard. *Could she be marking him for the cops? Naaah. She was a wreck.* "I'm waiting for a train," he said, pocketing the fossilized pretzel.

"Where to?"

"I'm going to . . . " He stopped. "Boston."

"I'm waitin' for a train, mythelf," she explained solemnly. "Right here. At the Grand Thentral Stathion." She dipped into the bag and offered him another pretzel. "Justh like you."

"Yeah," he said. "Just like me." Had she been a victim, a beaten wife, a throwaway, or had she willfully rejected the world as he was doing? If so, she was paying for her rejection. How would he pay? What would be the consequences of his actions? Where would he end up? A lunatic in the subway with a bag full of pretzels?

"Don't exthpect it to come, though." She rolled up the bag, very tight. "The train. It don't never come." She got

347

up and pushed her cart away, its wheels wobbling and squeaking down the marble corridor.

He watched her go, fatigue gripping the back of his neck and shoulders. Tired beyond caring, he brushed through the crowd of Sunday matinee goers, restless teenagers and retired couples returning to Yonkers and White Plains from "the City".

He stood before the box and dialed the combination, hoping the crowds would cover him. He swung the brass door open. Inside, tilted against the narrow confines of the box, lay a second envelope. He pocketed it, slammed the box closed and walked away.

Back in the labyrinth of the cross-town tunnels, he slid onto a counter stool at an underground Nedick's, ordered a hamburger and a vanilla shake, paid for it in advance out of his thin fold of cash, swallowed the hamburger in three bites and opened the envelope.

A three-by-five card stared up at him. The same hard-pecked typewriter had generated a second set of sparse characters.

> *New York State*
> *J5*
> *3214 Davenport*

J5? He took out the pocket atlas he had been instructed to buy and opened it. Ah. Each map featured a grid super-imposed on the geography, letters on the y axis, numbers on the x axis. He traced his finger to the intersection of the J and the 5. He sucked the dregs out of the vanilla shake glass, slid off the stool and climbed back up into the Grand Central atrium, where he purchased a one-way ticket to Poughkeepsie.

Once on board, he found a window seat and huddled against it. Poughkeepsie. A commuter sat in the adjacent seat, folding and unfolding *The Wall Street Journal* — a safe man, a sane man, a secure man with his well-ordered, adequately rewarded position in a murderous society. Exhausted, David dozed, suspended by the lulling rhythms of the train as it clicked over the maze of underground switches and rushed out into the cold night air. They rolled through the darkness, following the east bank of the Hudson northward.

POUGHKEEPSIE

Madeline hugged David at the door of a shabby, asbestos-shingled bungalow in the rundown outskirts.

"3214 Davenport, I presume," he said. Fondness and familiarity flowed over him. The arguments, the hurt feelings, the jealousy, anger and dismay, all gone. He had the urge to check his pockets, to see if the old emotions lurked in his jeans, but no. Nothing remained. Everything had changed and it was wonderful to see her. At least for the time being.

Quickly, she pulled him inside. "Neighbors," she whispered. He was the third stranger to arrive at the pink bungalow in as many weeks, a unique circumstance in a tight working-class neighborhood where no one ever left, no one ever came and nothing ever changed. She closed the door and they embraced, holding each other with no need to express feelings.

When David opened his eyes, he found Roger standing in the kitchen doorway, a strained grin on his face. "Hey, brother."

In the aftermath of the Chicago Convention, David had made a pact with Roger and Madeline. They'd sat on the grass and said 'I'm in' to each other and to their

349

comrades. Connie, Eddie, the others? They'd fallen by the wayside. But Mad, Roger and David had reunited — with themselves and with the others who vowed to push the resistance movement forward.

Now they were together, the three of them — Madeline, Roger, and David — subsisting on canned spaghetti, Wonder Bread and peanut butter, three newborn resistance fighters. Before they set out on their mission, they huddled over the kitchen table and began drafting a manifesto. Following the examples of the Vietnamese, they wanted to reach consensus on each action, how it supported their goals and principles, and how they would implement it.

They had no television, no phone. They were building a mass movement but they wrote and planned their assaults alone. The rest of the country seemed hopelessly bought off, and they clung to the understanding that they were acting in sync with cadres of other comrades, each following a different path to the same Revolution.

They understood the seriousness of their situation. They had no desire to unleash indiscriminate violence against ordinary people. Destroying lives had nothing to do with their goals. *No.* Their war was against property, against the state, not against people. They vowed that not a single life would be lost in their battle to destroy the biggest war machine in history.

They had planned to find work. Roger would teach David the lingo he needed to land a job as a gas monkey at a service station. Roger would use his mechanical prowess to fabricate the bits and pieces of the bombs they would construct as their first weapons. Madeline would get restaurant or store work, keep an ear out for any gossip that might sound an alarm.

Now, with the money that had fallen into Madeline's hands, they were free to move forward nonstop. Every afternoon they piled into the station wagon and canvassed the area, nearby at first, then circling outward, searching for hardware stores and scattered banks where they could cash another hundred dollar bill and, piecemeal, procure the tools and materials they needed to carry out the plan. From the list Roger had pilfered from the Pittsburgh office, they chose their first target — a Federal building in downtown Manhattan that housed the COINTELPRO offices of the FBI. If that Pittsburgh FBI office had yielded such a goldmine, what vital information would reside in the joint headquarters of the FBI and COINTELPRO? All we have to do is blow out the ceiling and the whole place will turn into a water-soaked, charred-paper mess. And nobody would be around.

They carefully delineated their roles — Roger the mechanic would prepare the package, city boy David would travel solo to New York to case the joint. They didn't want to be seen together in that building even once. Alone, David could wander until he felt suspicion at his back, bringing home what info he could gather with a casual snoop.

When it came time, Madeline would dress up as an office girl and deliver the package.

"Damn, guys." She smiled. "I've been in jeans and sweatshirts for so long, I'm gonna look forward to this."

Roger and David looked at her, puzzled.

"I'm gonna need a really, like . . . Madison Avenue outfit." She grinned, imagining herself gorgeous, with a whole different look.

She snickered at their shocked expressions. "Hey, you bumpkins. Some of those working chicks look pretty damned cute. Am I right?"

"Yeah." David and Roger grinned, nodded their heads in unison. "Working chicks."

"Uh huh," Madeline said. " So . . . " She stood and began packing the shabby kitchen. "I want a nice little working-girl sweater set, some . . ."

"Hey!" David said. "Don't get so you're turning heads. Can't you look kinda, like anonymous?"

"Screw that, Buddy. I'm gonna have fun with this. Besides . . . " She passed behind both her men, ruffling their hair. "I always turn heads." She shrugged, miming innocence. "Can't help it." She continued pacing. "Lessee . . . I'll need stockings. Sensible flats . . . "

"You're gonna have to wear a braaaaaa!" Roger taunted. "And pantyhose! Haw!"

"As to the bra? I'll survive," Madeline responded, "The pantyhose?" Eyebrow raised, she spat into the sink. "No way! The real thing. Silk, garters. That way, if I go . . . " She executed a perfect little wiggle. "I go out right!"

"Don't talk that way," Roger grumbled.

Madeline ignored him. "And a perky little pageboy wig. A nice little champagne-streaked 'fuck-me' thingie. You know . . ." She pushed demurely at her chaos of black curls.

The next morning they got serious. Over coffee they reviewed the plan, searching for any oversight that might jeopardize the action. Madeline would carry her payload downtown. They would stay separate, David leafing through a rack of informational brochures he had seen in the lobby. Roger would hang out across the street, begging for spare change. Regardless of their presence, Madeline would be vulnerable to any oversights or unforeseen events — a bureaucrat working overtime, an off-schedule security guard. She would linger in the ladies' room until the building had closed. Then, placing a chair on the receptionist's desk, she would clamber within reach of the ceiling, lift a panel and slip the package up and in. They were bringing the war home.

That last night, they slept together for the first time since they had gathered in Poughkeepsie. Without talking, they lay side-by-side, minds whirling. Thoughts, not desire, flew between them. David remembered his trip to Hanoi, to the machine shop, where young men and women had worked together, fought to survive together. There had been no hint of sexuality. Had they reached that level of commitment, of reality, where desire meant nothing?

Where is this going to get us? Madeline asked herself. Did any of them actually believe they could go up against the government of a United States at war? And create an alternative? Years of activism told them they had exhausted all options. They had no recourse. They must take this first step.

Yeah, it seemed futile. But look what had happened in Cuba. Thirty-six men escaped into the mountains, and two years later emerged victorious over one of the Caribbean's most vicious and heavily-armed dictators. In Vietnam, urban actions like theirs struck the first blow against the French in a campaign that ended in the death of Indochina's colonialism.

Be realistic. Expect the impossible. The slogan had caught in Roger's head. So what if it was impossible? They still had to jump on it. *If we fail, who knows what's going to happen to America in the years to come?* No turning back now. They were positioned to strike the first blow against the real bogeymen — the enemy within. Who wouldn't jump at a chance like this?

Alone together, they stared up into the darkness and waited for tomorrow.

Greenwich Village

The trio drove to Manhattan, buzzing with tension and excitement. With Roger behind the wheel, they cruised down a sedate Greenwich Village street. The station wagon was loaded with belongings typical of any itinerant student — boxes of books, clothing, cheap kitchen utensils, and the ubiquitous bricks and boards of a disassembled bookshelf. Beneath the books lay a flat wooden crate of dynamite, tools, a handful of windup alarm clocks, and coils of insulated, varicolored wire. They hid the address list that Roger had pilfered in the rocker panel of the driver's side door. The promise of the future — FBI and COINTELPRO would pay.

They pulled up to the curb in front of the Greenwich Village townhouse, where Madeline had stood just weeks before. Roger peered up at the three-story mansion. "This is it?" He whistled softly. "Man, oh man. Right in the middle of the ruling class."

"It's my home," Madeline said.

The dignified, Jamesian building, with its brick façade, wrought ironwork and worn granite steps, would afford cover, a privileged haven from which to launch their first attack. The trio paused inside the snow-and-salt-streaked anonymity of the station wagon, each caught up in the transformation they were about to make. A taxi whispered past under the leaden March overcast, tires hissing through ruts of wet, rotten snow.

"We'd better get this stuff inside," Madeline said. "The neighbors," old family friends whom she hadn't seen in years, people with time on their hands. Like the folks on the quiet street in Poughkeepsie, they would be curious.

David turned to Madeline. "Home, sweet home, huh, Mad?"

She nodded.

He squeezed her shoulder, moved by their shared past.

"We got work to do." Roger yanked open the door and stepped onto the sidewalk. "How do we get in?"

Free of the constraints of the Poughkeepsie house, Roger had trouble keeping his feelings in check. He adored Madeline and — although he could rationalize a notion of equality, that she belonged to no one — he wanted to chase after her, to possess her. But David . . . He had the advantage. He and Madeline were pals. Their previous relationship, the common denominator of class and shared experience — Bronco, Texas, versus Manhattan. No contest. No fucking contest. She was David's. He didn't exist, except as a revolutionary. *And how long would this revolution last?*

He shoved his hands in his pockets and watched his breath condense in the cold, wet air. He would have to grab hold of anger. He glanced up and down the street, forcing himself towards awareness, a primitive feeling that had come from the jeopardy of his past. *Get real,* he told himself. *Crank it uptight. Take control. He was the one with the skills. Madeline had the fire, David had . . . What did David have?* He shook himself free of it. They would assemble the first bomb that afternoon. They were tired but they had committed to this date, and by tomorrow night, after the bomb had been planted, they would be gone. Quickly.

"Let's go, *Amigo*," David said, nudging Roger back to reality. "We got things to blow." With Madeline leading the way, they lugged the box of explosives, the tools and wire and timers, gingerly down the crooked cellar steps, and shut the door on the harsh, spring day.

Roger moved the car to a space around the block and rejoined David in the basement. They had made dry runs of the assembly process in Poughkeepsie and Roger felt strong and confident again. Together, they cleared a scarred work bench. "We make a good fuckin' team," he said.

The work area was lit by a single glaring bulb that hung in a green cone from the ancient joists overhead. Perhaps a pool table had sat beneath its enameled hood. They laid out dynamite, batteries, the cheap alarm clocks, the blasting caps and the hand tools. Using needle-nosed pliers, matte knives and a bevy of screwdrivers and black tape, they began to assemble the first bomb. They knew the routine, but now they moved on to the real thing, a bomb big enough to blow out a whole floor of a Federal Building. And this time they would be using live batteries. "No more dry runs, Buddy," Roger whispered as they gingerly took inventory of the still-separate elements.

"Expect the impossible." David grinned and the two men embraced.

Filled with fear, excitement, and the taste of life-and-death resolve, Madeline struggled to get hold of herself. This was no boyfriend problem. She looked from her two men to the beams and shadows of the basement. *It's probably just being home,* she thought. *Naaah. It's because . . . because this is it! The first step that overtook the millions of steps and actions and people and places that had led them here.*

"Hey, Mad," Roger turned toward her. "Got any newspapers in this castle?"

Madeline woke from her reverie. "Newspapers?" She straightened up. "Shit, Man. My old man is a newsprint junkie." She started upstairs, stopped, afraid of what waited above. "Hey, guys. I'm gonna check out the kitchen. I'm hungry as hell!"

She climbed the basement steps and opened the door. Her heartbeat slowed. Her features softened. The room was cold, but it caressed her with the warm embrace of home. She tiptoed across the kitchen floor as if her parents were sleeping upstairs. *It's three in the afternoon. They're in Puerto Rico.* She stomped through the kitchen to the living room and scooped a stack of newspapers from the box by the fireplace.

Shivering, she cranked up the heater to ninety degrees on the hallway thermostat. The furnace woofed to life in the basement, and radiators began their familiar hollow knock, evoking more remembrance. *Things are moving quickly now. And with great finality.*

She entered her father's study and stood in the darkened room. *Even this feels gone. Like love lost. Like her men downstairs.* A terrific sadness overcame her. Even in the chill, the room smelled of his pipe tobacco, his books, and the pungent leather of the old club chairs. She needed to get back to the present. She fled her father's domain, rushed through the kitchen, and yanked open the basement door.

Downstairs, the furnace roared in the corner like an old bear, filling the pipes with hot water.

David turned to her, white-faced. "Jesus," he said. "You turned on that . . . that monster?"

"Yeah," she replied. "We're gonna spend the night. Did you want to freeze your butt off?"

"No, but when that thing ignited down here . . . " He laughed nervously.

"Never mind." Roger's voice sounded tight. "Maybe it'll warm up this cave." He rubbed his fingers together. "Kinda tough to work with frozen fingers."

Madeline took his hands between hers. "Poor baby," she said.

"Come on, come on!" Roger whispered, and patted the table.

She set the newspapers on the workbench. "And you don't have to whisper," she giggled.

"Nobody here but us guerrillas," David added.

Roger spread out the papers. "This is it, guys."

"Take a minute, Madeline whispered. "Stop. Everyone take a deep breath."

Both men straightened up, seduced by the calm in her voice.

Madeline came behind them, put an arm around each man, and brought them together in a triangle. "I want to seize this time, tell you both how much I love you." She kissed them. "How much I admire you." Another kiss. "And I want to hold you and smell you and remember all the things we have done. Personal and political. Together and alone." Kiss. "How much we learned from each other." Kiss. "We're doing something that we never did before. Weird. But it feels right."

"Fuckin' A!" Roger shouted. "It feels right."

"Right as revolution," David whispered.

The three revolutionaries embraced. Madeline began sniffing them. Roger and David reciprocated. The trio snorted and poked, licking and nuzzling until they collapsed into each other's arms. Laughter turned to tears and back to laughter. Exhausted, they fell silent, the furnace roaring in the background.

"Okay, Brother." Roger turned to David. "Let's slap this motherfucker together."

"I'm going to take a bath and then scrounge us something to eat." Madeline re-ascended the basement stairs. She paused at the top. "I love you both," she said. "I love you both so, so much." Without waiting for a response she opened the door and passed into what had been.

Touching each wall and banister as if it were a beloved and dying relative, she made her way up three flights of stairs to her secret bathroom, sitting in solitary elegance on the fourth floor. She turned on the taps. Hot water chortled into a claw-foot tub. She draped her grimy jeans and sweatshirt over the back of a wrought-iron chair. She loved her old sanctuary, the elegant tiled comfort, the rich enamel on the woodwork, the clarity of the beveled mirror over the sink. Yes, she would luxuriate, but she was there to ready herself. *It will be strange, staying here.* She sat on the radiator and listened to the tub fill.

Three floors below, an electric hacksaw rattled through a length of pipe. Her brothers-in-arms were assembling the bomb, small enough to fit in a purse, large enough to blow COINTELPRO right out its own windows.

After she bathed, she would take steaks or a chicken out of the freezer and cook a good meal. Screw the home-maker stereotype. The guys had worked hard, got along, no dueling dicks. They were a team and they all deserved a little luxury after their spartan existence in Poughkeepsie and the tense ride into Manhattan.

She would open a bottle of wine. Maybe two. But with the mission they faced in the morning, should they risk even a hint of hangover? She would sleep alone. She wanted to be left to her own thoughts, to fall asleep and dream in the abandoned comfort of her old bedroom. The boys could crash in the two guest rooms.

She studied her reflection in the mirror, the circles under her eyes gone blue to purple, the adolescence sucked from her cheeks. Only smooth, white skin and dark, curly hair remained of the child who had spent so many hours deciphering her identity in this same, flawless mirror. She opened the medicine cabinet. They were still there, a fine pair of French scissors, part of a gold-engraved ensemble her parents had brought from their honeymoon in Paris. She would cut her hair. She wasn't sure why. Maybe to ac-commodate the wig, perhaps as a ritual. *How strange,* she thought, and grabbed a handful of hair. "Fuck the good old days," she whispered, and she cut. Despite their age, the scissors carried a fine edge, and tight ringlets fell black into the white porcelain sink.

She turned off the water, climbed into the bath and sprinkled scented beads from a glass jar onto the rippling water. Aromas of vanilla and chamomile rose on the hot moisture from the tub. The room filled with a familiar scent, and she allowed the liquid warmth to lap over her body. She leaned back in the tub and let the wet embrace open her like an anemone. Tomorrow, she knew, she would feel very different.

CRACK! The nineteenth-century bathroom window blew out of its frame, splintering in mid-air. The ceiling flew upward. She clung to the edges of the claw-foot tub, engulfed in a tumultuous clatter of falling plaster, lath, splintered flooring and brickwork. An eternity later, she regained her senses to find herself on a narrow shelf of splintered floorboards and tile. Beneath her, two muffled, smaller blasts kicked the rubble upward in the dust-choked hole that remained of three floors and a basement. Water hissed. She couldn't breathe but knew she must move. Seeking air, she rose and steadied herself against the fractured walls. Plaster dust clogged her nose as she crept along the ledge. She could feel nothing in the soles of her feet as she picked her way through the chaos to a crooked stairway, skewed crazily downward into a maelstrom of dust.

David. She wanted David. She called his name. Nothing came from her throat. Her feet hurt. She wanted his arms around her. She wanted him to hold her, to lift her up, to carry her out, away, over the broken glass. There was no sign of him. No sound came from below.

More bricks slid clattering into the hole to her right. Her arms and knuckles bled. She seemed to be covered in flour. Naked. Spikes of cold, outdoor light pierced the jagged remnants of an outside wall. Where was the fourth-floor bathroom? The basement. The basement of her home. Her parents' home. *David?*

She crouched like an animal, trying to cover herself. Her newly shorn hair dripped with coagulated plaster dust. Vulnerable, numb, she walked bent over toward the shafts of outside light. *Outside of what?* She stumbled, fell on her hands, picked herself up and walked another step forward, onto cold concrete. Alone. The sky wet, gray. A red plaid blanket, warm, dry around her. She felt hands embrace her shoulders, turn her, guiding her away. *From what? From David. From Roger.*

She looked over her shoulder, searching for her comrades but the pull was too strong. She yielded to the sheltering arms on her blanket. A small woman, familiar-looking. *She mustn't know, this woman!* She mustn't know who the shorn, plaster-dusted body belonged to. She hid her face and let the woman guide her down the sidewalk.

They climbed a long flight of granite steps to a black enameled door, much like her own. But her own black enameled door was gone. Her feet grew cold. Her ears rang, oscillating in and out of tempo with her heartbeat.

The woman led her to a hallway bench and sat her down.

"Are you all right?" A voice thickened by traces of an Eastern European accent. "Madeline?"

Yes, Madeline knew. *This was Katherine.*

Not daring to look up, Madeline nodded her head. She might be dead but the blanket felt warm. She drew it to her. Her feet began to sting. "Something went wrong," she burbled. Her voice sounded thick, her lips felt fat.

"Don't move." Katherine patted her shoulders through the blanket and ran down the hall.

Madeline sat in the blanket. She could feel her knees. Her heart began to pound.

Katherine returned and placed a tumbler full of water into her hands. "Drink this," she said. "And no. I won't call the police."

"No! I . . . "

"Shhhhhh. I was the first one there. Nobody saw us."

Oh, David. David. Madeline looked toward the front door, willing him to open it, walk inside, hold her. Instead, a wolf stood measuring her, its head moving up and down. *Why a wolf?* She lifted the glass with both hands. They were trembling, but she wanted the water. She concentrated, found her lips with the brim of the glass and drank, tilting her head back. She heard airplanes. No. *Somebody crying. No. Something whining. The wolf. Oh. Sirens. A siren song. Coming here.* She stood on bare, bleeding feet.

"I'm going to hide you." Katherine gathered her in the blanket, pushed her up stairs and more stairs until they reached the height she had lost in the explosion. To the bathroom, the same bathroom as her own. *Strange.* Guided to the tub.

She watched water babble into the porcelain. *David. Roger.* She twisted, struggling to look out the window. Eyes burning bright, she clawed at Katherine's sturdy body. "Got to get them. Save them. Bring them here. Burnt. Hurt. Dirty."

Katherine yanked the blind on the window, closing out the gaping, smoking hole. "They'll be fine."

"No!" She collapsed against Katherine, who sat her down in the deepening warmth of the tub. "They have to run away! Now! Can't wait."

Katherine soothed her, sponging her. Keeping a hand on Madeline's shoulder, she placed a pill between Madeline's lips. "Swallow."

Madeline gagged, struggled to spit out the pill.

Katherine handed her the glass. "Drink," she ordered.

Madeline swallowed.

Katherine bathed the still-trembling body. When the glistening body was clean, Katherine could see that she — her lover's daughter — was whole. No swollen organs, no protruding bones, a million little cuts like lacework. The tub was full of plaster dust tinged red. For the moment, Madeline became Katherine's daughter.

Katherine had no need to mother. Her own had gone elsewhere, as had Madeline. Katherine and the girl's father had sought comfort with each other during that time, as they had before, but it meant nothing. This moment was beyond all that. This moment reminded her of Warsaw. The stinging zip of bullets, the compression of explosions, the shattered brick, the stink of explosives. The blood and bits of flesh that might, even now, lie scattered in the basement of her neighbor's home.

History tends to repeat itself. But always in different ways.

She wrapped Madeline in a towel and led her to a fourth-floor bedroom. She laid Madeline's head on the pillow. Covered her. Waited, watching the pill and the warm bath take effect.

Madeline struggled.

"Shhh," Katherine whispered. "You must lie still. I'll move you later, but for now . . ."

Below, a doorbell rang.

"Stay," Katherine's voice now stern. "Quiet." She fed her charge another pill. "Let this make you sleepy."

"But we've got to . . . "

"Soon," Katherine replied. "But first, the door."

Madeline lay under the covers, knowing no comfort, knowing no time. She knew loss. Only loss. Unable to withstand the emptiness, she dissolved into unconsciousness.

Bright daylight, another day. She could hear machinery outside and feel the woman sitting at the bedside. Hunger. Smell of food. Katherine. She had tea, and a clear broth in a bowl. Crackers.

Katherine fed her. She spoke softly as Madeline took the liquids, lifted the bowl with shaking hands and drank from it.

"The police are gone. Your parents will be home soon."

Madeline writhed.

"Yes, I know. They must not find you here." She put her arm on Madeline's wrist and took away the bowl. "I know what you are, Madeline."

Madeline closed her eyes, shook her head, tears squeezing from her clenched lids.

"I fought in the Ghetto, little one. Jews against the SS. We fought back, a few of us. Like you. We fought. We died. We watched each other die. I know what it looks like. I know what it feels like. Like you. Inside and out. But you are alive and you must take time."

Madeline embraced her.

"Your friends may be gone. I don't know. You don't know. You will learn when it's time to learn. But whatever happens, you will go on."

Madeline nodded her head and lay back on the bed. The soft voice resonated in her chest and the hairs on her arms prickled. She felt warm. She listened, the words coming and going.

"It starts with an assemblage. First information, Then knowledge. Then understanding. Then outrage. Something must be done. Strikes. Marches. Protest. Defiance. Resistance. The first step. We never got beyond it. Most of us died first. But you can move on from here. I see it happening with your Movement. You will learn. You must do more than expose the enemy. You can. You will."

Madeline felt Katherine move away from the bed. She brought more crackers, more broth, more water. "The solution will not come from you, not now. But you — and all the others — you have begun. You won't stop. People will learn from you, forget, then remember again. It's inevitable, like the laws of physics. The world is rushing toward a turning point. In time, others not yet born will reinvent society. You will live to see it, to join them. It's coming. There is no other option. So for now, Madeline . . . Sleep. And we shall see."

Charles Degelman lives in Los Angeles with his companion on the road of life and four cats.